Anna Abney is among the last descendants of the Abney family, former residents of Measham Hall, a lost house of Derbyshire. She taught English and Creative Writing  her PhD on the seventeenth-century lives in Kent with her husband.

Praise for the Measham Hall series

'It's rare for a historical novel to feel so timely'
Jo Baker, *Sunday Times*-bestselling author of *Longbourn*

'Political subterfuge and family secrets entwine in this tale of historical intrigue, set during the late seventeenth-century tensions between Protestants and Catholics. Meticulously researched and alive with intricate period details to savour, I raced through it, while learning huge amounts'
Lucy Ribchester, author of *The Amber Shadows*

'Impeccably researched and wonderfully atmospheric, with a heroine you can't help rooting for'
Frances Quinn, author of *The Smallest Man*

'Exciting and immersive. It took me straight into the heart of Restoration England in all its rich and vivid detail. I was gripped!'
Nicola Cornick, author of *House of Shadows*

'In elegant prose, this enthralling novel puts a human face to the trials, terrors and enduring hopes of the plague years'
Catherine Meyrick, author of *The Bridled Tongue*

'By turns humorous and heart-wrenching, impeccably researched and beautifully written throughout, this [...] demands to be read'
Lianne Dillsworth, author of *Theatre of Marvels*

Also by Anna Abney
The Master of Measham Hall
The Messenger of Measham Hall

The PRISONER of MEASHAM HALL

ANNA ABNEY

First published in the United Kingdom by Duckworth,
an imprint of Duckworth Books Ltd, in 2024

Duckworth, an imprint of Duckworth Books Ltd
1 Golden Court, Richmond, TW9 1EU, United Kingdom
www.duckworthbooks.co.uk

For bulk and special sales please contact info@duckworthbooks.com

© Madeline Dewhurst, 2024

All rights reserved. No part of this publication may be reproduced,
stored in a retrieval system, or transmitted, in any form or by
any means electronic, mechanical, photocopying, recording or
otherwise, without the prior permission of the publisher.

The right of Anna Abney to be identified as the Author of this Work has been
asserted by her in accordance with the Copyright, Designs and Patents Act 1988.

A CIP catalogue record of this book is available from the British Library

Typeset by Danny Lyle

Print and bound in Great Britain by Clays Ltd

1 3 5 7 9 10 8 6 4 2

Paperback ISBN: 9780715655344
eISBN: 9780715655351

A Note on the Text

During the time period of the novel, the British Isles were still using the Julian calendar (Old Style), although most of continental Europe had moved to the Gregorian calendar (New Style) at the end of the previous century. This meant that England (until 1752) was ten days behind the rest of western Europe. The civil year in England started on 25th March (at the Feast of the Annunciation), though New Year's Day was generally celebrated, as now, on 1st January, a system I have also followed.

Characters

Derbyshire
Sir William Hawthorne
Nicholas Hawthorne – his son
Percy Hawthorne – uncle of William
Abigail – servant
Ben – serving-boy
Palmes – the butler
Tickell – the cook
Goodwyn – the new steward

John Thornly – the bailiff
Sarah Thornly – wife
Eliza, age 22 – daughter
Kate, age 15 – daughter, works at Measham Hall
Alice, age 13 – daughter

Harrington – bailiff of William's farm in the Peaks

Lady Jane Pemberton née Sellwood née Calverton
Lord Ralph Pemberton – husband of Jane
Isaac Smith – Pemberton's secretary and son

Ireland
Major Tadgh O'Connor – Jacobite
Blanche Fitzpatrick – actress, spy for the Williamites
Francis Bedley – Jacobite, old school friend of Nicholas from St. Omer
Diarmuid O'Leary – lawyer
Úna O'Leary – daughter of Diarmuid
Mairead – the O'Learys' maid

Characters

Historical characters

James II and VII (1633–1701), King of England, Scotland and Ireland from 1685–1689

James FitzJames (1670–1734), Duke of Berwick, soldier and Jacobite, eldest son of James II and his mistress Arabella Churchill

Patrick Sarsfield (*d.* 1693), Jacobite, first Earl of Lucan, army officer

Richard Talbot (1630–1691), Earl and Duke of Tyrconnell, army officer and Lord Deputy of Ireland

Antonin Nompar de Caumont (1632–1723), Comte (later Duc) de Lauzun, commander of the French forces in Ireland

Boisseleau, Alexandre de Rainier de Droué (*c.*1650–1698), Marquis of Boisseleau, French major-general and Governor of Limerick

William III (1650–1702), Prince of Orange, Stadtholder of the United Dutch Provinces, King of England, Scotland and Ireland from 1689–1702 – a joint monarch with his wife, Mary II (1662–1694), daughter of James II and VII

Friedrich Hermann, Duke of Schomberg (1615–1690), second in command to William of Orange and one of the most experienced generals in Europe at the time

Meinhardt, Count Schomberg (1641–1719), first Duke of Leinster, third Duke of Schomberg, Williamite, army officer

Lanier, Sir John (*d.* 1692), army officer

Preface

Derbyshire, September 1690

Having forced himself up from the bed, William staggered over to the door and leant against the wall beside it. Trying to steady his ragged breathing, he pressed down on the handle. The latch lifted and dropped, but although he pressed with all his weight, the door remained steadfastly closed. He stared aghast at the lock, which he had long ago had fitted for his own privacy. The key, which he always left inside it, was gone. But he had no recollection of having locked himself in nor where he might have put the key.

Turning, he gazed around the shadowy room; there was no sign of the key on the chest next to his bed. Besides, over the last few days he vaguely recalled being visited by a procession of servants and doctors. How had they got in and out if he had locked the door? He hammered on the thick oak panels, shouting with all the strength he could muster, though the voice that emerged from his throat was little more than a feeble whisper. Could no one hear him? Where were they all?

At last, he sank to the floor and, not having the energy left to walk, crawled across it to the window opposite. Placing his hands on the window seat, he pushed himself up until he could reach the shutters. He managed to slide the bolt free, but though he clawed at the thin boards, the shutters would not open. They did not reach to the ceiling and from the narrow gap at the top of the windows, he could see grey clouds and a crow wheeling across the sky. It was only thanks to this exposed rectangle of glass that any light was let into the room. It was then he noticed the nails driven into the wood. Who could have ordered the shutters to be nailed closed? He plucked desperately at the boards, but he was too weak to force them. He tried to prise the iron nails out, but only ripped his own fingernails, leaving bloody smudges on the wood, like smears of rust.

What on earth had he become, that he must be caged up like a dangerous animal?

Chapter One

Dublin, Ireland, January 1690

'Am I dismissed then?' Nicholas was reluctant to leave the warmth of Blanche's bed.

'For now.' She gave him a lazy smile.

Rolling towards her, Nicholas began to kiss Blanche's neck, revelling in the softness of her skin and the rich, spicy scent of her perfume. She pushed her fingertips through his hair, caressing his scalp. 'I have an appointment,' she murmured.

'It can wait,' he said, his lips moving to her breast.

'With King James.'

Nicholas sat up. 'Far be it for me to keep His Majesty waiting.'

He tumbled out of the bed and retrieved his breeches from the floor. Once he had them on, he turned to look at Blanche, who was sitting propped up against the pillows, her glorious red hair loose about her naked shoulders.

'You should have your portrait painted exactly like that,' he said admiringly.

She laughed. 'Shall I ask the King?'

'Has he beheld you in dishabille?' Nicholas asked with a mixture of curiosity and mild resentment, as he pulled his jacket on over his shirt.

'Do you think I would tell you if he had?' Blanche raised her finely arched eyebrows. 'Put some more turf on the fire, would you? And pass me my shawl.'

Nicholas bent down to build up the fire. 'You're lucky to have so much fuel. I've had to stop my men from ransacking houses and felling trees for firewood. I can only hope more of them don't fall sick from the cold.'

He was not looking forward to returning to the damp room in Trinity College where he had been billeted. He did his best to stop the other soldiers from damaging the place, but still their contempt for such a venerable building pained him. Having been an academic at Oxford before joining the exiled King's army, he also felt for the scholars who had been thrown out of the college with nothing but the books they could carry. At least the King's chaplain was keeping Trinity's library and gardens secure from harm, though his celebration of Mass in the chapel had caused much outrage among the Protestants of Dublin.

'You can hardly hold me responsible for the shortages. If it weren't for the King's patronage I'd be shivering along with the rest of them.'

'God save you from such a fate!' Taking her shawl from the back of a chair, Nicholas wrapped it tenderly around her. 'Not when you must fall on your sword as Tarpeia or put an asp to your breast as Cleopatra, or will you be smothered tonight as poor Desdemona?'

Blanche had been an actress at the Smock Alley Theatre before it was closed down because of the Prince of Orange's invasion. Since King James's arrival in Dublin she had been entertaining his retinue with recitals. It was after one of these performances that Nicholas had introduced himself to her as an admirer of her art.

'Enough of death, I have written a comic speech especially to entertain and distract His Majesty's officers,' Blanche said.

'You have writ a speech yourself? I look forward to hearing that, though the King's commanders hardly need further distraction. I wish they would give more thought to training and equipping our troops, instead of wasting the winter gaming and whoring. The enemy have lost so many men to the bloody flux, our side has grown complacent.'

Chapter One

Blanche was looking at him in an oddly critical way. 'There is a letter for you in that cabinet.' She pointed to her dressing table.

'From you?' A feeling of unease pricked Nicholas's stomach.

'From Lord Pemberton's man.'

The unease turned to alarm and Nicholas's heart began beating hard. 'How did you come by such a letter?'

'Lord Pemberton is a former patron. He used to come to see me in Covent Garden. I was a great success in London and Saint-Germain, you know. I'm surprised you hadn't heard of me before we met. If my wastrel of a husband had not left me with so many debts I would never have been compelled to return to Dublin.' She wound one of her crimson tresses around her lily-white hand, looking up at Nicholas with indignant pathos.

But Nicholas was too disturbed by her association with the man who had coerced him into spying on the Jacobites to be moved by her plight. He fetched the letter from her dressing table, recognising the hand immediately as belonging to Isaac Smith, Pemberton's secretary.

'Don't read it here; I need to call in my maid to help me dress,' Blanche told him.

'Are you working as an intelligencer?' Nicholas asked her bluntly. He was trying desperately to think of all the things he had let drop that might have given his own double position away.

Blanche's eyes grew round with bewilderment. 'What on earth would give you that impression?' Nestling back into her pillows, she regarded Nicholas with an injured expression. 'I still correspond with Ralph Pemberton; he was an intimate friend and a generous benefactor. Knowing that you were also in Dublin, he suggested I keep an eye on you. He has concerns about your allegiances.' She gave him a sly wink.

'Did he ask you to seduce me?' Nicholas was aghast.

'Certainly not.' Blanche rose from the bed in one graceful movement, the shawl still secured around her. 'If you recall events correctly, I think you will find it was you who was the pursuer.'

Nicholas frowned. As he remembered it, after his initial approach Blanche had invited him to dine with her in her rooms, but he refrained from pointing this out. Instead he asked her if she was a supporter of the Prince of Orange.

Blanche shrugged. 'I must play to whomever has the power to pay me. At present that is King James, but if King William should prove victorious I will welcome him equally. I am a Protestant, though married to a papist, and I cannot afford the luxury of undying loyalty to either side.'

'Well, when you next communicate with Pemberton you can assure him that I have not forgotten my promise, or his hold over me,' Nicholas said resentfully, pulling on his boots.

'Tell him yourself, my dear,' she answered cheerfully. 'And don't forget my performance this evening. It will mean a great deal to me to know you are in the audience. I want to hear your thoughts on my new speech; you know how highly I prize your intellect.'

She placed a hand on his chest and looked at him with such warmth Nicholas found his hostility evaporating away. 'Of course.' He planted a kiss on her parted lips before hurriedly departing to find some private place where he could read his letter and reflect on the news that he shared a mistress with Lord Pemberton.

Not only was Pemberton's wife, Jane, an old family friend, but Nicholas had also come close to eloping with Pemberton's daughter, which made the fact that they had bedded the same woman all the more distasteful. What really concerned him, however, was whether Pemberton or, as was more likely, Isaac had discovered that the information he had been providing was not only limited, but also misleading. Unlike Blanche, Nicholas could not be indifferent to which side he was on, though he understood what it meant to have divided loyalties.

To his relief, the officers he shared a room with had gone out and he was able to read Isaac's letter unobserved. Isaac, as usual, opened with an enquiry after Nicholas's wellbeing. He hoped Nicholas would be delighted with his charming new courier. They were very fortunate, he wrote, that Mrs Blanche Fitzpatrick was now residing in Dublin, as she was a trusted friend, as well as an acclaimed actress. Nicholas's

Chapter One

correspondence had been somewhat lacking and he hoped that the lady might inspire him to write more fulsomely. Of course he appreciated that, it being winter, there was little news to relay, but he was sure Nicholas must have some stories of note, given the circles he moved in.

Isaac went on to describe the performance of a very moving new opera, Henry Purcell's *Dido and Aeneas*, which he had attended in Chelsea.

The secretary was such an eloquent and engaging writer that Nicholas found himself not only enjoying Isaac's letters, but looking forward to receiving them, despite the fact that they were written on Pemberton's behalf. Of course this was partly because Isaac also supplied him with news from home and sometimes included letters from his father, which would never have reached him otherwise. But he was also convinced that the various matters of mutual interest discussed in Isaac's letters were not there merely to disguise their true purpose, but because Isaac recognised him as someone with a similarly discerning mind.

Isaac was, like Nicholas, illegitimate, but where Nicholas's father had always acknowledged him, it was a poorly kept secret that Isaac, whose mother had been a slave brought over from Barbados, was also Pemberton's natural son. This illegitimacy, along with a shared sense of duty to fathers who depended on them, had created a bond between the two. Now, however, Nicholas understood the warning in Isaac's words. He needed to supply more valuable intelligence.

Nicholas was not a willing spy and would be the first to admit that, even if he were not acting under duress, he would probably not have been particularly adept at it. But Pemberton, as well as threatening to ruin his father, had also supplied him with money and for that he had to make some return.

Chapter Two

Derbyshire, May 1690

'Just go into the kitchen and talk to the man, master to servant. Tha's never had any trouble with that before,' John said playfully, running a finger round William's nipple.

Placing one hand on John's chest, William pushed himself upright and got out of bed. He squatted over the chamber pot to empty his bladder and then pulled on his shirt before returning to bed with his pipe and tinderbox. Cushioning his back with a pillow, he leant against the wall and lit the pipe, puffing slowly on it as he stared into the empty fireplace opposite. Despite the heat outside, the thick stone walls kept the cottage cool and damp, but even in the depths of winter they never dared light the fire in case the smoke drifting out of the chimney alerted others to their presence there.

John sat up beside him, wiping the spent seed off his belly with a corner of the sheet and continuing their earlier conversation. 'Cooper must have seen how the price of grain has gone up. Where did the man work before, Westminster Palace?'

'I don't recall. Crewe appointed Cooper. Tickell is supposed to be training him up. Tickell's never been a spendthrift.'

The truth was, apart from Tickell and Palmes, who had both worked at Measham Hall under his parents, William generally avoided the servants. Crewe had always dealt with them so that he didn't have to.

Chapter Two

'Tickell spends most of his time asleep by the fire, or so our Kate tells us,' John said.

William sighed. He was fond of John's daughter Kate, whom he'd known since her infancy; she was an obedient, careful maid, so it disappointed him that she was carrying tales back to her parents. It was only to be expected, he supposed. Perhaps it had been foolish to bring her into the house to work, but he couldn't see that there was much risk of her noticing anything untoward between himself and her father, for they were rarely together inside the Hall.

'Tickell must be seventy if he's a day, so I can hardly begrudge him a nap. He's a good cook and a loyal servant. Poor old dog deserves a rest.'

'It is odd Mr Crewe didn't appoint a new steward before he died,' John said.

'Crewe couldn't know in advance he was going to drop down dead all of a sudden.'

'Yes, but he was usually so thorough in his preparations for all eventualities,' John answered mildly.

William tapped his pipe out into a saucer with an angry jerk, stuffing fresh tobacco into the bowl and poking it down hard with his finger. He knew he ought to have anticipated Crewe's death. The man had reached his seventy-third year for Christ's sake and yet they'd continued on as if he was half that age. It seemed absurd now that they hadn't made plans for his successor. After all, even if Crewe hadn't died, he would have needed to retire at some point. Perhaps that had been Crewe's only weakness, an inability to imagine Measham Hall without his own presence; certainly it had been William's – one of his own many weaknesses, he thought ruefully. Yet Crewe had seemed immortal to him; the man didn't seem to age, his mind had been as sharp as ever and he rarely suffered any ill health. Crewe had once referred to William as his apprentice; it had irked William at the time, but he had come to understand the truth of it and also how much he owed his old steward. It was Crewe who had taught him how to govern his house and land; indeed, it was Crewe who had taught him how to behave like a gentleman, never once questioning the sex beneath the clothes. Perhaps Crewe had thought William ready to manage without him. William wished this were so, but the departure of his dear friend had only made it clear how impossible a task that was. Crewe had been his armour and he felt horribly exposed without him. It was as though all those years since he had returned home, a nineteen-year-old girl disguised as her brother, had melted away with Crewe.

'God rest his soul.' John understood how deeply William felt the loss of the man who had been his guiding light for the past twenty-four years, but the need to find a replacement was becoming urgent. 'What about that chap from Nottingham? They speak very highly of him at market and he carried good references. He seemed an upright fellow to me.'

'I didn't like the way he looked at me.'

William recalled the man's eyes, which, instead of remaining downcast as was expected of a servant, had stared straight into his own. He supposed Mr Cartwright had wanted to demonstrate his honesty with his level gaze and upright stance, but his probing eye had alarmed William.

What he needed was the impossible: a loyal, trustworthy, intelligent steward who could be left to run the household, but who would also overlook what others might consider peculiarities in his employer. A man with no interest in gossiping, but who had his ear to the ground and would alert William to any threats to his estate. Someone who would treat those below him with respect and fairness, who could quell discontents and quash any rumours circulating about the master of Measham Hall. A man who was pleasant company, but who did not mind living a secluded life. A man who, if he was not a Catholic himself, had no objection to papists. What he needed was Crewe.

'What about a housekeeper?' John suggested. 'More women are being employed in such roles now. The Langleys down at Ashby have a housekeeper as well as a steward, though ye could manage here with just the one.'

'You're not thinking of Abigail, are you? She's no head for figures.' William rolled his eyes.

Chapter Two

John laughed. 'Nay, not Abigail, fine woman though she is.'

Setting down his pipe, William studied his hands. One of his nails had torn and needed cutting. John slid his own hand around William's, caressing it gently before holding it up to his lips and kissing it. Very few people saw William's hands ungloved and it was a gesture as intimate as if John had kissed his breast.

'You underestimate the danger a woman would present,' William told him, staring earnestly into John's grey eyes. 'Women are more curious than men; they're not content with surfaces, wanting to know all that lies beneath. I couldn't work so closely with a woman; the risk of exposure would be too great.' He tugged the sheet off John's legs. 'And a housekeeper would notice the extra linen on washday and want to know where it came from. It's a wonder Abigail never asks about it.'

'It's not so often we dirty the sheets now, is it,' John said a little sadly.

William looked at his bailiff with a mixture of affection and remorse. They had been lovers for nine years and the irresistible fire that had once consumed them had bedded down to a steady glow, providing greater comfort and warmth and less of that all-consuming passion that had nearly undone them.

If it hadn't been for John, William would have been utterly bereft after Crewe's death. It was weeks since he'd last had word from Nicholas and he didn't even know if his son was still alive. He shuddered at the thought of Nicholas lying injured and left to die on some Irish battleground. Surely one of King James's officers would make sure Nicholas's family was informed if anything happened to him? William lived in constant anticipation of a messenger arriving, longing for a letter from Nicholas yet dreading he might receive instead the worst possible news.

John put his arm around William's shoulders. 'We'll find the right person, don't fret thyself.'

William let his head rest on John's shoulder. 'Sometimes I wish we could just live here, like a couple of old peasants, with only a simple potager and a few chickens to take care of.'

'Tha'd soon get bored of that.' John chuckled. 'Tha'd be riding out checking on cattle and protesting at any changes in the house.'

'Not if it were Nicholas taking charge of the place.'

'That day'll come, and in the meantime God will send the right steward to thee, tha'll see.'

William said nothing. Whenever John was tormented with guilt or the fear of damnation, William argued that the love they shared was so profound and their compatibility so complete, it could not be sinful. It was men who invented religious laws, which was why they were always disputing over them. God was not concerned with these petty affairs of human creatures any more than He was troubled by the rutting of beasts in the field. So long as they were discreet and harmed no one, why should it offend the Creator if they took pleasure in the bodies He had created? In this William was using the same arguments employed by the man who had first seduced him. Sometimes he believed them and sometimes, though he could not bring himself to admit this to John, he doubted there was a God at all.

Atheism, the sin of all sins, was too vile a word to apply to himself, yet it seemed to him that the Bible was full of inconsistencies and even downright absurdities, which only proved it to be the fanciful invention of human brains. His brother had been hung for being a priest by men who believed they were carrying out God's work. And as much as he would like to believe they would meet again at the Resurrection, William suspected it was more likely that men perished like every other living thing, disappearing forever into the earth from which they'd sprung.

Turning his head, he pressed his mouth against John's neck, just above the collarbone, treasuring the feel of the warm flesh against his lips and grateful for these moments of stolen intimacy. For who knew how long they might last?

John brushed his fingers over the stubble on William's shaven scalp. 'My dear jewel,' he murmured softly. 'My heart's joy.'

⇾ Chapter Three ⇽

Ireland, 30th June 1690

The day was uncommonly hot for Ireland. Nicholas squinted across the brown earth to the river below, which glittered alluringly in the bright sunshine. He could feel the sweat pooling in his armpits, cooling his flanks as it ran down his sides. Carraig, his stone-grey courser, whinnied and tossed his head. Leaning forward, Nicholas swatted at the cloud of flies that had gathered around the animal's face. It was hard going over the ploughed ridges, Carraig's hooves sinking into the soft ground, but they had been ordered eastwards to see if it was true that Prince William himself had ridden right down to the riverbank in full view of his enemies.

'Over there.' The usually imperturbable Major O'Connor pointed with excitement across the river to where, sure enough, a party had dismounted to sit on the grass while their horses grazed beside them.

Nicholas put his prospective glass to his eye. It was the Prince of Orange all right, surrounded by his blue-coated *Gardes te Paard*, their yellow sashes as bright as buttercups. The so-called King of England clearly thought himself invincible, for he was lounging quite openly on the high riverbank eating his dinner. Of all Nicholas's experiences in the war so far, this had to be the strangest. To watch the enemy dining in the sunshine, making toasts and drinking wine as though they hadn't a care in the world, even as their foes looked on.

They found it amusing, he supposed, believing themselves out of range and knowing that the land was too boggy to cross over, to flaunt their ease in this way. Such arrogance deserved to be punished, though he couldn't help feeling a twinge of admiration for their daring display.

O'Connor rode over from where he had been conferring with Brigadier Sarsfield. 'Spread out,' he ordered quietly. 'Don't let them catch sight of the field guns.'

The riders manoeuvred their horses to shield the two light cannons being dragged down the field behind them. The men's excitement buzzed in the air around them like a swarm of bees. What a feat it would be if they could rid themselves of Prince William so easily. He would be known forever after for this foolish act of hubris, shot dead while reclining on the grass.

'Wait until the Prince is mounted,' O'Connor cautioned.

The soldiers stretched in their saddles and their horses pawed the ground. They were all impatient for action and anxious in case this opportunity was missed. Carraig strained to go down to the water and Nicholas shared his thirst, licking his cracked lips with a dry tongue; he wished they too could enjoy a drink.

Across the river, the Prince rose and, along with his men, got back on his horse and began to move off. Sarsfield immediately called the order and the troopers dug their heels in, their horses parting swiftly before the guns, which had been loaded and charged. A deafening ringing screeched past Nicholas and the air filled with smoke and the smell of gunpowder as a cannonball soared across the river. On the opposite bank several horses collapsed and a soldier was sent flying not a hundred yards from Prince William. The gunner fired a second shot; his ball grazed the ground then rose and Nicholas watched in awe as the Prince was knocked backwards. He had taken a hit to his shoulder if not his chest, Nicholas was sure of it. The Dutch horse guards immediately closed ranks around their king, riding off with him at all speed. If the blow had been fatal, they didn't want the enemy to know it.

Chapter Three

A mighty cheer rose up around Nicholas and he found himself joining in with equal elation. 'The Prince of Orange is killed,' they shouted. 'Long live King James!'

Nicholas had not become entirely inured to the sight of men torn apart by musket and cannon shot, and the destruction of the poor innocent creatures that carried them still saddened him, but his only thoughts now were for victory. He had been in Ireland for over a year and had confronted death on many occasions fighting alongside these soldiers. He had trained with them, shared quarters with them, heard them cry out in their sleep and call for their mothers when they were wounded. He had gone hungry with them and got drunk with them, and though their lack of discipline often enraged him, he had learnt all he knew about soldiering from them, both good and ill. His reasons for joining the Jacobite army may not have been as straightforward as theirs, but he longed for an end to the war with the same gusto, for only then would he be released from the obligations that bound him here. If he survived that long.

There was a great deal of celebrating in the Jacobite camp that afternoon, not least among Nicholas's squadron. Messengers were immediately dispatched to Dublin to take the news on to the King of France that his arch-enemy was dead at last. Why Prince William had acted in such a foolhardy way was hotly debated. O'Connor thought he must have been testing his men's mettle, wanting to see how well they could withstand fire, while Nicholas suspected the Prince had been trying to draw them into attacking. Not that the Dutchman's reasons mattered now, O'Connor pointed out. With their paymaster gone, the Danish mercenaries would surely return home, along with the Dutch and Huguenot regiments. They would be required back in Europe to continue their war with France, leaving at the least a more equal playing field in Ireland. King James's chances of retaking his throne in England were looking stronger than they had since the disastrous siege of Derry. If the Scots Highlanders could rally themselves for another battle like their victory at Killiecrankie, there would be no stopping His Majesty's forces from sweeping him back into power.

As it grew dark, Nicholas left these increasingly rowdy discussions, ambling away from the tents to gaze at the hills that ridged the pale evening sky like the painted scenes in a theatre. Behind them was a similar camp to this one, only much larger and with far greater reserves of ammunition. And not only were the Williamites better armed, they were also far more experienced in warfare than his own side; indeed, their ranks contained some of the finest soldiers in Europe. Though Nicholas had known the exhilaration of victory, especially in the retaking of Sligo, he had tasted the bitterness of defeat too often to join in the merrymaking of his men.

He wished it was Blanche Fitzpatrick he had a rendezvous with now instead of the man he was supposed to meet. What bliss it would be to escape into the soft folds of her body for an hour or two. Though, of course, he wouldn't want her risking her life by following the army onto the battlefield. No, it was much better to picture her safely in Dublin. If all went well here and he made it back to the capital, he hoped to rekindle the flames of her passion. This prospect provided some light in his darkest moments and was one he fixed on when in need of hope.

Once he was clear of the tents and past the stench of the hastily dug latrines, Nicholas moved westwards, across a field and down towards a copse of trees by the river. Hearing sounds behind him, he turned to see if he was being followed, but it was only the dry ears of barley rustling in his wake. The senior commanders were engaged in a council of war with the King, and the soldiers, who had been up on duty the whole of the previous night, would have finished their rations of brandy by now and cast themselves down to seize what sleep they could.

As Nicholas got closer to the river, he heard a rumble across the hills, which at first he took for thunder, but as he listened he realised it was the sound of cheering. He must be mistaken surely? What had they to cheer about – unless Prince William had survived after all?

Checking his position by the stars, he surveyed the horizon before putting his hands to his mouth and giving out a low call, like that

Chapter Three

of an owl. He waited for a moment and then called again. At last there was a reply and a moment later a figure detached itself from the shadow of the trees and came towards him. The man wore a red jacket, like many of the soldiers from both sides, and his hat sported the white cockade worn by the Jacobites. When he pushed the brim back off his face, however, Nicholas recognised the English scout who had first made contact with him in Armagh.

'Kept me waiting long enough,' Wallis muttered.

Further raucous cheers punctured the air and, seeing Nicholas startle, he added with some satisfaction, 'Your Jacobite shot hardly touched King William; the ball just greased his coat, nothing more.' Then he jerked his head towards the camp behind them. 'So, what're they planning?'

'I am not party to their council. You can tell your commander I am kept in ignorance,' Nicholas whispered, glancing uneasily about him.

There were bound to be sentries out checking the riverbank. Two women, both camp followers, had been hung for being spies a few days previously. They were poor, emaciated creatures, but their strenuous cries of denial still rang in Nicholas's ears and the sight of their bodies, hanging like puppets from hastily erected gibbets, came vividly before his eyes. Even if his commanders spoke up for him, in the heat of the campaign he could easily be made an example of, that was if he wasn't killed outright.

'You're a captain now, ain't you? You must know something,' Wallis insisted.

Nicholas moved into the cover of the trees, forcing Wallis to follow him. 'Orders are issued at the last moment and even then they are often changed. King James is easily persuaded to alter his plans, first by Tyrconnell and then by the Comte de Lauzun, and then he must lend his ear to his son, Berwick.'

Since he was supposed to be spying for Pemberton under duress, Nicholas had to be careful not to give the impression he was an eager informant, leaking just enough information to keep Wallis and his superiors happy while not giving them anything too damaging to his own side.

'So they don't know what they're doing; why doesn't that surprise me?' Wallis spat into the grass. 'How many men have you got? How many horse and how much artillery? You can give me a figure for that at least.'

King James's intention was to fight a defensive battle; he was therefore eager for the Williamites to launch the attack. To this end, Nicholas had been told to lower their real numbers when reporting to Wallis. He had to be careful, however, not to raise the man's suspicions nor to be proven to be a liar.

'Less than forty thousand men all told and many of them are armed only with half-pikes. Most of the muskets we have are in need of repair and we've twelve pieces of small ordnance at the most,' he rattled off.

'A deserter came over to us a couple of hours ago and he puts your numbers at over fifty thousand.' Wallis insolently tapped a finger on Nicholas's chest.

Nicholas batted his hand away. 'Who was it? A foot soldier? The fellow was exaggerating, like deserters always do.'

Wallis just shrugged. Nicholas was right, then: the deserter wasn't an officer and wouldn't have any significant information to reveal.

'And what should we expect tomorrow?' he asked as carelessly as he could, though he doubted Wallis knew much more than he did.

'D'you think I'm going to give away our plans?' Wallis snorted and Nicholas could smell his putrid breath.

Stepping back, Nicholas found himself pushed up against a tree trunk, brambles ripping his stockings. 'And have you any message for me? Any letters to pass on?'

'Lord Pemberton tells you to keep up the good work. That's all. Maybe after tomorrow we can all go home and you can check on your old dad in person.'

The man spoke with derision, pressing his grubby palm briefly to Nicholas's cheek before pulling the French cockade off his hat

Chapter Three

and replacing it with a green sprig for Flanders, which he kept in his pocket. Then, turning to check his surroundings, he ran off through the trees and disappeared into the night. Nicholas waited, expecting to hear splashing, for how had the fellow got to him without swimming? But there was no sound; Wallis had disappeared as swiftly and quietly as was his custom.

I hope you end up back home in Hell, he thought bitterly, though he was sure Wallis couldn't have been made privy to his father's secret. It was far too valuable a piece of information for Lord Pemberton to share with such a man. It was just unfortunate he hadn't managed to winkle anything more out of Wallis on the enemy's numbers and position. He didn't like to disappoint his commanders.

There'd been no word from Measham for weeks and Nicholas prayed nightly that all was well there. Hopefully Father had received the letters he'd sent. It had been impossible to write since leaving his winter quarters in Dublin and besides it would have been too risky to entrust a letter to Wallis when they were about to go into battle.

He lingered under the trees, inhaling the rich, damp smells of moss and peat and considered the possibility that this might be his last night on earth. If he was to die, he prayed it would be swift and heroic – a death that his family (as he considered all the household at Measham) could be proud of. A quick end by sword or musket as he charged into battle, rather than the slow ebbing away of life from a wound or sickness.

The enemy had grown quiet and it was only the sounds of the night that he could hear now over the flowing water. Something rustled in the undergrowth as he moved and he looked about for a badger, but a chattering hiss gave away the presence of a frightened stoat, perhaps a female with offspring nearby. As he emerged from the copse he noted the tick tick of a bat, the one they called 'leather wings' in Irish, along with the whirring, clicking song of a nightjar. Perhaps, across the sea, Father too was listening to the call of a nighthawk or an owl as he smoked his last pipe before bed. The air in the gardens at Measham would be heavy with the fragrance of syringa and honeysuckle and

Nicholas was seized with a longing to be back in the safety of his childhood home, sleeping beneath the familiar bed-hangings with their embroidered deer, instead of under dirty canvas impregnated with the odours of unwashed men on a diet of ammunition bread and salted meat. He sighed; *self-pity will get you nowhere*, he told himself, bending his mind instead to the example of his martyred uncle, who had never wavered once in his faith and who, Nicholas firmly believed, would one day be sanctified.

* * *

After managing to snatch a few hours' sleep, Nicholas was woken by the sound of the enemies' drums beating the muster and he scrambled up, along with the rest of the men, stretching out his stiff and weary limbs. A thick mist lay over the land and it was impossible to tell where the drummers were or what the Williamites were up to, only that they were on the move. Everyone's blood was up and the men were impatient to get on with the fighting, but, to their disappointment, they were ordered to pack up their tents with all haste. The baggage and most of the cannon were to be sent down the road to Dublin and they were to follow, riding westwards first, before falling back to the south.

As they were mounting their horses, however, a messenger came galloping into the camp. 'Count Schomberg's men are fording the river,' he cried. 'O'Neill's dragoons held them off as long as they could, but they were outnumbered and outgunned. O'Neill himself has been shot and had to be carried from the field and his men have followed him.'

The King and his advisors disappeared into a nearby farmhouse to confer once again, though this time the alarm was clearly visible on their faces. If the Williamites were across the Boyne they could cut off their retreat and with it their line of communication to Dublin. O'Connor returned to Nicholas's squadron with new orders: Sarsfield's horses were to follow Lauzun's French brigade and block Count Schomberg's progress.

Chapter Three

They set off at all speed, galloping hard over the uneven ground. The mist had lifted, and, looking over to the north as he rode, Nicholas could see battalions of red-coated Englishmen marching to confront them. The strains of 'Lilli Burlero' drifted over and soon it was not just derisory words, but cannon fire that was being volleyed at them. The distance was too great, however, and all the enemy's cannonballs fell short. Digging in his heels, Nicholas let Carraig fly at full gallop, as he prayed to God to grant his side the victory, whether his own life was spared or not.

Lauzun's troops were lined up on the edge of a ravine, watching the Williamite troops below: cavalry, infantry and cannon – thousands of men had crossed the river, but now they were mired in the bog and unable to move forward. With a surge of excitement Nicholas believed his prayers might be answered and that though their own numbers were smaller they could still beat the enemy.

As the morning progressed the Jacobite side kept increasing, as more and more Irish troops joined them, until by midday the majority of the Jacobite army was there, led by King James himself. Nicholas had to move his men sideways along the ravine to make space and they sat in their saddles, as restless as their horses, packed together in battle formation, squinting down at the enemy in the blazing sun.

'If that's William's main force, we can easily take them,' one of the French officers observed.

Nicholas stared down his prospective glass, looking out for the bright blue and yellow uniforms of Prince William's *Gardes te Voet*. It was strange, he thought, that William had ridden right down to the river yesterday, but there was no sign of him or his Dutch guards here to oversee the bulk of his army. He did not seem the sort of leader to remain behind his men. Count Schomberg's father, the duke, was said to be leading a smaller force at Oldbridge. The bridge was being held by the Earl of Clanricarde's regiments and Lord Tyrconnell had been sent to observe them. William could surely not be north, at Oldbridge? If he were, Nicholas supposed Tyrconnell would soon send them word of it.

All along the ranks the soldiers began calling for the order to attack. Nicholas could hear the mutterings of discontent among his own men; they had not joined the Jacobites to stand around like spectators at a tournament – what the hell was the King waiting for anyway?

'Hold steady,' Nicholas told them, moving with difficulty along the tightly packed line. 'You can see for yourselves the trouble they are in. D'you want your horses to drown in the bog before they even reach the enemy?'

O'Connor rode up beside him. 'Sarsfield and Colonel Maxwell are going to test the ground. As one of our most skilful riders, they want you to go out further west to see if the land can be crossed there.'

Delighted to have been personally chosen, Nicholas looked to where Sarsfield was urging his horse down the ravine towards the enemy. Even in the saddle, the brigadier's height was imposing and his figure was unmistakable. He rode with an easy grace even over the most difficult terrain.

Murmuring encouragement into Carraig's ear, Nicholas leant back in his own saddle and hastened after his commander. The horses descended hesitantly, feeling for sure ground to tread on. Nicholas looked across the valley to where the Williamites and their guns were massed, then, bending low in his saddle, he directed Carraig westwards. The ground here was rough and marshy, better suited for defence than attack. At the bottom of the valley a little brook ran and above it were two double ditches with high banks. No horse could charge over such terrain. Turning back, he met Sarsfield and Maxwell, who had come to the same conclusion.

'Schomberg's men are already turning and looking for another way round. If we don't make haste they'll cut us off from behind,' Sarsfield said.

'What the hell are they doing?' Maxwell pointed up to their own side. The dragoons were dismounting and leading their horses forwards.

'The King must have given the order to attack,' Sarsfield cried with alarm. 'Ride out in front and stop them.'

Chapter Three

Nicholas dug in his spurs, forcing his horse to race at the ranks advancing in formation towards them. If he couldn't stop them, he would be mown down by his own side. His mouth was dry and his throat parched, but he let out a great shout, waving his arm in the air. Had he been alone, he had no doubt he would have met his death, trampled underfoot by his comrades, but on spying Sarsfield and Maxwell galloping up beside him, Lauzun ordered his troops to stand down.

'Why didn't the King wait for our reconnaissance?' Sarsfield demanded of the King's adjutant once they had re-joined their own side.

'His Majesty has received news from Tyrconnell,' the man said quietly. 'The enemy has forced the pass at Oldbridge, they've crossed the Boyne and our right wing is beaten. The King wanted to charge Count Schomberg before our troops got to hear of it.'

Nicholas's belly sank like a stone. He stared back down the valley at the enemy troops who had already left the bog and were steadily marching south. They numbered many thousands, but there must be thousands more to have defeated the Jacobite regiments at Oldbridge.

* * *

It was an angry and frustrated procession of men who took the road to Duleek. The soldiers had been eager for battle and considered it a terrible shame to their honour to abandon the fight now. Despite the King's wishes, rumours were beginning to spread about Tyrconnell's defeat at Oldbridge. Nicholas rode up and down beside his troop, offering words of encouragement and consolation and doing his best to maintain order among his disgruntled soldiers, although he was as disappointed as they were.

The trumpeters had just begun to play, raising the men's spirits somewhat, when several horsemen came galloping towards them in a great cloud of dust. Some of the Jacobites lifted their muskets in preparation to fire, thinking the riders must be Williamites, but seeing that at least one of the men was wounded, Nicholas shouted out for them to lower their weapons. He was very glad to have done so, for as they drew near he saw the white cockades in their battered hats. The soldier at the front shouted out that they were Lord Tyrconnell's men.

'We did our best,' he gasped as he came up beside Nicholas. 'But we couldn't hold them back; there are too many.'

'Is it true, then?' a soldier nearby asked. 'Our side is already defeated?'

'At this battle, yes,' another of the men answered. He carried a second rider before him; the man's bare head was matted with blood and his eyes were rolling in his skull like a terrified horse's.

From behind them came the crashing of cannon fire followed by the whistling of a ball flying through the air; it went right over their heads and landed in the midst of a group of soldiers further along the road. Many of them dropped to the ground, while others picked up their heels and ran. Bullets began to whistle past. One or more of William's cavalries must be circling them; they were going to be trapped. More horsemen were racing along the road from the Oldbridge direction, charging through the foot soldiers in their haste to escape the enemy, with no thought as to who they trampled over. Nicholas gazed with horror at the mayhem taking place around him. All discipline was lost; it was as though wild dogs had been let loose among the sheep. Men were fleeing in all directions; some had even dropped their weapons and were tearing off their coats in their desperation to get away.

O'Connor came galloping alongside him. 'Follow me,' he ordered. 'Sarsfield's horse are to escort the King to Dublin.'

'Aren't we needed here, sir?' Nicholas asked.

'The French brigade are holding off the Williamites at the rear,' O'Connor told him. 'Lauzun wants His Majesty to return to Dublin. If James is captured the war is over.'

* * *

It was night by the time they reached Dublin Castle. What a contrast their entrance was to the first time they had marched triumphantly

Chapter Three

into Dublin accompanied by the sound of pipers playing 'When the King Enjoys His Own Again'. It had been Palm Sunday and they had been met by jubilant crowds waving palm fronds and cheering for their king. James had been so overcome, he had wept quite openly. Now, in the courtyard, the King was met only by a group of anxious-looking servants headed by Tyrconnell's wife, Lady Frances.

Positioned nearby, Nicholas overheard James tell her, 'Madam, your countrymen run well.'

Giving him an arch look, she replied acerbically, 'If so, I see Your Majesty has won the race.'

It was true, they had raced all the way from Duleek. The road had been as chaotic as an overflowing river in a storm, with both soldiers and the local inhabitants fleeing the fighting, many running in nothing but their bare feet. But it was unjust of the King to blame the Irish. From the reports that had trickled through to Nicholas, they'd fought like lions at Oldbridge. It wasn't their fault if the commanders had got it wrong. They had been mistaken about the Williamite movements and completely outnumbered. Many were blaming Lauzun for sending them westwards instead of to Oldbridge and some said the French had been more anxious to protect their own artillery than to win the battle, a point that was hard to dispute given that half their field guns had already been on their way to Dublin before the fighting even began.

* * *

Nicholas was in the King's retinue when he addressed the Lord Mayor and Dublin's highest-ranking citizens at first light the next morning. James informed the dismayed men assembled before him that since he was now necessitated to provide for his own safety, they should make the best terms for themselves that they could. After this rousing speech, he left with all possible speed. Nicholas was sure he spotted drops of blood on the King's upper lip and imagined he was succumbing to one of his infamous nosebleeds, just as he had done at Salisbury when he had fled the field leaving the way clear for the Prince of Orange.

'The French wanted him to burn Dublin to the ground,' O'Connor murmured. 'I suppose it's a mercy he refused to do that.'

Nicholas thought of Blanche Fitzpatrick. There was no time to go in search of her and, despite his enquiries, no one was able to tell him of her whereabouts. She came from a Protestant family and although she had married an Irishman, would surely welcome the arrival of King William, who was bound to reward her well for her service to him. If anyone was able to make good terms for themselves, it was Blanche. She had probably forgotten him already, Nicholas supposed, dismissing him as firmly as she had done her errant husband.

If it hadn't been for O'Connor, Nicholas too might have been tempted to follow the example of his monarch and desert the Jacobite cause. But the Irish were undeterred by the loss of their leader and around the northern outskirts of the city their army was already regrouping. The order came from Tyrconnell: they were to make for Limerick where they would reassemble. It was one of the largest cities in Ireland and a good seaport, protected by the mighty Shannon River, O'Connor explained. It was from Limerick they would continue the war and prove victorious, he was sure of it.

Regardless of what Lord Pemberton might expect of him, Nicholas was no deserter. If his comrades were determined to fight on and believed they had a chance of winning, then he would be there, fighting alongside them.

⇾ Chapter Four ⇽

Measham, June 1690

There was an unexpected rapping at the front door and William's heart leapt. Could it be a messenger with news from Nicholas, or better still the lad himself? He couldn't help feeling disappointed, then, when Palmes came into the parlour to tell him it was a gentleman enquiring about the position of steward. He would try not to hold it against the fellow. At least it wasn't bad news, he consoled himself.

William moved to stand beside the bookshelf so that he was out of the light and could regard the man without being on display himself. It was a bit odd to turn up on the doorstep without having written first and now it was too late to send for John. William preferred having his bailiff beside him when interviewing for the post, not just because he trusted John's judgement, but also because it meant he wasn't the sole focus of the candidate's gaze. Now he felt put at a disadvantage.

Palmes had been accurate in describing the applicant as a gentleman. Fashionably dressed in a dark velvet suit, he cut quite a different figure from the other men William had interviewed. Sweeping his hat off his head, the man gave a low bow.

'Mr Goodwyn, at your service.' He had the clear, confident articulation of someone well-educated.

'Take a seat.' William gestured to the chair in front of the window.

Goodwyn moved elegantly, crossing his legs as he sat back with calm self-assurance. The sun shining on his face didn't appear to bother him in the slightest. He opened his bag and pulled out a folded paper. 'I hope you will forgive my unanticipated visit, but I have a letter of recommendation from Mr Crewe, God rest his soul, and I wished to deliver it in person.'

William was startled. Crewe had never mentioned anyone by the name of Goodwyn to him. Why on earth would he have written a letter on behalf of a stranger? Taking the document from Goodwyn, he stared at the familiar hand. It was Crewe's writing all right, though not so easy to read in this dark corner; still, he had no wish to move into the light and come under scrutiny himself.

'Mr Crewe was an old acquaintance of my father,' Goodwyn explained. 'I also have a testimonial from my previous employer, Mrs Powell. I was a member of her household for many years, but after her husband's death she decided to close up their property in Monmouthshire and move to Spain, where she has relatives.'

Goodwyn took another letter from his bag and as he leant forward, William caught a whiff of oranges and ambergris. It was an attractive fragrance and made a pleasant change from the more earthy odours that emanated from most of the men he had dealings with.

'Mrs Powell has been gracious enough to commend me very highly as their steward. Although it was not a large household, I had many and varied responsibilities, ensuring neither she nor Mr Powell were ever troubled with disputes or shortages. Mr Powell was elderly and had suffered from ill-health for many years. They left the running of their establishment entirely in my hands, though of course I would not expect every master to behave in the same manner.' Goodwyn smiled modestly.

From what William could make out, Mrs Powell's letter was indeed full of praise, though written in a serious and sensible style, without the sort of hyperbole that might give rise to suspicion.

He lit his pipe, drawing on it slowly. 'We are a very small household, with only eight servants in total. You are clearly a person

Chapter Four

of some refinement and may find the position here too parochial for you. Would you not prefer to pursue a placement in a grander establishment?'

Mr Goodwyn leant forward, an earnest expression animating his placid features. 'I am a man of simple tastes and few worldly ambitions. I prefer the peace of the country to the clamour of towns and cities.' He paused before continuing more softly. 'And while I am always discreet in my devotions, my adherence to the old religion is not something I can compromise. My understanding is that I would not be compelled to conform to the Anglican Church under your employment.'

'I encourage my servants to attend the local church services, in accordance with the law, but beyond that I do not concern myself with their religion. It is a matter for them and the Almighty,' William answered carefully.

He hoped he hadn't said too much and exposed his employees to danger, but he was convinced by Goodwyn's manner that his faith was genuine. Besides, the devout Crewe would never have written a character reference for a non-Catholic.

'Of course, sir.' Goodwyn lowered his gaze to his knees.

'I cannot pay you above twelve pounds a year,' William warned him.

'That will be perfectly sufficient for my needs,' Goodwyn responded without hesitation.

William ran through the list of questions he had presented to each candidate so far and Goodwyn provided exactly the sort of answers he had wished for but not yet heard. Goodwyn looked around the same age as William too, maybe a few years older, but definitely under fifty. It was a good age for a steward; he would have wisdom and gravitas while still being far from senility.

'Well, you certainly appear to be just the sort of man I am looking for,' he told Goodwyn. 'Are you staying nearby?'

'I have taken a room at The Barley Mow.'

'Excellent choice. It may be a humble country inn, but it is clean and the innkeeper is an honest host.' William nodded with approval.

He had thought Mr Goodwyn might consider himself too good for the local tavern and was reassured that this was not the case. 'I will read over these letters again this evening. Perhaps you would be kind enough to return tomorrow morning at ten of the clock?'

'It would be my pleasure.' Goodwyn gave another low bow before departing.

As soon as he had gone, William read through Crewe's recommendation again. Crewe's appraisal was short but fulsome. He had known Mr Goodwyn senior for many years and, as might be expected of so worthy a gentleman, had heard only good reports of his son, who had been an irreproachable servant to the Powells. Crewe had been assured that Goodwyn was discreet as well as capable and considered him eminently suitable for the particularities of the post at Measham Hall.

It was the next best thing to having his old steward back beside him. He supposed he had come to rely on Crewe too much and should have made better preparations for his eventual departure. To think how suspicious he'd been of the man when he first returned to Measham. Little had he known then that Crewe had been working on his behalf even when he'd believed him to be an enemy. Now it was time to extend that trust to a newcomer. Not an easy task when there was so much at stake, especially considering all his son had gone through in order to protect him from exposure. Perhaps sending Goodwyn to him was Crewe's final act of stewardship. He had not neglected nominating his successor after all.

As William stepped into the hall, he spotted the serving-boy rushing past. 'Ben,' he called, hoping that was indeed the boy's name. The lad approached him cautiously. 'You know the innkeeper at The Barley Mow, don't you?'

The boy nodded. 'He's my uncle, sir.'

'Of course he is.' If William had been told about the connection, he had forgotten it. 'Did you see the gentleman who just called in?'

'It was me as heard him knocking at the door and went to tell Mr Palmes, for his ears don't work so well no more,' Ben explained.

'Good lad, but did you see the man?'

Chapter Four

Ben glanced anxiously about him as if searching for the correct answer.

'No matter.' William stroked his moustache. 'Your uncle will know him. I have an important task for you.'

'Yes, sir.' Ben's pimpled cheeks flushed red.

'I want you to go down to The Barley Mow first thing tomorrow morning and ask your uncle for a report of the gentleman that was here. His name is Goodwyn. Say Sir William is asking, but don't let Goodwyn catch sight of you. Can you do that?'

Ben nodded solemnly. 'Yes, sir.'

'There's a shilling in it for you if you bring me back a report of Mr Goodwyn by eight in the morning.'

'Thank you, sir.' Ben sounded delighted, and no wonder, for his mother had told him not to expect anything from Measham Hall beyond his board and lodging; that was ample for a boy just starting out.

It was the longest conversation William had had with Ben and he hoped the lad would prove equal to the task. He certainly seemed willing enough. William wanted John's opinion too and would make sure he was at the house when Goodwyn called the next morning. He couldn't afford to take any chances and though he had Crewe's recommendation, he wished he also had his old steward's network of informants working for him. He knew no one in Monmouthshire and had never heard of the Powells, but then, apart from reading the newsletters Crewe had subscribed to and following the news from Ireland, he did not concern himself much with matters beyond his own parish.

* * *

Ben was waiting in the hall when William came downstairs the next morning.

'Mr Goodwyn retired early to bed last night, sir,' he said, forgetting to bow in his excitement at accomplishing his mission. 'My uncle says, more customers like that and he'll go out of business for Mr

Goodwyn hardly ate nor drank a thing. If it wasn't for his costly apparel he'd suspect Mr Goodwyn of being a puritan, he was that sober. But Uncle couldn't find any fault in him apart from temperance.'

'Excellent work, lad.'

William smiled, imagining well the innkeeper's attitude to men such as Goodwyn. Ben remained before him, looking up expectantly.

'Your shilling, of course, let me fetch my purse,' William said, remembering his offer.

Instead of his customary morning ride, William returned to his chamber to prepare himself for Goodwyn's arrival. Pulling off his wig, he scratched his shaven head. If he was still a woman he would grow his own hair and not bother with that thing. At least he didn't have to wear a bodice laced tightly at the waist, though some gentlemen chose to enhance their figures that way. Picking up the looking-glass Lady Jane had given him as a gift, he examined his reflection. It was difficult to see exactly how he would appear to others in the small rectangle of curved and spotted grey glass, but at least it enabled him to check that his moustaches were correctly in place and that his appearance was passable.

Balancing the glass back on his dressing table, he turned to the side in order to see his shape, then ran his hands over his chest and abdomen, a reassuring gesture that confirmed his broad masculine flatness. He had been wearing this waistcoat for several years now and would soon have to send his measurements to Ellen for a new one. It was a tricky and inaccurate business, using strips of paper to measure himself, but Ellen, perhaps because she had been the first to dress him as a man, always seemed to judge it right, sending him embroidered, quilted stays fitted with whalebone and designed to conceal his breasts and waist. They were always comfortable and made him feel almost invincible – his male armour was how he thought of them. Ellen was a fine seamstress and he paid her handsomely for her work, partly in acknowledgement of the risk she took in encroaching on what the guilds would consider a tailor's business. He wasn't sure if it was the money or their former friendship that ensured her continued loyalty

Chapter Four

and discretion. Quite probably it was the pride she took in her craft. She certainly didn't approve of his metamorphosis.

He caressed the soft material between his thumb and forefinger. Although he didn't care to admit it, it was also the knowledge that, despite their estrangement, it was Ellen's fingers that had cut and stitched this cloth especially for him that made the garment so comforting to wear. There were times when loneliness crept up on him despite John's company, which he only had on loan anyhow. He loved John deeply, but longed sometimes for the sort of friendship he had known with women, Jane especially, and Ellen before she turned puritanical. And at least they had been able to stay in the house instead of having to sneak about, fearing exposure.

He had certainly enjoyed playing the man with Jane and she had encouraged him in it. He couldn't help smiling at the memory. She had even promised to marry him if ever she was widowed. Of course it was out of the question; the risk would have been too great and if his imposture had been discovered the punishment would have been more severe for such an offence against the marriage rites. Besides, he could not have given Jane what she desired, for it was John to whom his heart belonged, even if he hadn't fully realised that when Jane was still visiting.

He had been a fool to fight with her. He'd done her an injustice in accusing her of betraying Matthew and she'd ended up married to an arrant knave, albeit a very wealthy one. Nicholas had assured him Lord Pemberton was a good husband, but he for one would never forgive the juggler for his treatment of Nicholas, let alone for conniving with the plotters against King James. Even Jane had agreed with her husband in thinking Nicholas an unworthy suitor for Pemberton's daughter. William straightened his waistcoat, tugging it indignantly. They would be lucky to have Nicholas marry into their family.

Tying his cravat carefully around his neck, he surveyed himself again. If it hadn't been for John's friendship, he would probably have ended up a misanthropical drunkard like many an Englishman before him. By encouraging Alethea to step forward, John had also coaxed

William into a gentler form, so that both the male and the female sides of him could coexist. He did not have to blot Alethea out entirely; she was still there, only William took precedence. She was the secret self he shared with John only and both of them took pleasure in this concealed female form. And for the most part Alethea was happy for this to be so. William stroked his moustache. Why would anyone choose to be a woman when they could be a man?

* * *

Goodwyn arrived punctually at ten. His manner did not alter on being presented with John Thornly, and he treated the bailiff with the same respect and courtesy he showed William, only he spoke to John more as an equal than an employer, which was fitting to both their stations. John approved of the man's candour as well as his familiarity with the current price of goods as varied as wheat and ink. William, meanwhile, was impressed by Goodwyn's evident expertise in managing servants, as demonstrated when he explained how he would deal with various scenarios, from thieving footmen to pregnant chambermaids. Not that either situation was likely to arise at Measham Hall.

'He seems almost too good to be true,' William told John, after that morning's interview.

'Lives up to his name.' John smiled reassuringly. 'There can't be any harm in hiring him on a trial basis; you could suggest four months.'

'He might refuse to leave.'

John laughed. 'Why then I'd throw him out. He's hardly a hefty-looking fellow. A bit of a dandy perhaps; I would have expected a more homely sort from Monmouthshire, but maybe they're all fine gentlemen over there.'

'He claims to have simple tastes,' William said thoughtfully.

'I know Mr Crewe is impossible to replace, but you'll have to take on someone and I can't see anyone better than Mr Goodwyn coming along,' John said more gently.

To this William could only agree. Measham was hardly the most fashionable location. He sent Ben back down to The Barley Mow

Chapter Four

with a letter for Goodwyn. He could move into Measham Hall the following day to begin a four-month probationary period as steward. Ben returned with Goodwyn's acceptance of these terms and Abigail and Kate were set to work cleaning Crewe's study and preparing his chamber for its new occupant.

It would be strange to have someone else in Crewe's rooms, but at least they were on the ground floor, at the other end of the house to his chamber, so his privacy would be preserved. He spent most of his time outside, anyway. Once Goodwyn had learnt the ropes, their contact should be minimal.

⇻ Chapter Five ⇺

Ireland, July 1690

The journey to Limerick took over a week and these were some of the worst days Nicholas had yet spent in Ireland. All around the countryside had been laid waste, the crops destroyed by both armies, and there was neither food nor shelter to be had. Since they had been ordered to throw down their knapsacks at the Boyne, they had nothing but the clothes on their backs. The baggage should have arrived in Dublin, but it never appeared and there were rumours that it had been plundered by officers from their own side. Many of the infantry were barefoot and coatless, but worst of all, they had discarded their weapons in the desperate madness that had infected them as they fled the Boyne. At least Nicholas still had his horse and he was prepared to fight to the death to keep him, for they were in as short supply as everything else.

He rode up and down with the other officers, trying to marshal his troop, but all was chaos. Groups of soldiers kept leaving the road in search of food and forage, only to reappear a day or two later, with sacks of provisions, sometimes with a hen tucked under an arm, sometimes dragging a cow or a sheep by a rope, despite the prohibition on plunder. And how was Nicholas to censure them when the army was unable to feed or quarter them?

Their progress was also impeded by the crowds thronging the road: men, women and children of all ranks and occupations, from

Chapter Five

the highest to the lowest, all desperate to escape the Williamite army and its supporters. Great carriages rumbled out of Dublin, throwing dust and grit over the people trudging by. Only the highest-ranking Catholics had been allowed to keep their horses; everyone else had to carry what they could on their backs or in hand-pulled carts. Nicholas hoped they wouldn't fall prey to the thieves who always lurked on the edges of the army followers, but there was nothing he could do to protect them; he had trouble enough keeping an eye on his own men.

As they marched across the country this exodus only grew; the city tradesmen, shopkeepers and priests were joined by farmers and peasants. Those who could not walk were either carried or fell by the wayside. Some of these desperate exiles had fled all the way from Ulster and had nothing but the rags on their backs. How and where they were all to be fed and accommodated, Nicholas could not imagine.

Along with the clouds of dust being kicked up by hooves and wheels and feet was the constant noise: the rumbling, thudding, tramping sounds of movement accompanied by officers shouting at their men, soldiers swearing and singing, children crying, babies wailing, people calling anxiously for one another. Some wanted to rush ahead, fearful of the Williamite forces in pursuit, while others were too famished and weary to do anything beyond putting one foot in front of the other, to the frustration of those anxiously trying to push past. Nicholas had never seen such mayhem or been in the midst of such a throng before and hoped never to be so again.

Beyond the road, across the fields and meadows, the *creaghts*, driven down from Ulster, could be seen moving slowly through the land. They were said to be like the Tartar or the Scythians – families who followed a chief and no other authority, setting up shelter wherever there was pasture for their cows, which they loved above anything, never killing them but living only on what they called 'white meat', or that which is made from milk. Sometimes they supplemented this meagre diet with blood drawn off from one of the cows. They used small horses called garrons, or else caried all they owned on their backs, sleeping in makeshift huts and dressing only in woollen cloaks, which they would wrap around themselves at night, sleeping in a circle with their feet towards the fire. Nicholas was fascinated by the *creaghts* and had made several entries in his notebook regarding them. The people of Munster disliked them for their lawlessness and accused them of stealing cattle, but to Nicholas, these nomads might have been figures from a legend.

An old man dropped suddenly to the ground in front of him and Nicholas had to pull hard on his reins to stop Carraig from kicking the poor fellow. Dismounting, he knelt beside the prone figure. The man's wig had tumbled off into the ditch where it was snatched up before it could be retrieved. Nicholas helped the man's relatives carry him to the side of the road. A woman knelt beside him, kissing his face and calling his name in an attempt to wake him, but taking the man's wrist between his fingers, Nicholas could detect no pulse beating there. The man's hands were soft and his fingernails carefully pared. Beneath the dust from the road they looked quite clean, only one fingertip was stained with ink, as though he had just been writing a letter. Staring down at his lined face, Nicholas was reminded of Crewe, who had been like a grandfather to him, and his eyes filled with tears. In his last letter from Measham, Father had informed him of Crewe's sudden demise. Nicholas comforted himself with the thought that at least Crewe had died in the comfort of his own home and not had to suffer such an ignominious death as this.

Someone must have sent for a priest, for one appeared led by a young boy and leaning heavily on a staff, to deliver the last rites. The people passing slowed and crossed themselves, bowing their heads at the grieving family, but no one could stop for long. Nicholas, too, needed to catch up with his squadron and, remounting his horse, pushed away all thoughts of how the grieving family might bury the body or whether they would be forced to leave it for the carrion crows.

* * *

On the third day it began to rain and the road soon turned to mud, making their progress even harder as people and animals lost their

Chapter Five

footing on the slippery ground. The only benefit of the rain was that it provided them with something to drink and many were reduced to drinking from puddles. After travelling for two nights without rest or refreshment, Nicholas was so famished and weary, he left the road in search of quarters, taking the few men he could muster with him.

They were riding towards the town of Athy when they heard women screaming. Spurring on their weary horses, they hastened towards the cries, coming to a busy green in front of a collection of cottages. In the midst of a crowd of angry villagers were a pair of their own soldiers, attempting to hold onto two unsaddled horses while fighting off their attackers with their swords. Like most of the Irish army, they appeared to have lost their muskets. The villagers, who were armed only with half-pikes, were getting the better of the soldiers.

Using his lieutenant as a translator, Nicholas called for peace, promising to discipline the soldiers if they had been plundering the village. The soldiers shouted in English that they had been requisitioning the horses, as was their right, since theirs had been taken from them by Lord Tyrconnell's men.

After some heated discussions, Nicholas ordered the soldiers to relinquish the horses, much to the disgust of his own company. In acknowledgement of this act of restraint, the villagers agreed to quarter them all for the night. Though their generosity was probably as much due to the fact that they were outnumbered and reckoned they might as well give freely what would otherwise have been forced on them.

Nicholas and Lieutenant Cosgrave, having been assured their horses would be safely stabled, were shown to a house on the outskirts of the village. The elderly residents were welcoming them in with a mixture of curiosity and apprehension, when Nicholas heard his name being called. He turned to see one of the horse thieves coming towards him, a plaintive look on his face.

'Captain Hawthorne! It is Nicholas Hawthorne, isn't it?' the man called in an English accent.

'Do I know you?' Nicholas asked.

The man had a smooth, boyish face and sandy-coloured hair. He looked familiar but Nicholas had met so many men in the past year, this could have been any one of them.

'I am Francis Bedley,' the man said eagerly. 'We were at college together. I showed you around on your first day at St. Omers,' he added with a slight note of indignation as Nicholas regarded him blankly.

'Bedley!' Nicholas said with astonishment. Bedley had been a deeply pious youth and Nicholas couldn't think of anyone less likely to go looting. 'Aren't you a priest by now?'

'I am still in training, but felt called to fight for my sovereign. God willing, once this war is over, I will return to the seminary at Valladolid,' Bedley said earnestly, as he pressed himself against Nicholas's elbow, unwilling to let his fellow alumni through the door without him.

The old man stood looking enquiringly at them.

'*Sagart*,' Nicholas said, pointing at Bedley.

At this, the old man, who had not witnessed the earlier altercation, gestured for Bedley to enter and the two English soldiers almost tumbled through the doorway and onto a floor of bare earth. It took a few moments for Nicholas's eyes to adjust to the darkness of the smoke-filled interior and when they did he was struck by the sparseness of the furnishings in what appeared to be a single room.

They were invited to sit on benches around a table that had been placed beneath a small window. Apart from a cupboard, the only other item of furniture was a bed, which stood in the opposite corner. The old woman brought them cups of sour milk and cakes of barley bread, explaining apologetically that it was all the food and drink they had. All three men were so famished, they devoured this repast in minutes and the woman immediately set about making more barley cakes, which she cooked over the open fire. She and her husband seemed oblivious to the smoke that was making the soldiers cough. Nicholas supposed they had grown accustomed to the absence of a chimney, for there was only a hole cut in the thatch to let the smoke out.

Chapter Five

The old man brought out a pipe, offering to share it with the company, but only his wife smoked with him and they drew on the pipe in turn, holding the smoke in their mouths until the pipe was passed back again.

'The Irish women all smoke,' Bedley exclaimed disapprovingly.

'And why shouldn't they?' Nicholas asked, thinking of his father, who could never be parted from his pipe.

Leaning across the table towards Nicholas, Bedley frowned and lowered his voice. 'I have never before seen such filth and nastiness as I have witnessed in Ireland.'

Lieutenant Cosgrave, who came from Galway, raised his eyebrows disparagingly. 'No doubt you've never seen such poverty either and why do you suppose that is? Could it be because the English have robbed us of all we had and reduced us to these sordid conditions?'

Bedley shifted uncomfortably on his side of the bench. 'Well, it is true that Oliver Cromwell's party did all they could to oppress and even eradicate the native Irish. It is no wonder so many of them are happy to join the army, for even the lowest soldier is better off than most poor wretches here.' Seeing that Cosgrave did not appear appeased, he continued, 'And while many of the Irish have been forced into ignorance and degeneracy, those lucky enough to be educated abroad can be counted amongst the finest of gentlemen. Indeed I have encountered several.' He smiled benignly at Cosgrave, clearly including him in the list of such gentlemen and was taken aback when Cosgrave merely laughed in response. 'I will say this for the Irish, they are most stoical, for despite all the hardships they bear I've never yet heard one complain.' Bedley gestured towards their hosts.

Nicholas pulled a face at Cosgrave and shook his head. He remembered from his schooldays how pompous Bedley could be and how pointless it was to argue with him.

The old man spoke suddenly to Cosgrave, who explained that he was asking Bedley, the priest, for a blessing. This was something Bedley was only too pleased to bestow at great length, adding his thanks to God for this propitious reunion with his old school friend – an act

Nicholas was starting to see more as a test of his endurance than a sign of divine favour. After these extensive prayers, they were all glad to retire to bed. Nicholas and Bedley lay on the benches, while Cosgrave wrapped himself in a rug and slept in front of the fire. This was by far the better option, Nicholas soon realised, but since he was the superior officer he felt obliged to remain on the hard, narrow bench for the remainder of the night.

The following morning, after rounding up the few soldiers they could find, they set off again. The missing men would either find their own way to Limerick or disappear into the hills; there was no point in pursuing them. Nicholas was just relieved to have Carraig returned to him. Bedley was equally pleased to see the horse.

'I can ride up with you,' he told Nicholas happily.

Nicholas looked around for Cosgrave, but he had been quicker off the mark and was already trotting up ahead. It would have been unfair to inflict Bedley on him anyhow, Nicholas thought. At least he was not a heavy fellow and though Carraig's pace slowed, the extra passenger proved a more troublesome burden to Nicholas than to the horse.

* * *

At last the high stone walls of Limerick came into view and Nicholas's heart rose at the sight, for the city gave every appearance of living up to its reputation as the strongest fortress in Ireland. It was almost entirely encompassed by a broad river, which he had been told ran on all the way to the sea and would provide good access for the French fleet. They could not be kept under siege here, for there was also a large bridge on the other side of the city, which led into County Clare and would ensure the passage of supplies and reinforcements, as well as a means of exit for those inside. It was surely the perfect sanctuary.

On their approach, they rode through several miles of suburbs and despite his weariness, Nicholas admired the orchards of apples and pears and the well-tended gardens filled with vegetables and flowers. They also passed some fine stone houses, which were already crowded with soldiers and though Nicholas offered to leave Bedley at

Chapter Five

a number of these, his companion refused to abandon him, insisting instead that he would accompany Nicholas all the way to the citadel.

They arrived at St. John's Gate only to find it crowded with people seeking entrance, most of whom were being turned away by the guards.

'All troops are to camp outside the city walls,' one of the guards shouted at them.

Nicholas explained that he and his passenger were officers and asked if the man knew the whereabouts of Major O'Connor. O'Connor had befriended him at Saint-Germain and had recommended him to Sarsfield; he was sure the major would help him find lodgings. Since his tent and belongings had been lost, Nicholas was determined not to end up sleeping on the ground or stuck in a mouldy tent with half a dozen other men; he'd had enough of such rough conditions.

'The major might be up at the citadel, or else over in English Town; mind you, it's already full of French soldiers and the commanders have requisitioned all the best houses, so if you're looking for quarters you'll be lucky to find anything,' the soldier told them.

They tried the citadel first, since it was close by. It was a smaller, less impressive edifice than Nicholas had expected and he noted uneasily how decayed the grey walls were. They may have been four feet thick and built to withstand arrows, but how would they resist persistent cannon fire?

There was no sign of O'Connor and they were directed to look for him in English Town. Nicholas reminded Bedley of his promise to part ways at the citadel, but Bedley once again insisted on accompanying him in search of the major.

Nicholas made him dismount, since the poor horse was almost spent, and they made their way slowly along the passageway between the houses that lined Baal's Bridge, walking on into English Town, which, being at the western end of King's Island and completely encircled by the river, was the most protected part of the city. No wonder it was where the commanders chose to lodge.

Bedley paused his incessant complaining to express his admiration for the great number of ecclesiastical buildings on the island – churches, chapels and abbeys, many of which appeared to be still in use, though some parts were little more than ruins. He was particularly impressed by Our Lady's Cathedral, which towered over the buildings clustered below.

They found Major O'Connor busy organising the stabling of horses close by King John's Castle. A much more splendid building in Nicholas's opinion.

'Ah, Hawthorne, I was beginning to wonder what had become of you. Survive the journey all right then?' O'Connor smiled warmly at him. He was a tall, slender man in his middle thirties, his expressive features enhanced by the lines in his face. Despite his evident fatigue, his eyes were bright with their customary perspicacity.

'Just about, sir.' Nicholas returned a wan smile.

'At least you've arrived on horseback; that's more than can be said for most.' O'Connor nodded at Carraig. 'And he looks like he's still got some life left in him too. You can tie him up over there, by the water trough. There's oats for him in the stables.'

'His name is Carraig and I'd like to keep him,' Nicholas said uneasily. 'I bought him off a dragoon in Sligo and he cost me eight pounds.' Money had grown scarce and all Nicholas had left was brass, which was of little value, though it wasn't the money that concerned him so much as the horse, of whom he had grown very fond.

'All the horses are being checked over and, if they're fit enough, redistributed, but don't worry, if you're in the cavalry you'll have a mount to ride.' Seeing Nicholas's expression, O'Connor added, 'I'll make sure it's known he's yours.' He took out a ledger and entered the horse's name. 'The cavalry are to set up camp outside the city, over on the Clare side. You need to go out over Thomond Bridge.' He pointed across to a fortified stone bridge.

'I was hoping for quarters inside the city, sir,' Nicholas said.

O'Connor surveyed their grimy, exhausted faces. 'This fellow a friend of yours, is he?' he asked Nicholas as he raised his eyebrows at Bedley.

'We were at college together,' Nicholas replied, not wanting to deny Bedley to his face.

Chapter Five

'And I'm a lieutenant, sir,' Bedley said. 'In the Grand Prior's regiment.'

'Well, Lieutenant, you and Hawthorne here can share my billet for tonight. I'm lodging with a cousin of mine, a Mr O'Leary. He's a lawyer in the city with a house in English Town. I daresay he can take two more. Tell him I've sent you. I've business to attend to here, but I'll return later.'

Nicholas and Bedley offered their profuse thanks and set off once more in search of Mr O'Leary's home. Bedley was convinced Carraig had been ridden too hard to be considered fit for service, though he did not consider himself to blame for adding to the horse's load.

'Both the French and the Irish eat horses; no doubt yours will end up on some Frenchman's plate,' he told Nicholas helpfully.

They soon discovered that it would have been impossible to navigate the warren of narrow streets with a horse. Following O'Connor's directions, they eventually found themselves, after several wrong turns, in front of a tall stone house with a lion passant carved into the lintel above the door.

After knocking loudly several times, the front door was eventually opened by a maid, a short girl in a rolled linen cap whose round face was as freckled as a trout's back. She stood staring at them with a mixture of incomprehension and insolence. A woman's voice called to her from within and the girl shouted back in Irish without moving her feet from the doorway or her gaze from the two strangers.

'We are here to see Mr O'Leary,' Bedley told her sternly.

Refusing to budge from her post, the girl shouted again over her shoulder to whoever was inside. Eventually a young gentlewoman, a richly jewelled carcanet glittering at her neck, emerged from a side door. She stood behind her maid, regarding them with equal wariness.

Nicholas gave a low bow, uncomfortably aware of his filthy and bedraggled appearance. 'Good evening, madam, my name is Captain Nicholas Hawthorne and this is Lieutenant Francis Bedley. We have been sent by Major Tadhg O'Connor, who said Mr O'Leary would be kind enough to provide quarters for us.' He spoke slowly in case she knew no English.

The young woman shook her head firmly and the maid began to close the door, but Nicholas, in his desperation, stuck out his foot to keep it open. He knew many soldiers would have forced their way in, and though such behaviour was not in his nature, he believed they at least deserved a hearing.

'We are gentlemen and will conduct ourselves as such,' he said quickly. 'We will pay our way and treat your persons and your property with the utmost respect.' Now they were in Limerick he was sure to receive some long overdue pay.

For someone of such short stature, the maid was surprisingly strong and Nicholas had to lean against the door to prevent her from crushing his foot as she tried to push it shut. He cursed his lack of Irish and tried the same speech in French, while behind him Bedley babbled something in Spanish. Through the gap in the doorway he could see an enormous hound had joined the women and was growling at him menacingly.

'Are you besieging the houses one by one?' a voice behind them asked in perfect English.

'We are officers in the army of King James,' Bedley told the enquirer, 'and require lodgings. We were informed the gentleman here would provide them.'

'Were you indeed?' A lean, white-haired gentleman was regarding them quizzically.

Nicholas, his shoulder still pressed to the door, hastily explained who had sent them and then almost fell through the doorway as the maid suddenly withdrew. She stood to one side, directing a hostile glare towards his midriff; rather like a diminutive Medusa who would like to see him turned to stone, Nicholas thought. The dog, which was as tall as she was, gave a deep, ferocious bark.

The gentleman moved nimbly round Nicholas, calling reassuringly to the dog in Irish. 'I am Mr O'Leary, the owner of this establishment. You had better come in and we will discuss terms,' he told them.

Chapter Five

The young woman of the house spoke fiercely to him in Irish, clearly unhappy with his invitation and he spoke as soothingly to her as he had done to the dog.

Nicholas and Bedley entered the house with some trepidation, following O'Leary into what appeared to be a study, the woman and the dog close on their heels. O'Leary sat down behind a large desk covered in books and papers, gesturing for them to be seated also. Once they had done so they found their heads were on a level with the dog's. It licked its giant chops, as if about to swallow them both whole, and then sniffed curiously at Bedley's jacket. He let out a little squeak.

O'Leary smiled. 'Don't mind Fionn, he's gentle as a lamb.'

Nicholas reached out to stroke the animal's narrow flank. Its dark grey fur was coarse and long, but otherwise it resembled a giant greyhound. 'I have been told about the great Irish hunting dogs and am pleased to finally meet one in person,' he said.

'The *cú faoil* is much too big for a townhouse such as this, but we have always kept them and though my ancestral property was stolen from me by Oliver Cromwell, I refused to abandon the habit,' O'Leary replied. 'We also adhere to the Irish tradition of hospitality and will provide quarters for you here for as long as they are required.' He looked sternly at the woman, who was frowning back at him. 'Though sadly, we are much reduced in circumstances and cannot entertain you as well as we would once have done. Tadhg O'Connor is a relative and anyone sent on his recommendation will be welcome.'

Nicholas and Bedley spoke over each other in their haste to introduce themselves and offer their heartfelt thanks.

'Well, at least there are only two of you, or are we to expect more?' O'Leary asked, a note of wariness in his voice.

'I don't believe so, sir,' Nicholas said.

No one alluded to the possibility that the house would be requisitioned and the present occupants turned out, but O'Leary said pointedly, 'I have conducted some business for Lord Tyrconnell; I hope he will bear that in mind when it comes to finding quarters for his men.'

'We are here to defend your city against the Prince of Orange,' Bedley reminded him unnecessarily.

O'Leary sighed. 'Pray God that will be possible.' He turned to the woman, speaking to her in Irish.

Nicholas picked up the word '*uisce beatha*'. The young woman pursed her lips but went over to a cabinet in the corner and took out three glasses and a bottle, which she placed on the desk. O'Leary poured them each a measure of brown liquid.

'*Sláinte*,' Nicholas said, raising his glass.

This Irish toast won him a look of indulgence from O'Leary and a grimace from the woman.

'To His Majesty's good health,' Bedley declared.

'*Séamas an Chaca*,' the woman muttered.

Nicholas was familiar with the name some Irish were giving to his king and did not entirely begrudge them the rude epithet. His own misgivings about James had increased on hearing that when he arrived in Kinsale, the King had insisted on being accompanied back to France by the entire squadron of recently arrived French frigates. A measure that was unnecessary for his own safety and deprived the Jacobites of vital naval assistance.

'Now, Úna, do not insult our guests,' O'Leary scolded. 'My daughter believes we Irish are fools to lose our lives for an English king. She thinks Ireland is just a battleground for foreign armies and that neither the French nor the Dutch, and especially not the English, have our best interests at heart.' He downed his drink and waved his glass at Úna, who obligingly topped it up.

'The Irish are flocking to join our ranks,' Bedley said indignantly. 'We are united in fighting for the one true religion.'

'So you are papists.' O'Leary nodded. 'I suppose that gives you a more pressing reason for supporting King James.'

'He is our rightful monarch,' Bedley retorted.

'And now his daughter and son-in-law rule England,' O'Leary said mildly, then shook his head. 'How sharper than a serpent's tooth it is to have a thankless child.'

Chapter Five

'Is that from an English play?' Nicholas asked with surprise, sure he recognised the line.

'*King Lear*.' O'Leary nodded.

Nicholas glanced at Úna, wondering if she had understood her father's reference to ungrateful daughters. She had seated herself on a stool on the other side of the room. The dog lay beside her, his huge head resting on her lap and she caressed his ears absentmindedly with one hand, while holding a pipe in the other. *That won't help to endear her to Bedley*, Nicholas thought with amusement.

'Shakespeare is one of the better English dramatists, in my humble opinion,' O'Leary said. 'Though not as great a poet as some of our Irish bards'

'It is certainly a tragedy that Princess Mary and Princess Anne have failed in their duty to their father, but I suppose a wife must obey her husband.' Bedley had no interest in playwrights or poets and wanted to return to the topic of their shared faith. 'God be thanked, His Majesty has a Catholic heir.'

'It makes little difference to us whether James sits on the English throne or William.'

To the astonishment of both Bedley and Nicholas, Úna spoke in Latin; not only that, but it seemed clear she understood English well enough to have followed their conversation.

'Neither king shows any inclination to return our lands or to free us from the usurpation of our enemies. James has already shown himself only too willing to appease the...' She paused for a moment, clearly struggling to find the right word, finally resorting to the Irish '*plandálaí*'.

'My daughter is referring to the English and Scotsmen given plantations in Ulster by James I and later by Oliver Cromwell,' O'Leary explained. 'Depriving the native Irish of their land and forcing them to go hungry.'

Úna nodded vigorously, continuing in Latin. 'While the French only want to detain William in Ireland to stop him from leading his armies against them in Europe.'

She was remarkably well informed and Nicholas could only agree with her assessment, though he did not say as much. He had long suspected that Louis was keen to prolong the war in Ireland in order to keep William distracted from Europe for as long as possible. He also knew that the French officers had been ordered to avoid any action that might incur the loss of their men and, more importantly, their artillery. It was no wonder the Irish did not trust them.

'Having only one child, I have raised my daughter like a son. I am only thankful she has not cast off her petticoats and put on breeches.' O'Leary chuckled, appearing to enjoy the young men's discomposure.

Nicholas thought uncomfortably of his own parent, who had done just that, but O'Leary seemed more amused than concerned.

'She might join the rapparees yet. What say you, *a leanbh?*'

'I am no bandit,' Úna retorted.

'It is a shame she cannot take up a profession, as I myself have done. Úna would make a fierce lawyer.' Undeterred by her scowls, O'Leary smiled proudly at his daughter.

Bedley had turned quite pale at the prospect of female lawyers and, fearful of what his compatriot might say, Nicholas interposed, speaking in Latin for Úna's benefit. 'My family home was also sequestrated under Cromwell's rule.'

The fiery maiden was unmoved by this admission. 'Though I imagine your property was returned to you,' she replied curtly.

'We did not get all our lands back. But it is true we regained Measham Hall, which means everything to my father.' The *uisce beatha*, consumed on an empty belly, was making him babble and Nicholas stopped himself from continuing.

Úna had turned her attention back to the dog and merely snorted in response, or perhaps it was the dog snoring. Her face was obscured by her dark hair, which she wore long and loose in the Irish fashion.

'If you take the road to Killaloe you will pass our family castle, Kilbawn, a grand stone building fit for Irish kings. I believe it stands empty now, since the adventurers who took it from us fled at the first sign of trouble,' O'Leary said.

Chapter Five

Nicholas considered it likely the house was now occupied by Irish troops, but wasn't sure if this news would be of any comfort, so merely nodded.

'The Prince of Orange certainly misunderstands the Irish people if he thinks they will turn against their own,' O'Leary continued. 'I expect he will be disappointed by how few take up his offer of a pardon, for his proclamation is obviously intended to bar any Irish Catholic lords from reclaiming their estates.'

William had issued a proclamation offering a full pardon to all the Irish now in arms who surrendered by the first of August, excepting the leaders of 'the present rebellion'. It was commonly understood that he had been influenced in this by those who had gained property and land under Cromwell and did not want to lose it.

Úna spoke to her father in Irish and they had a short and somewhat heated discussion, while Nicholas and Bedley, exhausted and hungry, sat studying the table with half-closed eyes. Nicholas hoped O'Connor would arrive soon, as his presence would surely increase their chances of some supper. They'd had nothing to eat since the previous day.

'Mairead will prepare the attic for you. You will find it quite comfortable,' O'Leary told them. 'Perhaps you would like some refreshment while you wait?'

'That would be most welcome,' Bedley replied, swaying slightly.

'We're sorry to cause your household any inconvenience,' Nicholas said, his heart lifting at the prospect of some food.

'Not at all, not at all. Úna my dear, can you send Mairead in with some milk for the officers.'

Úna rose and left the room without saying another word.

* * *

The attic floor was covered in rush matting, which in many rural houses the people slept on, but to Nicholas's relief there were also two narrow beds, both with flock mattresses and coarse but clean sheets and blankets. The mistress of the house might disapprove of them, but at least she had provided fresh bedding.

'What a strange household,' Bedley said. 'I suppose it is not surprising that the maid is so rude when her mistress is a termagant. And yet the father seems proud of his daughter's shrewishness. I know Irishwomen are said to be forward, but not even an Irishman would want a wife such as that.'

'I think we've taken the maid's sleeping quarters.' Nicholas threw himself onto the bed. The mattress was lumpy and his feet stuck out off the end of the bed, but after many nights spent sleeping on the ground it felt like heaven. He was sorry to deprive the maid of her chamber, but was too battle hardened and weary to offer to swap places with her and sleep in the kitchen.

'I wonder if her ill humour is caused by her plainness or whether her ugliness is a result of her foul temper,' Bedley mused.

'Are you talking about the daughter or the maid?' Nicholas asked, only half-awake, despite the grumbling of his belly.

'Miss O'Leary. It is clear from the pitting on her face that she has suffered the smallpox, but she should be grateful to have got off lightly. I've seen beauties whose otherwise perfect complexions have been ruined by the disease. Indeed, Miss O'Leary should count her blessings and be thankful to God that her life was spared.'

'I'm surprised you could see her face beneath all that hair.'

'Such a slattern.' Francis shuddered. 'Though it seems to be the fashion among Irish women not to dress their hair. Headlice must be rife among them. No doubt we'll be lousy too by morning.' He began to inspect the bedclothes.

But Nicholas had already fallen into a deep sleep.

⇾ Chapter Six ⇽

Measham, June 1690

William had to shed some of his natural caution in order to show Goodwyn the Measham account books and explain the composition of the household, its income and outgoings. He was grateful to Goodwyn for his tact. He kept a respectful distance, never looking at William directly and never questioning any of the decisions that had been made. Not that any money was wasted on luxuries or entertainments. Some men might consider William an overly generous landlord and an indulgent master, but his relatively modest largess kept the inhabitants of Measham loyal.

He thought of inviting Goodwyn to dine with him, as Crewe used to, but quickly quashed that notion. He did not want to set up a familiarity he would later regret. It struck him now how limited his knowledge of society was. He derived all his information from his own fireside and memories of the few months he'd spent living with the Calvertons as Jane's companion, but theirs was a much bigger and wealthier household than his and he had been but a girl when he stayed with them.

'Crewe kept excellent records,' Goodwyn noted with satisfaction, running his finger along the neat rows of figures and their accompanying explanations set down in Crewe's looping, secretary hand. 'While I can never hope to take the place of such a pillar of your family as

Crewe was, it is my desire to be equally useful to your house and your estate. Your ease shall be my ease.'

William was reassured by Goodwyn's words and pleased by the admiration he expressed for his predecessor. He also agreed with the sentiment expressed: Goodwyn would certainly not take Crewe's place; he doubted anyone capable of that.

Abigail knocked on the door and William took the opportunity of introducing her. Always dressed respectably, in simple, neatly fashioned clothes, she was a stout, comely woman and though she could be short-tempered and given to gossip, he would always be grateful to her for the love she had shown his son, as well as for her loyalty to him. She had turned down two offers of marriage that he knew of. John joked that Abigail saw herself as William's proxy-wife and would never submit to any husband but him. She certainly kept the other servants in order and though they sometimes teased her, they were as fond of her as if she was their own sister. As she curtseyed, her sharp eyes took in the new steward. Goodwyn half-rose from his chair behind the desk and nodded.

'Abigail has been with us for twenty-four years.' This was easy to remember because it was his Nicholas's age. 'She first came to us as a nursemaid and has been acting as the housekeeper here since Crewe's death.' He hoped Goodwyn would take the implied warning – Abigail had a proprietorial interest over the Hall and its workings and wouldn't take kindly to being crossed.

'And what a fine job you have done, Mrs Abigail. The cleanliness of the house is a tribute to you. I have entered grander mansions whose nobility is marred by dusty hangings and unswept corners. Here I see all is fresh and sweet.'

'Well, I do the best I can,' Abigail said with a mixture of deference and pride. 'Kate is a good lass, who works hard and does as she's told.' She directed this to William.

'I'm glad to hear it.' William realised too late that he ought to have lined the servants up to meet Goodwyn, instead of taking him straight into Crewe's study. 'We do not stand on ceremony here,' he

Chapter Six

explained. 'And you may find us a less formal establishment than you are accustomed to.' He turned back to Abigail. 'Since we are finished here, perhaps you might conduct Mr Goodwyn around the rest of the house, introducing him to each member of our Measham family.' Good God, he sounded like a parson.

'Of course, sir.' Abigail raised her eyebrows but looked pleased with this elevated duty. 'I came to ask where Mr Goodwyn will be taking his dinner.'

There was a moment's silence, which Goodwyn quickly filled by saying that if it wasn't too much trouble, he would take his meals in his own rooms. William assured him that this was no trouble at all. Abigail's expression was guarded, but William knew she would be chewing over the fact that the new steward considered himself above dining with her and the other servants.

* * *

On summer evenings, William liked to take a stroll around the gardens with Jove, his dog. While the spaniel snuffled in the undergrowth, he would stand inhaling the scents of the flowers and shrubs that released their finest perfumes before closing their petals for the night. A sense of melancholy had descended on him that particular evening, which was close to the anniversary of his brother's execution. He and Matthew used to walk the gardens together, debating matters philosophical and religious, discussing the future of the estate and the state of the country. Matthew, who had undertaken Nicholas's education, would keep him up to date on his son's progress in the schoolroom. Sometimes he and Matthew disagreed and sometimes they walked in companionable silence, but he had always admired his older brother and tried to please him. Now, he conversed inwardly with Matthew's spirit and this was for William, who was something of a sceptic, a form of prayer. He asked Matthew to keep Nicholas safe from the injuries of war and the diseases that accompanied it; to ensure, if he could, Nicholas's safe return to Measham.

His son had inherited William's love of the natural world, only Nicholas's interests were scientific, where his were of a more traditional nature. Every evening he visited the plants Nicholas had brought him from the physic garden at Oxford and was comforted to see them thriving, as though their fates were somehow linked to Nicholas's.

Crouching down to admire a bed of crimson, white-fringed gillyflowers, William was startled by Jove erupting into a volley of barks. He turned to see Goodwyn ambling down the path towards him.

'Please forgive me, sir, I did not mean to encroach,' Goodwyn said, stopping a few feet away.

William called the dog to his side and bade him be quiet, for Jove was still growling at Goodwyn.

'I would not deny the delights of the garden to anyone who can appreciate them,' he said, straightening up and reaching automatically for the pipe and tobacco box kept always on his person, setting the oval box on top of a hedge as he filled and lit his pipe.

'Who was it who wrote that the breath of flowers is like the warbling of music?' Goodwyn lifted his arms in a gesture of celebration 'I always think that one is never closer to God than when one is in a garden. It is such a balm to both the body and the soul.'

'Exactly,' William responded with enthusiasm. 'My cousin used to say that we find our natural home in a garden, because it was where God first placed us. So we strive to recreate the Garden of Eden, with its orchards, herbs and flowers.'

'What beautifully expressed sentiments,' Goodwyn said warmly.

'I wish I were as eloquent as Matthew was.' William sighed. 'He communicated his thoughts much better than I can.'

Although Matthew was in fact his brother, they had called themselves cousins. It had suited them both for Alethea to adopt her brother's identity, becoming William, while the original William had in turn followed his vocation and become Father Matthew Harcourt, a Jesuit priest. So the siblings had given themselves new selfhoods, one becoming a man, the other a man of God.

'Did your cousin consign many of his words to paper?' Goodwyn asked. 'Perhaps you might publish them if so. Only for circulation among a select audience of course.'

Chapter Six

'I do have a few of his sermons.' It had not occurred to William to share Matthew's writings, but he thought the idea would appeal to Matthew, who had devoted his life to spreading the word of God.

'Your cousin Matthew was a priest?'

'An exemplary one.'

Without noticing it, William was strolling side by side with Goodwyn down a shady alleyway towards the woodland garden. As their feet trod on the herbs planted underfoot the smell of thyme and chamomile rose up to mingle with the smoke from William's pipe. Jove, having dropped his guard, scampered on ahead.

'Matthew dedicated himself to all those who sought his ministry, choosing to follow his vocation here, when, with his capacious mind, he might have pursued a career in Rome or Paris, or even Whitehall. Somewhere close to the seats of power where he would have garnered greater recognition.'

'A man of God and of the people.'

Was that admiration, or was there a note of irony in Goodwyn's voice?

'He was a true martyr,' William found himself saying, although he had always been the first one to puncture such veneration.

'Was your cousin *the* Father Matthew Harcourt of Derbyshire?' Goodwyn came to a sudden halt. 'Pray forgive me, I should have remembered,' he said more earnestly. 'Indeed, I have in my small library the pamphlet containing his last speech from the scaffold. He was murdered during those terrible days of the so-called Popish Plot, was he not?'

William nodded, impressed that Goodwyn had kept Matthew's speech and pleased that it had been so influential. 'I suppose publishing his sermons would be a way of immortalising them, but it would have to be done in secret. I fear the times we are in make it too dangerous an undertaking, even if they were only copied out by hand.'

'They could be printed abroad and smuggled back into England, many papist texts are shared that way, but as you say, sir, the risks involved are far too great. I should never have suggested such a thing.'

'Are you involved in this trade?'

They had come to the end of the hedged walkway and passed into a glade surrounded by birch trees.

'I have purchased books from friends who have connections to the book trade. Indeed, I do have an associate in the printing business. He is a superior printer who produces small volumes of great quality.' Goodwyn took a round tortoiseshell box out of his coat pocket. 'Would you object if I indulged in a pinch of snuff?'

'Not at all.' William waved his pipe in the air. 'Though I thought snuff-taking was a city pastime, one for coxcombs and the like.'

Goodwyn smiled ruefully. 'It is a habit that is becoming more widespread, I believe.' Flicking the hinged lid open with his thumb, he took out a pinch of tobacco, which he inhaled with a quick snort. 'Perhaps I should substitute it for pipe smoking instead.' He sneezed before turning to spit into the grass, wiping his nose with a red handkerchief.

'New master, new method of taking tobacco,' William said with amusement. 'What type of leaf do you use; is it Virginia?'

'I find Havana-snuff finer; it is said to clear the lungs and refresh the brain.' Goodwyn held the box out to William, who took a pinch of the powder, smelling it with curiosity.

'Is it perfumed with lavender?'

'Yes, and bergamot.' Goodwyn flipped the lid shut just as a breeze set the birch leaves rustling. 'The powder is apt to blow away,' he explained, perhaps realising that the gesture might have seemed impertinent.

'And a very pretty box too,' William noted. 'Are those ancient gods?' He pointed at the scene engraved in silver, of two men outside a tent, one lying with his head in the lap of his comrade, their helmets on the ground beside them.

'The illustration comes from Homer's great poem the *Iliad*. They are the Greek warriors Achilles and Patroclus.'

Goodwyn stroked his thumb over the engraving with a tenderness that made William suspect the box was a gift from someone held dear.

Chapter Six

It was certainly an expensive receptacle and not something a steward was likely to purchase for himself.

'My tobacco-box is not so ornate, but no less precious for all that.' William fished the silver box out of his pocket. 'It has our family crest imprinted on it and was given to me by Matthew.' He rubbed his own finger over the demi-lion bearing an orb aloft.

'May I?' Goodwyn took the offered box from his hand, cradling it in his palms. 'It is beautiful in its simplicity.' After studying it carefully, he passed it back, holding the box aloft with the sort of reverence usually reserved for a holy relic.

William was touched by his veneration. 'I tried to persuade Matthew to take up smoking as a preventative against disease, but he never took to the habit, said it made him cough and croak like a frog.'

'And a priest needs a clear voice.'

'Which Matthew certainly had. I never heard anyone recite poetry or Bible verses better.'

'Which poems did he like to read?' Goodwyn asked.

They had begun to walk again, rambling through the trees towards the lake as though they were old friends who had trodden this path many times before.

'As a priest he kept to the psalms, but when he was young he used to compose his own sonnets and odes.' William turned to Goodwyn with some excitement. 'I had quite forgotten that Matthew was once a poet. Perhaps there might still be some of his verses written down somewhere. We could surely publish those without fear of arrest.'

'Indeed, sir,' Goodwyn responded with equal enthusiasm. 'I have a fondness for poetry myself and would be honoured to assist you in such a work.'

'I will search the attics in case any old scribblings have been kept up there,' William declared, forgetting that as far as the world was concerned, Matthew was only a cousin and not his brother.

Fortunately, Goodwyn did not seem to find it odd that Matthew's early writings should be stored at Measham Hall; he was only interested in finding and preserving them. It was very pleasant to have such an appreciative listener, especially in regard to William's memories of Matthew. Since Crewe had died he had no one to share these memories with.

John was not one for dwelling on the past; as far as he was concerned, Matthew had chosen his fate and was surely in Heaven now. To mourn excessively was a self-indulgence that could not be pleasing to God. It was better to be thankful for what they had been given than to rail against what had been taken away. John had lost three infants, so he knew whereof he spoke.

Unlike Crewe, John had never held Matthew in high esteem, perhaps because he had known Matthew since they were both boys. Not having any brothers to play with, Matthew used to go over to the Grange to provoke and tease John, who was three years older than him, and the two of them would end up rolling around on the ground, locked in combat, while Alethea looked on, fearing they'd kill each other but unable to stop them. That enmity had never entirely disappeared, despite the difference in rank.

Although he recognised the need for a priest to shrive the local population, John could not see that Matthew brought many benefits to Measham. He had resented Matthew's influence over William and his interference in what John considered his territory as bailiff. It was as hard for John to submit to Father Matthew's authority as an adult as it had been for him to bow to young Master Hawthorne's will as a child. Indeed, William sometimes wondered if John wouldn't have ended up on the side of Parliament during the late civil wars had he been old enough.

A breeze had sprung up as they walked, blowing clouds in over the lake and now it began to rain, the drops battering the ruffled surface of the water with increasing rapidity. They turned back to the house, but were soaked through by the time they reached the door.

'That was unexpected,' William exclaimed, stamping his feet and shaking out his arms.

Copying his master's actions, Jove also shook himself, spraying the two men with muddy water. Goodwyn cried out in dismay. In

Chapter Six

the flickering candlelight of the hall, William thought he saw a look of disgust cross Goodwyn's face and ordered the dog to lie down. Jove took up his place by the door with his tail between his legs. Bowing, Goodwyn retreated to his room to change out of his wet clothes. William, not bothered by a little dampness, grabbed a lantern and went straight up to Matthew's bedchamber, where he unlocked the door.

The room had been shut up for the past eleven years and no one had ever dared to suggest reusing it. He held his lamp aloft to survey the chamber. At least, apart from the dust, everything appeared to be in order. The mice had not got in; he would smell them if they had, besides there was nothing here for them. The hangings had been removed from around the bed and the mattress given to Palmes to help cushion his aging bones at night. Now the bedframe stood forlornly against the wall like the skeleton of some giant beast. Its only coverings were the grey cobwebs draped across its posts like the last remnants of skin or hide.

On the other side of the room, standing sentinel, was a large cupboard, emptied of its contents. William had taken most of Matthew's clothes, which were simple but of good quality. They were of similar stature; William's extra flesh made up for Matthew's additional inches in height. He had already taken up his brother's discarded person, so it was only natural to put on his clothes. Wearing them, William felt endowed with some of Matthew's confidence in the rightness of their lives at Measham. It was a comfort to feel his brother's lawn shirts, worn soft with age, against his skin.

The only objects of value had been a locket he had given to Nicholas and a gold crucifix he kept in his own chamber, along with a little statue of the Virgin Mary that had belonged to his mother. The books had all been added to Measham's library, which improved it significantly. William was not a great reader or buyer of books, though he did have a fondness for verse, shorter poems especially.

Matthew's papers had been left in a small desk that stood in his closet, covered with a Turkish carpet. William didn't recall these including any poems, but there could well be sermons.

Placing his lantern on the window ledge, he removed the rug and opened the desk. Beside a neat stack of notebooks tied together with a crimson ribbon was a pen-case full of quills and a small bottle of dried-up ink. Such ordered neatness was typical of Matthew. At the sight of the dirty bottle, encrusted with flakes of black ink, William was assailed by an unpleasant surge of guilt. How could he have left these words of Matthew's locked away without ever reading through them properly?

Watching Matthew's execution had been almost too much to bear. If it hadn't been for Nicholas's presence and the need to show some fortitude, he might have collapsed. He kept telling himself how fortunate they were that Matthew had been saved the torturous drawing and quartering he had been sentenced to, because the crowd, won over by Matthew's final speech, prevented the soldiers from dismembering him. His death by hanging had been mercifully swift and they had even been allowed to bury his corpse in Measham.

For years, anger and love had fought for precedence in William's heart. Anger with Matthew for choosing the path of martyrdom and love for the very same reason. He imagined their mother welcoming Matthew into Heaven, so proud of the son who had fulfilled all her greatest hopes. What on earth would she make of her daughter who lived as a man? It had been easier to justify the choice when Matthew was alive because William had been aiding Matthew's vocation. But with Matthew gone, his only defence was that he was holding Measham Hall safely for Nicholas, and now he feared that reason might be obliterated too. Then he would be forced to admit that his reasons were selfish ones; he lived as William for his own survival and no one else's. Since tasting life as a man, he could not return to the prison that was womanhood.

Perhaps all this stirring up of old memories was not a good idea after all. His discussion with Goodwyn had made him realise how much he missed conversing with Matthew. Talking to him in his head was all very well, but it was hardly the same as a conversation with a living person.

Chapter Six

Removing his gloves, William pulled on the bow that bound the notebooks and, despite the years that had passed, the ribbon slid easily through the knot. The first book had a yellowing vellum cover and felt soft between his hands. He was surprised by his own sense of trepidation as he opened it. He did not like to trespass on his brother's privacy. At the sight of the familiar handwriting his heart swelled with grief and it took him some time to decipher the words through his tears. At first, it seemed enough simply to trace his finger over the curling black lines that had been formed by his brother, but eventually he forced himself to sit down and read them properly.

Most of the pages were filled with religious meditations and he was struck anew by the beauty of their expression. There was nothing here to tarnish Matthew's memory. None of the revelations that, William had to admit, he had feared discovering. For in his youth, Matthew had not been so virtuous as he later became.

William continued to read until the oil in his lamp was almost spent and found no references to Matthew's earlier indiscretions in these writings, no hints of lust or weakness, no mention of gaming tables, strong liquor or pretty men. Just the humble reflections of a wise soul, one who strived to do God's will and wished to inspire others to do likewise.

On picking up the last book, several folded papers fell out. The writing on these was not in Matthew's hand. The tiny words slanting across the sheets made a pattern of verses, but they were all in Latin and William, never having learnt that language, was unable to decipher them. The few words he recognised suggested they were love poems. He could have fetched Matthew's Latin dictionary and attempted to translate them, but it seemed to him that such an invasive action would be tantamount to opening up the crypt and picking over Matthew's bones. Besides, they had been composed by some other party. That Matthew had kept them suggested the writer was someone he held dear, but William had no desire to pry further. He folded them up again and slid them under the sheet of blotting paper that lined the interior of the desk.

He had no qualms about showing the notebooks of Matthew's religious writings to Goodwyn, however, since Matthew had already delivered passages from these to any Catholic stranger who came to hear his sermons. These were public works, worthy of publication. Indeed, he was sure Matthew would want such illuminations to light up the lives of as many souls as he could reach. For the first time in many years, William felt a spark of hope igniting in his breast.

* * *

Goodwyn was equally impressed by Matthew's compositions. He had only had the books in his possession for one day, when he approached William with an unusually animated demeanour.

'Your cousin's writings are really quite exceptional, sir.' Goodwyn held one of the notebooks aloft. 'His style is so fluent and the images so well-conceived. With your permission I will make copies and send them to my associate in the printing trade. He will treat these works with the respect they deserve. We could start with just a few, for your approval.'

'Of course.' William, who had just come in from hunting, was rather amused by Goodwyn's excited enthusiasm. 'I must admit, I am ashamed now of having left them buried away when they could be a source of spiritual and moral succour to those in need. Reading them was like having my cousin beside me again; I could hear his voice rising up off the page.'

Then he caught Palmes's eye, for the butler was standing close by with a bemused expression on his face, and William experienced a sudden pang of misgiving.

'And you are sure your printer is trustworthy?' he asked, lowering his voice.

'I would trust him with my life, sir. Besides, the work is not overtly papist; I honestly don't believe there is any danger of it being picked up by the censors, and even if it was, I will ensure it is not traceable back to you.'

William nodded. 'They truly are the most uplifting of divine contemplations; it would be a sin to keep them from the world.'

Chapter Six

He had always relied on Crewe's judgement and his old steward had published Matthew's final speech. There could be nothing wrong therefore in printing more of his brother's writings. He was sure Crewe would have approved of the endeavour.

'Also, at the back of one of the books are a collection of excellent sayings,' he couldn't resist adding, his own excitement returning. 'What do you call them?'

'Aphorisms?' Goodwyn suggested.

'That's it, and very wittily expressed too.'

Goodwyn moved closer towards William, so that he was standing directly in front of Palmes. 'You mentioned your cousin's poems, sir; it was these you were originally interested in circulating.'

'I did not find any poems written by Matthew,' William said quickly.

'Perhaps there were some additional papers you would like me to sort through on your behalf?' Goodwyn suggested. 'Or works written in Latin that you would like me to translate?'

William began to think he ought to temper the steward's eagerness. 'That is quite all right, Goodwyn, copying out the notebooks is an onerous task in itself and it cannot distract from your duties as a steward,' he warned.

'No indeed, sir.' Goodwyn bowed. 'The work will be undertaken only once all the tasks for the day are completed.'

'Well, don't wear yourself out.' William smiled. 'The public can wait a while longer for Matthew's works.' His stomach was rumbling and he hastened into the parlour for his dinner. He had always been more a man of the flesh than of the spirit.

⇾ Chapter Seven ⇽

Ireland, July 1690

Nicholas slept longer than he had intended, waking to the sounds of people on the move – the rumble of cartwheels and the thudding of hooves, along with chattering voices, rose up from the street below. In the bed next to his, Bedley was curled up on his side, snuffling like a mole in its nest. Rising quickly, Nicholas washed himself as best he could with the water that had been left for them in a large earthenware ewer. He had hoped to be first, but judging by the murky state of the water, Bedley had carried out his ablutions the night before. Pulling on his boots and jacket, Nicholas tiptoed out of the room, eager to be free of his irksome companion.

Mr O'Leary was standing in the hall and invited him to take a breakfast draught of Xérès with him. But on hearing that Major O'Connor, despite his late return the previous night, had already left for the citadel, Nicholas declined the sherry and hastened out.

The streets were teeming with people – men from the country carrying pitchforks and scythes, eager to enlist to fight the English, were accompanied by the wives and children who had no option but to follow them.

The women had the haunted expressions of those who have lost everything and are still trying to comprehend the disastrous turn their lives have taken. Patrolling foot soldiers were trying to turn

Chapter Seven

them back, but they may as well have tried to turn the tide of the Shannon. Having nowhere else to go, the people were determined to seek sanctuary within the safety of the city walls and streamed around the soldiers in an unstoppable current. Some tried to impress upon the guards the extent of their sufferings, how they had been harassed by marauding soldiers who had stolen their cattle and their goods and burnt them out of their homes. Others just elbowed their way past, too grief-stricken for speech.

Navigating the crowds, Nicholas moved as fast as he could to get to the citadel and report for duty. Having been quartered in such pleasant conditions (even taking into account the disagreeable Úna and the tiresome Bedley), he was anxious to prove his worth to Major O'Connor so that he might continue to lodge there.

There was a great bustle in the courtyard as he passed in through the outer gate and he stopped to watch Lady Tyrconnell being helped into a carriage along with her daughters. Trunks and boxes were being stowed on the roof and loaded onto wagons behind. A considerable guard was assembling to accompany her on her journey. He enquired of one of the soldiers where she was going and was told that her husband was sending her to France along with all their own and the King's gold that she could carry.

As he watched, Sarsfield's young wife, Honora, came out on the arm of the Duke of Berwick and was helped into the carriage alongside Lady Tyrconnell. Honora was smiling and chatting animatedly, as though she were embarking on a pleasure trip, not escaping a war. She was probably excited to be going to the French court, Nicholas thought. She had already gained a reputation for her beauty and her charm, despite being only fifteen. They would surely embrace her in France. Berwick kissed her hand and gave a low bow. Nicholas wondered why it wasn't her husband seeing her into the coach. She and Sarsfield had been married less than a year, but she was at least twenty years his junior. Perhaps she found young Berwick more amenable; he was certainly closer to her in age.

Nicholas made a hasty bow as Berwick sauntered past him, whistling. *Stop speculating*, he told himself. He was getting as bad as those officers who were more interested in courtly intrigues than military affairs. Perhaps it was because the vivacious, rosy-cheeked Honora had brought to his mind an image of Lettice Pemberton, or Mevrouw Van Dorp as she was now called. Isaac had mentioned the wedding in a letter as though it were a piece of society gossip and Lettice was some distant acquaintance, instead of the woman Nicholas had almost eloped with. Lettice was 'happily settled in Amsterdam', he'd written. Nicholas hoped this was true and that Lettice was as content as Honora appeared to be. The difference in ages between spouses was similar, though Sarsfield was a great deal more spirited and handsome than the phlegmatic Van Dorp. Not only that, but Sarsfield was a celebrated warrior, while Van Dorp was esteemed only for his wealth and his collections.

Although he had considered himself heartbroken at parting from Lettice, Nicholas no longer regretted his failure as a suitor. His time at Saint-Germain had taught him that he was no courtier. Lettice was ambitious and would never have been content with the modest life he could offer her. His chest still ached when he thought of her, but memories of his former sweetheart troubled him less and less often. Indeed, on seeing Honora now, he realised that he hadn't thought of Lettice for some weeks. He hoped Lady Pemberton had been correct when she told him that some day in the future he would receive an invitation to attend a literary assembly hosted by Mrs Van Dorp, for it had been Lettice's dream to hold renowned society gatherings. Such occasions seemed a world away from the war in Ireland and now, even if he did receive such an invitation, he could not imagine being in a position to accept.

He stood to one side as the entourage rumbled out towards Mungret Gate. It came as no surprise that Lord Tyrconnell did not consider Limerick safe enough for his family and possessions, but if Sarsfield was sending his wife away as well, he too must fear the city would fall to the Williamites. Or perhaps he resented her departure and that was why he was not there to bid her farewell.

The inner hall of the citadel was full of officers waiting for orders. Tyrconnell and Lauzun were ensconced in a private meeting

Chapter Seven

and nothing could be done until they had finished. The sense of discontent and frustration among the men was palpable.

'Why are we waiting around for the English to arrive and dictate the terms of the battle, instead preparing to win it?' an Irish lieutenant grumbled, to general agreement. 'We should be fortifying the town and planning its defence.'

Spotting O'Connor in conversation with another officer, Nicholas made his way over, standing at a suitably respectful distance until O'Connor noticed him hovering and greeted him warmly, speaking to him in English.

'We've drawn the short straw, or been given the honour, of seeking an audience with Tyrconnell to request a council of war.' O'Connor gave his companion a rueful smile and the man raised his eyebrows.

Despite his advanced age, Tyrconnell was still an imposing figure and he was not used to being crossed. He was known for flying into rages, which was why there was some trepidation in approaching him.

'Can you believe it, after everything we've put the men and this country through, they're talking of giving in to the Prince of Orange,' O'Connor told Nicholas.

'Lauzun can't wait to get back to France and Tyrconnell has grown cowardly in his old age,' the other officer agreed.

But to everyone's relief, they emerged from their meeting smiling and announced that Tyrconnell had agreed to a council of war.

'Now we can plan our victory!' O'Connor declared, thrusting his fist into the air to a chorus of huzzas.

* * *

While his superiors were busy in the council, Nicholas snuck off for a walk around the city, retracing his steps over Baal's Bridge and onto the King's Island. Here, just beyond the walls, was a public house surrounded by carefully laid out gardens and a bowling green. All around him birds were singing and he could hear men calling out the scores good humouredly after each soft clunk of the bowling balls landing. It was as if they were oblivious to the cannonballs about to bombard them.

Around the ruins of an old fort, sheep and cattle grazed. *They'll soon be rounded up and consumed*, Nicholas thought. He had seen towns like Cavan burnt down to nothing despite the confidence of his fellow officers and could only pray that Limerick did not suffer the same fate.

He would have to make contact with the Williamites again soon, especially if he wanted letters from home, but he was in no great hurry to risk his life riding into the enemy's camp. Then it occurred to him, if he behaved discreetly and avoided any further advancement, escaping the notice of Pemberton's men, they might conclude that he was dead. And if he was, there would be no reason for Pemberton to expose his father. He knew he was not the only spy; there had been plenty of information leaked to the enemy that he was not responsible for and the garrison would have its share of informants and deserters. The trouble was, he would have to convince his own side that they no longer needed him to gather intelligence on the Williamites.

Nicholas had become friends with several of the Irish courtiers in Saint-Germain and had grown to esteem them highly. Not wanting to spy on his friends or undermine a cause he supported, he had chosen to confide in O'Connor because he knew him to be a compassionate and even-tempered man who would hear him out without rushing to judgement. Fortunately, he had been proved right in this, for O'Connor had listened carefully as Nicholas described how it was he had been coerced into spying. Lord Pemberton was married to an old family friend and had been a generous benefactor, making it difficult to refuse his request, Nicholas had explained, and when he had resisted, Pemberton had threatened to make life difficult for his father, who was a known recusant. This was convincing enough in itself, without having to expose his father's real secret and the reason for Pemberton's hold over him.

After promising he would not suffer for his revelations, O'Connor had presented Nicholas's case to his commanders, convincing them that Nicholas would make a trustworthy spy for their own side, while continuing to fight for the restoration of King James. So it was that Nicholas continued to act as an intelligencer, giving the enemy just enough genuine information to keep them content, while simultaneously

Chapter Seven

misleading them and learning what he could of their plans. He had been dancing on this precarious rope ever since he joined the Jacobites in France a year and half ago, but now he was so weary, he feared a fall.

Debates between the commanders usually lasted hours, but he arrived back at the citadel just as the door to the chamber opened and the officers came storming out, their voices raised in anger.

'It wasn't a council at all, Tyrconnell wasn't there to confer, he had it all planned. He showed us a declaration signed by all but one of the French officers, stating that Limerick would not be able to hold out for more than three days and we should surrender while we can get good terms. He says we'll get no more aid from France and must agree a treaty with the Prince of Orange,' O'Connor told him bitterly.

'If he thinks we'll submit to the treacherous English he must be even further along in his dotage than he looks,' an Irish officer spat.

'At least Sarsfield is standing by us; he won't capitulate,' another declared.

Although he disliked the bullying arrogance of Tyrconnell, Nicholas couldn't help hoping the viceroy would hold sway. His motives were both personal and practical; he considered it unlikely that they could hold out against the Williamites' forces, which were superior in both numbers and experience, and he was also desperate for an end to the war so that he could be released from his role as a spy. The sooner they made peace the better the chances, it seemed to him, that they would get good terms and he might be allowed to return to England.

* * *

Since no one had ordered him to re-join the cavalry, Nicholas returned to O'Leary's house that evening. He was aggrieved to find Bedley had had the same idea and was already there, ensconced in the parlour beside the long window, reading his Bible.

Mr O'Leary cheerfully invited them both to join him for supper. Nicholas had managed to secure a fairly substantial dinner in a tavern and was prepared to be offered only milk, but he was pleasantly surprised by the meal. Cold mutton, a salad of roasted root vegetables and a dish of artichokes were laid out on the table. There was also a large jug of ale.

'Major O'Connor isn't with you?' Mr O'Leary asked, evidently disappointed by his cousin's absence.

'He is in a meeting with Brigadier Sarsfield,' Nicholas explained.

'They have much to discuss, I'm sure.' O'Leary nodded. 'And what is the plan for the city?'

As it would soon become public knowledge anyway, Nicholas thought it could do no harm to mention Tyrconnell's declaration, but Bedley gave him a warning look and a sharp kick beneath the table.

'Peace is always preferable to war,' O'Leary said mildly. 'Better to negotiate than see our city in ruins.'

'But look how other cities occupied by the invader have been treated, with the people starved and dispossessed and the land destroyed.' Úna once more turned the language from English to Latin, though it was clear she understood what was being said.

'Our side has not been without fault there,' Nicholas couldn't resist interjecting. 'Newry, for example, a pretty little town, put to the torch under the Duke of Berwick's orders.'

'King James's bastard,' Úna said with derision.

Nicholas, being a bastard himself, smarted under her words.

'Brigadier Sarsfield is famous for his clemency,' she continued earnestly. 'It is said that when he retook Sligo he treated the Huguenots who had been holding it to dinner before giving them safe passage out.'

'That is true.' Nicholas set down his cup of ale. 'I was there when he offered them each a horse and five guineas' advance pay if they'd join us in fighting for King James. All but one refused, and that one rode off the next day with his horse and his money.' He laughed at the memory.

'Are you in Colonel Sarsfield's regiment?' Úna asked, her spoon halfway to her mouth.

'I am,' Nicholas answered, enjoying her look of surprise.

Chapter Seven

'Were you both reared for a career in the army?' O'Leary passed around the dish of artichokes.

'No indeed.' Using his knife, Bedley scraped half the vegetables onto his plate. 'I am a novitiate at the Jesuit seminary in Valladolid, but I was given permission to enter into King James's service.'

'We are honoured to have you at our table,' O'Leary said magnanimously. 'And you, sir?' He turned to Nicholas, who hastily swallowed a mouthful of mutton and wiped his chin.

'As I am the only heir to my father's estate he would prefer me safely at home, but the rebellion in England sent me to France and then to Ireland.'

'You were raised a gentleman, then.' O'Leary's bright blue eyes studied Nicholas with an astuteness he would not have wanted turned against him in a witness box.

'I am fortunate enough to have a worthy parent, one who was not ashamed to acknowledge me as their own,' Nicholas replied, still offended by Úna's jibe at Berwick's illegitimacy.

'You are your father's natural son?' O'Leary asked nonchalantly.

Bedley, however, looked uneasy and Nicholas realised that his old college associate had probably been unaware of his indeterminate status.

'I am a bastard, yes,' he said, shooting a defiant look in Úna's direction.

'Well now, according to Brehon law there is no such thing as a bastard.' O'Leary raised his bushy white eyebrows. 'Once a child is named and acknowledged by its father it has the same rights as any other offspring. These Irish laws were, of course, prohibited under English rule,' he noted sadly. 'And our traditions are all but dying out.'

'I have no objection to those born out of wedlock,' Úna said quickly. 'Only Irish wars should be led by Irishmen.'

'We had several Irish students at the Jesuit College in St. Omer,' Bedley said, aiming to change the direction of the conversation. 'Studious, thoughtful fellows. I think all except one found a calling to the priesthood.'

'Thaddeus,' Nicholas remembered. 'I'm surprised we have not encountered him among the officers here.'

'I heard he is fighting for the other side,' Bedley said, his voice hushed at the scandal of it. 'His father was slighted in a promotion by the King and so he went over to serve the Prince of Orange.'

'Traitor,' Úna muttered.

'I thought you considered both William and James to be as bad as each other?' Nicholas pointed out.

'I do, but I make an exception for those fighting under the likes of Sarsfield, men who have Ireland's best interests at heart.' She glanced at Bedley. 'Isn't it the case that the Pope himself favours William?'

'That is mere hearsay.' Bedley looked gravely affronted. 'His Holiness may be opposed to King Louis' territorial ambitions, but that does not mean he wants to see the Mother Church suppressed in Ireland, or anywhere else for that matter.'

'We are all at the mercy of more powerful rulers,' O'Leary said in a placatory tone. 'That is why negotiation and compromise are paramount if we are not to see our country devastated.'

'The Church has always followed the precept *"virtus stat in medio"*, but when it comes to defending what is right there can be no question. Did Christ not say, "I came not to send peace, but a sword."' Bedley responded with vigour, waving his knife in the air and inadvertently sending a lump of carrot flying across the table. 'We must execute the wrath of God against those that do evil, and the Protestant tyranny of the Prince of Orange is an evil to be fought against.'

'I am not fighting a crusade,' Nicholas countered, flicking the piece of carrot to the dog, who had been watching its progress with some interest.

'What are you fighting for?' Úna asked, suddenly curious.

Pleased by what appeared to be her genuine interest, Nicholas tried to answer as truthfully as he was able. 'I support King James and the right to practise our religion without being persecuted or penalised,' he said carefully. 'My grandfather fought for Charles I; we have always been loyal to the Stuarts. Besides, my cousin was one of those

Chapter Seven

priests executed in the so-called Popish Plot and I wish to honour his sacrifice.'

'Revenge, then,' Úna observed.

'Now, now, my dear, there is no need for such a severe assessment; Captain Hawthorne's motives might also be called noble,' her father chided. 'We do not want to see the Penal Laws reintroduced here either.'

Though Nicholas was offended by Úna's quick judgement, he also winced inwardly at O'Leary's kinder one, for he knew how far from noble his motives really were.

O'Connor arrived back and the conversation around the table, which was now conducted mostly in Irish, became more lively. The use of her own tongue seemed to melt Úna's frosty demeanour. Gold flecks sparkled in her dark green eyes, animating her expression and indicating a sense of good humour she was yet to share with her English guests. She had a wide, generous mouth and in contrast to her often harsh words, her smile was unaffectedly joyful. You could forgive her almost anything if she rewarded you with a smile like that, Nicholas thought. No wonder her father was so indulgent of her.

* * *

'What a virago that woman is,' Bedley muttered as they climbed the stairs to their room later that night.

Nicholas did not disagree, though it was clear her ill humour was reserved especially for them. His pride had been piqued by his inability to win Úna over, for he had become accustomed to being treated with a mixture of admiration and tenderness by most of the women he encountered. It was rather disconcerting to meet a woman who was resolutely immune to his charms. Not only that, but one who spoke to him as though she were his superior, despite her young age and her lack of rank or fortune.

Chapter Eight

Measham, 12th July 1690

William spread *The London Newsletter* across the table. It announced the King's victory in Ireland. The late King James's army had been defeated beside a river near a place called Drogheda. Many prisoners had been taken, including some inferior officers, but their names were not yet known. Might one of them be Nicholas? Better that than him being slain, for the article also claimed many had been killed. The late King James (as they liked to call him, as though he had died rather than been usurped) had retreated to Dublin and from there was believed to have gone towards Athlone and Connaught. Perhaps Nicholas had gone with him. His Majesty, King William, had issued orders for sparing all that laid down their arms. William prayed that Nicholas would surrender and be allowed home.

He was pleased when Goodwyn knocked on the parlour door; he was just the man to discuss these events with. Goodwyn's knowledge always seemed to be more current than the information in the newsletters, which were already old by the time they reached William.

'They have arrived, sir,' Goodwyn declared with the exultation of someone announcing royal visitors.

'What have?' William asked, distracted by Goodwyn's excitement.

'Father Matthew's books.' Goodwyn almost leapt across the room. 'If I may?' Moving the newsletter along with the dish of calves' foot

Chapter Eight

pudding it had been resting on, he wiped the table by William's elbow with his handkerchief, before removing a leatherbound quarto volume from his pocket. This he placed down ceremoniously in front of William. 'I had this one bound specially, with the Hawthorne crest imprinted on the cover.'

Appreciating Goodwyn's reverence for the little book, William washed his hands in a bowl of rosewater and dried them on his greasy napkin, before picking it up.

'The works deserve to be in folio, of course,' Goodwyn continued. 'But that would make it much harder to circulate them and discretion is the better part of valour, as they say. If you are willing to invest, I could order a folio edition, but it would be costly.'

William turned the book over in his hands, enjoying the feel of the soft crimson leather. 'I believe Matthew would have preferred these to some large and ostentatious volume.' Opening the cover, he understood a little of Goodwyn's delight. It was certainly impressive to see Matthew's words in bold black print, indented onto the paper indelibly, but such permanence was equally alarming. 'You don't think print too common? Perhaps we should have kept to handwritten manuscripts. Matthew was a refined gentleman after all. I wonder if he would have approved of our venture?'

'If I may speak freely, sir?' Goodwyn bowed and, when William nodded his assent, continued. 'Having laboured over Father Matthew's writings I have, without wanting to sound boastful, acquired a profound understanding of them, and this, coupled with what you have told me of his character, convinces me that for these particular works, print is the means your noble cousin would have chosen to spread his knowledge and share his message, were he with us.'

Goodwyn had pulled out a chair and now sat beside William at the table. Recognising the man's absorption in a subject clearly very dear to him, William chose not to take offence at his boldness, but instead offered him a glass of wine. Goodwyn, realising his indiscretion, coloured slightly and began to get up.

'Nay, nay, remain seated.' William waved him down. 'Truth be told, Crewe used to dine with me. I am not one for standing on ceremony and I miss sharing my repast with a companion.' He held out a plate of almond biscuits. 'Have you eaten? Do try one of these, they're quite delicious.'

'You are too kind, sir. Perhaps I might take one with the wine. In my haste to show you our new arrivals, I did indeed forget to eat.' Goodwyn dipped a biscuit into his glass. 'We had a similar arrangement in Monmouthshire; I used to sit at the high table with the Powells, while the rest of the household ate at lower tables. They liked to maintain the old traditions.'

'My father always insisted that the household were our family, a practice I too follow.' Lighting his pipe, William noticed for the first time the dark circles beneath Goodwyn's watery blue eyes. 'You look tired, Goodwyn; this extra work has worn you out. You are a fine steward and we can't have you falling ill with exhaustion.'

Goodwyn smiled. 'It has been a privilege to undertake the work. I only hope I haven't burnt through too many candles.' His fingertips hovered over the book's cover. 'As agreed, I have left it anonymous.'

William hardly noticed the next hour passing as they discussed Matthew's book, Goodwyn pointing out various phrases he considered particularly fine and William responding with his own favourite lines. They chatted as easily as if they were old friends and although William had enjoyed conversing with Crewe, he found Goodwyn to be a more entertaining tablemate.

It was only after Goodwyn had returned to his study that William realised he had left his gloves off, something he was never usually so careless with, for he always feared his slender hands and tapered fingers would give his sex away. He held them out in front of him, regarding them critically for the first time in a long while. The gloves had kept the skin pale and soft, but his fingers were thicker than they used to be and he cut his nails short. The span was narrower than a masculine hand, it was true, but otherwise they might pass as gentleman's hands. Besides, Goodwyn was so enamoured of his publication he was hardly

Chapter Eight

aware of his master's appearance. William had been successfully living as a man for the past twenty-five years; it was surely time to lower his guard a little.

* * *

''Tis very bonny.' John's reaction to Matthew's book was not as enthusiastic as William had wished. 'That's good quality leather, that is,' he added, seeing more was expected of him.

'I can give you an unbound copy to read,' William said.

'Ah, well, tha' knows I'm no great reader.' John scratched his beard.

'Sit awhile and I'll read thee some passages.'

Finding a dry patch of grass, William sat down. Jove quickly lay down by his side, but John was slower to join him. John enjoyed listening to him read poetry and he expected him to be equally responsive to Matthew's contemplations. But he had only read a few pages when John interrupted him.

'Wise words, I'm sure, but I need to be getting home,' he said apologetically. 'Sarah's not well and I must check on her.'

'What ails her?' William slipped the book back into his pocket. Goodwyn was right about the size; he couldn't have carried a folio around with him.

'She has taken a cold, it's not so bad now, but last time she was laid very low with it and I fear her being seized by the ague.'

'I have a fine elderberry and sage cordial for that; I'll give Kate a bottle to bring home with her.'

Although the making of medicinal cordials and flavoured waters was women's work, William took a special interest in it, which he explained to the servants as scientific experiments such as physicians and natural philosophers conducted. Inspired by his son's interest in botany, he had even had a laboratory built onto the brewhouse, where he liked to concoct all manner of efficacious drinks that benefitted the health of the entire household.

'Thank you, she'll appreciate that.'

William nodded. John's wife was a kind, hard-working woman and he had no personal resentment towards her. Mostly he felt guilty for stealing her husband's heart and his time. John said he and Sarah had not lain together since her last stillbirth, ten years ago. She had been approaching forty by then and they had given up any hope of producing a boy. Sarah had taken it hard, her inability to give him a son, and for this reason forgave his frequent absences more than she might otherwise have done.

As far as Sarah was concerned, John worked more hours than any other man she knew, but she was proud of the respect the squire showed him. They might have been kinsmen, their friendship was that strong, she'd say. Sir William would be lost without her John and she enjoyed the privileges this brought her family. Their youngest child, Alice, was Sir William's goddaughter and still attended the free school he had set up for the children in the parish, even though she was now thirteen years of age and old enough to be set to work.

This free school was somewhat contentious among the local population, being open to both boys and girls. If the girls had been taught only knitting, spinning and lacemaking, they would have welcomed it, but the girls were also taught reading and arithmetic alongside the boys and many feared for the future health and marriageability of their daughters. For that reason, attendance by the girls in the parish was much lower than that of the boys, though both sexes tended to leave by the age of ten, when their labour was needed by their families. Sarah Thornly was one of its stoutest defenders, however, pointing out the poor children the school fed and clothed, not to mention the apprenticeships and the superior positions in service gained by some of its alumni.

'The schoolmaster sent me a great report of Alice,' William told John. 'She is as diligent as ever in her studies and can write with a very fine hand. Her understanding surpasses that of any other child in the schoolroom.' He paused, knowing what he was about to say might alarm John. 'I have asked for her to be taught Latin alongside those boys who are capable of it.'

Chapter Eight

John, who had risen to his feet, sat down again beside William. 'For what purpose? What good'll Latin do her? If thou fills her head up with learned matter thou might drive out her senses and she'll end up more feeble-minded than our Eliza.'

John's eldest was a sweet girl, but weak-brained. She would never marry or leave home, but was a help to her mother around the Grange and on the farm and was cherished by all who knew her.

'I don't believe there's any danger to Alice. She's hungry for knowledge and her memory is capacious.'

William picked a dandelion, twirling the yellow flower between his fingers. In truth it was Alice herself who had asked to learn Latin and the schoolmaster had said that, with Sir William's agreement, she might sit in on the boys' lessons, so long as she remained silent and did not distract them by calling out the answers as she was often wont to do. William didn't want to get Alice into trouble with her parents for being too forward, so he kept this information to himself. His goddaughter had a special place in his heart and he wanted to assist her in any way he could, though as she grew older he sometimes caught her sharp eyes gazing at him with a questioning look and for that reason now maintained a distance between them.

'Discuss it with Sarah,' he said, knowing that John's wife was more ambitious for her daughters than her husband was.

'I believe she'll draw the line at Latin,' John grumbled, getting up again.

'Many popish gentlemen send their daughters to convents to be educated, and they teach them Latin there, you can be sure of it,' William told him, hoping this idea would get planted in the more receptive soil of Sarah's mind, for she was more devout a Catholic than either of them. 'My cousin Mary is an abbess in command of a magnificent convent in Rouen. Come to think of it, we could send Alice to her to be educated.'

John looked uneasy. 'That's a long way to go.'

'I'll look into it. I'm happy to pay for my goddaughter's education. I only have one child myself after all.'

John said nothing.

William had suggested once, in a moment of drunken passion, that they throw caution to the wind and try creating a baby together. He had concealed a pregnancy before; he could do it again. And John, in his desire, had almost given in, for William, when he was still Alethea, had delivered a healthy boychild. Fortunately sense had prevailed and John had refused to spend his seed on such dangerous ground. William had accused John of not loving him enough, since he did not want to sire a child with him and was capable of such cold restraint. The following day, however, he had been grateful for John's fortitude and sorry for his own intemperance. It was the moist humours of his femininity that drove him to such reckless desires. If only he could be rid of his womb, he would be freed of them, he was sure. At least now his menses appeared to have stopped. Perhaps his womb would shrivel up and disappear altogether.

William rode over as far as the Grange with John and then continued on, past the cottages of his tenants that skirted the village. Smoke was curling up from the chimneys and he could hear the excited shrieks of children playing on the green. A group of men tumbled out of The Barley Mow, laughing at some shared joke. As the door opened, music drifted out; a pipe and a fiddle were being played and someone was singing. He was almost tempted to join them, to take a tankard of ale and sit by the fire to listen, but he knew that his presence would subdue their merriment. They would wonder what Sir William was doing in the village tavern and worry that he'd come to observe the antics of his labourers.

He sighed and turned his horse homeward, Jove lying across his saddle. Jove was not an old dog but something seemed to be ailing him; he was not as sprightly as he should be and William feared he might lose him. His dogs had proved his most steadfast companions. Especially, he thought bitterly, since he was an outcast from the society of men, destined to be alone.

He knew John loved him, but would always belong first and foremost to Sarah and his girls. William's greatest hope had been that

Chapter Eight

Nicholas would return to live at Measham. That he might bring a sympathetic wife and raise a brood of children to fill the hall with renewed life. But the news from Ireland was not good. King James had fled once again, back to France and the court of King Louis. Even if Nicholas survived, he would never be allowed to return to England, not as long as William and Mary were on the throne.

Who then could inherit Measham? Who would love and care for it as he did? He did not want to become a miserable old recluse like his uncle Percy, surrounded by ancient retainers and living in filth as his house and lands fell into disrepair. He supposed he ought to go over there and offer his uncle some assistance, but the thought of having to spend time under the roof of the dotish old man filled him with dread. And then there was the land Crewe had acquired while working as his steward, which he had been good enough to leave to William in his will. That needed looking after too.

Rallying himself with a mixture of admonishment and encouragement, as he often did at times of crisis, William reminded himself that he had a capable new steward to support him in the management of his affairs. A man who was also proving to be good company. Goodwyn might even know of other trustworthy servants who could be sent to Uncle Percy's to get his estate in order. Perhaps he would see if Goodwyn wanted to join him for supper. They could continue their discussion of Matthew's writings. William would share some of his favourite poets with Goodwyn; the fellow was clearly learned and appreciative of verse. As Matthew had often pointed out, it was a sin to give in to despair. An evening spent conversing with another instead of sitting by himself would do him a world of good.

* * *

'Forgive me if I am being presumptuous, sir, but you seem somewhat downcast. Is there anything I can do that might lighten your burden?' Goodwyn's voice was full of solicitude.

William pushed a bit of bread around his plate, mopping up the leftover sauce before abandoning the sodden lump on the edge of the plate. 'I wish there was, but unless you can bring an end to war and my son home to me, there is nothing more you can do.' Despite his best efforts, he was falling into a deep melancholy, one that made conversation difficult.

'Not having a child myself, I can only glimpse at the suffering a parent must feel when their beloved child is far away and confronting danger.' Goodwyn refilled William's glass with wine. 'Your son is a hero and history will remember him as such. I realise that is little comfort to you now, but I feel certain Master Nicholas will not only survive, but return to you triumphant.'

'I wish I could share your convictions.' William took another mouthful of wine. 'What leads you to such certainty?'

'I spend a great deal of time in prayer – several hours each night seeking guidance from the Lord.' Goodwyn spoke hesitantly at first, his voice gaining confidence as he continued. 'Quite often I am directed to particular passages in the Bible. I have found that these passages invariably provide me with the answers I am seeking, not simply in spiritual terms but in practical matters also.' He held up one hand as if to ward off mockery. 'I am not a superstitious man I can assure you and I have no truck with witchcraft, but the consistent accuracy of these answers has convinced me of their validity. I applied this method in the service of Mrs Powell and she too discovered the Bible passages I showed her to be true indications of what would come to pass.'

Goodwyn pressed his hand to his heart. 'As your steward, I always pray for the wellbeing of you and your family. Two nights ago I was moved to turn the pages of my Bible and where should my finger fall, but on Luke 15 and the return of the prodigal son. Then I was seized with the knowledge that this was a message for you. Your son will come back to you and you will rejoice.'

William was so surprised by Goodwyn's speech, he was temporarily startled out of his despondent humour. 'I had not taken you for a fortune-teller,' he said with a laugh.

Goodwyn was gracious enough to laugh with him. 'Nor do I regard myself as either a prophet or a prognosticator. It is a practice I

Chapter Eight

have acquired after many years of religious devotion. I believe we can all hear the words God delivers to us if we meditate for long enough.'

'Matthew would be in agreement with you there, at least,' William allowed, lighting his pipe. 'I hope you are correct and that Nicholas does indeed return, not that he has ever been prodigal. No, indeed, he has always been an exemplary son.' He felt tears rising in his throat and took a hasty sip of wine to wash them down.

'Forgive me, sir, I did not mean to imply that your son was wasteful or disobedient, only that his return is assured. I can tell by the love, which not only his father, but the whole household bear for him, that your son is a true gentleman, one who will bring great credit to the Hawthorne name.'

'Nicholas has many virtues,' William agreed, pleased that Goodwyn appreciated Nicholas's character despite it being widely known that his son was base-born. 'He is very learned, in botany and natural philosophy especially. And though he is a fine swordsman, he is not at heart a soldier; it is these terrible times that have forced him to take up his sword.'

By the time William had finished extolling his son's praises, they had finished the first bottle of wine and started on a second. He even gave Goodwyn a detailed, if expurged, history of Nicholas's life so far. It was a long time since he had had such an attentive and appreciative audience. John was fond of the boy and understood his importance as the heir to Measham, while Matthew had been concerned with his successor's character and education, but only Jane had shared William's parental affection and it was a long time since he had been able to discuss his son with her. Now William discovered that talking about Nicholas brought his son closer, alleviating some of his fears and longings.

So when Goodwyn asked him if he had ever considered marrying and fathering more children, William did not take offence at the steward's curiosity. Goodwyn posed his questions in such a gentle manner that, instead of sounding prying, they appeared to stem from genuine Christian charity.

'I am not suited to marriage,' he found himself admitting. 'That is why all my hopes must reside in Nicholas. And what about you? Have you never wished for a wife?'

Goodwyn smiled so sadly, William fetched the bottle of brandy he kept in the cupboard and filled both their glasses.

'I was to be married once, but the lady refused me. The match had been arranged by her brother, who was a bosom friend of mine and thought us eminently suited, but alas, I did not please her. She had higher ambitions.'

'More fool her.' William rolled the brandy around his mouth. 'Though a lady should never be compelled to marry.'

Matthew had tried to marry him off and he'd been forced to reveal his pregnancy to put an end to the betrothal. Even then, Matthew had thought the suitor might still take him. It was only with Crewe's assistance that the impending nuptials had been stopped once and for all.

'I'm sure the lady in question was very sensible to reject me,' Goodwyn conceded.

'She must have married well then, to find a better husband than you.' William imagined some haughty gentlewoman of reduced circumstances who considered herself too good for the courteous steward.

'She did not marry at all.' Goodwyn let out a short laugh. 'I would have been a great asset as her spouse, but she was very headstrong.' He drank some of the brandy, murmuring his approval at the quality. 'I call her sensible because my heart was already engaged. I have only known one true love and, if I may quote from a poem by the late Reverend Donne, "My rags of heart can like, wish, and adore, But after one such love, can love no more."' He took a pinch of snuff and sneezed violently into his handkerchief. 'Forgive me, sir, I have no right to burden my master with my paltry sorrows.'

'It is no burden. Is your beloved deceased?'

With downcast eyes, Goodwyn gave a slow nod.

'I have a book of Donne's poetry; he is a particular favourite of mine. I take it you are also an admirer?'

Chapter Eight

Getting up, William opened the door to the library. He understood Goodwyn's embarrassment and wanted to alleviate any feelings of discomfort, but he was also delighted to find someone he could share his love of poetry with. Having located the book, he returned to the parlour and he and Goodwyn spent the rest of the evening as he had planned, in a discussion of the poetic arts.

William was touched by Goodwyn's moment of vulnerability. He recognised the man's grief, which time had clearly done little to soften, despite his piety. Goodwyn's inability to conceal the strength of his passions also encouraged William to trust the man; he seemed to be someone of a soft and open disposition. His devotion to his master's family was equally affecting and William was grateful for Goodwyn's prayers on their behalf.

Despite his usual scepticism, William found himself swayed by the strength of Goodwyn's convictions. Goodwyn was not the first person to have used the Bible as a tool for divination. Perhaps his mystical meditations did lead him to see events yet to come, to truths invisible in the ordinary way of things. Matthew had believed very strongly in the protection and guidance of a host of saints and angels. Now, William's need to believe that Nicholas was being defended by just such a spiritual army overcame his doubts and he allowed himself to be comforted by Goodwyn's adamantine faith. So much so that his mind was eased and he slept more sweetly that night than he had done for many months.

→ Chapter Nine ←

Ireland, July 1690

Ducking under the low doorway of The Mitre Tavern, Nicholas looked around the long, narrow chamber for O'Connor, his eyes slowly adjusting to the darkness of the interior. It seemed he had arrived first, so he took up a seat at the far end of the room, where they would not be overheard.

Because of his fluent French, Nicholas had been kept in the city to work with de la Vigne, the engineer recently brought over by the French. There were Irish officers who might have been more useful in this, speaking both French and Irish, but relations between the two nationalities had soured to such a degree that the viceroy, Tyrconnell, had suggested an Englishman would make a better intermediary. Sarsfield proposed Nicholas, who was already known to him as a reliable intelligencer. Now, instead of acting as an intermediary with the Williamites, Nicholas was to report to O'Connor on anything de la Vigne let slip that might be of interest. So far, however, de la Vigne's only concern had been the fortifications of the city. If they were to withstand the approaching Williamite army, they had a great deal to do and very little time to accomplish it.

'Good evening.' O'Connor sat down opposite him. 'They sell a passable claret here, so I've ordered a jug.'

Chapter Nine

'Excellent.' Nicholas smiled. It was a relief to see a friendly face again. 'Has your business today been as difficult as mine? Perhaps it's the hot weather, but the men seem especially discontented.'

'Well, you know, it's not easy for them having to wait for the enemy to attack.' O'Connor nodded at the innkeeper as he set down a jug and two drinking bowls. 'Soldiers prefer action on the field to defending against a siege.'

'I had to break up a fight between some Irish and French soldiers today.' Nicholas took a draught of wine. It was pleasantly rich and sweet and only a little rough on the tongue. 'The French had called the Irish cowards for fleeing the Boyne, while the Irish blamed the French for mishandling the battle.'

O'Connor waved a hand dismissively. 'Sure, the Boyne was just a skirmish.'

'And Tyrconnell?' Nicholas ventured. 'I've overheard mutterings that he's really in league with the Williamites.'

Divisions between the Jacobite factions in Limerick had been growing deeper and Nicholas needed to discover exactly what was being planned and by whom. There had been another council of war while Tyrconnell was out of the city and in his absence Sarsfield had been appointed second in command of the Jacobite army. Nicholas had heard whispers about an uprising against Tyrconnell and he wanted to know where O'Connor stood.

'Ah there's all sorts of stories going around. One is that Tyrconnell wants to hamstring the horses so they'll be useless to the enemy. I won't be permitting that order to go ahead, I can tell you that now, though I doubt there's any truth to it.' O'Connor shook his head. 'Another fellow told me that, being one of the only survivors of Cromwell's massacre at Drogheda, Tyrconnell has a lasting terror of sieges.' O'Connor chuckled with incredulity at such a fanciful notion.

Nicholas leant forward. 'Do you believe Tyrconnell will surrender to the Williamites?'

O'Connor's expression was guarded and Nicholas wondered if his friend harboured suspicions against him. He'd risked his life enough times for the Jacobites; he should surely have proved his loyalty by now. He took another mouthful of wine; the more he drank of it, the smoother it became. O'Connor was right to be wary, he supposed, since here he was, fishing for information when he had little to offer in return. He always bore Crewe's advice to him in mind, however – information is power; the more you have the safer you are.

'Tyrconnell comes from Old English stock; he has never been a friend to the Gaels, always favouring the English.' O'Connor looked down the room to where two men had recently come in, but they were engrossed in their own conversation and had no interest in what he might be saying. 'If Tyrconnell returns to France with Count Lauzun it's possible he'll slander the Irish, blaming any defeat on our inadequacies instead of his own poor judgement.'

'And you fear losing King James's support?' Nicholas asked.

'We still need his backing and that of the French, more importantly.'

'What about Berwick? If he were to replace Tyrconnell as viceroy you would be sure to keep the King's favour,' Nicholas pushed. He knew Sarsfield was friendly with Berwick and it made sense that they would approach the King's son to ensure any plot against Tyrconnell succeeded.

'That would be a bold move,' O'Connor replied, but he did not refute the suggestion.

When Nicholas took their jug up to the bar to be re-filled, he noticed that the men near the door had been joined by a woman. While he was waiting for the innkeeper, she began singing a slow lament, the notes vibrating in her throat to produce music of such sorrowful yearning it seemed to pour straight into Nicholas's heart and fill him with longing, though for what, he could not have said. He stood for a while in a state of near rapture, quite forgetting the wine set before him.

When at last he returned to O'Connor, the major was smiling at him. 'She's a fine voice on her all right,' he said, nodding over at the woman.

Chapter Nine

'Beautiful,' Nicholas agreed, still somewhat dazed by the extraordinary music.

Now she had stopped singing, the woman's face had taken on a hard, closed-off appearance, as though she were hewn out of stone. She sat very still, with her fustian mantle pulled tightly round her narrow shoulders. She could have been anything from thirty to sixty years old, for her face was marked with the kind of hardship that ages a person before their time. Her companions began a more merry tune and she tapped a bony hand on the table, her severe expression unaltered.

'And what of the indomitable Úna? I expect she has tested your mettle, eh.' O'Connor was regarding Nicholas with a wry sparkle in his eyes.

'Mistress O'Leary certainly has some strongly held opinions,' Nicholas conceded rather stiffly. 'She has no love for the English.'

'And why should she?' O'Connor raised his eyebrows.

'She is a great admirer of Brigadier Sarsfield,' Nicholas said, wanting to turn the conversation back to O'Connor's political allegiances.

'Which demonstrates her sound judgement,' O'Connor answered robustly. 'We have a great leader in Sarsfield; if anyone can take us to victory, he's the man to do it. Sarsfield won't squander the advantages we hold, as Tyrconnell would have us do.' O'Connor's former reserve melted away in the heat of his passion. 'We might have lost Dublin, but we still hold the ports at Cork and Kinsale in the south, along with Galway and Sligo in the west. The French navy can keep them supplied while preventing any supplies reaching the Williamites from England.' He traced the outline of a map in the dust on the table. 'Besides.' O'Connor gazed earnestly at Nicholas, wiping the map away with the palm of his hand. 'We won't have to hold out for long because the Williamite government in England is weak and a rebellion is expected any day. Then the English will be forced to withdraw from Ireland to deal with the civil war back at home.'

Nicholas hadn't received any news of an imminent rebellion in England, but then, he'd had no news of any sort. He had no idea how his father was or what was happening at Measham and could only hope that they weren't suffering under the rule of William and Mary.

'Are you certain that a successful rebellion in England is likely?' he asked.

'We seized some letters intended for the Prince of Orange. Not only are they fearful of a rebellion among their own people, the English believe the French are about to invade and want Prince William to return to defend them. Even if they've got that wrong, consider the French victory at Fleurus. If William's Grand Alliance suffer more defeats, he'll have to turn his full attention to Europe. Soon enough it will be the English begging us for favourable terms, that's what Sarsfield understands.'

* * *

Nicholas mulled over his conversation with O'Connor the following morning as he walked through the now familiar alleyways to the citadel. There was nothing he wanted more than the restoration of King James, but he had seen the might of Prince William's army and the prospect of civil war at home filled him with dread. If only the throne could be returned to James with as little bloodshed as when it had first been taken. The toll on Ireland had been terrible, but at least, he thought selfishly, his own family might be spared.

He hoped O'Connor was right when he said Prince William would be compelled to move his forces back to the Continent. Although the new recruits pouring into Limerick were full of enthusiasm for the fight, they had yet to experience warfare. Seeing how ill prepared these unarmed farm labourers and shopkeepers were, Nicholas feared for their chances. Most of them had no idea how to fire a musket or march in formation and none of them had experienced coming under fire. No doubt they'd make fine soldiers once trained, but there wasn't the time to train them up properly.

Chapter Nine

The sun was only just rising, but de la Vigne was already present and attempting to direct the hundreds of Irishmen who had been ordered to work under him. Nicholas hurried over, his head throbbing from the wine he had drunk the night before. De la Vigne wanted the ancient stone parapets demolished and replaced with earthworks strong enough to hold six cannons. Nicholas translated his orders to the English-speaking foreman, who in turn passed them on to the labourers, and the work of destruction began.

From the walls, Nicholas watched the French Brigade razing the suburbs around Irish Town to create a field of fire. The houses, gardens and orchards that must have taken decades to build and cultivate were all gone in a matter of days and their inhabitants sent to join the ever-increasing numbers of refugees. Although he understood the need for it, Nicholas couldn't help but be filled with horror at this ruination of so much productive land.

Somewhere down below, Bedley was employed in similar work. His regiment had been sent out into the countryside to fell trees and collect the wood for palisades to be erected around the city. Nicholas thought of the woods his father and grandfather had replanted after the devastation of the English civil wars and told himself these forests too would grow again. At least Bedley was now forced to camp with his men outside the walls and Nicholas was spared his chamber-mate's endless sermons and litanies of complaint.

* * *

Nicholas and O'Connor met again at The Mitre a few days later. Despite the sore head it had given him, Nicholas agreed to another jug of claret.

'Sarsfield is going to the aid of Athlone,' O'Connor told him. Seeing Nicholas's blank expression, he explained, 'The town forms a gateway across the Shannon to Connacht. It's strategically vital and is under siege from Colonel Douglas's troops.'

Nicholas had heard of the Scotsman, Douglas; his soldiers had become infamous for plundering and terrorising the locals. Nicholas's pulse quickened at the prospect of action. Despite longing for a release from spying, he had discovered that days spent on building works were dull in comparison to the thrill of battle or a clandestine engagement with the enemy. Now he relished the prospect of re-joining his squadron under Sarsfield for an honourable adventure.

He raised his cup. 'Here's to a victorious scrimmage,' he declared enthusiastically.

'But you are to remain in Limerick.'

Nicholas could hardly believe his ears. 'I'm as skilled a horseman as any.'

'The brigadier knows that, but you're needed here,' O'Connor replied with implacable calmness. 'Tyrconnell wants Sarsfield out of Limerick because he fears his influence; you can be our ears in the city, keep note of what the French are up to.'

Nicholas suspected O'Connor was merely being conciliatory. He'd rather be out with the cavalry than following Vigne around the walls of Limerick. He worried that Sarsfield had passed him over. A concern that only increased when the brigadier rode out of Limerick the following day with five battalions and a large escort of dragoons and cavalry.

* * *

'I thought you were in Sarsfield's cavalry?' Úna said pointedly, that evening over supper.

Nothing escaped her attention, Nicholas thought crabbedly. 'The brigadier hasn't taken the whole cavalry, just a few supporting riders. My work here is too important for me to go.' He chewed at a slice of salted beef, spitting a lump of gristle onto his plate before passing it to the dog. 'The Irish are so quarrelsome, someone has to help to keep the peace.' He stared belligerently at Úna.

'If we quarrel it is because we have been provoked. At least we have better table manners than the English.' She raised her eyebrows, looking pointedly at the dog, who was now resting his head on the table beside Nicholas's plate.

Chapter Nine

Nicholas looked at O'Leary with some embarrassment. 'Forgive me, I have become accustomed to eating with soldiers.'

'That's all right, my boy.' O'Leary smiled at him, but there was a sadness in his eyes and his face looked worn and tired.

'Are you unwell, sir?' Nicholas asked with concern, regretting his earlier rudeness.

'It grieves me to see our fine city wrecked and all the rich and fertile land about it turned to desert.' O'Leary shook his head. 'Limerick was once as grand a city as any you'd see in Ireland, second only to Dublin. You wouldn't find many better in England.'

'I can well believe it, sir. It saddens me too, I assure you,' Nicholas said ardently.

O'Leary nodded and patted his hand.

Rising from her chair, Úna threw her arms around her father's shoulders, pressing her cheek against his. 'We will build it up again, Daddy, every brick and stone.'

The two remained in this position, eyes closed and heads resting together for a moment. Nicholas was moved by the affection between father and daughter; it was clear that they derived great support and comfort from each other. His own father had been a remote figure until Nicholas reached adulthood and still maintained a physical distance, but they too shared a bond that went beyond duty and familial obligations. Nicholas recognised and understood the depth of love between O'Leary and his headstrong daughter. Picturing Father, dining alone in the parlour of Measham Hall, he experienced a sudden pang of anxiety. It was hard to imagine Measham without Crewe and Father must miss his old companion terribly. Nicholas wondered how he was managing and whether he had found a new steward. Even if he had, the new man could never become a close friend such as Crewe had been.

Úna said more cheerfully, 'How about a game of ombre? That will raise your spirits, Father. Do you play cards, Captain Hawthorne?'

'I do indeed.' Nicholas had been taught how to play at cards by a skilled gamester in order to befriend Lord Pemberton's son. And although that particular episode had painful memories, he was keen to do anything that might cheer his host.

As soon as Mairead had cleared the dishes from the table, Úna set out the cards, along with a bottle of *uisce beatha*, and O'Leary's face brightened. They were well-matched carders for all three had sharp memories and though each of them liked to win, none of them were so ambitious they resented losing. The next few hours passed swiftly and, being absorbed in the game, Nicholas forgot for a while his disappointment at being left behind by his commander.

'I do believe I've beaten you again, Captain,' Úna declared with delight at the end of their final round.

'You are indisputably the Queen of Hearts,' Nicholas said, indicating the card she had just played.

'Now don't play the gallant with me just because I have vanquished you,' she answered playfully.

'I wouldn't dare; your mind is far too sharp to fall for such flattery.' Nicholas had not intended any coquetry, but he was pleasantly surprised by Úna's light-hearted response to his compliment.

O'Leary chuckled. 'It will take a man of great sagacity and fine discernment to win this queen of my heart.'

'Now you are flattering me, Daddy!' Úna looked fondly at her father as she chided him. 'You must not indulge your only daughter with an excessive estimation of her worth.'

'You are too modest, Mistress O'Leary,' Nicholas interjected. 'Your father might speak out of paternal pride, but it is a pride deservedly placed in one of superior mental powers.'

'And let us not forget her physical charms,' O'Leary added. 'She is as beautiful as her mother was before her.' Lifting his glass, he nodded at Úna and his eyes glistened with tears.

Úna threw her hands up in mock alarm. 'I believe you gentlemen have imbibed too much *uisce beatha*; it has addled your senses. I shall retire to bed before any more nonsense can be spoken.' Collecting up the cards and replacing them in their box, she quickly rose from the table.

Chapter Nine

Nicholas would have contradicted her, for his admiration was genuine, but not wanting to offend his ticklish hostess, he wished her only a good night.

* * *

Rumours that the French intended to desert the Irish, taking much of their artillery back to France, were spreading throughout Limerick. And these rumours, as Nicholas discovered from Vigne, were not without foundation. Even some of the Irish officers were now suggesting they make terms with the Prince of Orange. Tyrconnell had received a letter from King James, stating that those who chose to remain in Ireland were absolved from their oaths of fidelity and were free to negotiate with William. Why continue to fight a losing battle? Better to get a decent settlement while they still could; at least that way they might get back some of their lands.

Nicholas was about to ride out to Athlone to warn Sarsfield when, just over a week after leaving, the brigadier returned to Limerick with his men. By the time they reached Athlone, O'Connor told Nicholas, the Williamite forces had already retreated back to Mullingar. Nicholas hadn't missed out on any action by remaining in Limerick, his friend assured him.

Sarsfield immediately got to work winning his fellow officers back over to the warring party. It took all his charm and force of character, but Nicholas was impressed by the way he managed it, even if this was partly because everyone knew that when it came down to it, Sarsfield had the support of the soldiers.

Regardless of any plans to leave, the infamously rude Count de Lauzun still demanded a tour of the outworks and fortifications. It was all Nicholas could do to hold his tongue as he and Vigne showed the count and his retinue around Limerick's walls. Lauzun strutted ahead, swearing loudly at the earthworks, the counterscarps and the palisades that had been so painfully constructed, some of them built out of the timber from the destroyed houses below.

After casting a disparaging eye over the ancient walls, Lauzun declared them untenable. 'They could be beaten down with roasted apples.' He kicked at one of the walls, sending stones skittering down its side, much to the amusement of the French officers accompanying him.

Nicholas felt the anger rising in his belly at this careless summation of a project that so many men had worked so hard on, indeed were still working on, for it was not yet complete, as Lauzun well knew.

'Never mind Lauzun,' O'Connor told him when they met later. 'The coward's just making excuses in order to leave; we'll be better off without him.'

And sure enough, the following day, Nicholas watched from the ramparts as the French officers marched their men, all three thousand five hundred of them, along with eight field guns, out of Limerick and onto the road to Galway, from where they planned to sail to France.

Seeing that the Irish army was firmly behind Sarsfield, Tyrconnell had no choice but to put everything into defending Limerick. He appointed the one remaining French commander, Major-General Boisseleau, governor. Though many of the Irish officers were unhappy about the appointment of another Frenchman, Boisseleau was, unlike the Comte de Lauzun, an extremely experienced general, especially in siege warfare. Nicholas continued to be employed as a translator for the French engineer and under Boisseleau's command the men were quickly set to work building up earthworks outside the walls. A great open ditch was dug, while bastions and small earth forts were reinforced with rubble. Fields were ploughed up and more trees felled to block the roads. Under the heat of the summer sun and the clouds of the Irish skies, the men were soaked in both rain and sweat, but still they laboured on, conscious always that William's vast regiments were drawing closer.

Berwick set his troops to work burning every house, barn and crop between Limerick and the advancing Williamite army. All that could be seen, stretching out for miles and miles, were clouds of black smoke rising from the inferno below. Nicholas was only grateful that

Chapter Nine

he wasn't one of the musketeers stationed behind every hedge and wall still standing.

* * *

Standing on one of the walls in Irish Town, close by the Devil's Tower, Nicholas was able to make out the lines of William's army progressing slowly over the rough terrain, hacking their way through the hedges in their path.

'They're pushing us back. We'll soon be forced to take shelter under the garrison cannon.'

Turning, Nicholas was startled to discover Bedley at his side. He hadn't seen his old compatriot in weeks and hardly recognised the man, who looked and smelt as rough as any campaign-hardened foot soldier.

'I've been allowed inside to report to Boisseleau,' Bedley said wearily, scratching at the unkempt beard that had grown on his chin.

Uncomfortably aware of his own comparative ease, Nicholas commiserated with the unfortunate Bedley.

'I have stood as close to the enemy as I am to you now,' Bedley told him, his voice tempered with amazement. 'I have listened to English infantry soldiers on the other side of the same hedge, discussing what they'd like for breakfast. That is the seriousness with which they undertake this war. They sat there in idleness while the Danish Brigade were busy clearing the way ahead. And before I could stop them, the Irish soldiers from our side of the hedge began shouting insults in Irish, to which the English yelled back "Ye toads, we'll be with you presently", and indeed they are.' He gestured to the advancing troops below. 'It was the behaviour of schoolboys not warriors.' Bedley shook his head. 'I tell you, Nicholas, I am tempted to throw it all up and go back to the seminary.'

Nicholas couldn't help being amused. As well as violence and confusion, there was an element of absurdity to war. 'Most of the English soldiers are fighting for pay, not for the liberation of their country or their faith, as you are,' he reminded Bedley.

Bedley failed to be roused, however. 'This is not the art of warfare as I understood it,' he said sourly. 'If Limerick falls, I will take it as a sign from God to return to Valladolid. The Protestants can have Ireland.'

'You have seen how the Protestant militias hunt down the native Irish; would you abandon them to such a rule?' Nicholas asked. 'All their customs, their language, as well as our religion, will be outlawed; they will never regain their properties nor be allowed to own any.'

'You have come under Mistress O'Leary's influence, I see. Beware the siren's call.' Bedley wagged a finger at him. 'Of course, the Ulster Protestants cannot forget the Irish Rebellion of '41 when so many Scottish and English settlers were massacred, women and children included. Theirs is not a forgiving religion.' Bedley gave a self-satisfied smile.

'Those accounts, which are so popular in England, were written to discredit Irish papists,' Nicholas said, indignation beginning to heat his blood. 'It is the Irish who were the first victims of such violence.'

Closing his eyes, Bedley held up one hand, preventing Nicholas from continuing his argument. 'Certainly there has been much butchery on both sides and the Irish reputation for barbarity is not entirely just. What is clear, however, is that the Irish should not be left to govern themselves.'

Bedley scratched at his beard again and Nicholas stepped away, partly to avoid catching lice and partly to stop himself from succumbing to the temptation to pitch his supercilious companion over the ramparts.

* * *

O'Connor was also out of the city most of the time, but returning to O'Leary's one evening, he beckoned Nicholas into his chamber.

'Have you had any communications from your former patron?' he asked quietly, closing the door.

'Nothing.' Nicholas walked over to the window. 'Perhaps they presume me dead.'

Chapter Nine

'Well, I'd be resurrecting myself if I was you.' O'Connor sat down on the end of the bed, stretching his long legs out in front of him and easing off his boots. 'Our kind host, Mr O'Leary, being a respected lawyer, has agreed to act as an intermediary with the English. Boisseleau is sending him into the enemy camp tomorrow to hear their terms and Sarsfield wants you to accompany him.' He waved at the only chair. 'Will you sit yourself down, Nicholas? You're making me dizzy with your pacing.' When Nicholas was seated he resumed. 'You'll need to seek an audience alone with one of their commanders and discover what you can of their strategy. You have a code word, don't you, that you can use?'

Nodding eagerly, Nicholas leant forward, pressing his hands against his knees. 'I assume Mr O'Leary knows nothing of my role?'

'Not a thing and it's important to keep it that way. I don't want Diarmuid being taken prisoner nor any harm coming to him at all.'

'Of course not, I'll protect him with my life,' Nicholas vowed solemnly.

'Take note of how their camp is laid out and where the Prince and the commanders' tents are, so that you can make a map of it for us. Our ammunition is running low and we need to know where best to fire it.'

'And what information can I offer in return?'

O'Connor smiled. 'Let them believe they've nothing to fear from us. That we're so preoccupied with fighting amongst ourselves we've no men ready to sally out against them. We want them to think there's no need to set up a line of contravallation. Also, encourage them to camp within our range by suggesting we're on the point of surrender. They'll have seen our cannon on the walls, but if they think we're unlikely to fire they'll be encouraged to come closer. Drop the bait to catch the rats.'

* * *

At dawn the following morning, bearing a white flag aloft, Nicholas and O'Leary, along with two other horsemen, rode out towards the enemy. The air was so thick with smoke, they had to move slowly to avoid the many hazards in their way. Trenches had been dug into the trampled earth, studded by tree stumps and broken hedgerows. The acrid air burnt the back of their throats and made their eyes stream. Up above, on Singland Hill, a row of Williamite soldiers could be seen ranged against them, muskets and flintlocks at the ready.

When halfway across this new-made wilderness, they spotted two Danish Guards coming towards them, their bright orange coats glowing like suns through the murky grey light. They were escorted into the camp, where they were taken to the tent of Colonel Sir John Lanier, who had once been a favourite of King James, but had declared for William on his invasion of England. Nicholas wondered if he might be one of the men Lord Pemberton had succeeded in turning.

Lanier, who had lost an eye in Flanders fighting for the French, surveyed them like a Cyclops, with his remaining eye. He was drinking brandy, and poured them each a cup.

'So, you wish to know what terms the King will offer for your surrender?'

'We are here to negotiate the terms for peace.' O'Leary smiled equably.

A soldier entered the tent and, approaching Lanier, whispered something in his ear.

'Well, you may hear what the King himself has to say on the matter,' Lanier told them. 'The sergeant here will take you to General Solms, who speaks on behalf of His Majesty.'

There was a note of discontent in Lanier's voice. It was well known that the Prince and his Dutch general did not trust the English serving under them. Nicholas saw his opportunity and seized it. As O'Leary turned to follow the sergeant, he spoke quickly to Lanier.

'I'm sure General Solms has no need of my presence, and there is some other business I have been asked to discuss with you.'

'Indeed?' Lanier said, scratching at the ribbon that held his velvet eyepatch in place. 'With me personally?'

Chapter Nine

Nicholas bowed by way of reply, hoping to appeal to Lanier's pride.

'Very well.' Lanier nodded.

To Nicholas's relief, O'Leary left in the company of the two Jacobite soldiers. He wouldn't come to any harm under William's protection, but Nicholas didn't want them overhearing what he said to Lanier.

'Perhaps you are acquainted with Lord Pemberton?' he ventured.

Lanier was watching him speculatively now. 'Ralph Pemberton? Yes, I have had the pleasure of dining with him.'

'His wife's family – the Calvertons – are old family friends of ours,' Nicholas said, affecting a careless air.

Henry and Margaret Calverton were highly respected and had been very influential at court. They had supported the Prince of Orange from the beginning, helping to pave the way for his usurpation of the throne. Nicholas hoped their names would buy him some trust with Lanier.

'Lord Calverton is a fine fellow, none better, gave me some very good advice.' Lanier nodded approvingly. 'There's a man who understands politics.'

'Yes, indeed, he has always been like a grandfather to me,' Nicholas lied. Though he had once saved the Calvertons from being robbed by highwaymen. 'It occurs to me that it might be preferable if we walk outside as we speak,' he added solicitously. 'It may appear somewhat suspicious if you are ensconced in private conversation with an officer from the other side.'

Lanier thrust back his head and snorted like a startled horse, but agreed that it might be better to talk out in the open as it were, and refilled his cup with brandy.

'Lord Pemberton is a friend and patron, but I have also been working for him in another capacity,' Nicholas explained quietly as they stepped out between the tents. Glancing around him, he just caught sight of his own party entering a large tent to his left. The Dutch King's banner fluttered above it. 'In fact, it was only with Pemberton's blessing that I joined the Jacobites. I have been sending him information on the enemy.' He did not like to use the term 'spy' in case it made him sound dishonest. 'I was in regular contact with one of the King's soldiers – a man named Wallis – in Dublin and arranged to meet him again just before the battle at the Boyne. I think my report proved useful.'

'I don't know of any Wallis, but will certainly consider any information of use to us,' Lanier said with guarded interest.

Nicholas fed him the intelligence suggested by O'Connor, all of which clearly pleased Lanier.

'I would be most grateful if you could also arrange for this letter to be sent to Pemberton.' Nicholas drew a letter he had written the previous night out of his pocket. Enfolded within it was a missive for his father. 'His Lordship is, no doubt, expecting some news from me.' He smiled apologetically before adding, 'Lady Jane Pemberton is my godmother and I promised her regular updates; she will grow anxious if her husband hasn't heard from me.'

'Very well, but I am no postman,' Lanier answered peevishly.

'Of course not. If the letter could be added to the post whenever that is collected, I am sure Lord Pemberton would be most indebted to you.' Nicholas knew they would have a regular post taking news across to England. He also knew the letter was likely to be opened and had made sure to include nothing incriminating.

While talking slowly, he was walking briskly, drawing Lanier along with him. He paid careful attention to the tents as he did so, drawing a map of the camp in his mind. His rigorous education at the hands of the Jesuits served him well in this. Now, he wondered where the Williamite armoury was, for he had not caught sight of any large cannon, only a few light field guns. It seemed odd not to have their heavy pounders up near the front.

'When the Irish see your cannons lined up against them, they'll run as fast as they did from the Boyne,' he told Lanier with a laugh.

Lanier gave out an exasperated harumph. 'Our train of siege equipment is still on the road from Dublin. A ridiculous state of affairs, to have an army arrive before its artillery.'

Chapter Nine

'But it must be close by surely?' Nicholas kept his voice steady despite his growing excitement.

'They're supposed to camp by Ballyneety Castle tomorrow night and all going well should arrive here the day after. The train's accompanied by the King's own comptroller of artillery; I'm sure you've heard of the renowned engineer and authority on sieges, Willem Meesters.'

'The very best,' Nicholas said admiringly, though the name was entirely new to him.

'And so he should be, he's costing us enough, highest paid artilleryman ever. Three pounds per diem – he's better paid than a colonel!' Lanier rolled his one eye.

'I hope both he and the train are well guarded.'

'I would have sent more than two companies of horse, but the opinions of the English are not valued here, no matter how many actions we have engaged in.' Lanier spoke bitterly. 'I secured Edinburgh Castle for King William, you know.'

'An impressive achievement. And the bravery with which you led your regiment at the Boyne is spoken of with admiration even by the enemy.' Nicholas was becoming quite adept at flattering army officers.

Lanier nudged him in the ribs. 'Not trying to lure me back over to King James, are you?'

'I wouldn't dream of it, sir,' Nicholas said, but noted with interest that Lanier referred to James as king. Perhaps the colonel was having doubts about his allegiance; he certainly seemed discontented with his current position.

* * *

O'Leary was not impressed with the terms Solms was offering them and did not believe they would be acceptable to Boisseleau. Back in the citadel, he went straight into a meeting with the governor. Nicholas begged some paper and a charcoal pencil from Boisseleau's secretary and found himself a corner where he could set down the map he was carrying in his head. He was eager to speak to O'Connor and

Sarsfield, but first he needed to draw a plan of the Williamite camp before he forgot any of the details.

'There you are, Nicholas.' O'Connor bent over him, studying the hastily drawn map. 'Very good, bring it through to Brigadier Sarsfield.'

'But I have something even more important to relay,' Nicholas told him eagerly.

On hearing that the Williamites' siege train was still en route, Sarsfield leapt up from his seat and began to pace around the room. If they could stop the train from reaching the Prince of Orange's camp, the whole course of the war could be turned in their favour.

'We'll have to move quickly and I'll need at least five hundred good men for the raid,' Sarsfield said. 'It'll mean removing the cavalry from their posts on the Shannon, including the regiments guarding the ford at Annaghbeg.' He ground his heel against the stone floor. 'What a pity it is the river's so low this year. We'll be leaving the crossing open to the English, but if we can destroy their artillery it'll be worth it.'

'You'll need Berwick's permission, won't you, sir?' O'Connor asked.

Sarsfield shook his head. 'He'll only want to lead the raid and he's too hot-headed. Besides, we'll be going deep into enemy-held territory; if we're to evade discovery we'll need rapparees to guide us and Berwick does not have my connections.' He gave a roguish grin. 'No, it's the viceroy's permission I'll need for this.'

O'Connor frowned. 'Tyrconnell vetoed Berwick's plan to raid Dublin.'

'Berwick wanted the entire cavalry and it was too risky a venture. For once Tyrconnell was right to stop him.' Slapping his slender belly, Sarsfield chuckled. 'At least Berwick can't call me fat and old, like he did Tyrconnell.'

'I hope you will include me among your horsemen, sir.' Nicholas spoke up, anxious not to be left behind again.

'The man who brought us the best bit of news in weeks? We wouldn't be without you, lad.'

Chapter Nine

Calling for his horse, Sarsfield set off at a gallop for the cavalry camp at Clare Castle, where Tyrconnell was staying, leaving instructions for messengers to be prepared to gather together a raiding party. He would send out scouts himself towards Clonmel to check on the progress of the train and to make contact with Michael Hogan, the chief of the local rapparees, who would be able to guide them through the difficult terrain of Tipperary.

Later that afternoon, as Nicholas was helping O'Connor prepare fresh horses in readiness for a raid, a trumpeter approached Limerick with a summons to surrender.

'There you go, Nicholas,' O'Connor said. 'The message you planted must've got through to the Prince of Orange; he thinks we'll give in easily.'

Boisseleau sent back a letter addressed to Robert Southwell, the Secretary of State for Ireland, expressing his surprise at the summons and telling Southwell he would best earn the Prince's esteem 'by a vigorous defence of the King's troops whom I have the honour to command'.

The Irish guns opened fire from the city walls. The siege had begun.

⇾ Chapter Ten ⇽

Measham, July 1690

'You're very quiet, John,' William remarked as they returned from checking on the sheep in the top fields, their horses ambling companionably along the green lane.

John was a man of few words and William was accustomed to his silences, but he had scarcely opened his mouth all day.

'It's hard not to be brought low by the state of the country,' John responded eventually, slumping forward in his saddle, his shoulders rounded. 'It's all anyone talks about – at church, in The Barley Mow, on the green. Everyone's feeling the pinch of want, what with fuel and food so dear. There's not many as will be celebrating Christmas this year.'

'Well, I hope they place the blame where it lies, at the door of Their Majesties. King William's promises about a new era of prosperity and liberty are proving false now, aren't they?'

Of course William sympathised with the plight of the people, but part of him also believed that by allowing the Dutch prince to seize the throne they had brought this misery on themselves. They should have defended their rightful king instead of welcoming in an invader.

'Some blame King William and some blame the Jacobites, along with the French that help them. The King promises trade will pick up again once the war is over.'

Chapter Ten

'He'd have to make peace with France and he'll never do that.'

John sighed. 'Sarah said the poor women in Leicester market were throwing stones at the millers and the bakers in protest at the price of corn. The mayor had to be sent for to quieten them.'

'Sarah is better then, if she is able to travel to market?'

'She is, God be thanked.'

And thank my cordials too, William thought. Usually Sarah sent him some token of gratitude for his medicines, a jar of honey, a cake or an extra cheese. Since he hadn't received any, he had assumed she was not cured.

'At least Goodwyn has shown me where we might make some savings,' he said, pushing a low-hanging branch out of his way. 'All these years and I hadn't realised that Tickell compensates for our lack of guests by serving up unnecessarily lavish dishes to the entire household. Goodwyn has impressed upon the new cook that simple hearty meals make much more wholesome food for servants. And Cooper's quite content with this since it makes his work less onerous. He's not so ambitious as Tickell.' Encouraged by their slow pace, the horses had stopped to browse the hedgerow and William was reminded of another saving. 'Goodwyn also knows of a wine merchant who will supply our cellars at a cheaper rate,' he added enthusiastically.

William had been disappointed to discover that, despite his initial approval, John did not admire Goodwyn as much as he did. This only made him more eager to prove the new steward's worth. The three of them had ridden out together on a couple of occasions in order to give Goodwyn a thorough tour of the Measham lands and though Goodwyn had been all courtesy, John had been particularly gruff in his responses. When questioned later, John had been unable to explain his dislike, saying only that Mr Goodwyn struck him as a gentleman who would be happier at court or in the city, rather than in the country. When William pointed out that Goodwyn had been full of praise for the beauty of the land, John had merely shrugged.

He and John rarely disagreed and it irked him that his friend did not share his high opinion of Goodwyn. It had been impossible to imagine anyone who could fill Crewe's place and he had been so anxious about giving a stranger the keys to his home, he had played out all sorts of disastrous scenarios in his mind. Now the reality was here, it wasn't so bad after all, quite the opposite in fact and William felt almost lightheaded with the relief.

Goodwyn was an easy fellow to get along with; he never imposed his company on William, but when they did converse he always had something noteworthy to say. He was calm and affable and William never felt that Goodwyn was looking askance at him. His greatest fear had been that a man intelligent enough to fulfil the role of steward would also detect the fact that William was not truly, at least in the physical sense, a man. But Goodwyn appeared to accept him as he was and had never once given the impression that he thought anything amiss about his master.

So Goodwyn had begun to fill the chasm left by Crewe. He now dined regularly with William and proved to be a highly entertaining and knowledgeable conversationalist. His access to information was almost as good as Crewe's had been and he kept William abreast of all the latest news from Ireland. Most important of all, however, was his unshakable certainty that Nicholas would return to Measham unscathed.

'Goodwyn informs me that King James's troops are fighting on without the King, under the leadership of the Earl of Tyrconnell. If the Scots rally again there is hope yet for the King's return,' he told John, happily imagining Nicholas returning to England at the head of a victorious army.

But John wasn't listening. 'Kate says the servants are not happy with the new diet,' he said abruptly.

'No one has mentioned any discontent to me. I didn't think Kate was the sort of girl to tell tales.' William tugged irritably on his reins, causing his horse to start back from a clump of wild cicely and turn his head enquiringly.

Chapter Ten

'Nor is she,' John said levelly. 'It was only her mother noticed how hungry the lass is when she comes home of an evening.'

'Does she not eat her dinner?' William frowned.

'She eats what little she is given.'

'Nicholas was always hungry at that age; no doubt she's growing, but I'll have a word with Abigail. She'll soon tell me if anything's amiss.'

'That she will.' John nodded in agreement and they rode on, their horses swaying amicably side by side.

William was not so content, however. The continual anxiety about Nicholas was bad enough; he didn't want to have extra worries added to this burden, especially when he had thought his domestic problems solved. Abigail never held her tongue out of deference. She would have been the first to come seeking an audience with him if the servants were being kept short of food. Kate was simply being fussy about the change in diet. He hoped Tickell hadn't ruined her appetite for the sort of fare most servants would expect as a matter of course.

* * *

He found Abigail at the far end of the Long Gallery, where she often used the superior light from the large windows to spin cloth, sew and mend the household linen. If he had had a wife it was where she might have sat, along with her maids. On rainy days the spacious passageway should have been full of children playing at skittles or shovelboard, practising their dancing or fencing, just as he and his siblings had once done. He could still hear the laughter of his little sisters, now long dead, as he chased them up and down, his stepmother's lapdogs yapping at their heels with excitement. Instead it was as quiet and decorous as a cloister, but perhaps it was no worse for all that. A gentle peace reigned over the airy space, which Abigail always kept clean and orderly.

Jove lay on the floor beside her, his head resting on his paws. William had wondered where the spaniel had got to. The dog looked up at William sadly, but didn't race to greet his master as he would usually do. Abigail stood and curtseyed as William approached, calling out an eager greeting. She clearly had something pressing to fill his ears with.

'You must let out my breeches, Abigail; they are growing tight, or rather I am getting portly in my advancing age.' William patted his belly, stalling the inevitable onslaught of her long tongue.

'You still cut a fine figure, Sir William, better than ever, I'd say, for a little weight suits a gentleman.' She adjusted her skirts, tugging on her apron with an agitated air. 'Of course I can alter them for you, sir, only Mr Goodwyn tells me I oughten to sit here, for this is a place for gentlefolk, but as you know, it being cloudy out and the light not so good and my eyes getting weaker, there is nowhere else where I can see so well for fine stitching. Now, I have been training up Kate, but there's that many other chores for her to tend to, she don't have time for all the sewing that's needed as well as everything else to be done when there's only the two of us. And anyway, by sitting here I'm saving on candles and the candlemaker is late calling to the house again so we're getting short on tapers.'

As she paused for breath, William seized the opportunity to speak. 'Don't fret, Abigail, I'll explain the situation to Goodwyn. I'm sure he will understand.'

But Abigail was not to be so easily appeased. 'That's just it, sir, I'm not sure he will understand, for he seems set against most of our ways here and maybe they're different to all the great houses he's served in, but they've worked well enough for us the past twenty-odd year, isn't that right?'

William turned to the window. 'But perhaps they can work better. Change is not always to be feared. With innovations come improvements.' He nodded at the gardens below and the lake he had created, whose waters could just be seen, glittering in the distance.

'I'm not afraid of change,' Abigail said indignantly. 'Only I don't like making things worse instead of better.'

'I don't see any deterioration of standards under Goodwyn, quite the contrary.' William took out his pipe and began to fill it.

'I don't suppose you do, sir, for you are still served meat every day and no shortage of cheese neither.'

Chapter Ten

William drew heavily on his pipe, feeling with relief the smoke enter his lungs. 'These are difficult times. Prices have increased and we must prune our outgoings. It is quite reasonable and more healthful to have eggs or fish on some days and meat on others. I too am forgoing some of Tickell's more extravagant dishes and there is always plenty left over from whatever joint of beef, mutton or pork that I am served, for the rest of the household to enjoy.' He wished now that he hadn't alluded to his widening girth.

Abigail shook her head. 'Eggs or fish would be a fine thing; we're lucky to see a bit of cheese. We are not rabbits, sir, to live on vegetives. Not that I'm complaining on my own account, but the youngsters are being kept short and they're the ones that need the most feeding. Now I don't know if that is Mr Goodwyn's doing or Cooper's, but it's not right and I have to bring it to your attention afore you lose good servants like Ben and Kate.'

If there was a fault, William was sure it must lie with Cooper. Goodwyn had explained the change in victuals to him in some detail and made it clear that the servants would if anything have more to eat, not less. There would be fewer dainty dishes, but ample bread, cheese and pottage, along with meat and fish on alternate days.

'Is it possible Cooper could be selling off some of our produce on the side?'

Abigail frowned. 'I always keep a sharp eye on the stores and haven't noticed anything amiss. I think you need to have a word with Cooper, sir, and Mr Goodwyn too, for he don't listen to me.' She gazed at him earnestly and William was troubled to see how tired her eyes looked. He still thought of Abigail as being young, but like him, she was now in her middle years.

'Of course, I'll talk to both Goodwyn and Cooper. I'm sure this is due to some misunderstanding and can be easily rectified.'

* * *

That evening at supper, William was more careful than usual in taking note of what was served. Supper was generally a lighter version of what they had eaten at midday and this was no exception; cold meat, salad, bread and fruit were brought to the table. He had invited Goodwyn to join him and as soon as Palmes had retired, he reported what Abigail had told him.

Goodwyn looked genuinely aghast. 'I will speak to Cooper first thing tomorrow. If you are not happy with his performance, we must find a replacement. I can make enquiries amongst my acquaintance.'

William was grateful to be relieved of the task of speaking to Cooper himself. It was Crewe who had appointed the cook shortly before his sudden death and he had never misjudged a man before, but perhaps his brain had not been as sharp as William had thought.

'Let's not act too hastily. Cooper has been satisfactory up until now; we should wait and see how he responds to our instructions.' William set his spoon down. The sliced beef had been tasty enough if a bit leathery, while the cauliflower salad was overly vinegary and the vegetable cooked almost to a pap. The stewed apples, on the other hand, needed more sugar. He missed Tickell's cooking.

'Very wise, sir. I will sound Cooper out and monitor his performance.' Goodwyn smiled and refilled William's wine glass. 'On a more elevating subject – I was wondering if you have any portraits of Father Matthew that could be added to a frontispiece for his book.'

'Alas I have not, which is a great source of disappointment to me.'

It never seemed to have occurred to their father to have a family portrait painted or indeed pictures of any of his children. Now William was left only with his memories of his mother and siblings to rely on and would have cherished such an heirloom. He did have a small portrait of Nicholas as a boy. When his son came home he would make sure to have him painted again; it had been foolish of him not to think of it before.

'Perhaps a description would suffice – a sketch can be based on a detailed description and if you believe it to be a fair copy, we can have it engraved,' Goodwyn said, delicately spearing a sliver of beef with his knife.

Chapter Ten

'I resemble my cousin very closely. When we were children we were often mistaken for twins. You could use my portrait.'

Turning, William pointed to the painting hanging on the wall behind him. In truth, not liking to be scrutinised, he had insisted on standing at some distance from the painter and then for only short amounts of time. He had not made it easy for the poor man. But Goodwyn seemed very taken with the picture.

'Your cousin must have been a handsome fellow indeed,' he declared and then laughed with embarrassment. 'Forgive me, sir, I sound like a flatterer, though I spoke straight from the heart. I am not usually so unreserved.'

'That's quite all right.' William drained his glass and reached for his pipe. Now he felt embarrassed too, but also surprisingly gratified by the compliment. It was a long time since he had received any and besides, it was a compliment on behalf of Matthew as well as himself. 'I can say without boasting that my cousin was a proper gentleman, with fine features and a noble countenance.'

'I do not doubt it, sir. His exterior must have been a fair reflection of his interior; revealing to all those fortunate enough to behold him, the beauty of his soul.' Goodwyn spoke softly, but ardently.

'Why, you are quite the poet yourself,' William said, moved by his words.

'But not half so skilled with words as Father Matthew was. You have not discovered any of his poems, the sonnets you mentioned him writing?'

William sucked on his pipe; he almost, but didn't quite feel ready to tell Goodwyn about the verses he had found, so he shook his head. Goodwyn could read Latin and might have translated the poems for him, but he was afraid of what they might reveal. It would be a shame to spoil Goodwyn's high opinion of Matthew.

Goodwyn patted his pockets. 'I appear to have left my tobacco in my chamber. If you will excuse me, I will go and look for it.'

'Why don't you try my pipe?' William held it out to him. 'Not so easy to misplace as a snuff box.'

'That is very gracious, sir.'

Stretching across the table, Goodwyn grasped the bowl of the pipe, his fingers lingering on the back of William's hand. His fingertips, though warm and soft, might have been the sharpest of arrow points, for it was as if they had pierced William's flesh and sent some venom coursing through his veins. Shocked by the sudden violence of the sensation, William looked up to find Goodwyn's eyes staring directly into his. Unabashed, Goodwyn kept his gaze trained on William as he sat back in his chair and inserted the pipe stem between his plump lips. He inhaled slowly, before removing the pipe and releasing a cloud of smoke. As if to break the spell he had cast, he coughed a little and took a sip of wine.

'The fumes are pleasant indeed and, as you say, have a more purifying effect than powdered tobacco,' he said in a calmly conversational tone. 'May I?' He held the pipe up.

'Be my guest.'

Goodwyn drew on the pipe again before returning it to William, who immediately placed it back in his own mouth. It needed relighting, but he ran his tongue around the damp stem, feeling suddenly more awake and more attuned to Goodwyn than he had felt towards anyone for a long while.

'I will have to make you a gift of a pipe.'

'You are too generous.' Goodwyn smiled. The tension between them might have become strained, but then Goodwyn asked casually, 'Do you play chess, sir?'

'I used to play with Matthew, though he had the infuriating habit of always coming out the victor, even when I thought myself on the verge of winning.'

'I think you will find I am not so skilled a tactician.' Goodwyn pushed his hair back over his shoulder.

'You mustn't give the game away out of deference. I only wish to win if I can do so by my own merits.'

Going over to a chest by the window, William picked up the heavy wooden board, carrying it carefully back to the table so as not to disturb the finely carved pieces laid out on their respective squares.

Chapter Ten

'Very good, sir, I will make no concessions.' Clearing the dishes to one side to make room for the chess board, Goodwyn carefully righted those pieces that had fallen over. 'May the best man win.'

* * *

William woke that night from a dream that he and Goodwyn had been fucking. It was so vivid he half-expected to find Goodwyn lying naked beside him and was relieved to stretch out his arm and feel only the familiar, bulky shape of his bolster. Rolling onto his side, he threw one arm over the soft lump. What had he done to summon these devils that filled his mind with lustful thoughts? He had not felt the slightest attraction towards Goodwyn until that evening and then he had only been responding to the sudden change in Goodwyn's manner.

Their game of chess had been good-humoured, though William suspected that, despite his protestations, Goodwyn had let him win. The rest of the evening passed easily and Goodwyn had not given the impression he viewed William as anything other than a respectable gentleman. He had certainly done nothing to incite such a lascivious dream. But then William recalled Goodwyn's fingers on his hand, Goodwyn's eyes fixed so intently on his; what had he meant by that? If Goodwyn had been his equal he would have said the man was flirting with him, but surely he must be mistaken. The steward would not be so forward with his master. The action was impertinent, however it was intended. Had Goodwyn seen through him? Surely he couldn't have discovered William's amour with John?

There had been many times when he and John had sworn they would conquer their terrible desires, but John was his lodestone and William could no more resist him than a fragment of iron could withstand the pull of the magnet. How could he be so disloyal now as to dream of fornicating with another man? It was iniquitous enough that he was committing adultery with John.

Or, by indulging his passions with John, had he opened himself up to desires for other men as well? Had he merely elevated his desire for John into an expression of love, when in fact it was only lust?

Rolling from one side of the bed to the other, William couldn't escape the thoughts and recriminations that hounded him. He must become more like his brother and drive these sinful thoughts out with prayer and mortification. When he first went through Matthew's things he had discovered a hair shirt; perhaps he should wear it now to scourge himself of his wickedness.

Although the night was cold, William's back was wet with sweat. He pulled his nightshirt away from his damp breasts and pushed the bedcovers down. Even his legs were clammy – the vapour had collected behind his knees in little pools. He had been suffering from these night sweats with increasing frequency over the past few months and was afraid he might be falling ill. It was a prospect that filled him with alarm, for if he became truly unwell who could nurse him without discovering his secret? He could hardly order John into the house to be his nursemaid. Besides John and Nicholas, only Jane and Ellen knew his secret and he had become estranged from both of them.

For the first few years of living as a man he had felt under perpetual siege, having to guard himself constantly against discovery, always alert for the monthly wounding, keeping rags to staunch the flow and then burning them. It had been easier when Jane stayed at Measham; with her at least he had an ally who could offer some moments of respite, who could act as his shield and his reinforcement. But he couldn't envision Jane leaving her husband to tend to him, not now.

Would Ellen come if he wrote to her? He had been generous to her family, paying for her son and her nephew's schooling. It wasn't that he had been paying for her silence; he had been very fond of both boys and wanted them to succeed in life.

Ellen was devout and might come to him out of Christian mercy. She had helped to deliver Nicholas and William knew she would be a dedicated and careful nurse. But she also disapproved of his religion and his way of life. Would she insist on converting him to her puritan faith? He didn't want to be preached to as he lay dying, no matter how plentiful his sins.

Chapter Ten

Pushing himself up against his pillows, he stared blindly into the dark room. It must be cloudy out for there was not so much as a sliver of moonlight breaching the gaps between the bed curtains. Nor could he hear the sound of any living thing, only the wind sighing through the trees. It was a night for desperate thoughts. And now he feared his dream might be some sort of premonition. As though he might end up in bed with his steward, despite himself.

'Oh, Matthew,' he whispered. 'I know I am beyond redemption, but I have never caused injury to another, not intentionally anyhow. Teach me how to be pure of heart. To trust in God to restore my son to me and to live chastely in my thoughts and deeds.'

⭢ Chapter Eleven ⭠

Ireland, August 1690

Sarsfield arrived back in Limerick late that night at the head of the cavalry troops that had been camped in Clare. Tyrconnell had agreed to the raid and was allowing him five hundred men, including the horsemen guarding the Shannon at Annaghbeg. They would assemble them all the next day and ride out under cover of nightfall.

Nicholas spent the last few hours before dawn tossed between feelings of elation and foreboding. He was hungry for adventure and thrilled to be part of such a vital and urgent mission. But what if Lanier had guessed what he was up to and given him false information? Sarsfield would never forgive him if the artillery train turned out to be hoax and they'd let the enemy cross the Shannon for nothing. If this was the case, instead of helping to save the city, he would be enabling its destruction. They would probably hang him as a traitor and he would deserve it too.

The thought of causing his friends such suffering and disappointment appalled him and he could imagine only too well how O'Connor would gaze at him with pity, even when he deserved the man's hatred. This image, which came so vividly into his mind, made his blood run cold. Even if he wasn't hung, it would be hard to keep the news of such an ignominious failure from O'Leary and Úna and then all her worst impressions of the English would be confirmed. Why the latter

Chapter Eleven

should hold any sway over his actions he didn't know, or didn't wish to dwell on; it was just that he couldn't bear to prove her right in her low estimation of Englishmen. She was always so infuriatingly certain that her opinions were correct.

He had to remind himself that he hadn't seen any large cannons at the camp. And his instincts told him that Lanier, who was clearly disillusioned with his own side and insulted by his Dutch commander's treatment, had spoken honestly, if carelessly. If they succeeded in destroying the enemy's guns, Úna would be forced to raise her opinion of him. Not, of course, that he gave a fig what she thought of him personally.

Nicholas eventually drifted asleep, dwelling on the satisfying scenario of Úna's derision being transformed into respect as he was hailed one of the heroes of the war.

He was woken an hour later by the thudding of the cannons on the walls. Dressing hastily, he rushed out to meet O'Connor, who was in high spirits.

'Well done on the map, my lad,' he cried. 'The English are already dragging their tents and field guns back away from our fire.'

At least, Nicholas thought, even if the raid did not succeed, he would have achieved something.

He was further relieved to be reunited with his horse, Carraig, who whinnied with excitement at seeing his old master. The stallion, despite having gone all the way to Athlone and back without him, appeared to have been well cared for and was in excellent condition. O'Connor must have made sure he got his share of provender, despite the growing scarcity of hay and oats.

The raiding party were ordered to rest for the afternoon in preparation for the journey ahead. They were served a substantial supper of meat and vegetables before leaving and everyone ate heartily, savouring what might, for all anyone knew, be their last meal. There was a sense almost of joy among them, as though this was a holiday they were celebrating, and in a way it was, for although they had all been involved in the constant skirmishes with the foe, everyone had grown sick of waiting for the siege to begin. It was far better to be on the attack than stuck inside a garrison. They were proud to have been selected for such an important undertaking and eager to prove themselves.

Nicholas was curious to meet the infamous rapparee leader, Michael 'Galloping' Hogan, as he'd heard tales of the bandit's extraordinary horsemanship.

'He'll guide us over the mountains; he knows every track and pass that runs through them, as well as every bog beyond. If anyone can keep us hidden from enemy patrols it's Hogan,' O'Connor had told him.

'So you're the young fella who found out about the siege train,' Hogan said when they were introduced, assessing Nicholas with sharp eyes. He had the bearing of a leader – confident of his prowess but not to the point of arrogance. Dressed in the close-fitting Irish trousers, which showed off his well-brawned legs, he walked with a wide stride and was clearly used to spending most of his time in a saddle, or more likely riding without one as the native Irish preferred. 'One of my men has spotted the train near Cashel, a massive great convoy it is, over a hundred wagons he said.'

Nicholas could have thrown his arms around the man in thankfulness. Lanier had not fed him a lie; his conscience was clear.

'I see my news has eased your mind.' Hogan nodded astutely. 'I'm glad Sarsfield hasn't relied on some pot-gun for his information. Always better to be wary.'

'Nicholas is no prater.' O'Connor slapped him on the back. 'He's as sound a man as any you'll find, especially among the English.'

Nicholas smiled; considering the reputation of the English among the Irish he could only be grateful for such compliments as came his way.

At last the moon rose, round and full, illuminating the land in its milky glow. This was both a blessing and a curse, for the light made it easier to navigate the country, but also made them more clearly visible. They would be passing through the estates of several Protestant gentlemen who would be only too ready to report their movements

Chapter Eleven

to the enemy so they needed to proceed with the utmost caution. Nicholas rode alongside O'Connor, glad to be in the company of someone who approached every obstacle with a calm and even temper.

It would be impossible to keep five hundred men from being spotted, so they headed westwards, trusting it would appear to any observer as though they were setting out to reinforce Athlone again. Once across the Shannon they could take cover in the forests that grew thickly over the Silvermine Mountains, before travelling back south. It was a detour and time was of the essence, but there was no other way of reaching the train without giving themselves away.

Sarsfield had hoped to cross the bridge at Killaloe, but Hogan told them it was being held by Williamites and led them on until they reached a ford an Irish mile north, out of sight of the troops on the bridge. Urging their horses into the water, they crossed in pairs. No one uttered a word and the only sounds came from the splashing of the animals.

A party of riders appeared suddenly from behind a grove of trees. The men, their forms broad and ominous under the woollen mantles that cloaked them, spread out across the path, blocking their way. The moonlight picked out the metal of their weapons – the daggers at their sides and the half-pikes resting on their shoulders glimmering like lanterns. Nicholas could see that several of them held muskets in readiness to fire and feared they had been betrayed. These men were clearly expecting them. He drew his pistol out of the holster tucked into his saddle-bow, but felt O'Connor's hand touch his arm. The major shook his head at him.

Hogan gave out a low call and one of the men responded in kind. He rode forward into their midst, where they greeted him like brothers. These must be his rapparees, then. Nicholas watched them with guarded interest. They might be skilled at evading and attacking the enemy, but rapparees were also notoriously bloodthirsty, with little loyalty towards the Jacobites.

Sarsfield signalled for the cavalry to proceed and they followed the outlaws into the darkness of the woods. If they were to be set upon, there'd be little chance of escape, Nicholas thought. But the pace remained steady and his horse followed O'Connor's as they made their way slowly along a narrow path, just visible between the trees. He was glad to be mounted on Carraig for he felt an affinity with the animal and knew it would react immediately to his most subtle command.

They rode on without speaking, the quietness broken only by the occasional snap of a branch breaking, the jingling of the soldiers' riding-gear and the muffled beat of hooves on earth. The rapparees used nothing but leather reins and their horses were unshod so they moved in silence. There was a strange beauty to the night, both mystical and sinister. Nicholas was conscious of the shadow of death cast all about them, but whether it foretold their own deaths or those they would inflict, he could not know.

After riding hard for many miles through the densely wooded Silvermine Mountains, they stopped in a clearing in the woods below Keeper Hill to let the horses rest and eat, but they could not tarry long. The enemy would soon learn that they were not on the road to Athlone and send out search parties in pursuit. So they continued on, guided by the rapparees, who made sure there was always a screen of hills between themselves and the plain.

As they passed beneath Mother Mountain, Nicholas heard barking. Surely the Williamites wouldn't use hounds to track them down?

'Are there wolves in these hills?' he asked O'Connor.

O'Connor grinned. 'Why, are you afraid of being eaten?'

Nicholas shook his head. 'I should love to see one. Our family steward, Crewe, said he saw a wolf in the Derbyshire Peaks when he was a boy, but it is generally believed there are no wolves left in England.'

O'Connor nodded. 'It's been many years since wolves were seen in Munster. They're mostly to be found in Connacht and Ulster, but with the bounty on their heads they're unlikely to last long, unless they can hide themselves away like a rapparee.'

Chapter Eleven

At daybreak they were rewarded with a view of the valley stretching out below them as far as the eye could see, the masses of heather and grasses glowing pink and gold in the dawn light. Taking out his prospective glass, Nicholas scoured the horizon, but the only movement he saw came from birds on the wing and the clouds moving slowly across the sky. Once they got to the cover of the wooded slopes around Glengar, Sarsfield gave the command to set up camp for the day.

'To succeed, we'll have to take the train of artillery immediately, before any of them can sound the alarm. The Williamites are bound to use a password to allow their men to leave and enter their camp; if we can discover what it is, we can pass ourselves off as the enemy and be upon them before they have the chance to turn their weapons on us,' Sarsfield told them. 'Otherwise we're likely to find ourselves at the mercy of their cannon and all will be lost.'

Several scouts were dispatched to check the surrounding area for the enemy and to find out, if they could, what the password might be. Nicholas was sent with O'Connor and one of the rapparees, a man by the name of Seán, to discover the whereabouts of the artillery train. It wasn't difficult to find – they heard it before they saw it, an almighty clanking of guns and cannonballs along with the rumbling of cartwheels, making the dry earth shake and sending up such great clouds of dust it looked as though they were a convoy of chimneys instead of wagons. Hogan's scout had been right: there were over a hundred carts all loaded up with ammunition and supplies, stretching along the road for almost two miles.

O'Connor gave a low whistle. 'Will you look at that, and by the looks of it only two troops of cavalry as escort.'

Watching these wagons of death as they headed towards Limerick, Nicholas thought of the gracious Mr O'Leary and his stubborn daughter. What would become of them under the onslaught of these weapons? They had already lost one home; now they would lose another and might well lose their lives into the bargain. He felt once more the old surge of enthusiasm for the fight he had embarked on and the worthiness of the cause. If they could deny the Williamites these weapons, there was a chance they might be victorious against the practised soldiers ranged against them.

Turning their horses, they sped back towards the camp to tell Sarsfield that the train of artillery was on the road approaching Ballyneety. They hadn't got far, however, when Seán suddenly held up a hand, pulling his horse to an abrupt halt. He put his finger to his lips and pointed down towards the river, where Nicholas was surprised to see a woman sitting on a rock and bathing her feet.

She wasn't dressed like an Irishwoman. A pair of heeled leather shoes, rather than the customary brogues, were placed beside her on a stone and instead of loose-fitting woollen garments, she wore a tightly laced bodice and skirts. Brown curls tumbled out from beneath a cotton cap, framing a rosy-cheeked, round face.

Seán whispered something to O'Connor, who in turn whispered the translation into Nicholas's ear.

'He thinks by the look of her she's English and I agree. You go down and talk to her, tell her you're a Williamite, see what she knows.'

Seeing Nicholas hesitate, O'Connor shrugged his shoulders. 'You Englishmen don't know how to talk to women. I'll go and show you how it's done.'

Before Nicholas had a chance to disagree, O'Connor had jumped down off his horse, handed the reins to Nicholas and scrambled down the bank to where the woman was sitting. Lifting his hat, he greeted the startled woman and gave a low bow.

'Forgive me if I alarmed you. My fellow soldiers and I are checking the area to make sure there are no Jacobites about planning to ambush the train of artillery,' he explained.

The woman gave a short laugh. 'Lord, you nearly had me jumping out of my skin. My husband's with the train, we were up at the front, but I was feeling poorly, so he left me in the village to rest. They aren't very friendly there though and I thought I'd come down to the river for a bit of fresh water to cool myself with. It's such a warm day.' She waved her hand in front of her face.

Chapter Eleven

'It is indeed,' O'Connor agreed. 'Would you mind if I joined you and dipped my hands in the river? It looks so refreshing.'

'By all means.' The woman moved over to make space on the stone beside her.

Kneeling down, O'Connor scooped up some water and washed his face. 'I must apologise for my fellow countrymen if they have not treated you with the hospitality you deserve. I hope King William brings them to their senses and restores order to this land; it needs to be ruled with a firm hand.'

'You're right there.' The woman nodded earnestly. 'Oliver Cromwell gave my uncle a big plot of land and a fine house in Armagh back in '52. He was doing very well 'til all this trouble started. We're hoping King William will reward his loyal soldiers in the same way.'

'A noble ambition,' O'Connor said with a tight smile. 'Is your husband an officer? What's his name? I might know him.'

'He's the cornet,' she said proudly. 'Albury is his name.'

'Albury, of course, a fine fellow, never seen a better flagbearer.' O'Connor slapped his knees. 'I certainly can't abandon his lovely wife out here in the wilderness; Albury would never forgive me. You must allow us to accompany you back to the village.'

In his alarm at this proposition, Nicholas accidentally dug his spurs into Carraig's flanks and the horse started forward with a whinny.

'There's our good Captain Hawthorne, another Englishman.' O'Connor waved merrily at him. 'Eager to give you a ride on his fine stallion.'

Nicholas raised his hat and Mrs Albury blushed.

'Now you mention it, I was wondering how I would find my way back and my legs are weary,' she said, drying her feet with her skirts and pulling on her stocking and shoes. 'La, I've spent so long in this country I'm showing off my bare legs like a brazen Irishwoman,' she exclaimed, as if only just noticing their naked state.

Ignoring this last comment, O'Connor beckoned to Nicholas and Seán. As he took the reins of his horse he whispered in Nicholas's ear. 'If she's part of the train she'll know the password; her husband wouldn't have left her here without it. Let's see if a dram or two loosens her tongue further.'

'What if we encounter enemy troops?' Nicholas whispered back.

'Then we'll let you do the talking.' O'Connor winked at him.

And so, Mrs Albury was helped up behind Nicholas, where she sat with her arms clasped tightly around his waist. He could feel the softness of her body pressing into his back as the horse swayed beneath them. She held him unnecessarily close, he thought, but perhaps she was afraid of being thrown; the road was rough and stony. He was more accustomed to riding with other soldiers than with women.

'Are you all right there, Mrs Albury?' he asked her.

'Oh yes, quite well, thank you,' she said, snuggling into him.

He was tempted to ask her for the password then, but didn't want to give the game away. He was sure his comrades intended no harm against her and besides, she was so amenable, if she knew the password he doubted it would require any coercion to get it from her. So the unlikely party trotted on to Cullen, where they stopped at the local tavern.

* * *

'You're a pretty fellow.' Mrs Albury smiled amorously at Nicholas as another cup of strong ale was set down in front of her. 'Where are you from?'

'Derbyshire,' he said, seeing no reason to lie.

'I thought I recognised your accent. I'm from Birmingham, so we're both from the Midlands.' She leant against his shoulder.

Sitting on a bench opposite them, O'Connor and Seán looked pointedly at Nicholas and O'Connor mouthed, 'Password.'

'We Midlanders have to stick together,' Nicholas agreed.

'That we do.' Mrs Albury squeezed his arm, leaving her hand resting on his wrist.

O'Connor and Seán turned away, speaking to each other quietly in Irish as they shared a pipe. The innkeeper looked over at them curiously and they went to join him at the counter.

Chapter Eleven

Concerned that his fair companion was growing sleepy, Nicholas shifted to face her so that she was forced to raise her head off his shoulder. Lifting his wooden cup, he gazed into her eyes over the rim. 'Here's to His Majesty's health.'

'Their Majesties,' she corrected him. 'Don't forget our good Queen Mary.'

Nicholas had in fact been holding King James in his mind, rather than the new regents. 'The proximity of a Venus such as yourself has displaced the rest of womenkind from my thoughts,' he declared, hoping he didn't go too far in his flattery. Though she was a comely matron, Mrs Albury was hardly a goddess.

'You cannot class the Queen among common women,' Mrs Albury chided, though her cheeks flushed pink with pleasure and she took another sip of ale.

'Forgive me,' Nicholas said, wondering how to turn the conversation round to the question of passwords. He drank a mouthful of the sour ale for inspiration. 'It will take a while to become accustomed to having joint monarchs; I don't believe such a thing has occurred in England before. And you know, I am a forgetful fellow; I'd forget my own grandfather's appellation if I weren't named after him.' Seeing Mrs Albury looking somewhat confused, he persevered. 'Why, I got our camp password wrong last time I returned and nearly had my head blown off.'

'Now that would've been a shame.' She tugged at a lock of his hair. 'To lose such a pretty head.'

Nicholas lowered his voice. 'I hope you know the password for the camp at Ballyneety; you will need it to re-join your husband there.'

'I can go back with you,' she said with great certainty.

'The major will not allow that.' Nicholas gestured towards O'Connor. Seeing her face fall, he added, 'I could take you along with me, but we'll still need the password, for as I mentioned before, I have forgotten it.'

'My husband did tell it to me.' She screwed up her face, then burst out laughing. 'What a pair we are, as bad as each other.'

'Quite right.' Nicholas joined in her laughter. 'It must be this Irish ale, but give me some clue and perhaps it'll come back to me.'

'Lord, what is it now?' She ran a finger over her jutting lower lip. 'It's the name of one of them Jacobite commanders, not Tyrconnell, the other one.'

'Berwick?'

'No, the other Irish one.'

'Sarsfield?'

'That's it, Sarsfield. It's a bit of a joke, see, for if anyone's likely to attack us, it'll be him.'

'Of course.' Nicholas nodded, trying not to show his surprise at what seemed to him such a laughable choice of a password. 'I won't be so foolish as to forget that again.'

'Another cup of ale, ma'am?' O'Connor re-joined them.

'If I have another, this young man will have to find me a bed and carry me up to it,' she said with some enthusiasm.

'We should be on our way,' Nicholas said hastily, raising his eyebrows at O'Connor. 'We must report back to Captain Poultney.'

'It doesn't need all three of you, surely? You could stay here and protect me.' She coiled one of Nicholas's locks around her finger.

'Captain Hawthorne is needed to guard those wagons,' O'Connor explained apologetically. 'We will tell your husband we left you comfortably at this tavern. I've spoken to the innkeeper and he assures me you'll be perfectly safe.'

'But the captain said I could ride with him.' She looked up at Nicholas, who was already on his feet.

Pulling a sorry face, he raised his hands to indicate his helplessness in the matter. 'I'll take you vaulting another time,' he promised.

Mrs Albury did not look appeased, but, making their excuses, the three men bade her a firm farewell. As soon as they left the tavern they rode as fast as they could back to Glengar, where the information they had gleaned was greeted with much delight and amusement by Sarsfield and the rest of the men. Many of the rapparees slapped Nicholas on the back, speaking to him in Irish, to which Nicholas

Chapter Eleven

could only raise his hands helplessly. If he got back alive from this escapade, he would endeavour to learn Irish, he vowed.

They rested for the remainder of the day and into the evening, waiting for darkness before moving on again. Two of the rapparees reported that the carts had stopped by the ruins of Ballyneety Castle and fires had been lit, so the English were settling there for the night. No more troops had been seen joining them. The Williamites, it seemed, were quite unconcerned about any risk to their armoury. Given how close they were to their army, they probably considered themselves quite safe, Nicholas thought.

By midnight, Nicholas was lying in a hideout above the road to Ballyneety, Carraig tied up with the other horses under the cover of some trees a few yards behind. He could see the carts and wagons of the artillery train drawn up in a meadow below, close by the ruined castle. They were being guarded by artillerymen, but as far as he could make out, there weren't above a dozen of them. The horse had been let loose and the cavalry escort were camping some distance away. Judging by the silence, they must have been sleeping. He surveyed the scene with rising excitement; victory seemed almost guaranteed, so long as they could keep an element of surprise.

It was then he recognised the soft hoot that was the rapparees' signal. Next to him, Seán pointed towards Limerick. In the distance, several troops of horsemen could be seen charging down the road towards them. Nicholas and his companions sank down onto their bellies. The smell of grass and earth filled Nicholas's nostrils and he could feel the ground shudder beneath him. The riders were bellowing some war song as their mounts pounded along the Old Limerick Road. It was clear both men and horses were well rested and ready for combat. As they came closer Nicholas recognised the familiar chants of the Enniskilleners. If these were reinforcements, the Jacobites' task had become a great deal harder. He had come up against the Enniskilleners enough times to know that they had earnt their reputation for fearlessness and ferocity. They were like a pack of mastiffs, he had heard it said, who would run against bullets when their blood was up.

Seán muttered some imprecation in Irish, to which Nicholas could only add his own in English. To their astonishment, however, the troops, instead of stopping, continued on past the stationary wagons and down the road towards Tipperary. Their purpose was clearly not to protect the train. Nicholas watched them disappearing into the darkness. Laughing with relief, he slapped a similarly mirthful Seán on the back.

Another signal was given, summoning them back to reassemble in the copse behind them. Here they joined the rest of their troop to be addressed by Sarsfield. He waved a hand to quieten their jubilation.

'The Enniskilleners, our old foe, may have moved off, but that doesn't mean there won't be further Williamite troops coming out on patrol. We can't afford to delay. Captain Fitzgerald will take an ambush party to follow the Enniskilleners and ensure they don't return.' Sarsfield pointed skywards. 'The clouds there are gathering; as soon as they're across the moon, the rest of us descend on the camp,' he told the men, speaking in both Irish and English by turn. 'I'll lead the way. Let's pray Captain Hawthorne got the password correct and the sentries will let us pass without raising the alarm. You're to follow as quietly as ever you can. If the sentries try to stop us, shoot them and we can still maintain our advantage.'

Nicholas was not far behind his commander as they descended towards the camp, every man bent low over their horse's withers, keeping the animals as quiet as possible. When Sarsfield and Hogan reached the gate to the meadow, they were stopped by two sentries. Nicholas could hear the men demanding the password and his heart beat violently in his chest. With one hand on his pistol, he felt for the charges hanging from the bandoleer strapped across his chest. His sword was heavy against his thigh as he pressed his legs lightly against Carraig's flanks. What if Mrs Albury had given him the wrong password? They could storm their way in anyway, but the alert would be raised and their chances of success compromised.

Chapter Eleven

'There have been reports of a raiding party in the area; we've been ordered to escort the artillery,' Sarsfield was telling the guards. They had accepted the password and were opening the gate. 'Leave it open for my men,' Sarsfield instructed them. 'Ye are woefully under-protected.'

Nicholas nodded at the surprised-looking men as he rode past them, his breath easing in his chest with relief.

Once inside the meadow, they were challenged again by a second guard.

'Sarsfield is the word,' the brigadier shouted, raising his sword. 'And Sarsfield is the man!'

At this Nicholas let his horse fly, as either side of him his comrades went charging through the camp with their swords and carbines raised. The ground trembled beneath their thundering hooves and the air was filled with smoke and the thud of bullets. It was impossible in the darkness to distinguish the wagoners from the half-clothed soldiers who were emerging belatedly from their tents, as their bugler finally sounded his trumpet. All around Nicholas, men were shooting and slashing at anyone before them.

The Irish shouted to one another in their own tongue so as not to be mistaken for Englishmen and Nicholas cried '*Nicolás Sgitheach*' with all his might, just as O'Connor had taught him to.

He could not have said how long the bloodshed lasted, though later he understood it had been but a few minutes. The memory of it, however, would remain with him always. As the smoke cleared he could see that the majority of those slain wore the clothes of common labourers. It seemed most of the soldiers had fled to the woods, leaving the wagoners to the mercy of their attackers. In fact, he could still see some of them, running barefoot across the neighbouring corn field.

Nicholas's horse stumbled and, looking down, he was horrified to see the body of a woman lying face down in the grass, a bloody slash across her exposed neck. Dismounting, he knelt by her side, turning her over as gently as he could. She had the light and slender form of a young girl. Her face was obscured by her hair, which was matted with some dark matter, mud or blood or both; in the darkness it was hard to tell. He lifted the congealed mass away from face and her lifeless eyes stared up at him, cold and accusing. Pressing his fingertips to her eyelids, he closed them and said a prayer for her soul. He was thankful now that Mrs Albury had remained at the inn and wondered whether her husband would make it back to her.

A hand clasped his shoulder. 'A sad loss, but don't take it too hard, lad.' O'Connor leant over him. 'She must have known the risk she was taking, to consort with the enemy. It is war and there are unfortunate casualties on both sides, deaths we wish we could have avoided. Besides, in the chaos, she might have been killed by one of her own soldiers; you cannot be certain who delivered the fatal blow.'

'Heer Meesters, we will offer you good terms if you come out from wherever you are hiding,' Sarsfield's voice called out.

'We need to capture the engineer,' O'Connor told Nicholas. 'But don't go poking about in the undergrowth; you might get your head blown off.'

A few prisoners had been taken and these were brought forward and questioned, but none of them could, or would, say where Meesters, the siege master, had got to. Nicholas was grateful that Sarsfield maintained his customary civility towards the prisoners, offering them no violence, nor allowing his men to do so.

'We found this fellow lying in bed in the little cabin over there.' Two soldiers dragged a shivering man before their commander. 'He's a lieutenant from Colonel Erle's regiment.'

'Set him down, gently,' Sarsfield commanded. 'What is your name, sir?'

'Lieutenant Colonel Robert Freke,' the man responded weakly.

'Have no fear, Colonel Freke, we'll have you back in your bed in no time. Now, as you can see, our raid, though risky, has proved successful,' Sarsfield told him cheerfully, adding, to Nicholas's surprise, 'Had it not, I might have returned to France.' Sarsfield crouched down

Chapter Eleven

in front of Freke, resting his hands on his knees. 'Have you any notion at all where your famous Heer Meesters might be?'

Freke shook his head, his eyes half-closed. He looked on the point of swooning.

'Return him to his hut and see he has all he needs,' Sarsfield ordered. 'Put everything we can't carry to the torch. Remember, we have to be swift. As soon as the gunpowder blows we'll have all the Williamite troops in the area after us.'

They raced through the wagons and the tents, searching for anything of value that was portable. The train had been carrying far more than anyone had expected. As well as six twenty-four-pounder cannons and two eighteen-pounders, there were mortars and metal pontoons that would have been used to bridge the Shannon, along with wagon after wagon packed with ammunition and supplies. There were enough rations to feed the entire Williamite army for several days. Nicholas stuffed some biscuits into his knapsack, along with a tinder box and a pouch of gunpowder. It was frustrating they couldn't take more with them; it was a terrible waste, but destroying the supplies was better than letting the enemy make use of them.

Some of the men took the camp's picks and shovels to the pontoons. Nicholas flinched as the clanging of metal rang out across the meadow, expecting half the Williamite army to descend on them. He joined O'Connor in rounding up the horses and loading them up with their booty. Once the wagons had been searched they were pushed together and overturned. Everything that could be moved was thrown on top, even the pontoons.

Under the advice of a captive artilleryman, they stuffed the cannons with gunpowder, then pushed them into a hastily dug pit. The muzzles were rammed into the earth, so that they stood almost upside down. Fuses were pushed into their touch holes and a powder trail laid. All the ammunitions and weapons that couldn't be taken were piled on top of them.

As soon as the men and horses were all assembled and ready to depart, the fuse was lit. They galloped away to the almighty boom of the cannons exploding. All around them the sky was glowing and Nicholas could feel the heat of the flames on his back. The horses skittered as the ground shook beneath them and the night air swelled with the roar of gunpowder. Nicholas was filled with a sense of elation at what they had achieved. To have destroyed the Williamite armoury, it was an incredible coup. Surely Limerick must be safe from their guns now.

⇾ Chapter Twelve ⇽

Measham, July 1690

After his shocking dream, William attempted to maintain a more rigorous formality with Goodwyn. However, he often found his reserve melting away under the warmth of Goodwyn's attention. His steward continued to pray for Nicholas every night, consulting his Bible and sharing the passages he was directed to with William. These, to William's great relief, continued to presage good tidings, and being the only information he had as to Nicholas's wellbeing, he held onto them with all the desperation of an invalid submitting to his physician's advice.

He was also deeply affected by the reverence Goodwyn held for Matthew's memory and could not resist being drawn into reminiscences about his brother. He explained to Goodwyn that Matthew had lived at Measham from childhood and was therefore more like a brother than a cousin. Perhaps some might consider Goodwyn's fascination with Matthew verging on the idolatrous, but William enjoyed discussing his brother too much to worry about such religious niceties.

Besides, Goodwyn was no pedant. When they supped together, Goodwyn's conversation was so witty it was impossible not to be entertained and William frequently found himself laughing heartily in spite of his best intentions. It did him good, he felt, to be drawn out of himself in this way. He hadn't laughed so much since he had parted company with Jane. Goodwyn's humour was of a more satirical nature than hers and his jibes were sometimes barbed, especially his witticisms regarding the other servants, but they were so perceptive that William couldn't help but be amused by them.

John was a considerate, thoughtful man, but Goodwyn's company made William conscious of how serious John was. He knew it was partly the weight of their clandestine relations that drove any humorousness out of their exchanges. They were gentle and kind towards one another and John had always been patient with his fears, especially regarding Nicholas and the future of Measham Hall, but their conversations were almost entirely of a practical nature. In that respect they did not differ greatly from any master and his bailiff and much of the time, had anyone eavesdropped on them, they would never have guessed that the pair were lovers. William was glad to feel his passions for his friend subsiding; he hoped this meant he was learning to be more continent. He had not dreamt again of Goodwyn and though the steward was often smart, he was never overly bold. If Goodwyn had been flirtatious with him, he too was showing greater self-restraint.

When asked, John said that Kate was no longer coming home hungry, though she had told her mother that the bread was often stale and the cheese full of maggots.

'Some consider cheese-grown worms a delicacy,' William observed. 'They are said to be proof of the cheese's richness.'

'Sarah prides herself on the quality of the cheese and butter produced at the Grange dairy; you won't find any better in Derbyshire or Leicestershire. None of it is old enough to have turned musty or grown worms,' John retorted.

There was nothing for it but to view the kitchens for himself. As William walked through the yard, he passed Kate plucking chickens and carefully storing the feathers in a sack for later use. A cat sat nearby, cleaning its paws and pretending not to watch her. Kate greeted him cheerily enough and certainly did not look in any way unhappy or ill-used. At the far end of the large low-ceilinged kitchen, Tickell was dozing in a corner by the fire as usual. Still refusing to retire, the old

Chapter Twelve

man had become a fixture of the house. Standing on the other side of the fireplace, young Ben tended to the meat that was roasting on a spit. Cooper stood at a table, pounding herbs with a pestle, a mound of chopped vegetables piled on a board beside him. The room smelt deliciously of rosemary, thyme, freshly baked bread and mutton juices. As far as William could see, everything was in perfect order.

'Good morning, sir.' Cooper looked up with surprise to see his master standing before him.

'Morning, Cooper. How goes it?'

'Very well, I thank 'ee, sir.' Cooper rubbed his brawny arms and, despite being built like a bargeman, looked shyly down at the chopping board, his cheeks reddening with the effort of conversation.

Ambling into the pantry, William regarded the loaves cooling on racks. Some looked like fine manchet while others were made of coarser wheat.

'There's household bread and the court-bread for your table, sir.' Cooper had followed him in and now hovered behind him.

'And the household bread is made fresh every day?' William asked.

'That it is.'

'And Kate brings the cheese fresh from the Grange.' William lifted the cloth off a slab of hard yellow cheese. Beside it was a soft white cheese wrapped in nettle leaves. Both cheeses looked and smelt just right, neither under nor over ripe. There was no sign of mould or maggots.

Returning into the kitchen, William glanced over at Ben, but the boy did not look up from his work. Tickell woke with a start and attempted to rise to his feet.

'Stay where you are, old friend, and I will come to you.' William bent down beside the man he had known all his life and Tickell beamed at him with fond recognition. 'Would you prefer your own fireside to retire to?' William asked gently. 'I can arrange it for you, along with a pension to provide for your needs.'

The smile fell from Tickell's face and was replaced with an apprehensive frown. Turning away from William, he took up a long spoon and began to stir the contents of the cauldron that hung over the fire. 'I've slept in this kitchen most of my life. I've no family left to care for me; where would I go?' He addressed the steaming pot.

'Why then, if you are comfortable here, this is where you shall remain. I have no wish to see you go,' William said, dismayed that what he had intended as comforting words had instead upset his old servant.

'Cooper's not learnt all my recipes yet.' Tickell pointed his spoon in the cook's direction, dripping broth onto the floor. 'And I'm keeping an eye on this lad here.' He jerked his chin at Ben, who grinned back at him, evidently not too troubled by Tickell's vigilance.

'We couldn't manage without you, Mr Tickell,' William assured him. 'Have you been using the salve I made you? To ease the pain in your joints.'

'Oh yes, Sir William. I rub it in every night after I've said my prayers.' Tickell lowered himself slowly back onto his chair.

'Is it helping?'

'I'm sure it is,' Tickell answered, staring down at the swollen knuckles of his hands. 'Will young Master Nicholas be returning home soon?' he added hopefully.

'God willing,' William said and Tickell crossed himself.

Nicholas had been an especial favourite of Tickell's, and the old cook had kept him supplied throughout his childhood with sweetmeats and tartlets.

Reassured by what he had seen, William was convinced that Kate, whatever her father might say, was overly delicate in her tastes. He had not thought her spoiled, but perhaps her mother indulged her.

As he walked down the passageway from the kitchen, Palmes came hobbling towards him.

'Ah, Sir William, I have been trying to locate your whereabouts. The schoolmaster is here to see you. He is very eager to speak with you on a matter of some importance, he says. I've left him waiting in the hall.'

Mr Rees was a tall, gangly man who reminded William of a heron. Now he flapped his bent arms anxiously as he bowed.

Chapter Twelve

'Mr Rees, what brings you to our door?'

Rees's reply was interrupted by Goodwyn opening the door to his office. 'Can I be of assistance, sir?' he asked William as he stepped into the hall.

'I'm sure you can,' William said with some relief, introducing Rees to him. 'There is nothing amiss at the school, I hope?' he added, looking at Rees.

'That is what I seek permission to discuss.' Rees ran his hat through his hands, bending the brim.

'Why don't you come into my study, Mr Rees, and we can discuss it.' Goodwyn held his door open, sweeping his free arm inwards to usher the schoolmaster inside.

Rees hesitated, looking to William for instruction.

'There is no need to bother Sir William; I am sure he has many other concerns to attend to,' Goodwyn said firmly.

'It doesn't concern my goddaughter, does it?' William asked Rees.

'No, sir, it is a financial matter.'

'Ah well, in that case, Goodwyn is your man.' William bestowed what he hoped was a reassuring smile and escaped into the parlour. Goodwyn would tell him later if there was any cause for concern. Rees, he suspected, was looking for more money, as was everyone nowadays.

All thoughts of the schoolmaster were driven from his mind by the arrival of a message from his uncle Percy, who lived some miles north of Measham, towards Derby. His uncle was ill and requested William's attendance. He feared the end was imminent. His uncle was given to exaggeration but he was also well advanced in his seventh decade, so it wasn't unreasonable to think he might be dying. Having to visit with the unpleasant old man was a prospect that filled William with horror, but he could hardly deny his relative's request. The Hawthornes were a small family; apart from Nicholas and William, Percy's only other relative was his daughter, the abbess, who lived in France. She was hardly able to travel to England when the two countries were at war and besides, if the way Percy spoke of her was anything to go by, she would probably be as disinclined to visit her father as William was. He told the messenger that he would be with his uncle the following day.

* * *

John insisted on riding part of the way with William. He worried about him travelling alone and being set upon by robbers.

'I have my sword and a pistol too.' William patted his side. 'Besides, there are few horses faster than Sans Pareil. I can easily outride any attacker.'

'Thou might have an accident, get thrown and knocked out.'

William laughed. 'You're worse than an old woman with all your worrying.'

'Thou used to enjoy riding out with me,' John said sorrowfully. 'I need to speak with thee alone anyhow, regarding Goodwyn,' he added more brusquely.

'Not more complaints from Kate?'

'Nay, not Kate, it's our Alice this time.'

'What has my goddaughter to do with Goodwyn?'

John released a heavy sigh. 'It's about the school. I cannot believe the orders to stop the clothing and halve the food for the poorer children came from thee, so they must be Goodwyn's invention. And folk are saying the rector is upset because Mr Rees has been told to teach the children papist prayers. Now I've no objection to that of course, but there's many as will have.'

William thought uncomfortably of Mr Rees's visit the day before. Perhaps he ought to have spoken to the teacher himself instead of leaving it to Goodwyn. But after their interview, Goodwyn had told him that Rees was demanding a higher stipend. He had not mentioned anything about the allowance for the pauper children or the school prayers.

'I hope Mr Rees has not been taking the money meant for the infants,' William said. 'He was complaining about his wages.'

'Why, thou wilt blame anyone but Goodwyn. What is this spell the man holds over thee?' John erupted with uncharacteristic impatience.

Chapter Twelve

'What are you talking about?' William replied with equal exasperation. 'Why are you always looking for reasons to find fault with Goodwyn?' If it wasn't so ridiculous, he would have suspected John of jealousy.

'I don't seek out faults in any man, but would thou bid me hold my tongue when a steward keeps making unneedful changes to the household and showing his economy to be wanting?'

William was brought back to the similar arguments he had once had with Ellen. How she had hated Crewe! And she wasn't the only one.

'When I first returned to Measham, your parents spoke bitterly against Crewe,' he reminded John. 'They accused him of selling off stock and taking profits for himself by falsifying the accounts. Indeed I suspected him too at first, but then I discovered that every action he took was for the good of the Hall and my family. I believe the same of Goodwyn. If I don't accuse him, it is because I know he is working to benefit our estate.'

'Goodwyn is a very different sort of fellow to Crewe,' John said stubbornly. 'Though truth be told, Crewe always made sure he was well provided for. How else did he buy himself that place in the Peaks?'

'Crewe deserved every penny he earnt. Loyalty doesn't come for free and I made sure his service was rewarded.'

William was immediately embarrassed by the implications of his words. He knew John's loyalty to him was unconditional, but couldn't bring himself to apologise and didn't know how to soften the apparent cynicism. So they rode on in a heavy silence, until he turned in his saddle and told John he might as well go home.

'Let me see thee through the woods at least.'

'That'll take you most of the way and it'll be evening by the time you're home again.'

'I'll see you to Repton,' John insisted. 'They'll tell us there if the ferries are crossing the Trent today.'

'I'm not a child,' William said irritably. 'Nicholas managed this journey alone as a young lad.' He longed suddenly to be travelling unhampered by John's sombre presence, free to enjoy the beauty of the trees and his own thoughts. Having spent several months living in a forest when he was young, he had no fear of the woodland. He was even tempted to gallop off down the path, leaving John's plodding steed far behind. 'Go home, John. I'll be quicker without you. I have no need of your protection.'

'Is that an order, sir?' John asked stiffly.

At any other time, William would have laughed and teased his friend out of his ill humour, but today he was not inclined to nurse John's wounded pride, so he answered simply, 'Yes,' and rode on without looking back.

⇥ Chapter Thirteen ⇤

Ireland, August 1690

Sarsfield's cavalry arrived back in Limerick to a hero's welcome and Nicholas was filled with pride to be counted among them. The governor ordered every cannon on the walls to fire at the besiegers as a riposte and crowds gathered in the streets to greet them. There was no time to waste in celebrations, however. Work continued at a frantic pace to build up the fortifications while the Williamites waited for new armaments to arrive. Meanwhile, the fighting beyond the walls of the city intensified. Every morning the residents of Limerick woke to find Williamite trenches dug a little closer and every night the Jacobites rode out to attack them.

Nicholas had not been able to return to the O'Learys' house and so had no opportunity to witness or enjoy their response to his recent adventures and the successful outcome of his intelligence. He had been ordered to remain with the cavalry, camped out in the countryside, and was too taken up in nightly skirmishes with the enemy to think much about his former hosts.

A week after their return from Ballyneety, Nicholas's squadron was ordered to retake some earthworks known as Yellow Fort, just outside the southern end of Irish Town. The fort had been seized by a force of Danes and Brandenburgers who had slaughtered every man defending it. The recapture of the fort would be no easy task; not only would they have to conquer these Saxon warriors, getting to the fort required riding out across a battleground dominated by the enemy.

As they prepared to leave, Nicholas prayed to Saint Michael to defend him, or if he must fall in battle, to bring him swiftly into the arms of his Maker. He stroked Carraig's neck as he prayed, asking for the horse to be kept strong and resilient so that they might both live to fight again.

On the signal from their commander, Lord Kilmallock, they charged at the fort, riding as fast as they could while the bullets flew at them from both the Williamite trenches on one side and the grenadiers on the other. At least the rutted earth here was firm; Nicholas knew that nearer the fort it would give way to treacherous bog. He had no choice, however, but to urge Carraig on, willing him to outrun the missiles tearing towards them from every direction. Between the blasts of gunfire, he could hear the bellows of injured men and horses. His nose filled with the sulphurous tang of gunpowder and his eyes stung. Despite keeping his lips clamped shut, his mouth was as dry as sand and his tongue burnt with an acrid taste. He prayed that if he reached the fort there would be enough of his own men still with him to overcome the soldiers holding it.

He was only a few yards from the fort when a second Williamite force came at them. The additional onslaught of bullets, grenadoes and choking clouds of gunpowder smoke was overwhelming. Nicholas could just make out Kilmallock signalling for them to retreat towards St. John's Gate. Reluctantly turning his horse, he plunged back into the maelstrom.

Caught up in the tumult and barely able to see through the smoke and the chaos of men and horses, Nicholas felt a terrible thud against the top of his right arm; it was so swift and so hard he dropped his reins, turning to see who had punched him. A bullet whistled overhead and would surely have hit him had he been sitting upright, but instead he found himself on the ground. His horse lay panting beside him and for an absurd moment he thought Carraig had fallen too out of an act of obedience and solidarity. But then he saw the blood pooling

Chapter Thirteen

around the animal's flank. Carraig's eyes were rolling back in his head and he was snorting heavily, his mouth flecked with foam. Whispering useless words of comfort and gratitude into his horse's ear, Nicholas struggled onto his knees, caressing Carraig's neck with his left hand. There was nothing more he could do for his loyal companion. If he stayed where he was he'd get his head kicked in by flying hooves.

At that moment a sabre came swinging through the air, missing his face by inches and, looking up, Nicholas saw an orange-coated rider, bending down from his saddle, his arm rising to strike again. Nicholas just managed to roll away, taking cover beside Carraig's heaving form. Drawing his own sword, he slashed defensively into the air above him, but the Danish horseman was now fighting with another rider.

Nicholas gazed about him. He needed to find another horse. Or perhaps he could fight his way on foot back to the city gate. He was sweating so heavily he could feel the perspiration running all the way down his right arm, soaking into his sleeve. When he tried to lift his hand, however, it refused to obey him and his arm remained dangling uselessly by his side. Glancing down he saw with a curious detachment that it wasn't sweat but blood that was turning his sleeve crimson. The pain was radiating up his arm and across his right shoulder blade now, making him gasp for air. His head was dizzy, but whether it was the smoke or an injury that was making him reel, he couldn't tell.

I must have been hit, he thought with a strange lack of concern, *but not as badly as poor Carraig. I can still make it back and perhaps on my way I'll kill a few Brandenburgers in revenge.*

'Come on, lad!' Someone was shouting at him. 'Give me your good arm. Stand on your horse and I'll pull you up.'

And there above him was O'Connor, appearing like an angel amid the dark clouds, stretching out his hand as if from Heaven. Swallowing down his rising nausea, Nicholas thrust his sword into its scabbard and stepped onto poor Carraig, using him as a mounting block; he clasped O'Connor's arm and was dragged up and across O'Connor's horse. He hadn't the strength to sit, but lay like a dead man, his head pounding with the horse's hooves as O'Connor made for the city.

*　*　*

Nicholas must have fainted, because the next thing he knew, he was being dragged through the doorway of the O'Learys' house by O'Connor.

'Bring him in here,' Mr O'Leary was saying and Nicholas managed to stumble, supported by O'Connor, into the small back parlour where he was laid down on a daybed, which had been pulled out into the middle of the room.

'Mairead.' O'Leary turned to the maid. 'You run down to the barber's and bring back the barber-surgeon. Hurry now.'

'Can I leave him in your care, Diarmuid? I need to get back to my men.' O'Connor knelt down next to Nicholas and, pulling the cravat from his neck, bound it tightly around Nicholas's arm, just beneath the shoulder. 'Keep your spirits up and we'll have you back fighting the enemy in no time.'

Nicholas listened to the clink of O'Connor's spurs as he left the room. The pain in his arm was now so great it was all he could do not to cry out. He swallowed the *uisce beatha* O'Leary fed to him in several gulps, hoping that if he could keep it down, it would bring him some respite.

'Don't you worry, Mr Mooney is the finest surgeon in Limerick,' O'Leary assured him.

Despite O'Connor's cravat, blood was still seeping out of Nicholas's torn sleeve. O'Leary raised the dripping arm, looked round for a support, discounted an embroidered cushion, and finding nothing more suitable to use as a prop, placed the bleeding limb gently across Nicholas's chest.

'I'll just ask Cook for a bowl and some rags to staunch the blood,' he said before departing with as much haste and as little commotion as possible.

Nicholas hoped the surgeon wouldn't find it necessary to cut his arm off. He might lose the use of it regardless. At least he was

Chapter Thirteen

left-handed; that was a small mercy. He felt with sudden urgency the need to return home and imagined Father's reaction to his dismemberment. Father had been so protective of him as a child; he would think him very careless to lose an arm. Still, so long as he could take over the Measham estate, that was all that mattered. Thoughts rolled round his head, oiled by the *uisce beatha* but disconnected by the pain. He was glad when O'Leary reappeared and gave him more sups of the fiery liquor.

Nicholas was even more glad of the drink when Mr Mooney, a large, red-faced man with arms like a butcher's, arrived. Nicholas watched out of the corner of his eye as the surgeon unpacked his case, laying out a curved dismembering knife, a pair of silver forceps and a gimlet with a conical screw.

'We'll have to cut more than the sleeve off his jacket,' the surgeon noted. 'A shame as it looks like good French cloth.'

Once the jacket and the sleeve of Nicholas's shirt were removed, the surgeon examined his wound. Nicholas closed his eyes as Mooney pushed an unexpectedly slender finger into the cavity and felt around. No one spoke and Nicholas was conscious of Mooney's laboured breathing. He hoped he was as skilled a surgeon as O'Leary had claimed.

'Can you save my arm?' he asked, his voice a feeble croak.

'I believe so. You are blessed indeed for the bone appears to be intact. If your arm had been raised and your body hit then things would be much worse. We must remove the musket ball lodged in your bicep, however. Though I knew a fellow who lived to eighty with a bullet stuck by his collarbone. It was very troublesome to him, but he had a terrible fear of the surgeon's knife. Better to take it out. If there is a small fracture to the bone it should fasten again with the right care.' He turned to address O'Leary and Mairead. 'Right, best turn him round and over on his belly so I can get at the arm more easily.'

He continued to issue instructions in Irish and Nicholas soon found himself face down and pinioned on the left by Mairead, who patted his left shoulder as she chanted Hail Marys. Nicholas wished he could join in, but he was too conscious of the *uisce beatha* burning in his chest and was afraid of vomiting. He reminded himself of the courage with which his uncle had met his death on the scaffold and vowed not to besmirch his memory by any show of cowardice.

A cool, damp cloth was pressed to his face. It carried the sharp resiny smell of St. John's Wort and the comforting scent of roses. He inhaled deeply and tried to cast all other thoughts from his mind as the pressure against his arm increased. He could feel the flesh and muscle tearing as the surgeon bore in with the gimlet and then a terrible wrenching as the bullet was grasped by the instrument. The pain was so excruciating Nicholas couldn't help but cry out.

'That's right, lad,' Mooney exhorted. 'Give it your all; the ladies will forgive a little cursing.'

Nicholas was sure he could hear metal scraping against his arm bone, a sound that seemed to be travelling internally up to his ear and echoing in his head. This was followed by a sickening squelching.

'There it is,' Mooney said with satisfaction, by which Nicholas assumed he meant the bullet.

More matter was tugged out of the wound as Mooney diligently removed every scrap of material dragged in by the musket ball, explaining as he did so that if any rags were left within they would most certainly lead to putrefaction. Finally, Nicholas felt the sting of padding being stuffed into his arm. He could smell turpentine and something even less pleasant, probably oil of whelps, he thought.

Once the surgeon was satisfied, Nicholas was carefully raised and turned onto his back again. Mooney, whose forehead was dripping with sweat, beamed at him and held the squashed lead bullet up for him to view.

'A little memento,' Mooney said, placing it on the table. 'Now, I've applied a tent to the wound, which will need changing twice daily. All being well and no sign of inflammation, I'll sew it up in a few days' time. If caution is taken and you remain at rest, you should regain full movement in the limb. Fever is the thing to watch out for.'

Mr Mooney turned to speak in Irish to the woman standing behind him. Nicholas was surprised to see Úna, a serious expression on her pale face, nodding intently as she listened to the surgeon. Had

Chapter Thirteen

she been present all along? he wondered, remembering the cloth that had been placed over his face.

They left him to sleep, but his arm throbbed so painfully it was a long time before he was able to descend into that welcome release. He was grateful to Fionn, who lay down at his bedside as though he were Nicholas's own faithful hound. He laid his left hand on the dog's back, finding it a comfort to run his fingers through the rough fur. He was sorry for the loss of Carraig and thought suddenly of his old spaniel Artemis. Father had a new dog but he'd forgotten its name; perhaps he could bring him an Irish wolf-dog as a gift. He wondered drowsily if Fionn had sired any puppies and hoped that if he had they had not been turned into whelp oil.

* * *

When he woke, O'Leary was sitting nearby, reading. He smiled when he saw Nicholas's eyes open.

'There is some broth here for you, if you can swallow it, and some wine cordial made by my daughter,' he said.

Steam was spiralling up out of the dish on the table and Nicholas could smell mutton, but he wasn't hungry and took only a little of the cordial to wet his dry mouth. It was sweet and soothing and he soon asked for more.

The lawyer, as well having an erudite mind, was a witty storyteller. Recognising that Nicholas was in no fit state for conversation, he kept him distracted from his injury with tales about his forebears and the history of Ireland.

'When we were in the mountains I had the good fortune to see an Irish hare, which is larger than the English hares and I am told does not turn white in the winter,' Nicholas said, wanting to make some contribution to their discourse despite his foggy head. 'I have also noted your *fionncholl gaelach*, a tree unique to this island that flowers very prettily in spring. I should dearly like to see a wolf.'

'And one day I am sure you will.' O'Leary nodded indulgently at him. 'I suspect you would rather be recording the beasts and vegetation of our country than engaging in warfare. My daughter is equally fond of the productions of nature. She loves to paint, you know, landscapes and such forth.'

'Is that so?' Nicholas wasn't sure why this information should surprise him, but he found it hard to imagine Úna with a painter's brush in hand; she seemed too quarrelsome to have the patience for studying landscapes.

'Though I speak as a proud parent, I am not the only one to admire her skill; she has a fine eye.'

As if summoned by their discussion of her, the young artist stepped into the room and spoke quietly to her father.

'And now she admonishes me for keeping you awake when what you need is the healing balm of sleep.' O'Leary stood up. 'We won't attempt to move you upstairs. You are welcome to make use of this room as your bedchamber for as long as it is required.'

'You are too kind. I can contribute for my upkeep and you must let me pay you for the surgeon's fee,' Nicholas said guiltily, though his army pay was late again.

'Ah don't worry about that now.' O'Leary scratched his chin. 'I still owe Mooney for my last shave; besides, I doubt he'll charge much, seeing as you were wounded in defence of our city.'

Úna picked up the half-empty bottle of wine cordial. 'You have given Mr Hawthorne far too much, Father; he should only take one draught three times a day,' she said in Latin.

O'Leary looked a little sheepish.

'It is my fault,' Nicholas explained. 'I asked for more as it is having such a beneficial effect.'

Úna stood, observing him with a critical eye, her forehead furrowed. Then, as if having arrived at some decision, she came over to him and placed a hand on his brow, studying his face and arm as she did so. Her palm was refreshingly cool and smooth and smelt of roses and St. John's Wort, like the cloth that had been pressed to his face during the operation. Nicholas felt all the muscles in his face relax and his eyes closed of their own accord. He could hear Úna and her

Chapter Thirteen

father talking quietly in Irish. He thought she was saying something about the danger of pain and the importance of sleep, but perhaps he only dreamt that.

* * *

Nicholas had no idea how long he slept for, though he was vaguely conscious of the light growing and fading away and someone putting drink to his lips. He woke intermittently to the thud of cannon fire, which set the windows rattling in their frames. Once there was an almighty explosion followed by what sounded like an avalanche of rocks. The whole house shook and he wondered if it really was any safer here than the camp out in the countryside. It was hard to distinguish between the external crashes and rumbles and the throbbing of his head and arm. Sometimes it felt as though someone was twisting a corkscrew into his bicep. It was especially bad when the dressings were changed, but he was too delirious to know who it was who tended to him.

An image of Measham Hall floated into his mind; the gardens were so beautiful in summer. Would he ever sit fishing on the riverbank again, chatting to Father as they waited for the trout to bite? How fortunate those in England were, that this war was being conducted on Irish soil. It was paradoxical that if his side was victorious, James would take the fight across the water and English fields and houses would be destroyed as well as Irish ones. Then he saw again the body of the woman killed in the ambush of the siege train. He could almost feel the weight of her body in his arms as he turned her over to reveal the young face and the look of accusation in her lifeless eyes.

* * *

He woke one morning to a softer drumming than usual and it took him a moment to realise it was the sound of rain. The weather must have been uncommonly dry for he did not recall hearing rain for a long time. There was a rap on the door and, to Nicholas's confusion, Francis Bedley stuck his head into the room.

'And how is our hero today?' Bedley asked, pulling a chair up by the daybed and sitting down.

'I'm hardly a hero,' Nicholas answered irritably.

'Since you are included in that pantheon of Irish saviours who raided the siege train, I think you will find that you are.' Bedley leant forward, placing his hands on his knees. 'And the arm?'

'Bloody painful.' Nicholas was getting a crick in his neck trying to look at Bedley and he resumed staring up at the ceiling. His right shoulder was hanging off the edge of the bed and he was afraid that if he tried to move he'd roll onto the floor.

'But God in His Mercy be thanked, you are alive and no longer feverish.'

Bedley's face loomed over Nicholas. His breath smelt like ditchwater and Nicholas was relieved when he resumed his seat.

'How have you been faring?' Nicholas asked. 'I did not expect to see you here.'

'I met Major O'Connor yesterday and he told me about your injury and subsequent fever, so I thought I must call on you in person. I've been hard pressed overseeing the unarmed soldiers in building up the earthworks. To give them their due, they have worked tirelessly, even as the enemy's cannon played on us night and day. Two of the towers were brought down, burying many of those who were defending them, God rest their souls. And now the enemy have got close enough to throw bombs and grenades over the walls. They've managed to set some of the thatched roofs alight, but have inflicted no substantial harm so far.'

'At least it is raining now.' Bedley's account was making Nicholas's head ache. He hated being an invalid, unable to take part in the battles raging outside.

'Indeed, the Almighty has seen fit to send us such heavy rain the enemy will be drowned in their trenches before long. It has certainly dampened their cannon fire,' Bedley answered with great satisfaction. His faith in the cause appeared to have been restored.

There was another knock on the door, to which Bedley responded with an imperious, 'Enter.'

Chapter Thirteen

Mairead came in carrying a tray, which she set down on the table. She was followed by Úna.

'How is our patient?' Úna asked in Latin.

'Much recovered, it seems,' Bedley told her.

Nicholas tried to push himself more upright using his left arm. To his surprise, Mairead was immediately at his side with another cushion, which she inserted deftly behind his back to prop him up. He thanked her in Irish and was rewarded with a smile, the first he'd seen on the maid's freckled face. Her angry defiance gone, she looked suddenly like one of the rural lasses Nicholas remembered from home. She belonged in a dairy or a country kitchen, not a besieged city, he thought.

'This is an improvement indeed,' Úna said with unusual enthusiasm. 'Can you manage a cup of milk and a little bread, perhaps?'

For the first time in days, Nicholas felt hungry and the women stood watching him eat with the sort of delight usually reserved by mothers for a sickly infant.

'*Quant je puis.*' Bedley quoted their college motto as he rose from his chair. 'I will leave you to the tender mercy of your nurses.' Bowing, he made a rather awkward exit. With the appearance of the women, all his self-assurance seemed to have evaporated.

'God save you,' Nicholas called after his retreating figure. It had been kind of Bedley to visit, after all.

'We must change the pledgets and dress the wound.' Úna brought over a tray bearing lint pads and a bowl of poultice.

Nicholas winced as the greasy pledgets were pressed into his wound, but Úna nodded with satisfaction. 'All signs of corruption have gone. I believe it can be sewn up now, but we must consult the surgeon.' She neatly bandaged his arm up again with dexterous speed.

'I am very grateful to you. Had I been out in the field, lying in the warm damp, I doubt I would have recovered.' Nicholas spoke sincerely; he believed he probably owed them his life or if not that, then at the very least, his arm.

'We must get you better so that you can re-join your company,' Úna responded briskly, returning to the table.

'Do you think that will be possible before winter sets in?' Despite his eagerness to return to the battle, Nicholas couldn't help being a little disappointed by her eagerness to be rid of him.

'I doubt it,' she answered more cautiously. 'Mr Mooney said you will need several weeks, if not months of convalescence if you are to regain complete use of your arm.'

Mairead had set about vigorously sponging the upper half of his body with a sopping wet cloth and the water was running off his chest and soaking the sheets. He was about to suggest wringing out the cloth when she began roughly drying him with a threadbare towel, humming a tune as she did so. Nicholas, feeling like a child's puppet, wondered uneasily about his lower half and wished he had a manservant to help him with his ablutions. His discomfort only increased when Mairead said something to Úna in Irish and they both chuckled.

'I am a source of some amusement to you,' he said.

'No, indeed,' Úna assured him. 'Mairead was just after telling me that for an Englishman you are a handsome fellow, and brave too.'

'You can speak English!'

'But the language of the oppressor burns my tongue,' Úna answered quickly in Latin, clearly aggrieved at having accidentally slipped into English. "Tis *garbhbhéarla*.'

'You're a fine linguist nonetheless, to speak three languages.'

'You would not be so impressed if I were a man.' Úna nodded at Mairead, who was holding up a shirt with a questioning expression. 'I know some Greek and a little French, too,' she couldn't resist adding.

'Why then, I am impressed regardless of your sex,' Nicholas insisted.

Mairead had dropped the shirt over his head and was trying to direct his left arm into the sleeve. He leant forward, getting the shirt on with some difficulty, though the right sleeve had been removed. Sitting back, he noticed that it wasn't his shirt – he had been reduced

Chapter Thirteen

to just two, both of the coarsest linen, whereas this was made of fine cambric, with delicate embroidery at the cuff.

'Someone has been kind enough to lend me his clothes,' he said, thinking perhaps it was O'Leary.

'It belonged to my brother,' Úna said curtly. She turned and abruptly left the room.

'*Deartháir?*' Nicholas looked questioningly at Mairead and pointed at the door Úna had just walked through.

Mairead nodded sadly before launching into a rapid speech in Irish, very little of which Nicholas was able to follow. He picked up the words 'dead' and 'sickness', but that was all. When Mairead had gone, he examined the shirt. The embroidery was done in coloured silks and depicted harps entwined with leaves and flowers along with the initials D. O'L. It was fine work and he wondered if it had been sewn by Úna.

She retuned that evening to administer his physic, which she no longer entrusted to her father, and he apologised for distressing her.

'You and your father have been so generous to me, a stranger from a country that has treated you despicably,' he said in Latin, not wanting to offend her with his native tongue.

He was pleasantly surprised when she sat down on the chair beside his bed. He was even more surprised when she began conversing with him in English.

'There were several times during your fever when you cried out to save a woman from being killed. You begged me to tend to her body, to keep it from the slashing swords.' Úna spoke with unusual reticence, looking away across the room as if to save him any embarrassment.

'Most of those killed during the raid at Ballyneety were common folk, not soldiers. It was dark and we had to act fast; there wasn't time to distinguish between them. It was Carraig, my horse, who stopped me from riding over the body of the woman.' Nicholas discovered it was a great relief to tell her what had happened. If she reacted with disgust, well, it was only what he deserved. 'I don't know if it was my sword that killed her, or someone else's, but either way, I am responsible for her death. I've seen women hanged, you know, for being spies, so she was not the first. But they were all innocent; that's what I believe.'

Úna did not answer him at once, but he had no sense of judgement or reprobation in her silence. If he had hoped to be punished for his sins, her tongue for once did not oblige.

'Even if it was your sword that ended that woman's life, it was not your intention to murder the innocent,' she said slowly, as if choosing her words with care. 'I was wrong when I suggested you had joined this war out of a desire for vengeance. I can see now how far you are from one who fights out of a love of violence. In capturing the train of artillery you have saved many more lives than you destroyed. Some, such as your friend Bedley, would argue that this, being a just war, is directed by God and therefore that it was God who smote down that woman. Certainly, in fighting to defend and protect you are, according to any of the treatises on warfare, free of any crime or transgression.'

Nicholas sighed. 'It is true I joined this war to defend my faith and protect those I love, but when I behold the terrible cost, well, I believe you were in the right when you said Ireland is being used as a battleground between two kings who care nothing for its welfare.'

'Then let us hope Sarsfield can lead us to victory despite them both.' Reaching into the box by her feet, Úna took out a piece of needlework, spreading the cloth over her knees. 'Do you have any brothers or sisters?' she asked, clearly wishing to turn the conversation away from subjects that might distress her patient.

'No, though as a boy I always longed for a brother,' he said, watching with admiration as a yellow primrose blossomed from her needle.

'Weren't you your mammy's darling, being an only child?' A smile played about her lips and Nicholas wondered if she thought him the product of a spoiled upbringing.

'Perhaps if I'd had a mother I might have been, but I grew up without one and found it a great burden – being my father's sole heir and the custodian of his estate,' he answered stiffly.

'There's many would envy you,' she chided, unmoved by his self-pity. 'But why didn't your father buy you a higher commission?

Chapter Thirteen

Then you could be taking your ease with the generals, sitting in counsel instead of riding against bullets.'

'He didn't buy me a commission at all; indeed, he'd rather I was at home with him than fighting here.' Nicholas had been proud of his swift rise to captain; she could hardly expect him to be a general at his age.

'Your father is not a supporter of King James?' Úna looked up from her sewing.

'Not especially. He thought the King was too hot in his promotion of Catholicism and I suppose he was right, for it turned the people against their sovereign. My father is an advocate of caution and moderation; he prefers a retired life over an active one.'

'If only all Englishmen shared his views and stayed at home, they would have spared us Irish a great deal of bother.'

'He would be in agreement with you there.' Nicholas refused to rise to her jibes. 'And what of you, do you have any siblings?'

'There were five of us, but I am the only one left. It is just Father and me now.' She bent her head over her work, tugging sharply on the thread.

'Was it the same illness that carried them all away?' Nicholas asked.

Úna's hand went instinctively to the scars on her face and she tapped on them lightly with her fingertips. 'My youngest sister was just newborn when three of us went down with the smallpox, so perhaps it was childbed fever that took my mother; it was a hard delivery and she was very weak after so we can't be sure. The baby too was a frail little thing.' She paused before stabbing her needle back into the cloth. 'I was nine years old and the first to catch it, so you could say it was me who brought the sickness into the house.'

'You cannot hold yourself accountable,' Nicholas said gently, then seeing her frown, added, 'That is unless you believe yourself to have divine powers. Humans cannot dictate the course of diseases, not as children anyhow.'

'But you think adults can?' she asked with genuine curiosity.

'Adults can take preventative measures. For instance, many of the enemy were destroyed last winter by the bloody flux and everyone put it down to the wet weather. But a deserter from their side told me that the Dutch soldiers, who built themselves huts and dug drainage channels around them, fared much better than their English comrades, who lay shivering in sodden tents.'

'Well, the English do not like hard work,' Úna replied acerbically, glancing sideways at him.

Ceding her parry, Nicholas merely smiled. 'And the brother who wore this shirt, he did not catch the smallpox?'

'My eldest brother died only a year ago. He was thrown from his horse and struck his head on a rock; we thought he might recover, but it was not to be.'

'God rest his soul.'

Úna crossed herself. 'So, like you I am now the repository of all my father's hopes and ambitions.'

'And you appear to be fulfilling them — at least, he is very proud of you.'

'Isn't your father proud of you?'

Nicholas considered this. 'I believe he is, though as a child I always doubted it.'

'Because you are his natural son?'

'I suppose so.' He was somewhat taken aback by the directness of her questions; he had never spoken so frankly with a woman, or perhaps anyone, before. Now he didn't want to dishonour or betray his father, but neither did he want to be dishonest in his response. 'I was always being told how fortunate I was that he acknowledged me, though he was cold as a parent and for many years I believed he would be glad to be rid of me. But then I discovered that he had good reasons for his reserve.'

'To protect you?'

'To protect us both.' Nicholas spoke more emphatically that he had intended and was relieved when she did not push him any further on the subject. 'Will you teach me Irish?'

Chapter Thirteen

She raised her dark eyebrows. 'You'd be better off asking my father; I am not a patient teacher.'

'I would rather learn from you.' He spoke teasingly, but he was enjoying their conversation. Drawn to the brightness of her intellect, he found himself wanting to prove his own intelligence to her. He had always been commended for his quick understanding and hoped to impress his hostess equally. Perhaps he might even coax one of her glorious smiles out of her.

'Well then,' she said, looking around her. 'We may as well start with the objects in this room.'

She began to name each item of furniture, getting him to repeat them after her. After about half an hour, however, she told Nicholas he was tired and must rest. She was a perceptive nurse. He realised suddenly how exhaustion had crept up on him and found his eyes closing involuntarily. He was vaguely aware of her moving quietly around the room as he fell into a heavy slumber.

* * *

The following afternoon, as Nicholas lay looking at a book on the natural history of Ireland lent to him by O'Leary, his reading was interrupted by several almighty bursts of cannon fire. His bed shook and a picture fell off the wall, landing with a crash just beyond his feet. The booms were much louder than usual and could only have come from the enemy's twenty-four-pounders, which must have been dragged right up to the city's walls. The even spacing between discharges suggested a signal.

Sure enough the cannon shot was followed by the loudest and most sustained gunfire and cracking explosions of grenades Nicholas had yet heard. He could see through the window that outside, despite the heavy rain, the grey light was obscured by thick clouds of dust and smoke. The room grew so dark, he was forced up from his bed to light more candles.

His sword was propped up in a corner. He hobbled over to it, his head spinning with the effort. Was he capable of fighting?

He suspected from the noise that the walls of the city must have been breached and wondered where the rest of the household was. Would the Williamite soldiers respect the women? He wouldn't be able to defend Úna and Mairead against a mob of infantry. At the thought of such an attack, the bile rose in his stomach. Boisseleau would hold the city secure, he told himself. Their garrison would see off the invaders. As for himself, he'd rather die fighting than be taken prisoner.

The room continued to shake with further volleys of cannon shot. Now Nicholas thought it must be his own side's guns firing from the citadel and King's Island. He couldn't bear being stuck inside while the fighting raged on around him. Spotting his boots at the foot of the bed, he shoved his feet into them, struggling to get them on with one hand. Wrenching the door open, he called out, but the house was eerily quiet. Where were they all? Mr O'Leary's study was empty and he turned to try the kitchen. Surely the cook had not deserted her post? A gush of smoky air blew down the corridor as the front door opened, closing again with a slam. Mr O'Leary came hurrying towards him. He was holding a handkerchief to his face and his bloodshot eyes streamed with water. Seeing Nicholas, he waved the handkerchief distractedly in the air.

'Oh, Mr Hawthorne, the enemy have got through the breach east of St. John's Gate and made it into Irish Town. It was all confusion with red coats being worn on both sides and some of the Grenadiers got as far as the main square before our soldiers took them. Then the Danes came storming in after them, ferocious fighters as history attests. And now my daughter and Mairead have gone out to join the men in defending the city. They say all the women of Limerick are there, throwing stones and bottles to repel the Williamites.'

'They've gone to fight?' Nicholas leant against the wall, feeling as though his legs might give way beneath him.

'I couldn't prevent them.' O'Leary pressed his hands to his cheeks.

'I must go to their assistance!' Nicholas cried, pushing himself away from the wall.

Chapter Thirteen

O'Leary shook his head. 'You're in no fit state to go anywhere.'

Taking Nicholas's arm, he steered him back into the parlour. Despite his frustration, Nicholas was forced to accept his own helplessness and found himself sinking back onto the narrow daybed under the direction of Mr O'Leary.

'What a strange turn of events this is, where the men must wait indoors while the women are out fighting,' Nicholas lamented.

'We can only pray our ladies are as invincible as the Amazons of old.' There was a slight quiver in O'Leary's voice. 'I shall fetch the *uisce beatha*,' he said, as though this would aid their prayers.

They had drunk most of the bottle by the time Úna and Mairead returned. Night had already fallen when Úna burst into the room, her reddened eyes glowing with excitement. Her long hair was wild and hung in tangled locks about her face, which was half-black with sooty powder. Nicholas and O'Leary beheld her with a mixture of awe, alarm and, on Nicholas's part, envy. He recognised the energetic euphoria imparted by a vigorous battle. Úna launched into a description of the fight in Irish, to which her father gasped and applauded by turn.

'The enemy filled the streets of Irish Town, all the way to the Baal's Bridge, and the women beat them back with nothing more than stones and broken bottles,' he translated for Nicholas.

'We were assisted by our own troops, especially the cannons, which swept those invaders off the counterscarps as they tried to climb over,' Úna explained in Latin as if just noticing Nicholas's presence.

'What was the tremendous explosion we heard?' he asked.

'The Brandenburgers were storming the Black Battery when the tower blew up and they were sent flying, but many of those defending it lost their lives as well.' Úna looked suddenly exhausted. She sank down onto a chair, pushing the hair back from her dirty face with an even dirtier hand. 'The roads are slippery with blood and there are limbs and the parts of bodies lying on the streets where they've been thrown.' She paused. 'And there are men blinded by powder, not knowing where they are.'

Her father handed her a glass of *uisce beatha*, squeezing her shoulder as he did so. She drank it down in one before departing to give herself a good clean, as she put it.

'Your daughter is one of the most extraordinary women I have ever encountered,' Nicholas marvelled.

O'Leary beamed at him. 'You'll not find another like her,' he said proudly.

* * *

Nicholas lay awake all that night, his mind besieged with conflicting thoughts. He had not felt such anxiety on anyone's behalf, apart from his father's, as he had experienced while waiting for Úna to return that evening. The constraints of his injury had been agonising and he considered for the first time that this forced passivity was frequently the lot of women. He understood more fully now why his father had renounced his own womanhood and embraced life as a man.

Though Úna could not be compared to Father; she was of a different order of being altogether. Bedley was a fool to value her worth so cheaply, for she combined honour and courage with wit and skill. It seemed there was nothing she could not turn her hand to; medicine, needlework, warfare and learning, the feminine and masculine virtues flourished equally in her. O'Leary even claimed she was as fine an artist as any of the Old Masters.

And now, God forgive him, he could not help but burn for her. What delight it would be to have her passions directed towards instead of against him; she was bound to be as fiery in love as she was in conversation. They could know great joy in each other's arms, he was sure of it. Instead of her student, he could become her tutor in the pleasures of the flesh.

Nicholas pushed himself upright and wiped his damp forehead with the sleeve of his left arm. It must be the *uisce beatha* working on him, to allow such wicked notions to enter his mind. 'Begone, Devil,' he muttered out loud. 'I am no seducer.'

Chapter Thirteen

Could he be Úna's husband instead? He almost laughed out loud as he imagined Bedley's reaction to such an announcement. It was a preposterous idea; the lady would never accept him — she made her disdain for his nation all too clear. She would certainly make a very trying wife anyhow. And what would she and Father make of one another? Though very different in temperament and interests, he could see an understanding grow between them, a mutual respect that could flourish into friendship. Father might not be so accommodating as Mr O'Leary, but he was hardly orthodox in his attitudes. Then again, O'Leary might not accept him as a son-in-law either.

Leaning over towards the table, Nicholas poured himself a cup of water from the jug that had been left there. He must stop this train of nonsense; these were just the sort of idle fancies to assault one's mind during sleeplessness. Yet, even as he argued with himself, Nicholas could not dislodge the conviction that even if he searched the whole world over, he would never find Úna's equal.

⇾ Chapter Fourteen ⇽

Measham, August 1690

William had not intended to be away from Measham for so long, but Uncle Percy clung stubbornly onto life and it was two weeks before he finally departed this world. It took another two weeks to see him in the ground and sort out his affairs. The house was in a terrible state of disrepair, tended to only by a handful of elderly servants. For William it served as a stark warning of what could have happened to Measham Hall if he hadn't found a replacement for Crewe.

The reward for his attendance on Percy was that his uncle left all his property and its contents to Nicholas – with the exception of the family Bible, which was to be sent to his daughter Mary, and a coach that was fit only for firewood, which he bequeathed to William, along with an old mare who would not survive the winter. Percy's will also, to William's great relief, included annuities for the servants, who seemed to be well provided for, though determining where they could retire to was not such an easy matter. The butler and the serving-man wished to remain where they were and in the end William agreed that they should stay on in one wing, while the rest of the house was shut up. They certainly weren't capable of looking after the entire building. The land too was turning into a wilderness. Percy had enclosed most of it so that it was no longer being tilled by local farmers, many of whom had been driven away, unable to sustain themselves on the few

Chapter Fourteen

plots of marshy land left them. Having taken over the fields, Percy had failed to look after them; the walls were only half-built and the hedges sparsely sown, so his sheep and cattle roamed freely, eating the crops that had once been planted. William could only hope that Nicholas would be able to return and claim the property soon. He had enough on his hands with Measham to care for.

Most of the country was in a state of panic over rumours that the old king, James, had landed somewhere in England at the head of a French army, though exactly where his armada had come ashore altered according to the newsletter or teller. For those in the West Country the invaders were in Kent or Sussex or sometimes Hampshire, while the people of the southern counties were convinced the previous king was leading his avenging army eastwards from Plymouth or Torbay. William didn't much care where they were, so long as they brought his son safely home.

Despite having no address nor word from Nicholas, he had sent a letter via the same intermediary he had used before, a Mr Isaac Smith, informing Nicholas of his inheritance. In coded language, he had urged his son to abandon the Jacobite cause and return home. No one need know where Nicholas had been or that he had been fighting for King James. Who would inform the authorities? There must be boats that could smuggle him back to England. William directed Nicholas to write back to Measham Hall as he did not expect to remain for much longer at Percy's and now he was impatient to get home to see if a reply might be waiting for him.

How wonderful it would be to have Nicholas living a few hours' ride away. He could just see the place transformed under Nicholas's care into a thriving household with beautiful gardens. As he walked around the crumbling mansion and overgrown grounds, he imagined Nicholas with a kind and compatible wife, strolling through arbours of flowers, their numerous children running before them to play hunt the fox or catch-ball, their laughter ringing out in the air as their mother called for them to take care. The land around them fruitful and prosperous.

On the south side of the house, in an area now taken over by brushwood and brambles, Nicholas could erect greenhouses like Lord Pemberton's, or even better – like the Dutch ones he had described with such admiration. He would have all he needed for his botanical pursuits and could send for specimens instead of travelling across the world to discover them. Oh, he knew it was all idle fancy, but what would life be without daydreams?

A large tawny-orange butterfly with black-spotted wings landed on William's arm and he stood immobile, watching the delicate creature twitching on his sleeve. He was not a superstitious man, but he had heard that the Irish believed butterflies to be the souls of the dead waiting to pass through purgatory. The butterfly took to the air, landing on a nearby witch-hazel and William was seized with a sudden unease; his mouth grew dry and his stomach sickened. Was it an omen? Could it be Nicholas who had died?

He shook his head and told himself to stop being a fool. If the butterfly represented anyone it would have to be his uncle. Goodwyn had been keeping him updated on affairs at home, writing regularly to assure him that life at Measham Hall continued in an orderly fashion and that there was nothing that required his attention. The only sad news had been the demise of poor Jove. The dog's distemper had finished him off. Considering how poorly he'd been before William left, this news had not come as a surprise, but was no less unwelcome for that. He went to the stables to check on his horse and was glad to see Sans Pareil looking sleek and healthy. Still, he could not dispel the fear gripping at his insides.

* * *

It was a dreary, damp day when William finally rode back to Measham. Swollen grey thunderclouds smothered the August sky, but without any wind they neither released their cargo nor blew away. Even Sans Pareil could do no more than plod along, tossing his head at the flies. Still, after the dirt and dust of Percy's house, William was looking forward to siting down to supper and a glass of claret in his own clean

Chapter Fourteen

and tidy parlour. Cooper might not be a great cook, but he was a damn sight better than Percy's.

It was late evening when he arrived home. He dismounted stiffly, cursing the fact that his limbs were not so nimble as they used to be, and called for Jasper. The lanky, sandy-haired groom, who had worked in the Measham stables since he was a boy, emerged from the stables with an uncharacteristically gloomy expression.

'It's a mercy you're back, Sir William.' Taking the reins, Jasper leant into Sans Pareil's neck, running his hand over the horse's side with slow, even strokes. Sans Pareil nickered in response. 'Such a shocking business about Mr Thornly, none of us can understand it, he was a good bailiff, one of the best. Not like this new fellow, if you'll pardon me for saying so.'

'What are you talking about? What has happened with Thornly?' William demanded, panic rising in his belly.

Jasper looked stricken. 'I thought you'd have heard, sir. Didn't you hire the new bailiff?'

'I most certainly did not. Where's John?'

Lifting one of Sans Pareil's legs, Jasper carefully inspected his hoof, taking a picker out of his pocket to clean it. He spoke softly all the while to the animal, as though he could no longer hear or see his master.

Knowing when he'd get no more information from the groom, William ran into the house, all stiffness forgotten. As soon as he was through the door he shouted for Goodwyn. The steward emerged from his study, smiling calmly, and gave a low bow.

'Welcome home, Sir William. I hope your journey was not too arduous. Perhaps you would like to take some wine in the study. We were not expecting you back for a few more days.'

'What the hell is going on? Jasper tells me we have a new bailiff.'

'A most unfortunate occurrence. I did not like to trouble you with it while you were detained on family matters. Pray come and sit down, sir. Rest your legs and take some refreshment, then I can explain all.'

Goodwyn gently ushered a bewildered William into the parlour. 'I will fetch the wine myself.'

William sank down onto his usual chair. At least the fire had been lit, even if they weren't expecting him. His worst fear was that John had been taken ill, next that their affair had been discovered and Goodwyn had taken it upon himself to dismiss John. He would have to be reinstated; William couldn't possibly work with anyone else. And what of John's family? The disgrace of it. He needed to use the privy but could hear Goodwyn's steps outside and didn't want to delay hearing the news.

'Here we are,' Goodwyn said soothingly, setting a tray down beside him and pouring out a glass of sweetened wine.

William took a large mouthful. He hadn't yet eaten that day, but had lost the appetite he had worked up riding home. He couldn't even bring himself to light his pipe.

'May I?' Goodwyn gestured to the seat opposite.

William nodded and Goodwyn settled himself down. His calm, self-possessed manner reminded William of a priest or a physician when counselling a parishioner or a patient.

'I must ask you to be brave now, my dear master, for I have something terrible to relay. Something that will wound you deeply.'

William felt all the blood in his body sinking down into his feet and was afraid he might swoon.

'Some weeks ago, as your uncle lay dying and you were occupied in nursing him so faithfully, John Thornly disappeared. Not being well acquainted with the man I thought perhaps this was something he was prone to doing. Some men do go off on bouts of drinking or whoring or the like.'

William flinched. 'John was not like that.'

Goodwyn gave a conciliatory nod. 'His wife and daughters assured me of that. But we needed someone to manage the land until Mr Thornly returned and knowing of a very experienced and reliable fellow who could help temporarily, I asked Mr Latham to step in during Thornly's absence. As the days went by and Mrs Thornly grew

Chapter Fourteen

increasingly distressed, Latham organised a search for him. It grieves me deeply to tell you how he was found.' Goodwyn stopped to take a pinch of tobacco.

William was incapable of uttering a word; he could only listen on in silence, dreading what was to come next.

'There is a small cottage in the woods, I am sure you must know of it.' Goodwyn's voice was soft and slow. 'One of Latham's men stumbled across it. None of the villagers would venture near the place because they believe it to be haunted. Alas, I fear now it may be.' He paused and stared into the flames. 'Mr Thornly's body was found inside, hanging from one of the rafters.'

The light in the room was strangely dazzling and the fire seemed suddenly to throw out a scorching heat. Though he sat quite still, William's whole body was throbbing. It was as if every atom of his being was fighting against this extraordinary news. An image of John's body flashed into his mind before he could dispel it.

'Your man was mistaken.' But even as he spoke the words, William knew that resistance to this tragedy was futile. His fate had been enacted in his absence and his life lay in ruins.

Goodwyn shook his head. 'A physician was summoned. It is his view that Thornly hanged himself.'

'John would not commit self-slaughter.' This much, William was sure of.

'Who knows what drives men to such desperate acts.' Goodwyn raised his hands in a gesture of incomprehension. 'Perhaps he was plagued with a guilty conscience for sins known only to himself. His desperation must have been terrible indeed to throw away his life in that manner.'

For a moment, William thought he might vomit the wine he had drunk onto the hearthstone. He took a deep breath to steady himself. 'And his body, what has been done with that?'

'Thornly's widow asked that he be buried in the garden of the cottage, since that was the place he had chosen to die. A Christian burial was out of the question of course. I hope you won't consider it impertinent, but I took it upon myself to see that her wishes were followed. It seemed the least we could do for the poor woman and her daughters. Since the ground had been abandoned long before and you had never expressed any plans for it, I did not think you would object.'

William could not stop the tears from coursing down his cheeks, though he knew such a display of emotion must appear excessive. 'Forgive me,' he managed to say at last. 'I knew John all my life.'

'Of course, sir. I understand completely,' Goodwyn said kindly. 'Pray take a little more of the wine. It will soothe your spirits.'

William forced himself to swallow another mouthful of the spiced liquid and presently a calmness did indeed come over him, only it was accompanied by such a potent drowsiness that he found his eyes closing and his limbs growing heavy. He tried to rouse himself, but was unable to resist the sleepiness that was weighing him down. He felt as though a feather quilt had been thrown over his head and was slowly smothering him.

When he woke it was dark and he was lying on his bed. He had a vague recollection of Goodwyn helping him up to his chamber. Had there been another man assisting him too? William couldn't be sure. Out of the corner of his eye, he thought he saw a figure hovering in the shadows and he almost called out John's name, but was overcome again with weariness and sank back into sleep much as a drowning man, having lost all hope, might sink beneath the insistent waves.

→ Chapter Fifteen ←

Ireland, 31st August 1690

Nicholas woke late on Saturday morning. He lay for a while listening to the rain drumming on the windows, trying to work out what was different. Then it struck him: the rain was all he could hear. The incessant crackling of the guns had stopped.

'Have they agreed terms?' he asked Úna when she came in with his medicine. 'Are they collecting their dead?'

'I don't believe so. People are saying the enemy stole away in the night. Their trenches are lying abandoned along with their dead.'

Nicholas insisted on going outside to see for himself and they set out together after a breakfast of watery porridge. The end of the siege had come just in time, for supplies of food and fuel were getting very low.

Despite the heavy clouds, the daylight made him blink and he stepped cautiously out onto the muddy street, feeling as weak as a newborn lamb. Still, it was impossible not to rejoice at the sensation of raindrops against his face and the gentle warmth of the murky sunlight on his eyelids. He inhaled deeply, but was assaulted with the smell of gunpowder layered over the sickly tang of decomposing flesh.

'Have you heard any news of Lieutenant Bedley?' he asked, feeling guilty that he had not enquired about his old companion before. Major O'Connor was out in Clare with their squadron, but Bedley had been engaged on the city's ramparts.

Úna shook her head. 'I've not seen him these past three days.'

They said nothing more on the subject but at the back of their minds they were both wondering whether Bedley's body was among the corpses that were being piled onto carts for burial, and their eyes were drawn unwillingly to the face of every red-coated cadaver they passed.

They made their way up to the walls of Irish Town from where they could see across the river to the devastated countryside stretching out for miles. They were an island on a sea of brown mud and blackened, burnt-down crops. The enemy's cannon could still be heard firing from Cromwell's Fort. They stood in silence watching the bedraggled mass of William's army marching slowly away, their cannons dragged by oxen behind them. Below the walls soldiers were busy destroying the enemy's earthworks, searching their trenches and stripping their dead. Anything of value would be claimed, but the plunder appeared to consist mostly of shovels and pickaxes, items that would be handy enough for rebuilding the city.

'Where is the cavalry?' Nicholas wondered out loud. 'They could finish off the Williamites if they were here.'

'I believe they're busy elsewhere.'

'Did you receive news from O'Connor?' Nicholas was curious as to where she got her information from.

'I know he is at Sixmilebridge.'

Nicholas detected a note of hesitation in her voice, but perhaps it was because they were speaking in English. Remembering how animated she had been in O'Connor's company, it suddenly occurred to him, with an unpleasant constriction in his chest, that Úna might be a little in love with O'Connor. He was after all a handsome, gallant fellow, who knew how to charm the ladies; but Úna must know that he already had a wife and children in Mayo to whom he was, by his own account, quite devoted.

* * *

'I don't care if you speak French like a native, your Irish pronunciation is horrible!' Úna told Nicholas, but the harshness of her judgement was at least sweetened by a peal of laughter.

Chapter Fifteen

'I thought this poem would please you,' he replied, looking at his teacher with what he hoped was an appealingly wounded expression. 'It heaps praise on the ladies of Limerick.'

'It could have been a list of insults for all I could recognise from your mangled delivery.' Úna was immune to his attempts to win her sympathy. 'You are clearly not ready yet for the great Irish poets like Dáibhí Ó Bruadair. We will have to find you something simple enough for the English mind to comprehend.' Usually she refused to speak in anything other than Irish during their lessons, but now she lapsed into Latin in her impatience to communicate with him.

'It isn't more than two weeks since we started our lessons; I think I have been doing rather well considering how different Irish is from Greek or Latin,' Nicholas said indignantly. He had been accustomed to impressing his tutors with his quick apprehension.

'I did warn you I would be a hard taskmaster.' Despite her words, Úna's expression softened and there was a note of contrition in her voice. Picking up the manuscript volume she had lent him, she turned to an even more densely written page of verse. 'This poem praises an Irish judge for acquitting two men accused of treason by the same rogue who brought about the execution of your cousin.'

'Titus Oates?' Nicholas leant over the page so that their arms were touching. 'I'm pleased my account made such an impression on you.'

'I have a good memory, unlike some.' Resuming her schoolmasterly attitude, Úna tapped his hand with her quill. 'You can translate this poem into English.'

Nicholas was about to object when Mairead marched into the room, pushing the door open without knocking.

'There is a woman here to see you, Captain Hawthorne.' She glared at Nicholas disapprovingly and he wondered what he could have done to reignite her animosity.

Then the strong and familiar fragrance of the visitor's perfume reached him — civet and musk and other expensive ingredients that had been kept too long and grown stale, though she evidently still applied them liberally. Nicholas's heart began to race; surely it couldn't be Blanche Fitzpatrick. Why would she have left the protection of Dublin now that it was under English control?

'Nicholas!' An attractive woman, around thirty years in age, with elaborately curled auburn hair, swept past Úna and leant over Nicholas to kiss him on the cheek.

'Mrs Fitzpatrick,' he said faintly, rising from his seat.

'Pray do not get up on my account.' She pressed a hand to his left shoulder, compelling him to sit down again.

Though he had been fond of her, Nicholas had scarcely given Blanche a thought since arriving in Limerick and her appearance now was both alarming and inconvenient. How on earth had she found him?

'What brings you to Limerick?' he demanded somewhat ungraciously.

'The same circumstances as have brought most of Ireland here,' Blanche exclaimed, withdrawing a fan from her pocket and waving it vigorously in front of her face as though his question had distressed her. 'I was dismayed to hear that you had been injured and came as soon as I discovered your whereabouts.' Turning to Úna, she pointed to a chair on the other side of the circular table. 'May I?'

'Of course.' Úna pulled the chair out for her.

Blanche moved the chair closer to Nicholas and then, gathering up her skirts, sat down beside him. The inner folds of the pink mud-splattered material were still crimson where the sun had not faded the dye and though her bodice was richly embroidered in gold silk thread, the stitching had frayed in places. Her attire had certainly deteriorated since Nicholas had last seen her, or perhaps it was only that he had never viewed her in daylight before. Beneath the table, her leg touched his.

Blanche gave a heavy sigh, letting her shawl slip from her shoulders. Her breasts, which were barely covered by the lace on her chemise, quivered magnificently. A black patch in the shape of a coach and horses appeared to rear up as the breast on which it was stuck trembled. This was an old trick with which Nicholas was familiar and he couldn't help smiling at it.

Chapter Fifteen

'I cannot tell you the ordeals I have endured.' Blanche's voice was rich and sonorous and Nicholas half-expected her to launch into one of the tragic speeches she had delivered for the courtiers in Dublin. Instead, she looked across at Úna and asked in a plaintive tone, 'I hope you won't consider it an affront if I ask to speak privately with Captain Hawthorne?'

'Of course not.' Úna bobbed a small curtsey before striding out of the parlour, shutting the door with an emphatic click.

'That was rude,' Nicholas chided, getting up from the table and retreating to the daybed.

Blanche, however, was not to be deterred and took up her chair, placing it back down beside him. She pulled a folded piece of paper out of her bodice. 'I have a letter for you.'

The paper was still warm from her body and smelt of her perfume. Nicholas was delighted to see his father's handwriting and unfolded it eagerly. It was a long missive and Father had taken care to write in small letters, the lines running closely together across the page.

'You can read it later at your leisure. It's just as well your father has used a cypher, for he is rather indiscreet in what he says. And his hand is very poor for a gentleman. I suppose he is accustomed to using scribes.' Leaning forwards, Blanche stretched one arm across the curved bedhead so that her sleeve brushed the back of his neck.

'Your friends have been most concerned as to your wellbeing.' She spoke so softly now he was forced to turn towards her to hear her words and was almost overwhelmed by her heady scent. 'You have been very negligent in communicating with them. Indeed they believed you must have perished, only news came of a Captain Hawthorne who had been part of the raid on the artillery train.'

The porridge Nicholas had eaten that morning turned cold and slimy in his belly. Had Colonel Lanier admitted passing the information about the ammunitions on to him? It would cast the colonel in a bad light, but worse, it would expose Nicholas as a traitor to Lord Pemberton.

He pressed his head back away from her face. 'I had no choice but to take part in the raid. I couldn't refuse an order. Since then, as you know, I was injured and have been confined to bed.'

She ran her right hand over his chest and stomach. 'And I am heartily relieved to see your person still complete and as handsome as ever.'

Her hand moved down to his thigh, pressing lightly upon it as her fingers curled in towards his groin and to his shame he felt himself becoming aroused. Gazing up at the ceiling he began conjugating irregular Greek verbs – it was an old technique that had served him well in the past.

'The siege may have been halted, but the war is not over,' Blanche continued, now feeling for his cock.

Nicholas grasped her hand with his left one, his right hand being still out of use. However, since she was sitting on his right side, this left him with nowhere to place her hand and he was forced to hold it up in the air, away from his body.

'Are you not desirous of a little relief?' she asked tenderly, wriggling her suspended fingers.

'I am not well enough,' he moaned.

'Your prick disagrees.'

'My prick doesn't know what is good for me. I must rest or my fever will return.'

'Well, God forbid I should be the cause of any inflammation.' She gave him a saucy look. 'If I promise not to enflame you further, will you release my poor trembling hand? My fingers are prickling all over.'

He let go of her wrist and she placed her hands demurely in her lap. His heart was still racing, but it was the thought of Úna returning and finding him in a compromising position that was causing him the greatest anxiety.

'To return to more pressing business.' Blanche raised her eyebrows archly. 'The raid at Ballyneety cost the Williamites dearly. You can make amends by reporting on the comings and goings here in Limerick. They want to know what Sarsfield is up to and who backs him. Tyrconnell would have surrendered weeks ago if it wasn't for him.

Chapter Fifteen

The Williamites need to know whether the French plan to send more aid or if they are giving up on Ireland and are withdrawing completely.'

Despite his dismay, Nicholas was reassured on one point at least: he had not been connected to the discovery of the train. If he had, Blanche would have warned him his life was forfeit. She might even have been dispatched to finish him off. He knew she carried a dagger concealed somewhere on her person.

'It'll soon be winter and everyone will be dispatched to quarters,' he told her.

'I don't think the Irish will rest so easily as that. There'll be further efforts made to regain ground. Darling Sarsfield especially will want to encroach on Dublin. Berwick too is as young and eager as a wolf pup. If Tyrconnell returns to France, won't Berwick be placed in command of your army?'

'Most likely, but with your talents you will have no difficulty in discovering such information for yourself. Weren't you the belle of Dublin last winter? You are far more likely to gain such men's confidences than I am.'

Her expression changed to one of injured disappointment and he felt another surge of shame, only for the discourtesy of his words this time.

'You overestimate my powers. Besides, the mood is very different now that King James has departed. Less whoring and more warring.' She gave him a withering glance before rising to stand behind her chair. 'When you are recovered you must discover the answers to my questions, otherwise I can't answer for what actions Lord Pemberton might take. You know he does not take kindly to being crossed.' She walked over to the door with a regal bearing worthy of a Cleopatra, her stateliness undiminished by her threadbare garments. 'Now I've discovered your lair, I will become a frequent visitor. Do you think your little friend will be put out?' She stopped and pressed the fingertips of one hand to her lips. 'I hope I haven't sullied your reputation.' And she curtseyed before leaving Nicholas in a state of physical and mental torment.

⇾ Chapter Sixteen ⇽

Measham, August–September 1690

When William woke again it was daylight, but whether one night had passed or several he could not say. His whole body ached horribly. As he shifted onto his left side, a sharp pain stabbed him in the arm, forcing him to turn onto his back. He felt as though his brain had been replaced by a huge bowling ball that knocked against the sides of his skull as he moved, but after lying prone for a while, he managed to push himself up to a sitting position. Lifting his sore arm to examine it, he saw that his sleeve had been rolled up and a mark left from where he had been bled. He was sure he had been wearing his jacket when he lay down to sleep. Someone had removed it, along with his wig, which had been placed on its stand on his dressing table.

All his worst nightmares had come to fruition. Weak and incapacitated, he had been exposed to the ministrations of others. He must have been seized by a terrible fever to remember so little. Who had summoned a doctor to bleed him? What had they seen? Had he been ranting? His only comfort was that the rest of his clothes remained on. His waistcoat had not been undone and he assumed from this that his female form had not been exposed. But this didn't lessen the fact that someone had accessed his body, had lifted him up and held his arms as he lay sleeping. Had they taken their time, examining his narrow wrists and dainty bones? He prayed

Chapter Sixteen

that it was Abigail who had nursed him, but feared it might have been Goodwyn. And was it the local doctor who had come to him? What tales might he spread?

All these fears were as nothing, though, compared to the loss of his beloved. His last words with John rang round and round in his mind until he thought they would drive him insane. He had been unforgivably harsh. Why had he sent John back to Measham when he could have taken the opportunity to speak further with him? Now that opportunity would never come again. He could never make amends for his disdainful treatment of one who had only ever shown him tenderness and respect. It was unbearable that he had dismissed John's company and sent him packing like a common servant. What right had he to laugh at John's fears and accuse him of jealousy? He was a worthless wretch who deserved to be exposed in the pillories, to be mocked and pelted with dung.

No longer caring how much outward pain he suffered, William curled up on his side and almost screamed into his bedclothes. As his sobs subsided, John's face appeared, reclining on the pillow beside him, his thoughtful eyes bright with questions, a curl of brown hair spread out on the blank pillowcase. He almost fancied that if he reached out his fingers he might touch again the soft bristles of John's beard, stroke the cheeks stained russet by sun and wind, and provoke John's lips into curling upwards in one of his cautious smiles. What wouldn't he give to press his lips to John's open mouth again.

He had led his friend into sin, but John was not a bad man. He had been a good husband and father; William was sure Sarah would testify to that. If anyone was deserving of God's mercy, it was John, who had acted always out of love and never out of hatred, anger or villainy. He was guilty of adultery, that could not be denied, but so were half the great men of England. It was the breaking of this commandment – the act of suicide – that William couldn't fathom. John was not a man to flee from trouble and though he had been unfaithful, he would never desert his wife and daughters, no, nor William neither, whatever cross words might have passed between them. Could he have underestimated the depth of John's passions, that he had been driven to despair?

No, the more he considered it, the more he was convinced that John would never have taken his own life. Though of a serious disposition, he was not a man given to melancholy brooding. His sense of duty, to the land and to his family, came first with him.

Dragging himself out of bed, William splashed his face with water from the jug that had been left out and placed his wig on his thumping head, adjusting it in the mirror so that it sat correctly. Beholding his bloodless countenance in the dusty glass, he could see only the hollow sockets behind his eyes and the loosening teeth embedded in his jawbone, as though his flesh had melted away to reveal the skull beneath the skin. He grimaced at his reflection, as if he needed another *memento mori*.

Was it grief that had made him so ill or had he caught some contagion at his uncle's house? Perhaps there had been an evil miasma lurking in the thunderclouds as he rode home. If God had struck him down as a punishment it was no less than he deserved.

He crept through the house, relieved not to encounter Goodwyn; he couldn't face the man now. All the energy he had was required for one purpose, to speak with Sarah. But first he must try to replenish himself.

The silence that fell on the kitchen as he entered only confirmed his sense of ghostliness.

'Give me a cup of ale,' he told Cooper, leaning on the table for support.

'Sir.' Cooper laid the sheet of pastry that was hanging from his rolling pin across the top of a pie and hurried out to the brewery.

'Where's Tickell?' William asked Ben, who was sweeping the floor.

The boy glanced nervously at the empty stool by the fireplace. 'Gone to the poorhouse, sir,' he whispered.

William's legs almost gave way beneath him. 'Who the hell sent him there?' he demanded.

'Mr Goodwyn, sir.' The boy was clutching his broom as though he'd like to ride away on it.

Chapter Sixteen

'Well, he must fetch him right back out again.' Seeing the look of terror cross Ben's face, William added, 'Don't worry, I will speak with Goodwyn. You go out to the stables and tell Jasper to saddle a horse for me.'

William sank down onto Tickell's usual seat, hardly noticing Cooper, who set a tankard of ale, along with a plate of bread and cheese, down beside him. After forcing himself to eat, William felt strong enough at least to ride over to the Grange.

Ben must have mentioned William's feeble state to Jasper, for instead of Sans Pareil, he had prepared the steadiest mount in the stables. The mare stood patiently while Jasper helped William into the saddle as though he were a child just learning how to ride. Ordinarily William would never have allowed such close contact, but he was grateful to the three of them for their silent understanding.

As the old mare lumbered over the hill, William stared about him in amazement. How could Measham exist without John? He was as much a part of the place as the soil and the rocks, the rivers and the trees. Goodwyn might as well have told him that the air had departed from the land, that the sun had burnt itself out or the rain drowned in the lake.

When the old farmhouse came into view, he fully expected to see John striding out of the door, pulling his coat on. William's mouth had grown dry again and he swallowed uneasily. He must not give way to his emotions in front of Sarah. He had always maintained a distance with her and no doubt she thought him very haughty, but he could not relinquish his defence in the face of their joint mourning. He dreaded especially seeing John's daughters in the throes of grief, for it would be very hard not to share their tears and succumb to womanish lamentations. But perhaps they had cried up their store of tears and he would find them already in a state of wretched submission to their tragedy. That, he thought, would be even worse. He hadn't seen Kate in the Hall and assumed she was staying at home to comfort her mother. How had they explained John's death to sweet, simple-hearted Eliza? he wondered.

He rode round to the back of the house and tied the horse up in the yard. The place appeared deserted. The door usually stood open, but finding it locked, he rapped on the knocker. A dog began barking from within and eventually he heard a man shouting roughly at it to be quiet. The farm dogs slept in the stables and this didn't sound like one of John's dogs; it had the deep baying of a mastiff.

When the door opened, William was shocked to be confronted by a stranger: a hard-faced man with a thrusting chin and anger in his eyes, like a dog that's been bred to fight. Was this some relative of the Thornlys?

'How can I help you?' Pulling the door shut behind him, the man looked William up and down, adding 'sir' when he took in William's apparel.

'I wish to speak with Mrs Thornly.' William didn't see why he should introduce himself to this knave.

'She's gone. Mr Latham's the bailiff here now.'

When William had been told there was a new bailiff he had assumed the man had been housed in one of the Measham cottages, not in the Grange. Why had no one said that the Thornlys had left? He was feeling dizzy again, but knew this was not the sort of fellow to reveal any weakness to.

Inhaling deeply, he said in as magisterial a manner as he could summon, 'Mr Latham was appointed in my absence and I'll decide whether he stays on as bailiff or not. I never gave my permission for him or you to move in here.'

The man bowed, but there was still an insolence in his manner. 'Pardon me, Sir William. I'm Mr Baines, Mr Latham's serving-man. Mr Goodwyn installed us here, said it only made sense since the widow and her daughters left it empty.'

'Where have they gone?'

Baines just shrugged.

'You're the fellow who found John Thornly?'

'That's right.' Behind Baines, the dog began to bark again.

William supposed the dog was the reason Baines was keeping the door closed. It was clearly as hostile as its master. He wanted to question the man further, but was interrupted by the sound of

Chapter Sixteen

hooves trotting into the yard. He turned to see Goodwyn arriving on horseback, followed by another man, who looked almost as ruffianly as Baines only slightly better dressed. He wore a dark purple coat and his beaver hat sported a peacock's feather.

'Sir William,' Goodwyn called, his voice full of concern.

The second man had slipped down off his horse and now helped Goodwyn to dismount. Goodwyn came straight to William's side, his arms held open. 'I did not expect you to leave your bed today. You are not well, my dear sir; you should not be out unaccompanied.'

'What's this fellow doing in the Thornlys' house?' William demanded. 'And where have the Thornly women gone?'

'They did not wish to remain in a place with such terrible associations,' Goodwyn said softly. 'I believe Mrs Thornly was so ashamed of her husband's actions, she preferred to go somewhere new, where no one would know them.'

'But their family and friends are all nearby; no one hereabouts would judge her so harshly.'

'I did my best to persuade her to stay, but she was adamant, as were her girls. Why don't you return to the Hall and compose a letter to them?' Goodwyn turned to the man in the purple coat. 'May I introduce Mr Latham, the new bailiff.'

Sweeping his hat off his head, Latham gave a low bow. 'It is a great honour to work for you, Sir William; I will ensure your beautiful lands are maintained to the highest standard. Indeed I have already noted some areas where productivity might be increased.' Like Baines, Latham spoke with a London accent, or at least one from the south-eastern counties. He did not sound like an upland man.

Goodwyn tapped Latham's arm to silence him and the three men stood watching William. How he missed having John by his side. Now he felt usurped on his own land.

'You were very quick to find a replacement, and to house them here,' he told Goodwyn. 'You should have waited for my return.'

'Forgive me. I could find nowhere else to accommodate Mr Latham and did not think you would want him in the Hall. However, if you are unhappy, I will move him elsewhere.' Goodwyn nodded at Latham.

'You can get him lodgings in the village for now, but I want to see his testimonials and I will question him myself before he continues as bailiff.' William glared at Latham, who blinked his hooded eyes slowly, a look of indifference on his face.

'Of course, of course,' Goodwyn soothed. 'All these were just temporary measures to ensure standards were maintained in your absence.'

William felt too weak to insist on entering the house and instead returned home with Goodwyn. Every ounce of vitality had drained from his body and as soon as he got back, he allowed Goodwyn to usher him up the stairs to bed.

'I'll send the boy up with some cordials for you and when you are well enough, you can write to Mrs Thornly,' Goodwyn assured him.

'Send Abigail,' William said.

But it was Ben who arrived with a jug of something sweet and a plate of biscuits. After drinking a little, William succumbed to sleep again, grateful to drift free of his agonising thoughts.

This freedom was short-lived, however. His mind was dragged up from the depths of oblivion by countless figures darting round him like fishes. They moved so fast it was hard to see them clearly in the murky waters, but sometimes as they passed he recognised a familiar face. There was Jane, sixteen again and untouched by sorrow, her limp gone and her feet skipping wildly in their silk slippers as her skirts billowed round her. Now here came Ellen, her pretty hazel eyes hard with puritan disapproval. She paused long enough to thrust her face into his. 'What of the poor folk whose land you've enclosed? You offer their children alms as a salve to your conscience, but now you've withdrawn even that. Where's the food and clothes you promised them? What has become of Tickell, who worked so hard to provide you with sweetmeats?'

Suddenly his stepmother whirled before him, hand in hand with Lady Margaret, dancing a furious courante, their shrieks of derision

Chapter Sixteen

rising above the beating of a tambour and shaking everything around him until he felt the curds in his belly rising up into his throat.

Round and round they all swam, reaching out their hands and throwing back their heads, their mouths wide with laughter, their hair floating behind them in yellow and brown strands that merged with the fallen leaves sinking through the green water. Their teeth were pearly white and sharp as arrows. Now they were throwing darts at him — tiny fire-spears that flashed like shafts of light but burnt into his flesh like brands. 'You are not William,' they chanted. 'You are just a weak and foolish woman, as sinful as Eve and as easy to tempt.'

'Alethea, Alethea.' Now he saw his mother, but though he could hear her voice calling to him, her mouth was still. It was as if she were a painted figure, trapped behind a layer of varnish. She stood flat against a mud-brown background. Gradually the picture receded so that more of it was visible and his father was revealed, seated beside his mother, who stood, one alabaster hand placed on her husband's shoulder. 'What have you done now, you mischievous girl?' He could hear their thoughts echoing inside their painted heads.

'She always was a tom-boy,' his stepmother chimed in. 'Wild and unbiddable, a hoyden, a strumpet.'

With a great effort, he forced himself awake and the noisy clamouring faded alongside the frenzied images. It was hard to believe they were figments of a nightmare, or even of a feverish brain; he had never dreamt up anything so lifelike before.

The curtains had been closed around the bed and from the little light seeping through the gaps in the hangings it was impossible to tell if it was an overcast day or a moonlit night. As his eyes adjusted to the murky light, however, he made out the familiar, homely figure of Abigail, sitting on a stool by his bedside. He was so thankful to see her, he stretched a hand out to grasp hers, but the hand that took his was gloved. It squeezed his palm painfully hard.

'You look so like him, you have even adopted his mannerisms, but you are nothing compared to the true William,' he heard a voice say. 'No thing at all,' the voice sneered.

A fingernail was pressing into the pad of his thumb, poniard-sharp despite its covering; without the glove it would have pierced his skin. William tried to withdraw his hand and it was released with a sudden jerk so that it fell back onto the coverlet.

Then Goodwyn was holding him up and a cup was placed to his lips. 'Drink a little more, sir,' Goodwyn said with his customary solicitude, and William was compelled to swallow the syrupy liquid. It burnt his throat, leaving the taste of something bitter in his mouth. Goodwyn settled him back on his pillows and he felt himself falling through thick layers of cloud, until all was black again.

* * *

And so it went on, for hours, days or even weeks, William could not have said. He was tormented by visions of John. There were episodes when he was convinced John had returned to him, that they were lying together, wrapped in the close comfort of each other's arms. John stroked his hair and called him 'my own sweet lass', just as he used to do when they were alone together and William would step out of his manly self along with his clothes, becoming Alethea again. Resting his head on John's shoulder, one hand pressed against his warm breast, his fingers trailing through the dark hairs as though they were the grass in a meadow, he experienced such deep joy, grateful for each rise and fall of his beloved's chest, each beat of his heart. He drank in the mossy, bark-like smell of John's sweat and vowed never to leave his side again.

Then they were riding out above the hay meadow and he must have said something that tickled John, for in one of those rare moments he delighted in, John threw back his head and laughed with pure, full-hearted abandon. His collar fell open and as his neck was exposed so too was the noose tied round it, the thick rope chafing at his skin, causing red welts to appear as it tightened its grip. William tried to turn his horse, to ride back to cut the rope that was dragging John away from him, but the animal would not, or could not, move and he was stuck fast to his saddle. John's face swelled, livid spots appeared

Chapter Sixteen

around his bloodshot eyes, his tongue was forced out of his mouth and his head fell forward in surrender to the death-dealing knot.

Once, waking with a raging thirst and sick of the physic he was being given, William drank the water from his washing ewer. It cleared his head enough for him to stagger to the door. He was determined to escape this incubus-ridden cell and find Abigail. She would tell him honestly what was happening in Measham. Goodwyn was full of reassurances, but he no longer trusted the man's platitudes. He was also sure that Abigail would make a better nurse than Goodwyn, that her rough and practical ways would prove more efficacious than his ministrations, which William now found as cloying as the medicine.

His limbs were so heavy, getting across the room was like wading through mud. He staggered and almost fell, but forced himself on, lurching from table to bed to chair until he was finally in reach of the door handle. He lifted the latch and pushed, but the door resisted all his efforts. At first he thought it was because he was so weak, but at last he had to accept the terrible truth. The door was locked. He was a prisoner in his own chamber.

⇥ Chapter Seventeen ⇤

Ireland, September 1690

At Nicholas's urging, Úna continued with his Irish lessons, but relations between them had become strained since Blanche Fitzpatrick's visit. He wanted to explain that his dalliance with Mrs Fitzpatrick had been the result of loneliness and idleness during a long and trying winter and that he no longer had any interest in the woman, but feared this admission might cast him in an even poorer light, so he said nothing. Besides, it was better Úna thought of him as a libertine than as a traitor. He lived in dread now of Blanche's reappearance. Mr O'Leary still treated him with the same courtesy, but Nicholas didn't think that would last long if the actress became a frequent visitor to his house and especially not if he discovered the real reasons for her attendance.

His only consolation was that the letter Blanche had delivered brought some very favourable news. Not only was Father in good health, but his great-uncle Percy had died, leaving his entire estate to Nicholas. Though Father warned him that the inheritance included a great many debts and that the house and lands were in a poor state and would require further funds to restore them, he couldn't stop his heart from expanding with jubilation. He was now a man of substance. As soon as he was well enough he would go to the cathedral to request a Mass in honour of his uncle. The man had had a long life and was of a difficult disposition, so Nicholas did not mourn his soul's passing

Chapter Seventeen

to eternity, but was grateful to his great-uncle for his beneficence. He wished he could tell O'Leary about the inheritance, but that would involve explaining how the letter had reached him. He could inform O'Connor, however, and this new source of income should enable him to secure more credit from his fellow officers, though with the King's retinue gone, there were few men left with any money to lend.

Father, of course, wanted him to abandon the Jacobite cause and return to England. Even if such a journey had been as easy to undertake as Father assumed, Nicholas could not have done it. He would not desert his comrades. Although the siege was over, he had been hoping to remain with the O'Learys for the winter. He cared deeply for the old man and enjoyed the comfort of his home, but it was the daughter's company he could not bear to relinquish.

One afternoon, as Nicholas lay reading, he noticed that Úna had fallen asleep in a chair by the window. She had a large drawing book open on her lap and her pens and ink lay on the table beside her. He tiptoed over, curious to see a sample of her work. To his surprise he discovered a portrait of himself. He had presumed she'd been drawing the vase of wild flowers she'd placed in the centre of the table, but they, it seemed, were a diversion. He moved round beside her so that he could see more clearly. She had not put in any of the details of his face, but the proportions were all correct and the lines fluid and dexterous. It was impressively executed.

She must have been exhausted to have fallen asleep mid-drawing. He studied her face. There were dark shadows beneath her long black eyelashes and he feared she had not been eating adequately, for she seemed even thinner than when he had first met her. Bedley had been wrong about her, though; she was far from ugly, or even plain. In repose, with her oval face and slender hands, she reminded him of the marble monuments of great ladies carved onto the tombs in cathedrals. She had the same still dignity, a grace that a little superficial pitting could not erase and it now seemed to him that the scars on her face only ennobled it, for they were testimony to the suffering she had endured and overcome. His fingers itched to pick up a pencil again, to recreate the image before him with a few simple lines. Yes, he would return Úna's compliment by drawing her. He thanked God once again that it was not his left hand that had been injured, for he still had little movement in his right.

He used his own notebook, which he always kept close by him, and sat down opposite her at the table, moving as quietly as he could so as not to disturb her. He did not attempt any colour, using only some charcoal to create a rapid sketch. But he was only halfway through when she woke with a start, her drawing block falling to the floor.

'What are you doing?' she asked.

He clumsily shut his notebook. 'I thought I might try my hand at drawing again, but I am out of practice.'

'Were you drawing the flowers?' She bent to pick up her own picture, keeping it tilted away from him.

'Just the vision of loveliness before me,' he couldn't resist saying.

She darted a scornful look at him. 'Do you mock me?'

Nicholas was mortified. 'Mock you? No, I should never stoop so low.'

'I see.' She nodded and, picking up her book, went to the door. 'You consider me too sorry a creature to satirise,' she said in Latin, departing before he had a chance to refute her suppositions.

Really, she was the most contrarious, impossible creature he had ever met, he thought, snapping the piece of charcoal in frustration, all notions of ancient ladies and chivalry gone.

* * *

That evening O'Connor joined them for supper, considerately bringing most of it with him. No one asked where he had obtained the mutton and the hens, they were too hungry, but at the back of their minds was the knowledge that such produce could only have been requisitioned from some poor farmer who would now be going without so that they could fill their bellies.

Nicholas was very glad to see his old friend, not only because he enjoyed the man's company, but also because O'Connor should be able

Chapter Seventeen

to provide him with the information that would satisfy Blanche. He had decided not to tell O'Connor about Mrs Fitzpatrick for fear of placing her in danger. The memory of the dead woman at Ballyneety still haunted him and he couldn't bear to be responsible for another such death. It meant he would have to keep quiet about his inheritance too, but so be it.

'You are looking much improved,' O'Connor told Nicholas. 'We weren't sure you'd pull through.'

'It is thanks to the O'Learys for their care of me,' Nicholas said warmly.

'I knew I had left you in capable hands.' O'Connor smiled. 'Úna's reputation as a healer is widespread; she is more knowledgeable in the application of medicine than most physicians.'

Úna smiled back at O'Connor. 'You only say that because I once cured you of the colic, though it was with a common remedy.'

O'Connor replied in Irish and they both laughed, much to Nicholas's discomfort, though he knew he should not care about being excluded from their familiar jests. It was frustrating that his comprehension of Irish was progressing so slowly. Now Úna was giggling like a young girl; it was quite unlike her and unbecoming too. He looked at O'Leary, but her father was smiling indulgently and joining in the merriment.

'Have you been able to visit your family?' he asked O'Connor. 'Your wife and children must long for your return.'

'As I long for them,' O'Connor answered with reassuring fervour. 'It is many months since I was last with them, but I hope to rectify that soon.'

'Will you be able to spend the winter at home?' O'Leary asked.

'God willing, though we cannot afford to rest throughout the season. No matter how harsh the weather gets we must push on with the fight to reclaim our land. The Prince of Orange may be returning to England, but his troops here will be reinforced. Our greatest difficulty is finding food and shelter for the men and forage for the horses. Connacht and Clare have been utterly devastated.'

'By the Williamites?' Úna asked.

'By both sides,' O'Connor answered sadly. 'The Duke of Berwick is particularly enthusiastic in his desire to destroy anything that might give shelter to the enemy, from entire villages to ancient castles.'

'The King's brat needs to be restrained,' Úna said hotly. 'He is like a child playing at soldiering. That is all the Irish are to him, puppets at his disposal.'

'Is Berwick likely to be made commander in chief?' Nicholas took the opportunity to ask.

O'Connor nodded grimly. 'Tyrconnell is going to France on an embassy to Louis and has already appointed Berwick commander, so now the young fellow will be able to level all around him to his heart's content.'

'Still, it will be good for us if Tyrconnell secures more help from the French,' Nicholas said.

'It's hard to know what game Tyrconnell is playing. He is very thick with Lauzun, who will paint our situation in the worst possible colours. Tyrconnell might have hoped we'd lose the siege so that he could surrender, but our success must prove to Louis that we are still worth supporting.'

If Nicholas had been ambitious, he would have asked if there was a way for him to join Tyrconnell's embassy. It would certainly be a means of appeasing Lord Pemberton. But his shoulder was not yet fully healed and the very thought of a sea voyage filled him with exhaustion. Besides, he had no appetite for the machinations of courtiers and little patience for or skill at the requisite affectations and flattery. He had found all the politicking during his previous sojourn in France both tedious and dispiriting. There may have been less bloodshed than on the battlefield, but the savagery was just as prevalent.

'And Kilbawn?' O'Leary asked. 'Have you seen it with your own eyes? Is it gone completely?'

O'Connor reached a hand out and placed it over his cousin's. 'I am so sorry, Diarmuid, only a few stones remain. Perhaps one day you might regain the land and rebuild the house.'

Chapter Seventeen

O'Leary shook his head, his eyes downcast. 'I do not believe I will live to see such a thing.'

Úna, who was sitting next to him, grasped her father's other hand, speaking softly to him in Irish. He smiled at her absentmindedly, his eyes full of tears. Nicholas thought of the house and lands he had recently acquired and wondered at the justice of it. What had he done to deserve such riches and what was O'Leary guilty of that his home should be stolen from him? A sense of shame came over him suddenly and he was glad he had not rejoiced at his inheritance in front of the O'Learys.

As he was leaving, O'Connor asked Nicholas if he was well enough to ride out the next day. All the troops in the garrison were to assemble on King's Island to be reviewed by Berwick and Nicholas might like to join them. Nicholas assured him that he was most certainly well enough and could ride one-handed. He was eager for some exercise in the fresh air and also hoped he might secure further information to satisfy Blanche. Though he was determined to give her nothing that would prove detrimental to the Irish cause.

⇾ Chapter Eighteen ⇽

Measham, September 1690

Resting his head on his arms, William knelt at the window seat. He could not die here, like a trapped moth or a fly battering itself uselessly against a window. He had to honour John's memory, to discover what had really happened to him. He gave even less credence to the idea of suicide now. There was a distinctly unsavoury air about the new bailiff; he was not a man William would ever have employed, and his servant was clearly a ruffian itching for a fight. What could have induced Goodwyn to hire such men? They looked better suited to soldiering than managing farmland. The thought of Baines finding John's body and lifting it from its noose filled him with disgust, for he could just picture Baines's lack of respect as he hauled John about like a carcass of meat.

Eventually footsteps could be heard in the passage outside – the firm tapping of a gentleman's heels, followed by the turning of a key in the lock.

'My dear sir, what are you doing over there on the floor?' Goodwyn rushed to his side and, lifting him under the armpits, helped him back to the bed.

'Why I am being kept a prisoner in my own house?' William demanded, as he sat down.

'No one is keeping you imprisoned. Why would we wish to do that?' Goodwyn spoke to him reprovingly as though he were a

Chapter Eighteen

spoilt child, lifting his legs so that he was forced into a reclining position.

William realised with horror that he was now dressed in his nightclothes. Could he have changed into them himself without remembering it? It was an action that he performed every night, so it was possible he had done it unawares. He clung to the likelihood of this because it was too overwhelming to consider any other.

'All our concern is for your own safety, especially after your fall on the stairs,' Goodwyn continued smoothly.

'What fall?'

'Don't you remember how we found you on the stairs?' Goodwyn pushed him forward slightly in order to arrange the pillows behind his back. 'And on another occasion you were discovered wandering through the house in nothing but your nightgown, raving like a lunatic.'

The thought of such exposure filled William with dismay and he feared he might give way to tears. He wanted to ask who the 'we' was, who else had witnessed his delirium, but Goodwyn was prattling on, apparently oblivious to his distress.

'The doctor advised tying you to your bedposts, but I was loath to enact such extreme measures.' Goodwyn refilled the cup by his bedside and handed it to him, his voice growing more severe. 'If you don't keep to your bed, however, the physician will insist we resort to the rope.'

William flinched as the words conjured up an image of John, hanging from the rafters of their cottage. He stared down at the beaker in his hands; he had spilt some of the sticky liquid and the drops had spattered like blood across the white sheet.

'You must have plenty of other work to do; why don't you send Abigail to nurse me?' he asked, pushing the horrible vision of John out of his mind. Why had Goodwyn taken it upon himself to perform the duties of a valet?

Goodwyn was studying him carefully and William found it difficult to read the expression in his pale blue eyes – he would almost have said it was one of contempt or even derision. Then Goodwyn took the liberty of sitting beside him on the bed. 'Would you really wish for another personal attendant? Another witness to your secrets?' he asked, his voice now sly and insinuating.

William felt as though all the blood in his body had turned to ice and each of his organs was slowly freezing. But he would not be cowed. He might still have the body of a woman, but he had lived for twenty-five years uncontested as a man and during that time he had developed the will and the pride of a gentleman. He was accustomed to living as he wished, to having his orders obeyed, indeed to all the privileges that men enjoyed, and would find a way to bind Goodwyn to him. Besides, he had sacrificed too much to relinquish his manhood now. He would rather die than be forced back into skirts, to live at the whim of others.

His brain prickled with fear, his senses fighting the torpor that engulfed them. If only he were not so enfeebled by sickness. He should have taken Abigail into his confidence long before. He needed more allies to shore up his defences, to guard him in times of weakness.

'Of course you have proved yourself invaluable and I will reward you handsomely for your loyalty and discretion,' William forced himself to say. 'Disclosure would not benefit either of us.' He took a sip of the perfumed wine.

Goodwyn patted his thigh. 'I have no desire to see you unmasked. Rest here and leave everything to my management.'

William was nettled by Goodwyn's reference to masks, but managed to remain placid. 'You must have enough to oversee without having to watch me. Why not send in Abigail to be my nurse?' he repeated.

'Does she know?' Goodwyn asked curiously.

William swallowed. Was it safer to have Goodwyn believe Abigail knew? He could imagine Abigail's incredulity if Goodwyn were to tell her, but then, perhaps she did know and had chosen to ignore it. For what was there to know really? He was almost tempted to put the question to Goodwyn but was afraid of what he might say. He felt suddenly overcome with a terrible weariness, as though the toll of a quarter of a century of subterfuge was extracting all its payment now.

Chapter Eighteen

'I don't know,' he said simply.

Goodwyn smiled pleasantly. 'In this instance, ambiguity may be our friend. People are often more accepting of those things that aren't named outright. But why are you so eager to have her wait on you? I could send the new man in to you, Baines. You might enjoy his attentions more.'

'What do you mean by that?' William felt thoroughly nauseated now.

'You appear to have a predilection for men of the lower orders. Baines would be the perfect groom of the bedchamber for someone of your tastes.'

'How dare you speak to me like that!' But William's outrage was tempered by the drowsiness that had come over him.

Somewhere above him, he thought he heard Goodwyn laughing softly. 'That's right, go back to sleep.' Goodwyn's voice drifted over him. 'I am fulfilling the role William always intended for me and you will fulfil the role intended for you.'

⇾ Chapter Nineteen ⇽

Ireland, September 1690

The foot soldiers who lined up for review were a motley pack, dressed in a variety of uniforms, many lacking jackets and even more without weapons. They were eager, but lacking in discipline and training. Due to the intemperate weather, Berwick did not keep them long.

At least several tons of Kilkenny coal, along with numerous bombs and grenades had been discovered buried in the enemy encampment. Some had exploded since the Williamites had left a lit powder trail, but many were salvageable and O'Connor and Nicholas rode out to take a look at what was left of the Prince of Orange's camp.

As they approached the site of the ammunitions they saw a great flock of crows. These birds had become very common around the city, drawn by the plentiful carrion. Out in the field, the birds were so tame and so intent on their booty they scarcely bothered to move out of the way of the horses' hooves. Instead of taking to the air, they strutted about, pecking at the ground like chickens in a farmyard.

'How fat they are,' Nicholas observed with disgust, for he knew what meat had made them so plump.

'A murder of crows,' O'Connor remarked. 'Isn't that what they call a flock in England?'

'Birds of ill-omen, and no wonder.'

Chapter Nineteen

Glancing down, Nicholas almost fell from his horse. At his feet a skeletal figure clawed at the earth, hands outstretched as if reaching out to him for mercy, its charred flesh half burnt from its bones. Ahead of them, outlined against the leaden sky, stood the few remaining timbers of a burnt-out hall. It stood at crooked angles like the blackened hull of a shipwreck washed up on a shore of ash. Spreading out from it were more corpses and parts of the bodies of men who must have tried and failed to escape the flames that had engulfed the building.

Nicholas and O'Connor rode forward in silence, their horses picking their way daintily over the cadavers and swishing their tails at the flies. The closer they got to the ruin, the more burnt the bodies were, until it became difficult to distinguish them from the grey soot blowing about in the wind.

A soldier was searching the area, sifting through the ash for anything salvageable. When they called out to him, he came over and grasped O'Connor's stirrup, staring up at him with desperate, wildly starting eyes, as if seeking absolution.

'Bastards set the hospital alight before marching out. Left their wounded there to die,' he said.

'It was burnt down deliberately?' Nicholas could hardly believe it.

'On Prince William's orders, or so the deserters told us. There were at least three hundred men inside, they said.'

'It could have been accidental. The Prince of Orange doesn't have a reputation for barbarity.' Nicholas shuddered. The now familiar pain was gnawing at his shoulder again.

'And Tyrconnell wants to make terms with him?' O'Connor shook his head. 'Who can think such a man would show mercy to the defeated?'

* * *

Nicholas arrived back at the O'Learys' to find Blanche ensconced in the parlour with Úna, sipping a cup of cordial. The two women were illuminated by the light from the long window, and the differences between their dress and deportment were quite stark. Blanche was like some exotic bird with her rich and colourful plumage, while Úna was more like a hedgerow songbird, small and somewhat dowdy but with a voice to surpass all others. To his surprise, they appeared to be very amicable and were chatting together in a mixture of English and Irish.

'Dear Captain Hawthorne.' Blanche reached out a hand to be kissed. 'How good it is to see you up and about.'

All he really wanted to do was return to bed, but he bowed stiffly before joining them at the circular table, seating himself uneasily on the remaining chair.

Blanche squeezed his arm as she glanced towards his lap. 'You are out of practice at riding, I see, but any aches will soon wear off.'

Nicholas kneaded his left thigh self-consciously, while his right hand rested uselessly on his other leg.

'How is your arm?' Úna asked with proprietorial concern. Since she had nursed him, she took an almost professional pride in his recovery.

'Painful, and still very weak.' He wasn't given to complaining but he didn't want Blanche to think he was capable of resuming his duties.

'But you have been reviewing the troops, I hear,' Blanche said smoothly.

'Berwick soon discharged them as the weather was so foul,' he answered grumpily, the image of the charred corpses foremost in his mind.

'And is Tyrconnell still in Galway?' Blanche lifted her cup to her lips, gazing at him over its rim.

'He will return to Limerick for a few days before sailing for France with Count Lauzun, or so I have been told.' Nicholas stared fixedly back into her eyes as he conveyed this information.

'I hope he comes back at the head of a mighty French army,' Blanche said, pressing her hands together in front of her heart and gazing heavenwards as if she were playing the part of Joan of Arc. 'And does not abandon our cause.'

'God willing,' Úna agreed fervently.

Chapter Nineteen

Nicholas raised his eyebrows. 'Unfortunately, I believe that outcome is unlikely.' He disliked holding this double conversation, but he needed to offer Blanche some military intelligence.

'Mrs Fitzpatrick has been telling me all she has suffered since the start of these cruel wars,' Úna told him suddenly.

'Is that so?' Nicholas responded with some alarm.

'Your gracious hostess has been so kind as to lend a sympathetic ear to my tales of woe. I am not usually given to recounting them, but her gentle encouragement has induced me to quite pour my heart out.' Blanche sighed and dabbed at her eyes with her handkerchief, which had clearly been much in use as it was ready in her hand and quite damp with tears. 'Like so many others forced to seek refuge in Limerick' – she lowered her eyelids – 'I was brutally accosted on the way here by enemy troops.'

'She has lost everything,' Úna said when Nicholas failed to respond. 'And since Major O'Connor no longer requires his room, I have suggested Mrs Fitpatrick lodge with us.' Úna gazed levelly at Nicholas, as though challenging him to either object or to reveal a liaison with Blanche. 'I will of course have to seek my father's permission, but I am sure he will agree.'

'You are an angel.' Mrs Fitzpatrick smiled beatifically at Úna. 'And please call me Blanche.'

'Do you not have lodgings already?' Nicholas asked, his voice sounding somewhat shrill.

Blanche shook her head sadly. 'The house in Irish Town where I was staying has been destroyed by cannon fire and now I am quite homeless.'

Nicholas wondered what he could say to Mr O'Leary to induce him to refuse Blanche Fitzpatrick sanctuary. Despite his earlier misgivings about visits from an actress, Nicholas could just imagine how delighted his host would be to extend his hospitality to an Irishwoman in distress.

⇾ Chapter Twenty ⇽

Measham, September 1690

William lay in the dark, listening to the rain pattering against the window. The sound of all that pure, clean water dropping from the heavens made him painfully conscious of how thirsty he was. If only he could tilt his face up to the sky and fill his parched mouth with rainwater. What he wouldn't give just to stand outside in the open air, to feel the earth beneath his feet and a crisp, cool breeze against his flesh. To smell all the scents of the natural world; hay, blossom, even the dung of cows would be better than the fetid smells of this locked chamber. He swallowed, trying to moisten his tongue with spittle.

He drank as little of the concoctions Goodwyn brought him as he could manage, sipping the stale water left for him to wash with instead, for he was now convinced that he was not ill at all, but being kept in a mixture of delirium and sedation by artificial means. At present Goodwyn still considered his requests for water to wash himself with reasonable, since his fevers made him rank and sweaty. But he didn't like to ask for fresh water too often in case Goodwyn became suspicious. He knew only too well, now, how conniving the man's mind was. Soon, William also feared the pool of medicine he had been pouring into the chest by his bed would start to seep out onto the floor and give him away. He couldn't empty the evil stuff into his chamber pot because Goodwyn always checked that with

Chapter Twenty

the thoroughness of a physician. In fact, when Goodwyn referred to the doctor's visits, William suspected he was lying and that the only medical attendant was Goodwyn himself.

He hoped the victuals he was given weren't laced with poison, though it was quite possible, especially since he suspected Cooper was also in league with Goodwyn. He ate only enough to keep himself alive, but it was impossible to fight off the lethargy that consumed him. He tried to keep a clear head, to plot a way out of this ordeal, but all too often his thoughts dissolved as he was claimed by sleep once more.

* * *

Something was scratching at the wainscot. At first he thought it was a mouse, but now it was growing louder, becoming an insistent tapping. Could it be a rat, or a bird stuck in the chimney?

'Sir William, Sir William, can you hear me?' a woman's voice called, urgent but low.

He rolled off the bed and forced himself to stagger to the door. 'Who is it?'

'It's me, Abigail. I feared as you was dead.'

Perhaps I am and this is Hell, William thought. 'Can you get the key and unlock this door?'

'Mr Goodwyn says you're contagious.' Her voice was hesitant. 'He says he's willing to risk his own life to tend to you, but he doesn't want anyone else catching your sickness.'

'The lying devil,' William muttered. 'The only disease I have is the one Goodwyn is giving me. I think he's dosing me with an opiate or some other soporific. Can you get some uncontaminated food and drink to me?'

William had the idea that if he could get his strength back, he could force Goodwyn to release him. He had been imagining locking Goodwyn up in his place, but he would need assistance, especially in dealing with Goodwyn's myrmidons, Latham and Baines.

'He makes up your physic himself, in your laboratory, Sir William. Won't let anyone else near it. Same with the keys, always keeps them on his person.'

'Doesn't Palmes have a set?'

'Goodwyn has them too,' she whispered.

Pressing his ear to the keyhole, William heard her sigh. 'See what you can do,' he told her.

'I'm so thankful you're alive, sir.' Even through the wooden door, William could hear the emotion in Abigail's voice. 'That new bailiff is a swaggering ruffian and Mr Goodwyn allows him all sorts of licence. The pair of them act like they're the lords of the manor.'

What a fool he had been to place so much trust in Goodwyn. If only he had listened to John. He had allowed a snake into his paradise and it was destroying all he had created.

'Get me out of here and we'll oust the lot of them,' he promised.

'Why don't I go for the constable? Tell him you're being kept locked up against your will? Or I could fetch Cooper and Jasper; they could hack this door down.'

But William could just imagine Goodwyn successfully persuading the men that he was raving and had to be constrained for his own protection. He didn't want to back Goodwyn into a corner either, for fear the devil would expose him.

* * *

Abigail was as good as her word. A few days later, when the door opened, instead of his tormentor, William was overjoyed to see Abigail entering the room.

'Oh, Sir William!' she cried. 'You're as pale as a ghost and there's scarce a peck of flesh on you.' She set down the basket she was carrying. 'I found a bottle of your own walnut water, as you made last summer and some good, sweet wine to mix it with. And I've a bowl of pottage here too, along with some fresh bread.' She placed the food on the chest by his bed and took the bottles over to his dressing table, where she filled a tumbler with a mixture from them.

'Where's Goodwyn?' William asked anxiously.

'He's gone to Leicester on business, along with that Latham. They won't be back afore nightfall. He let me into his room to clean it and

Chapter Twenty

I found the second set of keys.' She held them up triumphantly. 'He thinks I'm just a foolish woman, not worth paying any mind to. Did you give him permission to move into Father Matthew's bedroom?'

'I certainly did not. What a strange fellow he is.' He saw Goodwyn's publishing project in a different light now. Odd things Goodwyn had said regarding the 'real William' drifted back to him. Was it possible Goodwyn had known his brother before Matthew became a priest?

William carefully adjusted his nightclothes, uncomfortably aware of Abigail's perception of him. She, however, was busy trying to open the shutters. For once, William was glad of the murky gloom they imposed on the room.

'Don't bother with them,' he said. 'They're nailed shut and besides, we don't want to draw attention to the windows.'

'Well I never.' She examined the boards. 'Just wanted to let in some air.'

She handed him the tumbler and he drank from it gratefully. The smell of the pottage was turning his stomach, but he knew he must eat and once he'd quenched his thirst, he managed a few mouthfuls. After a while, his belly settled and he began to revive a little.

'I must get away as soon as possible. Can you help me down to the stables?'

'Mr Goodwyn has taken your horse,' Abigail said indignantly. 'Besides, sir, you look too weak to ride. Jasper could take the carriage out and drive you instead.'

William shook his head. 'Better to use the cart in case we meet Goodwyn on the road. I can hide under a rug. Where's the other fellow, Baines?'

'He'll be down at the Grange, I expect.' Abigail shook her head. 'It's not right, you having to skulk about like a common thief on your own land.'

'We'll have to evade the cook too.'

'Cooper's not a bad sort; he's been as unhappy as the rest of us with Goodwyn's orders. He wanted to make you all sorts of delicacies, but Goodwyn wouldn't hear of it.'

William wasn't convinced. 'We can't risk trusting him. This might be my only chance to escape. Goodwyn will take extra precautions if he catches me and then I'll have little hope of regaining my liberty. Better to keep Palmes out of it, and what about Ben, where's he?'

'Ben is Mr Goodwyn's lackey now and accompanies him everywhere. Goodwyn says he's training the lad up to be a valet.'

William looked at Abigail with concern. 'What will you tell Goodwyn? I don't want him punishing you for letting me go.'

'Punish me for obeying my master! What a topsy-turvy state of affairs this is.' She shook her head.

'There's no reason why I shouldn't own another key. I might have kept it hidden and only just remembered it,' William said, thinking out loud. 'You should feign ignorance, Abigail. Remove all trace of what you've brought up here and return the keys to Matthew's chamber.'

'Or I could come with you. You shouldn't travel unaccompanied, not when you're so poorly.'

'That is very kind, but it would be better to have you stay here. I don't suppose you've heard if Lady Jane is at Castle Rufford?' he asked hopefully.

Jane's mother had died the previous year and he knew she sometimes stayed with her father in their Nottinghamshire residence. It would be a much shorter journey than travelling all the way to her house in London or Kent, but he didn't want to risk going there unless he could be sure of being met by Jane. Her father was quite capable of handing him over to Goodwyn. The prospect of several days' travelling was overwhelming in his current condition and he longed only to find somewhere safe to recuperate.

'I hope you'll forgive me, sir, but I took the liberty of writing to her, I was that worried about your health and what Mr Goodwyn was up to and I didn't know who else to turn to. She used to visit so regular, I thought she'd understand. But I've had no word back and I don't believe she's there.' Abigail thought for a moment. 'What about going back to your uncle Percy's house?'

Chapter Twenty

William shook his head. 'That is the first place Goodwyn will look and the few remaining servants are too elderly to protect me. Goodwyn will not relinquish me so easily as that.' He thought of Goodwyn's malign determination and couldn't help shuddering. 'There is Crewe's farm up in the Peaks. The man he left in charge is a stout fellow and one I believe I can trust.'

'Is he known to Goodwyn?' Abigail asked uneasily.

'I don't think so. Harrington has managed Crewe's farm for years.'

William had told Goodwyn about the farm he had inherited from Crewe, but he didn't think Goodwyn had had any dealings with Harrington yet and now he recalled Goodwyn seeming surprised to hear of the bequest, for he had commented that Crewe must have been devoted indeed to leave his master his property.

William pressed his hands to his face. 'I wouldn't be surprised if Goodwyn's letter of recommendation was a forgery. I don't think he knew Crewe at all.'

'Mr Crewe never made mention of any Goodwyn in my hearing,' Abigail agreed.

'It's a risk,' William continued, half to himself. 'But perhaps less of one than travelling all the way to London when I don't even know where Jane is.'

Abigail had repacked the basket. 'I'll go and find Jasper. Just as well he's still here. He's been threatening to leave, you know, and he's been here since he was a little lad.' She paused at the door. 'Would you like me to help you dress, sir?'

'That's all right, I can manage,' William said, though he was feeling quite light-headed.

Abigail gave a little curtsey and he wondered again whether she had guessed his secret. Either way, it was immaterial now; he had to make haste to leave before Goodwyn's return.

* * *

It seemed to take an age before he and Jasper finally set off. The cart had to be got ready and Abigail insisted, quite wisely, on packing enough provisions to last a few days. When William finally emerged into the daylight he had to close his eyes it was so dazzling. How incredible it was to feel sunlight on his face.

Jasper and Abigail helped him onto the cart and it was a relief when they pulled a rug over him and he could rest his eyes along with his aching limbs. It was an even greater relief when Jasper called to old Dobbin and the cart began to move. William could hardly believe he was finally escaping Goodwyn's control or that he was having to leave his own home hidden in the back of a haycart. At least Jasper had made him a comfortable nest of straw so that he was cushioned against the jolting of the wheels and though he still felt every hole and stone on the uneven road, the shaking helped to relax his limbs and he soon found himself drifting towards sleep.

He was woken by the sound of voices. The cart had stopped and he had no idea how far they had travelled.

'What you got there then?' a rough voice asked.

'Just some extra feed for the sheep in the top field,' Jasper replied.

'Is that on Mr Latham's orders?'

William had the horrible feeling the voice belonged to Baines.

'He agreed I should take some extra up to them. They're out of grazing up there and it'll save you having to move them all.' Jasper's voice was gruff but calm.

'All right then. I'm off down to the Hall for my dinner anyhow.'

The man was clearly more interested in his belly than the farm, William thought. But he was aware of Baines's horse moving only a few paces and then stopping right beside the cart. He heard it stamp its hoof and snort. Then a sword descended, just below his feet, straight through the rug and into the hay. He almost pissed himself in terror, convinced he was about to be exposed. Could he and Jasper take on Baines? They were both unarmed, for Goodwyn had taken his sword. He should have asked Abigail to find him another, or at least to give him a kitchen knife, but he had been in too much of a hurry to think straight. Jasper probably had a pocket-knife of some sort, but what good would that be against a sword?

Chapter Twenty

The blade was withdrawn, lifting the rug slightly, but Baines can't have been looking down because he rapped the side of the cart.

'Off you go then.'

William felt the cart lurch forward as Dobbin plodded off again. They weren't even beyond Measham yet. William stretched out his cramped legs. This was going to be a long journey.

⇝ Chapter Twenty-One ⇜

Ireland, September 1690

To his dismay, Nicholas's assumptions were proved correct. O'Leary was not going to turn away a woman in need and the very next day Blanche joined the household. At least Nicholas was deemed well enough to return to the attic and was no longer on public display.

'What game are you playing?' he hissed at Blanche when they were left alone together in the parlour.

'Why are you so cruel?' she responded with a wounded air. 'Do you think you are the only one entitled to lodge here?'

'I don't see why you wanted to come to Limerick; surely you'd be much better off in Dublin.' He pushed the rug back off the harp that stood in a corner of the room and plucked idly at the strings with his left hand.

'Protestants who stayed in the city under King James are treated very harshly by our new governors. They call us traitors and refuse to have any dealings with us. It seems we were all expected to transplant ourselves in English soil; that was the loyal thing to do.' Going to the window, she folded back the shutter that had come loose. 'I now rely on Lord Pemberton's generosity. At least he does not forget an old friend, but don't worry, I won't besmirch your reputation or reveal you to be a spy. You might have more faith in me than that.'

Chapter Twenty-One

'I am not going to resume our amour,' he warned her, adjusting the rug back over the harp.

'You have a mighty high opinion of yourself, Captain Hawthorne. I can see your affections lie elsewhere and have no interest in pursuing you.' She paused, then turned to examine him with curiosity. 'You will have to marry her of course and she is not a great catch as far as society is concerned, but as a love-match, well, ye are certainly well suited, I can see that. She is quite the learned lady.'

'I am not considering matrimony,' Nicholas replied, considerably nettled.

'I hope you have not turned into such a rake that you would bed and then abandon a young maiden?' she declared with mock outrage.

Úna entered the room just as Blanche was speaking and looked from one to the other of them with concern.

'Mrs Fitzpatrick is jesting with me,' Nicholas said quickly. 'She was an actress on the stage, you know.'

'She did inform me of that,' Úna said warily.

Blanche went over to Úna and, putting an arm around her, drew her to the table. 'You offered to show me some of your watercolour pictures,' she said. 'And I am most desirous of seeing your work.'

Nicholas joined them, also curious to see more of Úna's drawings, for she had never made such an offer to him. But Úna looked suddenly abashed.

'They are simple, clumsy pieces, done for my own amusement,' she said.

'Let us be the judge of that,' Blanche told her. 'An artist never knows their own worth until they are put before an audience.'

Úna reluctantly took some pictures out of a drawer in the dresser and placed them in a pile on the table. 'This one is of Lough Derg.' She hastily put it to one side and drew out another. 'And this is our old home, drawn from memory.' She was about to turn that one over too when Blanche stopped her.

'But they are beautiful,' Blanche exclaimed. 'Such fine details and the colours are so clear and true; you have captured the place perfectly. Though I have not seen your previous habitation myself, I can tell it is a genuine likeness.'

She did not exaggerate; Nicholas was taken aback by the excellence of the small paintings. He was a competent draughtsman, but could never produce landscapes of such depth and luminosity as these. To look at them was to step inside the scene and feel oneself there, gazing from under the shade of a copse as the sunlight played on the blue-grey waters below, or walking up the avenue of beech trees to the imposing front door of an ancient house.

'They are exquisite,' he mumbled.

Blanche chuckled. 'Captain Hawthorne is quite overcome by the power of your work, I believe.'

Ignoring Blanche, Nicholas turned to Úna. 'Though the mansion and lands of Kilbawn are destroyed, they are not lost to you, for you have captured them here in paint for all eternity. This must be of some comfort to your father, that he can visit the places he loved whenever he beholds your pictures.'

Úna seemed momentarily startled, catching his eye with a look of recognition. 'Small comfort,' she retorted, quickly regaining her habitual gruffness. 'My daubings cannot house or feed us.'

'Ah, but now you have hit upon something,' Blanche said, quite undeterred by Úna's acerbity. 'When times are better you might well make some income from your art. There are many who would be pleased to part with money for pictures like these.' She gave a little laugh. 'But I speak as one who has been forced to earn her own keep; your father has a good profession and someday he will be supplanted by a worthy husband to provide for you.'

This was followed by an uncomfortable silence as neither Úna nor Nicholas could think how best to respond.

'Well, show us another,' Blanche commanded gaily, pointing at the pictures.

Chapter Twenty-One

Encouraged by their praise, Úna presented the rest of her paintings, vividly describing the places and her reasons for drawing them, all her previous discomfort forgotten. And so an hour or more passed very pleasantly as the three, united by their appreciation of the arts, chatted as if they were old friends, forgetting temporarily any previous entanglements that might come between them.

⇾ Chapter Twenty-Two ⇽

Derbyshire, September 1690

Old Dobbin could only manage a slow pace and it was dark by the time they reached Crewe's farmhouse the following evening. They had spent the night sleeping in the cart, as William did not want to risk stopping at an inn. Once they had put a good distance between themselves and Measham, he sat up beside Jasper, but despite pulling the rug around him, he was shivering uncontrollably and he couldn't help longing for a drop of Goodwyn's physic, whatever was in it.

The downstairs windows of the house were illuminated by the glow of candles and William could smell the woodsmoke curling up from the chimneys. At least the house was inhabited, hopefully by Harrington and not another of Goodwyn's cronies. Then again, perhaps it would be better if it was empty. His stomach lurched as he envisioned walking into a den of Goodwyn's associates. He didn't think he would survive if he was recaptured.

Jasper had stopped the cart in the front yard and William clambered down awkwardly. The cold air sliced into his emaciated flesh like carving knives as he hobbled, bent almost double, to the front door. He could hear dogs barking excitedly and suddenly two spaniels came running round the side of the house, almost knocking him over. He recognised their markings, for his own dogs had come from the same family and he reached out a hand to be sniffed at. It was a good sign,

Chapter Twenty-Two

to see them here. The dogs were followed by a tall, broad-shouldered man of middle age. He held up a lantern, eyeing William with a mixture of suspicion and pity.

'If you're looking for alms, I'll show you round to the kitchen.' He stared at the cart. 'You're out very late if you're wanting to peddle your wares.'

'I realise my appearance here is strange and unbecoming of a gentleman, but I am Sir William Hawthorne,' William announced as robustly as he could, though he was barely able to stand.

'Sir William?' the man said with astonishment.

'The same man that Crewe passed this farm on to,' William answered, not having any other means to prove his identity. 'And if I am correct, you are Mr Harrington?'

'That I am.' Harrington bowed. 'May I help you inside, sir?'

When William nodded, he hastened over to his side, shouting to the boy who stood behind him to show Jasper and the haycart round to the stables at the back. Offering one arm for support, he opened the front door and led William into the house. They stood in a small entrance hall and from the next room William could hear women's voices chatting.

'Mrs Thornly and her daughters are residing here, sir.' Mr Harrington spoke quietly, with a note of wariness in his voice. 'Sarah Thornly is my wife's cousin and when they were turned out of the Grange they sought refuge here. We could not deny them.'

'Turned out?' William exclaimed with horror. 'I was told they had left of their own volition.' Now his position was doubly uncomfortable. 'Can you make up a room for me? I'm very weary from my journey and have been unwell.'

'Of course, sir. Will you come through to the fireside while you wait?'

Harrington had already opened the door to the parlour and William had little choice but to accompany him in. The room fell silent as he entered and numerous pairs of eyes, all glittering in the candlelight, or so it seemed to William, beheld him with varying degrees of surprise and discomfort. There were more people here than he had seen in a long time, and most of them younger by a generation too. In addition to the Thornlys, several of the Harrington brood were present. The warmth from the blazing fire, the candles and the bodies made him so giddy he was afraid of fainting.

Mr Harrington whispered in his wife's ear and she hurried out of the room, curtseying to William as she went. He hoped that he would soon be shown to a more private apartment.

'Sir William.' Kate jumped up from her chair to curtsey and the rest followed suit.

'Please, sit down,' William managed to say, gratefully sinking onto the seat offered to him.

'Is he going to send us away again, Mother?' Eliza clutched her mother's arm and Sarah drew her into an embrace, her arms wrapped tightly round her daughter's shoulders as if to shield her from William.

The women once again turned their eyes on William and he felt a rushing in his head as though a gale was blowing inside his skull. He swallowed down his rising nausea.

'I can assure you, you were not sent away on my orders.' His voice emerged as little more than a whisper and he was very grateful to find a cup of ale being pressed into his hand. He drank it down swiftly, trying to hold the beaker still so as not to give away the trembling of his hands. He hadn't realised how parched his throat was, but now his thirst was awakened he longed even more for some of Goodwyn's damned cordial. At least, fortified by the ale, he was able to explain that he too had been forced to flee.

'Goodwyn and his men have taken over Measham Hall and were keeping me prisoner there. But I will get it back from them and you will return to the Grange, if you wish to.' He glanced uneasily at Sarah Thornly, but her face was averted from him.

'Thank you, sir,' she murmured, stroking Eliza's hair.

'That's monstrous, Sir William,' Alice, always the boldest among her sisters, declared, her eyes round with wonder. 'How did you escape?'

His audience watched him expectantly.

Chapter Twenty-Two

'Ah, with Abigail's assistance,' William said, somewhat shamefacedly.

'Is Abigail safe, sir?' Kate asked anxiously.

'You know Abigail.' William managed a watery smile. 'She won't let anyone get the better of her.'

A young girl ran into the room and over to Kate and Alice. 'You're to be bedfellows with me and Mabel tonight,' she informed them with great satisfaction.

'Of course.' Kate smiled brightly. 'The more the merrier.'

William thought guiltily of how he had accused Kate of being overly fussy when John told him about the new diet in the kitchen. His heart was full of grief and remorse to be seated here in the midst of John's family and John snatched away from them. He wanted to tell them he would clear John's name, that he didn't believe him guilty of self-murder, but was overwhelmed by the large audience and couldn't find the right words. Eventually, to his relief, Mrs Harrington returned and offered to show him to his room.

* * *

He didn't venture forth again until the following afternoon, fortified by some dinner, which he took in his room. Sarah and Mrs Harrington were busy in the kitchen and their daughters were occupied with sewing and mending, so it was easy to evade them. William went in search of Mr Harrington, whom he found in the stable block talking to the blacksmith.

'Might I have a word with you?' William asked him.

'Of course, sir. Would you like to come into the house or do you prefer to take in the air?'

After his days of captivity, William preferred to be outdoors, though he was still very weak. Mr Harrington led him to a long bench that ran along the back wall of the house and they sat facing the autumn sun, which was bright and pleasantly warm.

'I need to gather some brave and trustworthy men together to take Measham Hall back from the villains who have seized it,' William explained. 'Goodwyn is not a strong-looking fellow, but he has hired two rough knaves as his confederators. They will put up a fight, I am sure.'

Harrington nodded pensively, gazing out over the garden to the wild hills beyond with narrowed eyes.

'I will recompense whoever helps me very well,' William continued. 'Indeed, I need a new steward; perhaps the position could make up part of the reward for regaining my estate.'

'You'll be needing a new bailiff too,' Harrington observed.

'That is true,' William agreed, though the pain it caused him was hard to bear.

Harrington lowered his voice. 'Mistress Thornly believes her husband was murdered. She says that though he had been downcast since Goodwyn's arrival, he was not in such a state of despair that he would contemplate taking his own life.'

William swallowed. His throat was dry and the craving for Goodwyn's stupefying drugs gnawed away at his mind. 'Those are my thoughts also. You can assure her that I want to see his murder avenged as much as she does.'

'If you don't mind me asking, sir, why don't you go to the local constable or the Justice of the Peace and explain what has happened? They would raise the hue and cry to get back your property and arrest the men involved.'

'They'd want to consult with lawyers and such forth.' William shook his head.

It wasn't as if Goodwyn had seized his estate by force; he had done it by deception – through forgery and flattery. He'd exploited William's love for his brother and wormed his way into William's affections. He would probably find some other poor fool to practise his trickery on if he wasn't stopped. For that reason alone William supposed he ought to have the rogue arrested. Other witnesses might come forward, Mrs Powell for example; who knew how Goodwyn might have manipulated her – that was if she wasn't a fabrication. But then, Goodwyn would have no qualms about revealing his true sex. If William could be sure Nicholas could step in and take Measham Hall, he might be willing

Chapter Twenty-Two

to undergo the humiliation of public exposure, but to allow Goodwyn to rob him of everything, that was inconceivable.

'Knowing Goodwyn, he will have falsified documents to make it look as though I have handed Measham Hall over to him. Besides, we have nothing to prove John Thornly was murdered, unless Mrs Thornly has some evidence?'

'Nay, she has only her own knowledge of the man she was married to this past twenty-odd years.' One of the dogs had come over to lean against its master's knees and Harrington fondled its ears absentmindedly. 'But how can Goodwyn claim ownership of the Hall when you have a living heir? Isn't there an entail or such like?'

'Nicholas is fighting for King William's enemies and will have to lay down his arms and swear allegiance to the new monarchs if he is to come into his inheritance – that's if he hasn't forfeited his rights to it.'

'And I suppose that puts you at odds with the courts,' Harrington said.

'It does not help my case. The local Justice of the Peace is a supporter of the Prince of Orange; he would be only too pleased to see me ousted from my country seat.' William grimaced. In his hurry to leave Measham Hall he had not been able to find his tobacco tin and now he was torn between his desire for Goodwyn's liquor and a longing for a pipe of tobacco. 'Do you ever smoke a pipe?'

'I don't, but there is a pedlar expected tomorrow who usually carries such commodities.'

'If you can supply the pen and paper, I will write you a bill of exchange to cover all my expenses here,' William told him eagerly. It was hard to think straight without his pipe to clear his mind.

'The farm is yours to do with as you wish, Sir William,' Harrington pointed out.

'And I have no desire to make changes; I can see it is thriving under your good husbandry.' William gestured to the well-tended garden and the land rolling away beyond the hedgerow, though he had yet to inspect any of it. 'I should be happy to return home and leave the management of this farm in your capable hands, just as Crewe did before me.'

'Thank you, sir. Besides the millstone quarry, it is mostly sheep-walks, as you know.'

The trees in the garden were already decked in gold, while across the Peaks the heather was turning from purple to russet. The season was more advanced here than at Measham.

'Have you written to me since Crewe died?' William asked uneasily, for he did not remember having received any letters from Harrington.

'I sent the accounts down to you at the end of August and received a letter back only last week telling me someone would be up to fetch the profits. I was going to raise the matter with you last night, but you looked so poorly I didn't like to bother you. I was sorely troubled, though, I must tell 'ee, since the letter, purporting to be written on your orders, demanded most of the takings be handed over in coin and not only that, but it said we must start paying rent, and though I know rents have been going up all over, they are not summat Mr Crewe ever asked for, not since we were working here on his behalf.'

'Damn Goodwyn, the letter was another of his own wicked devices. Rest assured, I will not be changing the arrangements set up by Crewe.' William looked about him, almost expecting to see a rider approaching. Would his escape delay the arrival of Goodwyn's man, or would he dispatch him more quickly to see if William was here? 'We need to surprise Goodwyn and the sooner it can be done the better our chances,' he told Harrington.

'I know some loyal fellows who aren't afraid of a fight,' Harrington said. 'I can lead them myself; I was a soldier in my youth.'

'I will go with you.'

William knew it was probably foolhardy, but he couldn't bear to stay behind like a coward while other men risked their lives for him. Goodwyn would expose him if he got the opportunity, but that was a risk he would have to take. During the previous long and sleepless night, the realisation had come to him that he had neglected his responsibilities for too long, allowing Goodwyn to gain control

Chapter Twenty-Two

because it was easier to leave his affairs to another's management, instead of listening to those he had a duty to and taking charge himself. He was not going to make that mistake again.

'I mean no disrespect, sir, but wouldn't it be better if you rested here until you are well again?'

'I won't be a hindrance,' William promised. 'I will obey your orders like a good soldier and remain at the rear of any action if you prefer it, but I must accompany you.'

'Very good, sir. If you allow me a few days, I will seek out the men I have in mind and work out our best plan of action.'

'Thank you, Harrington, I am indebted to you.' William rose unsteadily to his feet and with as much dignity as he could muster, made his way back to his room.

* * *

William must have fallen asleep because he was woken by a cautious tapping at his door. Pushing himself up, he called for whoever was knocking to enter. He was relieved when it turned out to be Alice, the person here he felt most at ease with.

'I hope you'll forgive me for interrupting your rest, sir, but my mother is very anxious to speak with you and asked me to request an audience.'

His heart thudded in his chest. He could hardly deny Sarah Thornly an interview, but he dreaded having to speak with her. He wondered if her grief equalled his. John had always spoken of his wife with respect and admiration, but more as if she were a work-fellow than his darling. She had never been his passion, not like William was. And William had never wished to hear of any intimacies that passed between them.

'Of course,' he said. 'Just let me prepare myself and I'll see her in a few minutes.'

As soon as Alice left, he put on his padded waistcoat and jacket. It was a mercy Goodwyn had left his clothes discarded in a corner of his chamber at Measham and had not destroyed them. Perhaps he had intended to use the waistcoat as evidence of William's disguise.

It was already dusk and the room was growing dark, which was to his advantage. Sarah would have to take the only chair, while he sat on the bed, but it was not unusual for grand figures to receive guests in this manner.

His heart started jumping again at her knock, but he managed to answer her with a steady voice and she came in carrying a candlestick, which she placed on the rickety little table beside the bed. Illuminated by the glow of the taper, it was clear how much she had aged since John's death. Furrows were etched along her cheeks and across her brow and her mouth appeared as one thin, tight line among many. Dark shadows circled her eyes and her usually upright posture sagged as if weighed down with sorrow.

'Please be seated,' William said hastily. 'Pray let me express again my heartfelt condolences on your bereavement. Like you, I don't believe for a minute that your husband took his own life,' he added to save her from having to saying it.

'Thank you, sir, I appreciate your kind words.' She arranged her skirts around her, anxiously pleating the woollen folds over her knees as she spoke. 'After myself, I reckon as you knew John better than anyone, so you'll recall him to be an honourable man and a devoted servant. No one could love the Measham living more than he did; the land was in his blood and bones, the same as his father's before him.'

'And yours too, I imagine,' William said gently.

'Aye, indeed. And John was the kindest of husbands and fathers; he'd never have abandoned us, not in this life or the next.'

'Of course not,' William agreed with some discomfort.

Her head bent, Sarah pinched and then straightened the creases in her skirts. Her fingers were not used to being still. 'No, he'd never have left us, not even if he kept a mistress and was quite besotted by her.' She looked up at William and there was both a question and a challenge in her eyes. When he remained silent, she continued softly. 'He was your bosom friend, I believe.'

For a moment William thought she knew the truth about their relations. He sat motionless, waiting for her to go on.

Chapter Twenty-Two

'Men consider it a loyalty to keep each other's secrets, especially where women are concerned and I don't expect you to give me her name, nor do I want to know it. John always treated me like a duchess and I was a good wife to him in return, as good as any man has a right to expect, even if I never was able to give him a son.' Her voice became clogged with emotion.

'John never held the lack of a boychild against you, Sarah. Why, he had nothing but love and respect for you and spoke often of how fortunate he was to have you for a wife. There was no other woman to drive him to despair and, as you say, he'd never have deserted his family.' William spoke sincerely, but somehow the words rang hollow in his ears; he hoped they did not sound false to Sarah.

She nodded as if she was satisfied, at least to have said what she needed to and proved she was no fool, if nothing else. But this was not all she had come for.

'I understand you don't want to go to the constable, so all I ask is this: don't let Goodwyn die before you get him to confess to John's murder.' She stared out of the small window as she spoke, her eyes fixed on the first star to appear in the blue-black sky.

The starkness of her words caught William short. Although he had pictured Goodwyn's demise in various different ways, it wasn't his intention to kill the man. That would be murder. As for Baines and Latham, he suspected that when faced with a superior force they would flee rather than put up a fight. No, he simply wanted to force them out of his home and off his land and once he had done so he didn't believe they would return, though of course he would have to hire servants who could also act as guards.

Like Sarah, he wanted John's name cleared. He wanted to dig up his body and bury it in the village graveyard. But how could he make Goodwyn confess to his crimes without being unmasked himself? And the pain it would cause Sarah to know her husband, far from keeping a mistress, had in fact been his master's lover, surely outweighed all other considerations. He had thought long and deep about what John would choose and knew in his heart that John would rather stay where he was, in an unmarked grave, than bring shame and ridicule to his family.

When Sarah had gone, William sat on in the dark room. He imagined sliding a knife between Goodwyn's ribs and silencing the villain forever. Only then could he rest easy. He would be saving potential future victims as well. He was surely damned for his double life; why not add another crime to his transgressions? He just had to work out how to get close enough to his enemy to kill him.

⇾ Chapter Twenty-Three ⇽

Ireland, September 1690

When he heard a light knock on his bedchamber door late one night, Nicholas couldn't help hoping it might be Úna, though he knew a midnight visit from her was far more likely to herald an emergency than anything amorous on her part. So, despite being a little disappointed, he was not entirely surprised when his visitor turned out to be Blanche. Afraid of giving Úna the wrong impression, he had been doing his best to avoid being alone with Blanche. If he had known this would incur a more furtive visit he would not have made himself so elusive during the day, but at least his former lover was still fully clothed and not in her night apparel. He glanced down the staircase behind her; all was dark and quiet.

Blanche stepped into the attic room, carrying her candle aloft. 'I have a letter for you and since there was no opportunity to give it to you earlier, I have been forced to come to you now,' she told him somewhat accusingly. 'It is urgent.' She thrust the letter into his hand.

He could see from the handwriting that the letter was from Pemberton's secretary, Isaac, and hastily prised it open. Blanche lit the candle that stood on the cupboard beside his bed from her own and then left both candles there for him to read by, sitting down on the other bed in the semi-darkness. Nicholas was so absorbed in the letter he hardly noticed her waiting there, with the blanket drawn up over her knees.

Isaac wrote using their usual cipher:

Dear Nicholas,

I write at the bequest of your old friend Lady Pemberton, who has received some very concerning news from Measham Hall. The source is a maidservant named Abigail, who I understand is well known to you. She sent my mistress a letter which is not entirely legible, but the gist of it seems to be that your father is lying gravely ill while his new steward has forbidden anyone from waiting on him in case they catch his sickness. Abigail fears something is amiss for the steward has brought two rogues into the Hall and the three of them are treating the place as if it were their own, while Sir William, to use her expression, lies dying upstairs.

I have sent a man over from Castle Rufford to discover what is taking place at Measham Hall, but my lady will not rest until you forget the lost cause of the late King James, return home to your father and restore order to his estate. Abigail's letter has alarmed her greatly and she fears for Sir William's safety. Not only that, but she is afraid he will be swindled out of everything he owns, which of course includes your own inheritance.

Out of concern for Lady Pemberton's ease of mind and in acknowledgement of our friendship, which I hope you still honour, I have enclosed a pass for you to return to England. Your passage from Dublin aboard The Royal Oak *has been arranged. My lady and I have agreed that there is no need to trouble Lord Pemberton with this matter. You can report directly to me on your return.*

Your faithful friend,
Isaac Smith

Nicholas had to read the letter twice before he could fully comprehend its contents.

'*The Royal Oak* is due to sail in four days' time.' Blanche's voice emerged from the shadows. 'You had best leave at dawn if you are to ensure you catch it.'

'How will I explain my sudden departure?'

'I'm sure you can come up with a plausible reason.'

Chapter Twenty-Three

Nicholas nodded. It would be easy enough to convince his comrades that he was on a mission for Sarsfield. He would be given one of the best horses in the stables. It was a question of getting to Dublin without being caught by the enemy or being set upon by rapparees, who, even if they didn't kill him, would severely impede his progress.

Blanche rose and took her candle from his bedside. Suddenly conscious of his debt to her, Nicholas thanked her sincerely.

'God keep you safe,' she said with real concern and for once Nicholas didn't think she was acting a part.

Her large, expressive eyes took on new depths in the candlelight and he was struck anew by the beauty of her high cheekbones and shapely mouth. Taking a step towards him, she went to kiss his lips, but he turned his face and her kiss landed on his cheek instead.

'Forgive me,' he said, feeling he had been ungracious. 'Should you ever require my services beyond the bedchamber, they will be yours to command.' He gave a low bow.

'And likewise, I am sure.' Blanche's hand brushed his as she turned to leave. 'I hope we meet again in happier circumstances.'

Instead of getting dressed, as soon as Blanche had gone, Nicholas sat down to write a note for Úna. He didn't have time to compose the kind of letter he wanted to write and feared Úna would read his declaration of love with either suspicion or contempt, but it was preferable to leaving without any explanation. Being as short of paper as he was of time, he could not afford to make a mistake; taking a deep breath, he loaded his quill with black ink and began to write in Latin.

Dearest Úna,

I hope you will forgive my writing to you in this clumsy and furtive manner, but I have been called away on a matter of great urgency and could not depart without entering this plea. Being no poet I will not attempt to list your remarkable qualities for fear you will take my praise as empty flattery; let me tell you only that my admiration for you grows with each day spent in your company. Indeed I would happily endure further injuries should they prolong my time under your care. It might please you to know that you have brought an Englishman to complete surrender. I am yours, for your wit and beauty have conquered my heart. Now all that I desire is to serve you for the remainder of our days. Pray do not kill me off entirely with a refusal. Incomparable one, you would do me the greatest honour if you would become my wife; say yes and I will move heaven and earth to return to you.

Your humble servant,
Nicholas Hawthorne

P.S. If you can give me some indication of your acceptance then I will approach your venerable father for his consent to our union. Please give him my heartfelt thanks for his goodness and generosity and my apologies for departing so rudely.

God save and protect you both.

Once he had dressed and packed the few possessions he owned into a knapsack, Nicholas made his way carefully down the attic steps to the first floor. He had memorised which chamber each family member inhabited. Úna was sharing her room with Mairead and he could only hope that if one of them woke it would be the mistress rather than the maid. He stood for a moment in the passageway. A rumbling snore was coming from O'Leary's room. Crouching down, he slid the note under Úna's door. If she didn't spot the folded sheet of paper in the morning, surely Mairead would find it and give it to her mistress. He hoped O'Leary would not be offended by this address to his daughter.

Fionn was standing in the hall looking up at him questioningly as he descended the stairs. He stroked the dog's rough fur. 'Keep them all safe,' he whispered. Then, opening the door as quietly as he could, he slipped out into the street.

Now he must turn all his attention to getting back to Measham Hall as quickly as possible. He felt sure Father would rally if he was beside him and prayed for an unimpeded journey by land and favourable winds at sea.

→ Chapter Twenty-Four ←

Derbyshire, October 1690

'Are you ready, sir?' Harrington asked with concern.

'I am all prepared and as eager for action as a young soldier.' William slapped his thigh and gave what he hoped was a convincingly hearty smile. He had bought a knife, as well as a pipe and tobacco, from the pedlar.

It had taken an agonisingly long time for Harrington to assemble a suitable band of men. Due to the wars, most men of fighting age and disposition were employed in Their Majesties' army and it was not easy to find men they could rely upon, men who would not take their money and desert them. Many of those Harrington first approached had been free miners forced out of work by landowners who claimed all the profits from the lead and coal unearthed on their land. These men had no love for the gentry and would not risk death or gaol to return a baronet to his property.

In the end Harrington had ridden down to Measham and enlisted the service of four local farmers – men who were equally keen to get rid of a steward who seemed intent on enclosing more and more of the common land and thus depriving them of their furlongs. It had been a stealthy operation in order to avoid alerting Goodwyn, and William felt the humiliation of his position very keenly. He knew all the men by sight, though only one, a Mr Topliss, by name and he wished he'd been able to undertake the task himself, but it had taken the past two weeks for him to recover fully from the poison Goodwyn had been dosing him with. Now at least he felt stronger and more alert.

He promised the men that when he was back in charge he would sign a binding treaty to ensure they kept their own plots and also that the village oxen would be maintained for the use of all. It was another local grievance that Goodwyn claimed the oxen were too expensive and must be sold off. Goodwyn insisted that once the fields were enclosed, horses would be used to plough the land instead, in keeping with modern innovations.

The news Harrington brought back from Measham was as troubling as William had expected. Abigail had left the Hall and was living with her parents, but they feared eviction from their cottage. She told Harrington that Goodwyn had scoured the area for William and had sent Baines up to Percy's house to look for him there. William could only hope he had not mistreated or distressed the old servants.

He looked at the men assembled in the farmyard. They were stout, solid fellows and outnumbered Goodwyn's villains two to one; it should be easy for them to take back the Hall. Restoring his finances and regaining the trust of his tenants would be a more complex affair.

They set out not long after midnight, travelling by moonlight and stopping at dawn to rest the horses and refresh themselves. It was just after midday when the old chestnut tree came into view and they turned onto the road to Measham Hall. Harrington had insisted they sing some rousing ballads for the last few miles and all, apart from William, were looking forward to a hearty set-to. William had spent the journey anticipating Goodwyn's reactions and rehearsing every possible outcome. Now a grim determination had settled on him. Whatever Goodwyn said, however he might denounce William to the others, William would not be deterred. He must not allow Goodwyn to intimidate him. His heart and his mind were masculine and he would act with manly daring. He was the master of Measham Hall and a snivelling wretch like Goodwyn was not going to take his inheritance from him.

Chapter Twenty-Four

Dismounting, they led their horses round the back of the house to the stable yard. William had managed to get a message to Jasper, telling him to continue working at Measham until he returned, when Jasper's help would be vital. The groom was mucking out the stables when they arrived, his body hunched over like that of a much older man. Looking up at the sound of hooves and seeing who it was, a huge grin spread across his face and his back straightened.

'You've come at the right time, sir. They're all in the house eating their dinner and drinking your wine.'

'Is it just the three of them?' William asked, fearing Goodwyn might have added to his entourage.

To his relief, Jasper nodded.

'And have they their weapons with them?'

'They never go unarmed. Goodwyn wears your sword now, sir, makes me sick to see it. He struts around in your clothes like he's a Hawthorne.'

'Who serves them at mealtimes?'

'Young Ben, for they say Mr Palmes is too slow; Goodwyn only keeps him on to fetch the wine from the cellar.'

'Do you think Ben could take their weapons without them noticing?'

Jasper looked doubtful.

'You don't want to put them on their guard,' Harrington warned.

William was tempted to try Goodwyn's own trick on him and adulterate the wine with a soporific. There would be some of Goodwyn's concoction left in his laboratory, he was sure, and he could get Palmes to carry it in to them, but the men behind him were eager for action and such a strategy might seem cowardly to them.

'Right,' he said. 'Are we ready to take them?'

The men responded with a quiet chorus of approval.

'I'll fetch my axe.' Jasper hurried back into the stables, reappearing with an axe and a cudgel.

'We need you to distract Cooper while we go in through the kitchen,' William told him.

'Cooper will join us; he hates them fellows as much as I do,' Jasper insisted.

William hesitated, but since Abigail had also spoken in the cook's favour he decided to take the risk in trusting him. Once the horses were stabled out of sight, they moved silently into the kitchen. Cooper was carving up a calf's head and he gave a small cry upon seeing them, his knife raised in his hand. Jasper motioned to him and Cooper closed his mouth. Topliss carried an old musket and he used the kitchen fire to light a cord in readiness for firing it. An action William hoped would not be necessary. Grabbing the copper spit from beside the fire, Cooper followed them down the passage, his carving knife in one hand and the spit in the other. If he did turn against them, he was well-armed.

William could hear Latham's voice coming through the open parlour door. He was recounting some story and his tale was punctuated by Goodwyn's shrill laughter. The sound turned William's stomach. To think he had once enjoyed the devil's company. With one hand on the dagger he had bought, he strode into the parlour with as much rage and force as his own father would have done.

Goodwyn sat at the head of the richly laid table; numerous platters, piled high with a variety of meats and pastries, were illuminated by the best beeswax candles. Ben stood at his elbow, dressed in a new velvet suit. Ben's face had been scrubbed clean and his hair, which had always been mousy brown, was now a glossy gold. He was carrying a silver pitcher and his mouth fell open at the sight of his old master. Latham and Baines grabbed their swords and were about to jump to their feet when William's men leapt towards them brandishing their weapons. Topliss pointed his musket at Baines, who immediately resumed his seat. Lunging forward, Cooper knocked Latham's sword out of his hand, using the copper spit like a pike.

Goodwyn did not show the least unease; leaning back in his chair, he surveyed William with a look of amused contempt. 'I am overjoyed to see you have recovered, sir. We have been deeply concerned as to your whereabouts and your welfare.'

Chapter Twenty-Four

'Don't play games, Goodwyn; you're lucky I don't have you clapped in irons.' William turned to Baines and Latham. 'You have no right to be on my property. Tell me what you did to my bailiff, John Thornly, and I'll allow you to leave unharmed.'

William hadn't really expected them to do as he ordered, so he wasn't surprised when instead of obeying him, they looked to Goodwyn for instructions.

'Dear Sir *William*.' Goodwyn laid special emphasis on the name, as if to remind William of what he knew. 'We are aware of your friendship with the late Mr Thornly, but I think you are forgetting that you made over your house and lands to me. I have the documents, signed and sealed by your good self, to prove it.' Goodwyn turned to Ben, tugging on his sleeve. 'Go and fetch the documents; you remember where they are, don't you?'

'Yes, sir,' the boy whispered before running around the back of the men towards the door, the jug still clutched against his chest.

Harrington was about to stop him, but William shook his head.

'Let the boy fetch the documents. They're forgeries, just like the letter this scoundrel claimed was written by Crewe.'

Goodwyn sighed. 'If you have changed your mind that is regrettable, but I'm afraid it doesn't alter the deed, as witnessed by both Mr Latham and Mr Baines. Mr Latham is a lawyer, as you know, trained at Gray's Inn.'

This was news to William, but he wasn't going to let Goodwyn get the better of him this time. 'You can trot out every lie in your repertoire; if you don't leave peacefully, we will make you leave with force. Neither my men here nor I give a damn about any faked deeds. But first you must tell us the truth regarding Thornly's demise.' William's heart was beating so fast he feared it might explode in his chest. Whatever Goodwyn threw at him, he must brave it out; he could not risk giving away the slightest sign of weakness.

His Measham comrades had all known John well; they had grown up in the same parish and even played together as children. They were partly here on his account and now they muttered imprecations and raised their weapons in readiness for use. Latham looked a little nervous now, but Baines was like a fighting-dog straining at its chain and looked ready to strike the musket from Topliss's hands.

Goodwyn's lips were stretched into a pitying smile and if he felt any fear he did not show it. 'You know full well the reason poor John took his life, along with your own complicity. Would you really wish me to divulge it to the assembled company?'

'I have no idea what you are alluding to, but your wicked brain has no doubt invented all sorts of depravities. You seek to besmirch the reputation of an honest, upright man, to cast aspersions that will veil your own misdeeds, but the fellows here all knew John Thornly too well to believe any vicious lies that drop from your lips. Indeed, as Catholics we have, since the Reformation, endured all the blasphemy and filthy slander our enemies like to throw at us and cannot be tainted with it now. We haven't forgotten the slurs put upon the Jesuits during the so-called Popish Plot, lies that caused the martyrdom of my own cousin, Father Matthew. Do you take these fellows for fools who will swallow your falsehoods?'

At these words, William thought he could detect a change in Goodwyn's complexion, a slight reddening of the cheeks, a wince even. He had known a reference to his brother and their faith would be the likeliest way to pierce Goodwyn's stomach, or at least to pinch it.

'I did not think an untutored mind capable of such eloquence, though you overreach yourself with the hyperbole.' Goodwyn turned to address Harrington, while pointing at William. 'If there is any devil here it is this person, who goes by the name of Sir William. They are the imposter who abuses your good natures and who caused the downfall of your friend Mr Thornly. I advise you all to return to your dwelling places and there will be no punitive action taken against you for the offences you are committing. Remain here and you will soon find yourselves in the stocks, for I expect the constable and his militia to arrive at any moment. And when they do this he-she will be unmasked.'

The men looked about them a little uneasily, but then, to William's surprise, Topliss spoke out. 'Sir William is no imposter. He may not be

Chapter Twenty-Four

a commonplace gentleman, but he's a Hawthorne like his father and grandfather before him. We'd rather have him as our squire than you, for he respects the land he was bred in and the men who work on it.'

There were murmurs of agreement from the other local men and Harrington demanded scornfully how Goodwyn planned to conjure up the constable.

'Young Ben understood my command and will have gone with all speed to fetch him,' Goodwyn said calmly.

'If I am an imposter then the deeds you claim I have signed are worthless,' William expostulated.

'I believe a court will find them legally binding,' Goodwyn replied with infuriating smugness.

At that moment, as if conjured by Goodwyn, there was a thunderous knocking followed by the creaking of the front door being thrust open.

Goodwyn smiled. 'And here they are now, our worthy bastions of the law come to see that justice is done.'

↦ Chapter Twenty-Five ↤

Measham, October 1690

The gods had answered Nicholas's prayers and his ship not only left the port on time, but was blown across to Holyhead so rapidly he landed the following day. The knowledge of the roads he had gained riding out with Sarsfield's cavalry had ensured he reached Dublin safely, but once across the sea he had to negotiate the mountain tracks of Wales before he could get onto the road to Measham. After changing horses at Llangollen, he made good speed, but his mount threw a shoe and it was early afternoon, four days later, by the time Measham Hall finally came into view.

Leaving the horse tied to a tree, he ran up the path to the house. Bounding up the steps, he pushed on the front door and, finding it had been left unlocked, went straight into the hall, where he almost collided with Palmes. He had to catch the ancient butler as he staggered backwards in shock.

'Master Hawthorne, what a joyous surprise,' the old man gasped. 'But terrible events have occurred here. Sir William is missing, the new steward claims the house is his and now there is some commotion in the parlour and I am too afraid to go in there.'

Palmes was shaking so violently, Nicholas whispered to him to take shelter in his room and rest there until he was sent for. Keeping out of sight of the parlour door, which stood ajar, he made sure his

Chapter Twenty-Five

pistol was charged. He was wary of going in unaided and cursed the weakness in his right arm that prevented him from carrying weapons in both hands. Pressing himself against the wall nearest the door, he listened to the voices coming from the parlour. The first voice was familiar, but he couldn't quite place who it belonged to. The sneering tone reminded him of someone, but who? Then, to his delight, he heard his father's voice. So Palmes was mistaken; William wasn't missing.

Nicholas was about to enter the parlour when hoofbeats resounded outside, followed by rapid footsteps. A band of men came charging into the hall, the front door slamming behind them. For a terrible moment Nicholas was taken back to the day the pursuivants came for his uncle. He was somewhat reassured to recognise the red-cheeked constable leading them as the village baker.

'Mr Wragg,' Nicholas said, lowering his pistol and striding forward so as not to be taken for a robber skulking in the shadows.

Wragg's plump face grew even redder. 'Why, Master Hawthorne, I did not expect to encounter you here.'

'I have just arrived, under orders from Lord Pemberton. What in heaven is going on?'

A well-dressed young lad stepped out from behind Wragg. 'Your father is crazed, Mr Hawthorne. Mr Goodwyn is the master now and he bade me fetch the constable to take your father away.'

'Who are you?' Nicholas demanded in astonishment, not recognising Ben, who was several inches taller and much better dressed than when he had previously encountered him.

Then that familiar voice came out of the parlour again, louder this time. 'If you will permit me, gentlemen, I will fetch the deeds myself.'

At this sound, Mr Wragg puffed out his chest and marched into the parlour, calling for his men to follow him. Nicholas hurried in alongside them, determined to protect his father.

'Mr Goodwyn is attempting to defraud me of my property. He imprisoned me here and murdered my bailiff,' William roared at them.

Despite his joy at seeing his father on his feet and not his deathbed, Nicholas was shocked by William's gaunt, sallow-faced appearance. It was clear that raising his voice was taking every ounce of his strength.

'Now, now, Sir William, calm yourself,' the constable ordered. 'Gentlemen, I insist you all lower your weapons and behave in a lawful manner.'

William had already put away his knife and rushed to embrace Nicholas. 'My son, my darling son,' he cried, his face wet with tears. 'You were correct in one thing,' he shouted in triumph at Goodwyn. 'My son has come home to me!'

Nicholas looked at the man his father was addressing and froze with horror at the sight. Now he knew to whom the familiar voice belonged. He hadn't considered it possible, but there he was, like a ghost returned from Hell, Lawrence Gascoigne, sitting at the head of the table in his own parlour. And on seeing Nicholas, Gascoigne did indeed turn as a pale as a ghost.

William, arms still outstretched, turned to see what it was that appalled Nicholas so, and caught sight of the small pistol in Goodwyn's hand. The gun was cocked and Goodwyn was pointing it straight at Nicholas.

Without hesitating, William threw himself in front of his son. There was a resounding crack and the room filled with the smell of gunpowder. Nicholas just managed to catch his father as he fell.

'Mr Goodwyn!' the constable yelped indignantly.

'It was self-defence,' Nicholas heard Gascoigne's voice reply. 'Hawthorne was reaching for his gun.'

'Murderer,' another man shouted.

On the floor of the parlour, amid a sea of legs, Nicholas gently set his father down. He could feel the warm blood seeping out of Father's back onto his hands.

'My boy,' William gasped, and his eyes shone with joy as he reached a hand up to touch Nicholas's face. 'You are unhurt?'

'I am quite well,' Nicholas reassured him, ignoring the commotion above them. He had to bend his head close to Father's to catch his words.

Chapter Twenty-Five

'Bury me as William, beside my brother, and our tomb will tell the truth at last.'

'Hush, Father.' Nicholas's tears were dropping onto William's face, so that their tears ran together. 'We will fetch a surgeon; you will survive this.'

With great effort, William tilted his head from one side to the other. 'No surgeons or doctors. Let no one tend to me but Abigail.' His breath was ragged and his stare had grown wild.

Someone handed Nicholas a scarf and helped him lift Father enough to bind it across his back and around his chest. As they pulled it tight, William groaned. Blood was dribbling from his mouth now.

'Stay with me.' Nicholas cradled his father in his arms.

The man kneeling beside them began to pray and it seemed as though time had stopped, for no one in the room moved and the only sound was the chanting of the Lord's Prayer. William's eyelids fluttered. He gave out a terrible hissing croak and his head fell back over Nicholas's arm. Then his face relaxed and his expression fell into serenity. He looked suddenly like a youth, freed of all the sorrow and conflicts the years had burdened him with.

Staring desperately about him, Nicholas caught sight of a silver plate on the table.

'Pass me that platter,' he told the man next to him.

When it was handed to him, he held it over his father's mouth. But no breath misted the polished surface.

'My father is murdered,' Nicholas cried in a great howl of anguish.

As he rose to his feet, Nichoals saw Gascoigne standing at the head of the table. A brawny man had him by the arm and must have forced him to drop his gun, for his hand was empty.

'I will have you for this!' Nicholas drew out his sword and made to leap towards his foe, but found himself held back as his own arms were seized by two of the militia.

'There will be no more violence committed here,' Wragg stated. 'Mr Goodwyn must be brought before the sheriff to answer for this death.'

'This man' – Nicholas jerked his chin to indicate the man the constable referred to – 'may be going by the name of Goodwyn now, but that is only the latest of many aliases. He has called himself Staley and Waddington and has even faked his own death, but his true name is Lawrence Gascoigne. He is a Jesuit who has committed many crimes, the gravest being treason against our current monarch. Lord Pemberton will want to question him.' Nicholas knew that Wragg could not ignore an accusation of treason and hoped Pemberton's pass, which he carried in his pocket, would keep him safe from the exact same charge.

There were shouts of outrage from the other men in the room, some for and some against Goodwyn. Mr Wragg stared with bulging eyes from Goodwyn to Nicholas, his crimson face shiny with sweat.

'The son is as pernicious a liar as his sire, or should I say his dam?' Undaunted, Goodwyn sneered at Nicholas. 'If anyone here is a traitor to Their Majesties it is he, who has been off fighting for the Jacobites in Ireland.'

'Take my letter of passport from my pocket,' Nicholas instructed one of his captors. 'I have other witnesses – Lord Pemberton's secretary, Isaac Smith, for one, who suffered cruelly at the hands of this villain.'

Wragg studied the letter that was handed to him. 'Well, we will see what the sheriff has to say on the matter. In the meantime, Mr Goodwyn, as he calls himself and is known by me, will be committed to the county gaol. And if you don't keep the peace you will be locked up too, Master Hawthorne, and that goes for the rest of you as well.' Wragg looked sternly at Harrington and his men.

'Constable Wragg, I humbly request that you take the deeds whereby Sir William made over his house and lands to me, into your custody. If they remain here that treacherous cockerel will destroy them.'

If anyone looked like a cockerel it was Wragg, who thrust out his chest with self-importance as he agreed to show the documents to the sheriff and sent one of his men to fetch them from Goodwyn's desk.

Chapter Twenty-Five

'Are you going to believe a man who just murdered the supposed signer of these deeds in front of you? It is clear I was his intended target for he knew I would unmask him,' Nicholas argued.

'We'll let the sheriff make up his own mind on this matter once he has all the evidence afore him,' Wragg responded.

'Be careful what you accuse me of; you may regret it,' Goodwyn told Nicholas as he was escorted from the room by Wragg's men.

'By murdering my parent you have killed the only hold over me you had,' Nicholas answered softly, staring him in the eyes. Then he nodded to Latham and Baines, who remained seated at the table as if hoping to escape the constable's notice. 'What about these other two – his accomplices?'

'We have committed no crime,' Latham said. 'I understood that I had been employed under Sir William's orders and took up the post of bailiff in good faith.'

'These scoundrels killed John Thornly,' Harrington swore.

'Lord Pemberton will wish to question these men too,' Nicholas quickly added. 'His secretary will recognise them if they were his torturers.'

Wragg looked uncomfortable, but Pemberton's name carried enough weight for him to take Latham and Baines into custody as well. Baines seemed about to fight his way out, but Latham bade him behave, insisting that their names would soon be cleared.

* * *

Harrington and Topliss helped Nicholas carry William up to his chamber, where they laid him carefully on the bed. The room was in darkness and Nicholas went to open the shutters but found them nailed shut. He gripped the edge of one shutter in both hands and tried to wrench it away from the window, the wood cracking and splintering around the nails. It was only when he felt Harrington's hand on his shoulder that he became aware of the pain in his right arm and let his hands drop to his sides.

'We'll see them hang, all three of them, for the murders of your father and John Thornly,' Harrington said.

Nicholas stared at an iron nail protruding from the broken wood and imagined it being hammered into Gascoigne's skull. He closed his eyes; he would not allow that devil to dominate his thoughts now. Harrington was right; justice would come. The training he had received in the army asserted itself and a kind of numbness settled over him as he set his mind to the most pressing practical issues.

'Are you acquainted with Abigail Palmer? Can you send her over in the morning to prepare the body for burial?' he asked.

'I know Mrs Abigail. I'll call in and tell her directly,' Topliss said. 'Shall I fetch the parson as well?'

'Thank you, but I'll speak with him tomorrow.'

William had been on good terms with the rector at Measham, attending his services despite never having formally renounced his Catholicism and Nicholas was sure the parson would agree to William's burial in the family tomb, but he could not face talking to the man now.

When at last he was left alone, he drew a chair up beside the bed. Candles had been placed around the room and the fire lit in preparation for a night's vigil. Someone, probably Palmes, had placed a rosary in William's folded hands. Nicholas gazed at his father-mother in the flickering candlelight. He had never seen William in repose before and had never had the opportunity to study his face closely. His father had always maintained a strict distance from him, had never dandled Nicholas on his knee or cherished him like a mother might, yet here was the body that had first housed him, that had laboured to bring him forth into the world and had refused to give him up. The body that had belonged to a girl, but grew into a country squire and became the very pattern of an Englishman.

The moustaches that had always been glued to William's upper lip with mastic were gone and in their place was a fine, dark down, like that of a boy just coming into manhood. His jaw was still firm and square and he had the fine Hawthorne nose, which people said Nicholas had inherited. William's thick black eyelashes rested on cheeks as weathered and leathery as a shepherd's who spent all his

Chapter Twenty-Five

time in the fields. But this ageing seemed only to enhance his beauty, for it bestowed an appearance of wisdom and indicated a lack of vanity. Surely the serenity of his expression was an indication of his contrition and absolution?

Nicholas sat for a long while, too dazed and shocked by the reappearance of Gascoigne and the murder of his father to do anything other than go over the afternoon's events in his mind. Instead of saving his father, he had caused his death and this terrible fact undermined everything he had done in the past and all that he might do in the future.

At last, recalling himself to his obligations, he prayed to his uncle, Father Matthew, that he might travel to purgatory to act as an intercessor for William's soul. Father had not been given the chance to confess, but Nicholas entreated God, in His love and mercy, to accept William-Alethea into His eternal kingdom. Despite knowing that according to Catholic doctrine, Father was guilty of a cardinal sin, Nicholas found it impossible to believe his father's soul was destined to burn forever in the pits of Hell. Perhaps this made him a sinner too, but he had been a soldier long enough to know his parent was not confirmed in evil.

It was true Father had been weak and had fallen into temptation. He had failed to master his passions, but they had never moved him to violence, only to love. William had striven to protect those around him, never to destroy. Surely sacrificing his own life to save his son had earnt him his passage to Heaven. As for passing himself off as a man, Nicholas had never heard that listed among the sins.

'Be not afraid,' he told Father. 'In the Lord's house are many mansions; there will be a place for you there.'

A sliver of moonlight framed the shutters and the last candle guttered and went out. How many days and nights had Father spent confined to this room? He must have suffered punishment enough at Gascoigne's hands to make him penitent. Getting down onto his knees, Nicholas redoubled his prayers, asking God what he might do to save his parent's soul. There was no penance or mortification he would not undertake to rescue Father from everlasting death.

Abigail arrived with the dawn, her ashen face streaked with tears. Dropping her basket, she kissed Nicholas's cheeks as though he were a child again, crying with joy to see him and with grief and anger that Sir William had been taken from them so brutally by that devil, Goodwyn.

Nicholas had not expected the profound comfort his old nursemaid's presence would bring him and found himself sobbing with her.

'I failed him, Abigail. It is my fault he's dead.'

'That's nonsense. You are not accountable for what happened here and you must put all such thoughts from your mind.' She sat Nicholas down on a chair and stood observing him sternly. 'Your father beat that wicked man and if he had to give up his life to do it, well, that's exactly as he'd want it. You know as well as I do how precious you were to him. Seeing you return was all he desired and he lived to see his wish fulfilled; that's as much as any of us can hope for. Do you think he was going to let that villain take you from him? Be proud your father died a hero.'

Never before had Nicholas received one of Abigail's scoldings with such gratitude. What comfort it afforded could not last long, though, for now he had to prepare her for the revelation of his father's body. She had never given the slightest indication that she suspected her master might not be entirely as he presented himself and Nicholas could not imagine how she would react to such a disorientating sight. He feared the shock might strike her down with apoplexy or a palsy. Or worse, that her respect for her master would be destroyed by his deception and turn instead into scorn or hatred.

When at last Abigail's barrage of words, both loving and furious, petered out, she and Nicholas stood awkwardly looking down at the body on the bed.

'I understand Sir William's dying request was that I wash and shroud his corpse ready for burial.' She picked up her basket. 'I've got a winding sheet here, along with the necessary herbs. I'll fetch a bowl of water for the cleaning.'

'I can get that for you,' Nicholas offered.

Chapter Twenty-Five

'Well, you might bring it up for me, that would be a kindness, then you can leave me to it.'

'Can you manage on your own?'

'Oh yes, your father was quite wasted away; it won't be hard to turn him.' Abigail began to cry again.

'There is something I must explain to you regarding my father's body. There is a reason why he stipulated that no one else was to attend to his remains. It may come as a grave shock to you...'

Abigail raised her hand. 'There is nothing for you to trouble yourself with here, Sir Nicholas.'

Her use of his father's title gave him a jolt – of course, it belonged to him now, for better and worse.

As Nicholas had failed to move, she continued. 'I believe I know what you allude to, sir. You cannot serve in a house for a quarter of a century without noticing a few things and, well, I've lived here longer than you have. Sir William was always Sir William to me and always will be, don't matter what lies under them clothes.' Abigail nodded at the bed and then gazed with candid sincerity into Nicholas's eyes. 'Aren't we taught that the body is just a house for the soul anyway? People set too much importance by what shape it takes; it's what's contained within that matters, in my humble opinion.'

Nicholas was humbled by her wisdom, which he realised now he had undervalued. 'I did not know you were a philosopher, Abigail.'

'There's much you don't know about me, Sir Nicholas.'

Nicholas managed a smile. 'I'll go and get that water.'

She smiled back at him approvingly. 'You do that, sir. And tell Cooper to make you some breakfast; you need to keep your strength up.'

* * *

Nicholas rode out to consult with the parson later that morning. After dinner, feeling consumed with tiredness, he lay down on his bed to take a nap, but as soon as he closed his eyes, his brain began to teem with so many disturbing images he thought he might never sleep again. Every meeting he'd had with Gascoigne returned to him, the man's sneering, self-satisfied countenance looming before him in the silent room. The audacity of the scoundrel, to take advantage of his absence in order to beguile his way into their home and try to steal it from them. And what of the body that had been dragged from the Thames and identified as Staley? Who had that belonged to? If only he had known he was dealing with a villain as slippery as Gascoigne, he would have taken a more cautious approach instead of blundering into the parlour alongside the constable.

Rubbing the crusts from his eyes, Nicholas went down to Crewe's old office to search through the papers there. A small leather-bound book lay on the desk. Nicholas was moved to see that on the frontispiece was a portrait of his uncle. It was a good likeness of Matthew, though he looked more like a young gallant than the austere priest Nicholas remembered. Father had referred to the publication of Matthew's sermons in one of his letters. Nicholas put the book in his pocket; he would read it later.

He was not surprised to find that Gascoigne had kept meticulous records of all the transactions in and out of Measham Hall. Though he was perplexed by the amount of produce that had been sold to a grocer in Leicester. He hadn't thought Measham capable of producing so much surplus. He wondered that there had been anything left for the household to eat.

There were two sets of accounts, one kept in ledgers on the desk and another that he discovered in a locked drawer. He had to break the lock to open it. Gascoigne probably still had the key on his person, or if not, he had hidden it so well Nicholas could not unearth it. The hidden ledger listed monies Gascoigne had invested in both his own name and William Hawthorne's. There were shares in the Royal African Company and the Hudson's Bay Company and Gascoigne had also invested money with a Mr Sweetapple, a goldsmith. Nicholas would have to write to these companies and demand the money back, though he doubted they would be willing to oblige. He could sell the shares, he supposed. Perhaps he should consult Isaac Smith on the matter; he was just the person to know how best to proceed. Nicholas

Chapter Twenty-Five

was certainly not going to allow Gascoigne to profit from them and neither did he want any involvement in that wicked trade. Though he knew Lord Pemberton had gained much of his wealth from the buying and selling of slaves.

Beneath the ledger lay another sheaf of papers. These contained sonnets written in Latin, which formed an exchange between two characters from Homer's *Iliad* – Achilles and Patroclus. Most of the poems were written under the guise of Achilles, who described his love and yearning for his 'beautiful boy' Patroclus. A few were responses from Patroclus and expressed his gratitude for his friend's bountiful heart and unceasing affections, despite his own unworthiness. By Achilles' divine hand he had received such heavenly joys, yet now he must die for the last time and become a being incorruptible. He exhorted his beloved friend not to mourn his loss so violently, but to rejoice at his salvation.

Nicholas recognised the hand that had composed these, for it belonged to Matthew, who had been his first tutor. He guessed that his uncle was referring to his calling to the priesthood when he wrote of his salvation and that this was the reason he was lost to Achilles, but he also understood the pun on the little death that came from pleasure. Thank God his father couldn't read Latin; that at least was a small mercy.

He could also guess who 'Achilles' was, but he compared the writing with that in the ledger to make sure and as he expected, it resembled Gascoigne's. He had received letters from Gascoigne himself, but the man was adept at changing his hand, as he knew to his cost.

Although he had understood before that Gascoigne bore a violent and jealous love for Matthew, one that would not burn itself out, Nicholas had not realised the lengths to which Gascoigne would go to claim what had once belonged to his dead lover. Matthew had tried to marry Alethea to Gascoigne but she, having become William, had refused. All these years later, Gascoigne had still been determined to subdue Alethea and take Measham Hall.

But how could Matthew, a man Nicholas had always revered as a martyr, have been seduced by a cockatrice like Gascoigne? Yet his father too had been cozened by the monster. Nicholas had never liked Gascoigne, not when he was pretending to be the bookseller Waddington nor when he presented himself as Staley, but then Gascoigne had never attempted to win him over. He had been a boy and beneath Gascoigne's respect. The rogue must possess the ability to charm even intelligent, modest men, which made him all the more dangerous. Nicholas began to fear that Gascoigne would cast his spell over a judge and jury and not only evade justice but deprive him of his birthright.

He had been about to cast the poems into the fire, when it occurred to him that they might help prove Gascoigne's true identity, though he was not sure he could bear to expose such writings to public scrutiny. He still had the locket of Matthew's that father had given him. It contained a portrait of Gascoigne. And surely there must be other victims who could be brought forward as witnesses.

His speculations were interrupted by Palmes, who explained that the serving-boy, Ben, had returned escorted by his mother, who was hoping Sir Nicholas might be so good as to hear his plea. Nicholas hastily put away the papers and told Palmes to send them in.

'That's a very fancy suit of clothes for a Measham servant,' Nicholas observed, as Ben stood shamefacedly in front of him. Now that his hair was unbrushed and his complexion muddied, Nicholas recognised the young serving-boy and couldn't help being somewhat amused by his blue velvet attire and fine lace collar.

'Mr Goodwyn was training Ben up to be his valet,' Ben's mother explained. 'He's a good lad who only ever did as he was bid and never meant for any harm to come to the master, God rest his soul.'

'What exactly did Gascoigne – Goodwyn tell you was wrong with my father?' Nicholas asked Ben, trying to gauge the right level of severity or latitude.

'He said Sir William was sick and needed locking up for his own good. I never thought Mr Goodwyn would shoot the master; I'm right sorry, Sir Nicholas, that I am.' Tears welled in Ben's eyes.

Chapter Twenty-Five

'Did you ever witness Goodwyn bringing any papers to Sir William?'

Ben shook his head. 'Only the master's medicine.'

'I might need you to testify to that in court; do you think you can do that?' Nicholas tapped a quill on the desk.

'Yes, sir,' Ben whispered.

'Well, I'm happy to keep you on here, but there are too many other tasks for me to require a valet de chambre; you'll have to make do with being a menial for now.'

'That'll do him fine,' Ben's mother answered. 'He were getting too many airs and graces anyhow.'

Ben thanked him keenly, though Nicholas detected a note of disappointment in his voice and assured the lad that not only could he keep his fine suit, if he was loyal and worked hard he would promote him. He hoped Ben might prove a useful witness against Goodwyn.

* * *

William's funeral was better attended than Nicholas had expected. Despite the rain, the residents of Measham lined the road to the church to pay their last respects, following the hearse to the village church. There were so many mourners some had to stand in the porch. Nicholas was heartened to see Lady Jane already seated on the Hawthorne pew. Her small body was engulfed by her cloak, with only her face emerging from it. Her silver walking stick rested against the wooden bench. She was staring straight ahead, but turned as they entered and gave Nicholas a sad smile of acknowledgement. Her swollen red eyes were made all the more prominent by the pallor of her skin. Nicholas knew she would be grieving now almost as much as he was, for she had loved his father, even if they had never been reconciled after Father accused her of betraying Matthew to the priest hunters.

Isaac was sitting beside Jane. Nicholas supposed he had come to discuss their mutual enemy, Lawrence Gascoigne. He was glad to see Isaac and looked forward to conversing with him. Then he recalled

Blanche's warning and thought uneasily that Isaac probably knew he had been working for Irish interests.

Isaac stood up and bowed, causing some excitement among the congregation, who had never beheld a man of his colour before. Ignoring the whispering behind them, Nicholas slid onto the space next to Jane. She reached out a gloved hand and, taking his, held it lightly in her lap.

'My poor boy,' she murmured. 'Forgive me for not intervening sooner. If I'd had any idea what was going on I'd have summoned the militia, but the man we sent over to Measham was well received by Gascoigne and assured that all was well.'

'You mustn't blame yourself. Gascoigne is a master contriver and outwits everyone he encounters. But we won't let him away this time.' Nicholas nodded at Isaac, who inclined his head in response.

Although he would have liked his father to receive a Catholic funeral, Nicholas was moved by the parson's eulogy, for it was clear from his words that the man knew and esteemed Sir William. He spoke of William's benevolence in setting up the school, his charity to those in need and his equitable treatment of his tenants and labourers. He was a fair master and an upright servant of the Lord, the parson said, and there were murmurs of agreement among the congregation. As Nicholas had requested, he made no mention of the manner or circumstances of William's death. Nicholas did not want Gascoigne to sully the collective memory of his father. He had seen John Thornly's family were present and hoped they wouldn't take it amiss that no reference was made to the murder of their relative.

All in all, it was a fitting tribute and Nicholas took solace from the knowledge that Father would have approved. He had worked so hard to be a true English gentleman it was only right that he should be buried as such. Besides, he had no interest in the niceties of religion, as he used to call them.

Jane went to take Nicholas's right arm as they left the church and he moved to present her with his left.

Chapter Twenty-Five

'Received a bullet in the right one,' he explained. 'And it is still weak.'

'Does your surgeon believe you will recover full use of the arm?' she asked with concern.

'He is confident I will in time.'

'I am glad to hear it; you don't want to end up an old cripple like me.' She raised her stick.

'Does your leg trouble you?' he asked. He had never heard Jane refer to her injury before. She had been lame for as long as he had known her and it had simply been part of who she was.

'It is not the physical pain I mind so much as the memories it provokes.'

Jane had been much abused by her first husband, who had thrown her down the stairs and broken her hip. Nicholas had learnt this from Abigail when he was a boy and had once dreamt of slaying the monster on Jane's behalf, but the man had died of an apoplexy and Jane had finally been freed of him without Nicholas's intervention. They had almost reached the graveyard and both fell silent at the sight of the old yew tree that shaded the corner where the Hawthornes were buried.

It wasn't until Father was interred in the family tomb that Nicholas became conscious of the agitation that had been gnawing away at him. When he was laid to rest at last in the monument that carried both names, William and Alethea, Nicholas finally felt that Father's identity was safe and his body was where it should be.

It had been summer when they had buried Matthew here and Father had stood beside him. Now, despite Jane's company, he felt quite bereft. The wind stirred the fallen leaves on the grass, sending a sycamore leaf spiralling across the inscription on the tomb, drawing Nicholas's eye to the familiar carvings. He recalled Father explaining to him what they symbolised – the caterpillar at the bottom does not die, but is metamorphosed into the butterfly in the top corner. *You are transformed now, Father*, he thought, *and will be resurrected along with Matthew.*

He invited Jane and Isaac back to Measham Hall and was pleased when she consented to stay for a few days before returning to her father's house in Nottinghamshire. Isaac thanked him but said he must travel straight on to Derby, where Gascoigne and his accomplices were being held, in order to question and identify them.

'I will call in on my return, however, if I may?' Isaac said, taking his horse's reins from the servant who had been waiting for him.

'Of course, I won't hear of you continuing your journey without stopping here. I owe you my thanks for arranging my passage home.'

'Her Ladyship was most insistent.' Isaac nodded towards the Pemberton coach, where Jane was being attended to by her maid.

'I can follow you up to Derby if you think my evidence is needed there,' Nicholas said, looking up at Isaac, who was already in the saddle.

Isaac shook his head. 'There is no need for you to attend. I am meeting our lawyer in Derby. He will insist Gascoigne is tried for treason and murder and I want to see the other two get the same treatment.'

'Good luck and God be with you.' Nicholas patted the horse's neck.

'I have no need of luck; the constable witnessed Gascoigne kill his master – that is petty treason in itself.'

Placing a hand on the reins, Nicholas spoke so quietly Isaac was forced to bend over towards him. 'What if Gascoigne tells them my father was not Sir William? Do you think they will exhume his body to see for themselves?' It was a scenario that had kept Nicholas awake all the previous night.

'We will prove Gascoigne is a hardened fraudster as well as a papist; no judge or jury will believe a word he says. I give you my word, your father will rest in peace.'

These words provoked a surge of emotion that threatened to engulf Nicholas. Fighting down his tears, he let go of the reins and went to join Jane in her carriage.

* * *

Once all the funeral guests had left, Nicholas and Jane settled themselves in front of the parlour fireplace with a glass of Hippocras

Chapter Twenty-Five

wine. The new cook had made it very sweet, with plenty of honey and a warming hint of cinnamon and cloves.

'There's nothing like Hippocras to fortify one in times of trouble.' Jane, who had requested the drink, raised her glass. 'Or so my father always says.'

'How is Lord Calverton?' Nicholas asked her.

'Extremely well. He has the vigour of a man half his age. He still goes out riding every day and his mind is as sharp as ever, though he no longer attends court.'

'Is he not in favour with the King and Queen?' Nicholas asked in surprise.

'They would listen to his counsel, of course, out of respect for the service he has done King William, but he prefers to spend his final years enjoying his leisure.'

'And your stepchildren? I hope they are all in good health.' Nicholas was genuinely fond of the Pemberton offspring, but he was also angling to hear more of Lettice without offending Jane by asking after his old sweetheart directly.

'Richard is excelling at Eton and shows no signs of his brother's weaknesses, which is a great relief. I was uneasy about sending him there as the place certainly did Edward no good, but Richard is of a very different temperament as you know. The girls are well. My husband is already considering a suitor for Dorothy.' Jane sighed, before adding somewhat accusingly, 'After your entanglement with Lettice, I cannot prevail upon him to wait until she is older.'

Nicholas felt stricken. 'Poor little Doll,' he said impulsively. 'I hope she likes the fellow.'

'He is a young man of good family and they will have an extended betrothal,' Jane answered somewhat sharply. 'Besides, Doll is fifteen now, the age her mother was when she was married.'

These sounded like Lord Pemberton's words and Nicholas suspected the betrothal had caused some discord between Jane and her husband. She was devoted to her stepchildren and the youngest three were equally fond of her.

'I hope Mrs Van Dorp is in good health.' Since Jane had mentioned her, he felt it was safe to refer to Lettice.

'She is coming close to her confinement. I did offer to attend her lying-in, but she declined,' Jane said sadly.

Nicholas felt suddenly nauseous. 'I didn't know she was with child.'

'We hope she is blessed with a healthy boy this time. Her first was born too early and did not survive. But Lettice is strong and as determined as ever.' Taking pity on Nicholas, Jane smiled at him. 'Mr Van Dorp dotes on her and allows her every freedom she desires. She is quite the toast of Amsterdam and has already hosted several assemblies. She has even had a printed book of poetry dedicated to her, and instead of objecting, her husband takes great pride in it. He sent us a copy bound in leather.' Jane spoke with some amazement. 'And she conducts a correspondence with a respected philosopher. Mr Van Dorp considers this a beneficial education.'

Lettice had clearly won over the dour Dutchman – Nicholas had hardly got a word out of him when they had met. Perhaps, Nicholas reflected now, his judgement of Heer Van Dorp had been somewhat clouded by jealousy. He hoped the man was not as repulsive to Lettice as the picture his own memory provided.

'I am very glad Lettice is fulfilling her ambitions,' he said sincerely. 'I will pray for her safe delivery.'

'Do you remember when we were last together, I promised to find you a wife?' Jane swirled the cloves around the bottom of her glass. 'When you are out of mourning there is a gentlewoman I should like to introduce you to. She combines all the qualities to bring you much happiness. Indeed, as soon as I met her, I thought of you.'

Nicholas stared into the fire. He had not expected Jane to pursue her promise, especially not when he was in Ireland fighting for the other side. Úna was never far from his thoughts and he was plagued with fears that Blanche might have told her about their liaison in Dublin. He had still had no word from Úna in response to his proposal. It would be a great relief to confide in someone, however, and he could think of no one more suitable than the wise and maternal Jane.

Chapter Twenty-Five

'I have proposed to a young woman in Ireland,' he blurted out before he could stop himself.

Jane set down her glass. 'And has she accepted?'

'Having to depart so hastily, I only had time to leave her a note. I await her reply, but she is in Limerick and it may be difficult for letters to reach England from that city.'

'Her family support King James, I suppose. Are they Old English?'

Nicholas swallowed. 'They are Ancient Irish and very proud of it.'

There was silence for a moment and then Jane said softly, 'She is unlikely to settle here, then.'

'I hope that she will. She is very refined and has a tender heart. She nursed me through a fever after I was injured; if it wasn't for her ministrations I doubt I would have survived. You might find her somewhat haughty on first acquaintance, but with familiarity I know you would grow to love to her, as I have done. Her father is a lawyer, held in such high esteem that he was sent to negotiate with King William before the siege of Limerick. He is a very kind and hospitable man, descended of a noble family. I shall invite him to live here too, since his home was sequestered by Cromwell.' Nicholas's face had grown very hot and he pushed his chair back away from the fire.

'That is generous of you, Nicholas, but, and you know I speak as one who has your best interests at heart, this does not sound like a compatible match. How will a proud Irishwoman win over the trust of your servants and labourers? You need a wife bred to managing an Englishman's estate. One who brings a dowry that will help to finance it – have you considered the upkeep of both Measham and your late uncle's estate? You cannot afford to marry out of love alone. It is time to rein in those youthful passions and consider your responsibilities.'

Nicholas sighed; he should have anticipated this response. 'I wasn't expecting to step into my father's shoes so soon and the outcome of the wars in Ireland are as yet undecided. King James might regain his throne yet.'

'From what my husband tells me, that is highly unlikely. The English people will not stand for it, no matter how they grumble about the current sovereigns.' Jane rose and refilled their glasses from the pitcher on the table. 'Your father took a sensible approach to religion and I thought, given his funeral, that you too might conform to the Church of England, at least outwardly.' Handing Nicholas his glass, she gazed into his eyes with a pleading expression. 'It may not appear to you now as a heroic sort of life and I am not suggesting you confine yourself to the country as your father was compelled to. You could sell your uncle's property and buy a townhouse in London. You could even stand for parliament and look to implement change that way.'

All these things seemed a world away from the sort of life Nicholas had envisioned for himself, though he was sick of warfare and the misery it caused.

'Forgive me, your father is only just buried; it is too soon for you to think of such matters now.'

Instead of resuming her seat, Jane walked around the room, looking at the pictures and trailing her fingers over the ornaments. Thank God Goodwyn hadn't sold any of them off — at least Nicholas hadn't noticed that anything was missing.

'It is all just as I remembered it,' Jane said, echoing Nicholas's thoughts. 'I passed so many happy hours here with William. I keep expecting him to open the door and walk in, his pipe in his mouth and a spaniel at his feet. I suppose I am as eager as he was for you to take his place and enjoy the legacy he bequeathed you. He could be severe, I know, but he always dreamt of the family you might one day have, of the guests you'd invite, the learned companions who might assemble here, the musicians you'd employ and the dances you'd hold.' She stood gazing up at William's portrait. 'Though no great company-keeper, he was not naturally reclusive. He sought seclusion out of necessity rather than desire.' Her voice became clogged with emotion. 'I cannot bear to think of William being kept prisoner while that malevolent creature used his beloved home as though it were his own.'

Nicholas's head ached and he felt suddenly overcome with exhaustion. He could raise the question of his father's double identity

Chapter Twenty-Five

with Jane, he knew she was aware of it, but there seemed no point in raking over that now. He suspected that at the back of her mind dwelt the same horror he kept trying to supress — the thoughts of what Goodwyn might have subjected William to. Not necessarily of a corporal nature, but the humiliation of exposure and the ridicule of the person William had created would be enough. Nicholas could imagine only too well the manner in which Goodwyn might have tortured his father.

'God willing, Father is at peace in the bosom of his Maker and all his mortal sufferings have been washed away,' Nicholas managed to say, though his voice was unsteady.

'The Lord is gracious and full of compassion, slow to anger, and of great mercy,' Jane responded.

'I keep hoping Father sought forgiveness for his sins. There must have been time for reflection and prayer during his captivity. Prisoners are often drawn to repentance.'

Jane placed a hand lightly on his shoulder. 'I am sure of it,' she said confidently. 'Your father's behaviour and views may not always have appeared orthodox, but his heart was pure.'

Nicholas put his hand over hers, squeezing it gently. 'Thank you, that is a great comfort.' He spoke honestly, but could not help reflecting that Jane was not aware of William's relations with John Thornly. He doubted her faith would withstand such knowledge as that.

* * *

Jane's warnings had the opposite effect to the one she had intended and, instead of inclining Nicholas towards a more advantageous match, made him long for Úna's spirited company and disputatious conversation. Not caring whether she was a suitable bride or not, he wrote to Úna the very next day, repeating his offer of marriage and inviting her father to take up residence in his great-uncle's house. He addressed the letter to Mr O'Leary, in the hope that, given his position, O'Leary might have access to the postal service, though it was rarely used by the native Irish and had been disrupted anyway by the war.

He considered enclosing some money, but, since the letter was likely to be opened by the postmaster, decided against it. He would have to reimburse them in person, an action he was determined to undertake. Once he had sorted out his father's affairs and Goodwyn had been dealt with, he would return to Limerick and beg Úna to marry him. With every day that went by, his longing for her grew. Without Úna he felt as though half his heart had been torn from his chest and the pain radiated through all his being with an ache that was greater by far than the bullet wound in his arm.

* * *

After days spent listening to the complaints of the Measham residents, most of which he was unable to address having no money at his immediate disposal, it was a great relief to see Isaac. Pemberton's son came striding across the hall towards him, his elegantly dressed form exuding energy and determination. It was as if a gust of fresh air had blown in through the door behind him, stirring up the ancient dust that had settled over every surface in the house.

'Palmes, can you tell the cook we have a guest for dinner,' Nicholas called to the butler. 'Come into the parlour; you must be weary after your ride and in need of refreshment,' he said eagerly.

Strictly speaking Isaac should count as an enemy, but Nicholas had always felt an affinity with the fellow who was, like him, illegitimate, but more than that, had a discerning mind and a capacious memory. Not only did Nicholas want to hear about Isaac's visit to Derby gaol, he was also desperate for conversation with a like-minded individual. He had to wait until dinner, however, for Isaac requested politely that he might be shown to his room in order to wash and change out of his riding clothes. Only once they were seated at the parlour table did Isaac begin to describe his encounter with the prisoners in Derby.

'Latham was not known to me, but I recognised Baines at once as the ruffian Gascoigne employed in torturing me.'

Nicholas winced, for it was he who had originally alerted Gascoigne to Isaac's activities in support of the Prince of Orange.

Chapter Twenty-Five

But Isaac, apparently unaffected by the memory, was carefully cutting himself a neat slice of pigeon pie.

'The procedure took longer than it should have done; Gascoigne tried to undermine my testimony by calling me a treacherous Moor, and the sheriff, being a simple man who had not encountered anyone of my hue before, was inclined to believe him.' Isaac sighed wearily.

'It must be infuriating to have your way continually impeded by such ignorance.'

'It can be aggravating,' Isaac responded with his usual composure. 'It is certainly tiresome. Fortunately, Lord Pemberton's authority outweighs such preconceptions. The sheriff has agreed that there is a case against Gascoigne, and that Latham and Baines should be tried too as his accomplices. They're to be held in Derby gaol until the Lent Assizes. I'm sure Lord Pemberton can have a word in the ear of whichever judges are on the Midlands circuit then.'

'And not being native to the county, the jury are unlikely to look kindly on them,' Nicholas said with a mixture of hope and anxiety.

Isaac had been chewing slowly on a mouthful of pie, which he now appeared to swallow with difficulty. He took a hasty gulp of wine to send the morsal down.

Nicholas, who had been enjoying a piece of trout, looked at him with concern. 'Is the pie no good?'

'It is not the sort of fare I am accustomed to when at home.' Isaac gave a forced smile. 'But no doubt I have been spoilt; Lord Pemberton only hires the very best cooks.'

'Cooper's dishes have been my only pleasure since returning home, but then, even the simplest of meals would seem like a feast after the meagre diet we were reduced to in Ireland.' Nicholas thought guiltily of Úna and her father and hoped they were getting enough to eat.

Pushing his empty plate to one side, he continued, 'I have heard a litany of woes regarding Gascoigne and have made a list I can furnish you with. Correcting his evils will be a time-consuming business and requires recouping money he has spent and invested elsewhere.

I still have no firm proof that John Thornly was murdered, only testimony to his reputation, along with hearsay and speculation.'

'Baines is the sort whose tongue will loosen after a good dose of his own medicine and Latham seems a weak-willed rogue. I don't believe it will require much pressure to get him to confess; a small financial inducement may work best.'

Isaac took an enamelled toothpick out of his waistcoat pocket. It was shaped as an arm, the hand clasping a golden sickle. Above the arm was a gold death's head, which Isaac held delicately between his thumb and forefinger, working a piece of gristle from between his teeth with the blade.

'So you pick your teeth with the reaper's sickle,' Nicholas remarked, momentarily distracted by the ingenuity of the jewel's workmanship. 'That's quite a *memento mori*.'

'A gift from Lord Pemberton to remind me to avoid death by toothache.' Isaac raised his eyebrows. 'Which also reminds me — I was able to retrieve this from Mr Gascoigne.' Feeling in his coat pocket, Isaac drew out a silver box, which he passed across the table to Nicholas. 'It bears your family crest so I knew it must have belonged to your father and insisted on taking possession of it.'

Nicholas cupped the familiar box in his hands. 'His tobacco box — Matthew had it made for him.' Grief rose up in his chest, threatening to overwhelm him.

Isaac discreetly looked away. 'No wonder Gascoigne coveted it. He has convinced himself that he is the rightful owner of your property. He insists the true Sir William promised it to him and concludes that, because your uncle offered him your mother's hand, he is as much her husband as if a priest had legally joined them.' Turning back to face Nicholas, he paused, taking in Nicholas's horrified expression. 'There is no need to look so stricken. Gascoigne would not have had any carnal interest in your mother's body and I'm sure his devotion to your uncle kept him from inflicting too much suffering on her.'

It was very strange to hear his father spoken of in this way, as though he was still Alethea, the woman Nicholas had grown up

Chapter Twenty-Five

believing was his dead aunt. Nicholas could only think of him as Sir William, for that was the father he had always known and that was how he would remember him, no matter whose body lay beneath the clothes he had worn. And he would certainly not allow Gascoigne to decree otherwise. It was some comfort to him that Abigail, in laying out his parent's body, had found no signs of external violence, only the wasting brought on by the opium Father had been fed.

'But Gascoigne's claims work to our advantage,' Isaac continued. 'For they appear so wild, they'll bring him down if nothing else does. Gaol has worn away much of his former subtlety and he has lost any support he once had from the Jesuits. Oh, there is plenty of dirt to be dug up yet.' Isaac looked as though he relished the task.

'So long as it doesn't tarnish my father's reputation, or my family's name,' Nicholas insisted.

'You can rest easy on that count,' Isaac assured him. 'Though it is only thanks to Lady Jane that you are sitting here a free man in possession of two manor houses.' Isaac gave him a reproving look. 'You have hardly endeared yourself to Lord Pemberton by your antics in Ireland. Your intelligence was sporadic and of little value to our side, while we strongly suspect you were in fact spying for the Jacobites. If we did not have a mutual enemy in Gascoigne, I would not be dining with you now.'

'That is a groundless accusation.' Knowing he would be questioned over his allegiance, Nicholas had prepared his refutation. 'Lord Pemberton is not a soldier and has no knowledge of the battlefield.' He refrained from adding that neither had Isaac. 'Chaos reigns supreme and its attendant, misinformation, runs riot. In addition to which, King James's commanders are a fickle bunch who change their minds as often as their loyalties. I would supply some useful fact only for it to be changed into fiction the very next day. I understand from Mrs Fitzpatrick that I am held responsible for the discovery of the Williamite siege train. I only wish I were so skilled a spy, but as you know, it is not a profession I am naturally suited to. Had I been the one to bring such invaluable information to the Irish they would have promoted me to a major and my name would be eulogised in their songs.'

Isaac smiled and took a sip of wine. 'Your oratory has improved at any rate. Perhaps we should employ you as a pamphleteer, a few choice letters denouncing the Jacobites would help win back Pemberton's regard.'

Nicholas's disgust must have shown in his face for Isaac laughed.

'Lord Pemberton has more pressing matters on his mind; I think you are safe for now, though if you are to remain in England you will need to do him some service. But tell me, how is the lovely Blanche?' Isaac raised his eyebrows.

'She appears very well, having ensconced herself in the house where I was residing.' Nicholas paused before adding, 'I'm sure Lord Pemberton will want to keep his amours with actresses from his wife.' He hated to stoop so low, but he needed to ensure his safety.

'It is your benefactress you would wound if you decide to make such information public,' Isaac warned him.

'And if Lord Pemberton releases me I will not have to resort to hurting anyone.'

'Such threats are beneath you and will not further your cause.' Isaac dislodged another bit of debris with his golden sickle. 'Lord Pemberton does not take kindly to coercion, as you know. I suggest you do not raise the subject again, especially since you have swum in the same waters.' Isaac spoke as severely as a schoolmaster. 'I hear you have fallen in love with an Irishwoman, one who may be equally displeased to learn of your communications, both carnal and otherwise, with Blanche Fitzpatrick.'

Nicholas's belly constricted. How was it that Isaac always had the upper hand? He had thought him a friend when it was clear Isaac saw him as nothing more than a puppet.

'Come, let us not fall out over affairs of the heart. You can trust in Blanche's discretion; I hope we can trust in yours.' Isaac smiled at him magnanimously.

Begrudgingly Nicholas agreed, feeling more than ever like a petulant schoolboy.

Chapter Twenty-Five

'You are going to require more servants, not only a steward and a bailiff, but a butler too quite soon – if I am not mistaken. I can make enquiries on your behalf, if you wish,' Isaac offered, apparently wanting to placate his disgruntled host.

It was true that Nicholas couldn't manage the place without new servants and he knew Isaac was the best person to recommend them, but did he want to end up with more of Pemberton's spies in his household?

'Reliable, well-trained servants are not easy to come by, especially those of the right calibre who are willing to work in such an out-of-the-way place,' Isaac continued, glancing around the room. 'It's just as well you like the food; good cooks are as rare as hen's teeth.'

'Your assistance would be greatly appreciated,' Nicholas conceded. It would serve his interests to go along with Isaac for now, especially if he wanted to avoid Pemberton's retribution.

* * *

Abigail had come back to Measham Hall and ran the house so well, with the help of Kate and Ben, that Nicholas saw no reason to look for another steward. But perhaps his standards were not as high as Father's had been. He supposed he might have to employ a steward at some point, especially if he were to go overseas again. To his relief, Harrington found a bailiff to manage the farm. The man was lodged in the village since Mrs Thornly had agreed to return to the Grange. She said it would be too much for Eliza to start anew elsewhere.

Despite being kept very busy, Nicholas was often lonely and he missed the company of his friends and comrades in Ireland. His father seemed to haunt every room in Measham Hall, and being outside was no better, for every landmark served only to remind him of Father's absence.

He longed for some word from Úna and was overjoyed when, at the beginning of November, a letter finally arrived. Taking the travel-stained, much-folded parchment into Crewe's former office, which now served as his study, he began to read. Racing impatiently through her words of condolence, though her sympathy and horror were tenderly expressed, he slowed only when he reached her response to his proposal.

When I discovered the note you had slipped under my chamber door, I was so amazed by what was written there, I was inclined to think you mocked me. Mrs Fitzpatrick, however, convinced me that the sentiments expressed were genuine. (I hope you will forgive me for confiding in her, but I was in desperate need of female guidance and Mairead, being so young, has not the same experience as Mrs Fitzpatrick.) You will be pleased to learn that she is a staunch ally of yours.

Your second letter was proof, if I still needed it, as to the sincerity of your intentions. Father and I give our humble thanks for your generous offer of a home for him either at Measham Hall or as custodian of your late great-uncle's property. Father was so deeply affected by your kindness that he wept.

A ghrá, if you knew how tortured my heart is you too would weep for me. To win the love of a man of courage and nobility, of gentle understanding, of looks impeccable and fortune assured, should be the triumph of any woman's life (or so we are taught); certainly it is more than I had ever expected to achieve. And yet I cannot marry you.

We are Irish and our home is in Ireland; we cannot desert her now when she needs us most. I will never swear an oath to the English monarchs, not even by proxy through the vows of my husband. I cannot live in the land of our oppressor, enjoying my ease while my countrymen are dying to free our land.

Pray do not write to me of love, for I cannot bear it. Write with news of your health and your home. Tell me what you are reading so that we might converse on matters literary and philosophical. Then, when I hear of your marriage to an English gentlewoman I will be ready to receive such news with all gladness for you.

Blessings to you,
Your loving friend and servant,
Úna O'Leary
P.S. I had writ several pages on the news from Ireland and the torments that beset us, but on Mrs Fitzpatrick's advice I have removed them.

Chapter Twenty-Five

Nicholas was plunged into a state of great misery by Úna's refusal. There must have been some spark of hope residing in his heart that had been keeping him buoyant and now it was extinguished he felt all the light had gone from his life. How could he remain in England, enjoying a life of plenty, while she was faced with violence, hunger and destitution? If it hadn't been for the impending trial of his father's murderer, he would have shut up the house and returned to Ireland straight away, Lord Pemberton be damned. But he couldn't leave until he had seen Gascoigne hang and the Lent Assizes didn't begin until March, which was exactly when the battles in Ireland would resume.

He stared wildly round the room, and, feeling as though the wainscoted walls were closing in on him, went out to the stables. Sans Pareil, his father's horse, was still there, so he rode out on him, galloping blindly over the parkland, not caring where the horse took him.

Eventually Sans Pareil slowed to a walk and Nicholas realised they were approaching the Grange. Eliza was in the yard feeding the chickens. She looked up at the sound of the horse and smiled at him, her expression as sweet and guileless as a child's. Dropping her bucket, she ran over with great excitement.

'Mary's had pups, come and see,' she called.

Glad of the distraction, Nicholas dismounted and followed her into the house, leaving Sans Pareil tied up outside. Mary was Eliza's spaniel; it was an odd name for a dog but no one had been able to dissuade her from it. The dog looked up from her place in the corner, the puppies wriggling around her.

Eliza lifted a black and white one. 'We're keeping him. I shall call him William after your dad,' she told Nicholas solemnly.

Mrs Thornly, who had been kneading dough at the table, wiped her hands on a cloth and gave a curtsey. 'Please have a seat by the fire, Sir Nicholas, and Eliza will bring you a cup of ale.'

Nicholas sat down, uncomfortably aware that he was taking John Thornly's old chair, and Eliza dropped a liver-and-white spotted puppy onto his lap.

'You can have this 'un,' she said. 'He's got the same colouring as your old dog.'

Nicholas fondled the animal's silky ears. They certainly needed a dog about the Hall, though he'd had more of a guard dog in mind. A spaniel might at least warn them of intruders, he supposed.

'Eliza, go and fetch the ale for the master,' Mrs Thornly told her daughter. 'Forgive her, sir, she doesn't mean to be disrespectful,' she added as soon as Eliza had left the room.

'There's no need for apologies; I'm grateful to Eliza for bringing me some much-needed cheer.' Nicholas placed the puppy back down by its mother.

'You look tired, sir.' Mrs Thornly said with concern, though she looked as fatigued as anyone could. 'You've had to take on a great deal. It must be hard not having any kin to share the burden with. And then there's the waiting for the trial...' Strands of floury hair had stuck to her forehead and she pushed them away with the back of her hand.

'Gascoigne and his men will hang for what they did,' Nicholas promised her.

'I won't rest easy in my bed until they do,' Mrs Thornly admitted. 'Sometimes I fear they'll come back here to finish us off.'

'I'd see to them first. Haven't you heard about my reputation as a swordsman?' Nicholas was trying to make light of her fears, but her look of alarm only increased.

'We can't afford to lose you, sir. If anything happens to you, we'll be turned out of here.'

'I've made a will, Mrs Thornly, and left this house to you. No one can take it from you, or the girls – I've made provision for them too.'

'Well, that is very generous of you, sir.' Sarah Thornly flushed red, but she looked as though a great weight had dropped from her shoulders. 'Very kind indeed.'

'It's no more than you deserve,' Nicholas answered gruffly, looking down at the dogs.

'May you live a long life.' She smiled sadly at him. 'This place needs you here; it's where you belong. Your father, God rest his soul,

Chapter Twenty-Five

always dreamt of the day you'd settle here with a family. You're the last of the Hawthornes now, just as we're the last Thornlys of Measham.'

Eliza returned with a jug of ale and, after taking a mouthful, Nicholas hastened to his horse.

'Don't forget your puppy.' Eliza followed him out. 'He'll be drowned with rest of the litter, if you don't take him.'

'I'll come back for him; keep him for me,' Nicholas called back to her.

'You can call him John, after my dad.' Eliza beamed. 'Then John and William can play together again.'

Dear God, Nicholas thought, what had the girl seen? He'd have to convince her to pick some other names. He dug his heels into Sans Pareil's flanks and rode off at a gallop, as if he could outride not only his sorrows and disappointments, but his responsibilities too.

* * *

It was evening by the time he returned home. Palmes came hobbling towards him; the poor butler was bent almost double.

'Eliza Thornly delivered a dog, sir; she said it belongs to you. It's in the kitchen, but Cooper says the whelp's in his way.' Palmes's voice trembled with anxiety. Old age had made him prone to panic at the slightest irregularity.

Wearily, Nicholas followed Palmes into the kitchen. The puppy had been penned into a corner with a couple of stools laid on their sides. Tickell, restored to his customary seat by the fire, was watching it with a bemused expression. His wits had been eroded by his incarceration in the poorhouse and his mind often wandered.

'I can mind the dog for you, sir,' Ben said eagerly. 'It can sleep alongside me.'

'I'm not having it making messes in my kitchen,' Cooper warned.

'I'll clean up after 'un. I can train him too,' Ben insisted.

It was the first time Nicholas had seen the boy lifted out of the despondency that had come over him since his demotion from valet to scullion.

'Miss Thornly said the dog is called John after her late father,' Palmes told Nicholas with an expression of amazed horror.

The puppy looked up at Nicholas with inquisitive eyes and wagged its tail.

'We'll call him Jack, and he's your charge, Ben, so you must make sure he behaves himself.'

Ben beamed at him. 'He'll be the best dog you ever owned, sir.'

Nicholas couldn't help smiling back at the lad. Ben's delight was infectious.

'You'll be wanting your supper, sir; I was about to bring it through to the parlour,' Palmes said.

But looking around the kitchen, with its roaring fire and glowing tapers, Nicholas told them he would take his supper there, for he was in need of company. In truth, he was sick of dining alone, with only his father's and grandfather's portraits to keep him company. His forebears always seemed to be looking down at him reproachfully, while the many lectures Father and Matthew had given him over the years, on his role as custodian of Measham Hall, resounded in his ears.

Abigail came into the kitchen and Nicholas insisted they all sit down and break bread together. Instead of objecting, as he thought she might, Abigail took a seat beside Cooper. The two seemed very comfortable together, he noticed, teasing each other affectionately. There was a tenderness in Cooper's manner towards her that Nicholas had not expected the gruff cook capable of. He was glad of it; Abigail deserved a lover who knew her worth.

As if conscious of being observed, she caught Nicholas's eye and smiled warmly at him.

'You take after your mother.' Abigail paused for a moment. 'Ellen,' she added with some emphasis. 'Ellen was always happiest in the kitchen. Do you remember,' she called over to Tickell, 'how Mrs Liddell used to help you with the cooking? She had the nimblest fingers and could shape pastry and dough into such dainty figures.'

'Mrs Liddell.' Tickell nodded in recognition. 'Is she coming back?'

Chapter Twenty-Five

'She lives in London now, along with her sister,' Abigail reminded him.

Abigail couldn't still believe Ellen was his mother, Nicholas thought. In truth she had only been his wetnurse, but it had suited Father to let the world believe Ellen was Nicholas's mother; he'd let Nicholas believe it too, for his whole childhood. Nicholas felt a sudden surge of anger with William for all the subterfuge he'd imposed on him. He still didn't know who his real father was, only that he had been some sort of unorthodox preacher.

He drank down his ale and wished they had some *uisce beatha* to go with it. What were the O'Learys doing now? Playing cards perhaps, or receiving a visit from O'Connor.

At the other end of the table, Abigail was explaining to an astonished Cooper how Ellen Liddell had been one of them Leveller types who believed everyone was equal before the Lord and made no distinctions between nobility and common folk. Ben, having long since stopped trying to keep his blue velvet suit clean, was sitting in the corner stroking the puppy and feeding it scraps. Palmes was valiantly attempting to remain awake, while Tickell had dozed off with a contented look on his face.

Gazing around at them all, Nicholas realised, with a mixture of affection and despair, that this was his family and he could not leave them, not yet anyhow. His anger with his father subsided as quickly as it had risen. How he wished William was here to see his home restored to the sort of peaceful domesticity that he had valued above all else.

He would keep on writing to Úna and, when affairs were settled here, he would go back to Ireland, even if it meant he must live as an exile from England. And once in Ireland, he would convince Úna to marry him. Then, if God and the wars between the two kings allowed it, he hoped she would agree to return here with him as his wife. For she would fit in perfectly as the mistress of Measham Hall, he was sure of it.

Acknowledgments

Huge thanks to all the team at Duckworth Books, and a special mention to my editor, Daniela Ferrante, for her brilliant and supportive editing. Thanks also to Becca Allen for her copyediting.

Many thanks to John Maloney for his thoughtful and perceptive feedback and to Simone Maloney for her enthusiasm, support and encouragement.

I am grateful to The London Library for their extensive and impressive collection of books and online resources and for being a great place to carry out research. Thanks also to The Limerick Civic Trust and The People's Museum of Limerick for their very informative walking tour.

Thank you always to Colin, for everything.

Also available

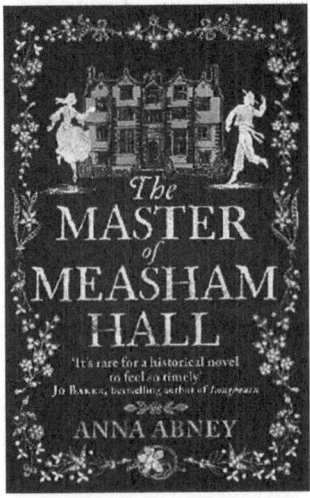

The Master of Measham Hall
(Book I in the Measham Hall series)

1665. It is five years since King Charles II returned from exile, the scars of the English Civil Wars are yet to heal and now the Great Plague engulfs the land.

When Alethea Hawthorne suddenly finds herself cast out on the plague-ridden streets of London, a long road to Derbyshire lies ahead. Militias have closed their boroughs off to outsiders for fear of contamination. A lone woman, Althea must navigate a perilous new world of religious dissenters and charlatans, and a pestilence that afflicts peasants and lords alike.

Page-turning yet exquisitely observed, *The Master of Measham Hall* captures the religious divides at the heart of Restoration England in a timeless story of survival, love and family loyalty.

OUT NOW

The Messenger of Measham Hall
(Book 2 in the Measham Hall series)

For Nicholas Hawthorne, the Catholic heir to Measham Hall in Derbyshire, subterfuge is part of everyday life. But there are deeper and darker secrets even than his family's outlawed religion: why is his father, Sir William, so reclusive? What became of his mother, and his aunt Alethea? And who fatally betrayed his cousin Matthew?

Nicholas is determined to find out, but as England slides towards invasion by the Protestant forces of Prince William of Orange, he becomes entangled in conspiracies within King James's court – and soon learns that both truth and love come at a high price.

OUT NOW